SILVER AND SAPPHIRES

There was no mistaking the tall, broad-shouldered silhouette that filled the doorway.

He didn't move for a long moment. When he finally stepped inside, he crossed the cabin in three strides and scooped her into his arms. His silvered gaze shone like a blade, sharp with desire.

"Please, my lord. D-do not—"

He laid a finger on her lips to silence her. He nuzzled the edge of her jaw, her throat, her hair. "I promise," he whispered. "I promise, Ashiana. I will not hurt you."

A tiny sob welled up from within her. She opened her mouth in a soundless plea, but wasn't sure whether she meant to beg him to stop or continue. She tensed, but then . . . then she felt his touch, so sure, so gentle . . .

SILVER AND SAPPHIRES

SHELLY THACKER

AVON BOOKS NEW YORK

SILVER AND SAPPHIRES is an original publication of Avon Books. This work has never before appeared in book form. This work is a novel. Any similarity to actual persons or events is purely coincidental.

AVON BOOKS
A division of
The Hearst Corporation
1350 Avenue of the Americas
New York, New York 10019

Copyright © 1993 by Shelly Thacker Meinhardt
Published by arrangement with the author
Library of Congress Catalog Card Number: 92-90418
ISBN: 0-380-77034-2

First Avon Books Printing: February 1993

AVON TRADEMARK REG. U.S. PAT. OFF. AND IN OTHER COUNTRIES, MARCA REGISTRADA, HECHO EN U.S.A.

Printed in the U.S.A.

RA   10 9 8 7 6 5 4 3 2 1

To Suzanne Brown, LaVerne Coan, Carol Lucas, Linda Pedder, and Angie Thayer, for sharing five years of insights, critiques, laughter, chocolate, and dreams.

Acknowledgments

Writers the world over are blessed with exceptional librarians who make our lives easier. I'd like to say thank you to all who spend their days behind a reference desk, never blinking when a stray writer asks for advice on eighteenth-century explosives or the raising of baby tigers. A special word of praise to Marilyn Gurney of the Maritime Command Museum, Halifax, Nova Scotia, for her research-and-rescue mission.

Thanks also to Kelly Norman, MIRLYN wizard, and U-M library guide extraordinaire; Kusum Mongia, Nidhi Nigam, and Aruna Ravishankar for their assistance with the Hindu language; and the Government of India Tourist Office, Port Blair, Andaman Islands.

My deepest, most heartfelt thanks, always, to Mark, whose love makes everything possible.

Prologue

India, 1743

The July sun sizzled over the Bay of Bengal, the acrid smells of gunpowder and cannon shot clinging to the heat-thickened air. The residue of violence mingled oddly with the more piquant scents of pepper, cinnamon, and cloves. Broken casks of spices, dropped by the English pirates in their greedy eagerness, littered the deck of the Portuguese merchant frigate.

Like a sailor's rum-induced nightmare risen from the sea, the English buccaneers had reduced the *Adiante* to a tangled ruin of torn sails and rigging, splintered masts, and blood-washed oak in a matter of minutes. Thankfully, none of them had given so much as a glance to the capstan, the slim barrel beside the mainmast used for storing cable.

Hidden there, six-year-old Ashiana de Canto e Calda trembled, her blue eyes squeezed shut, her boyish white shirt and breeches stuck to her pale skin in the sweltering heat. She must not let the pirates know she was here. Papa had said she must not.

He had asked her to be a brave girl, in that split second when he realized the ship approaching under a friendly Portuguese flag was not friendly at all. He had only enough time to whisk her inside the capstan before the *Adiante* took a full broadside.

He gave her a reassuring flicker of his usual reckless

1

smile, just before he replaced the lid and drew his saber to fight.

She only heard what happened next: swarms of men coming over the railings, shouting in a guttural language. The clash of swords. The sharp pop of pistols. Screams— *Deus,* the screams!

Then, for a few minutes, an eerie silence reigned.

Papa, she thought, terrified. *Papa! Are you all right?*

Her heart had thudded a dozen unsteady beats before she heard his voice, shouting curses as the pirates helped themselves to the cargo he had worked so hard to get.

Now Ashiana could hear muffled sounds from the holds below. She struggled to catch her breath, trying not to cough. Smoke tortured her lungs with every gasp, and that frightened her even more. This smoke wasn't coming from the ship's spent cannons; she had smelled that more than once in the past. This was much stronger, and she could guess its source.

The *Adiante,* her birthplace, the only home she had known, the ship where she had scrambled through the rigging, journeyed to all the ports of India, and sung songs with her father's sailors all her life, had been set ablaze.

She heard the pirates on deck again, yelling in that awful, unfamiliar tongue. From the responses shouted by her father, it sounded as if these Englishmen were looking for some treasure they had not found. She heard Papa say the word "sapphires" several times.

It made no sense in Ashiana's spinning, aching head. Her father did not trade in jewels. He was a spice merchant, sailing between Bombay, Madras, and their home port at Goa. They had been on their way to the Andaman Islands, where Papa would stop to trade with his friend who lived there, the Maharaja of Ajmir. She had always liked visiting the Maharaja and his palace. He and his people were of the warrior tribe called the Rajputs, but they did not frighten Ashiana. The Maharaja always gave her sweet nougats and let her play with the peacocks and baby *chital* deer in his menagerie.

The *Adiante* had been within sight of the Maharaja's

islands when the English pirates attacked; now it all seemed impossibly far away.

She could hear her father speaking again. His voice was more angry than she had ever heard it.

"Destroying my ship and slaughtering my crew will not change the truth! The Nine Sapphires of Kashmir do not exist. It is only a legend!"

This time one of the pirates responded in Portuguese so heavily accented that Ashiana could barely make it out.

"Damned lies," the man snarled. "You're good friends with them Ajmir, so you must know something. They're the ones what guard the sapphires. Everybody from here to Brazil knows that. Now start talking!"

Ashiana heard her father utter a painful grunt, as if someone had hit him, hard. She whimpered despite herself. It was very hard to remember that he wanted her to be a brave girl. She blinked as smoke stung her tear-filled eyes.

The fire was getting closer.

"You cough up the truth right quick, Cap'n, else there won't be enough pieces left of you or your ship to feed the fishes."

Ashiana heard what sounded like a kick, followed by more blows. She stifled a sob. Papa swore at them savagely.

There was the sound of cloth tearing. "Maybe me cat-o'-nine tails will loosen your tongue!"

Ashiana, to her horror, heard a whip singing through the air.

Papa shouted in pain.

She clapped her hands over her mouth to keep from crying out. Her cheeks wet with silent tears, she huddled into a smaller ball, shaking uncontrollably. Her body jerked as the lash landed on her father's back again and again with a vicious *crack ... crack ... crack*.

Then Papa stopped shouting. He stopped making any sounds at all.

Ashiana gasped.

"Had enough, Cap'n? Tell us what you know about the sapphires!"

He uttered only a weak groan. The pirates laughed. It almost made Ashiana's racing heart stop beating. She had never heard anything so cruel and horrifying in all her life.

In that moment, an overwhelming emotion seized her, a feeling she had never experienced before. She *hated* these Englishmen! Hated them so much she could taste it like something foul and bitter on her tongue. She would kill them if she could!

The pirate called out something in English.

The whip cracked again. Papa screamed.

"*Nao!* No!" Ashiana sobbed, unable to stand it a second longer. She threw her full weight upward against the capstan lid and tumbled from her hiding place. Her eyes took in the ghastly scene in a single second: smoke poured from the *Adiante*'s bow. Torn bodies lay strewn across the deck—Gaspar and Diogo and Martim and others—every one of her friends! Two men held her father by the arms while a third raised a lash over his bare back.

"*Nao!* No! No! *Papa!*" She threw herself at the astonished pirate who held the whip. "*Filho da puta!*" She beat at him with her small fists, yelling curses she had heard the *Adiante*'s sailors use so many times. "*Va para o diabo! Chega!* No more!" She grabbed his arm with all the strength she possessed, to keep him from hurting her papa anymore.

The pirate shouted at her in English and shook her off with a snap of his arm. The whip, still gripped in his hand, snaked sideways and struck Ashiana as she fell, opening a line of red from her wrist to her elbow. She landed on the deck with a cry of pain.

In the confusion, her father threw off the men who held him, his face contorted with fury. He launched himself at the one who had hurt Ashiana. "*Gajo refugo!* I will kill you!"

One of the pirates behind him drew a pistol.

"*Papa!*" Ashiana screamed in warning.

She was a second too late. The gun went off, spewing

fire and noise. The horrible smell of burnt gunpowder laced the air. Papa staggered, his body suspended for a moment against the clear summer-blue sky, his handsome features a mask of agonized surprise. He crumpled to the deck.

The pirate leader swore and began yelling at the man who had fired.

Ashiana, sobbing, ignored the cursing Englishmen and scrambled to her father. He lay unmoving on a jumble of canvas and rigging, his black hair and neatly trimmed beard slick with sweat and blood, his back crisscrossed with slashes, a round hole just beneath one shoulder.

"Papa? Papa!" Ignoring the fiery pain in her left arm, Ashiana touched his cheek. His brown eyes flickered open. A bright-red stain was spreading quickly on the white sail-cloth beneath him.

"I am sorry, *minha cara,*" he gasped.

She tried to bunch up part of the canvas to pillow his head. A shadow blocked the sun. Ashiana looked up to see one of the pirates looming over her. With his pale face, matted blond hair, and bushy beard, he was the ugliest, most frightening thing she had ever seen.

"So this little sea whelp be yours, Cap'n?" He laughed, speaking mangled Portuguese. "Well, maybe we'll get the truth from you now!"

Ashiana spat at the man. He only laughed harder. Reaching down, he grabbed her by her thick black hair and jerked her up against him. "After you've tasted me lash, you won't be so—"

Suddenly, his voice choked out. As if from the clouds above, an arrow had whistled across the deck and pierced his throat. He dropped Ashiana, grabbing at his neck as he toppled over.

The men around him fell back in shock. A spear killed another of their number before they could think to draw their weapons. Ashiana crawled back to her father and huddled over him protectively.

The pirates crouched and whirled to face their unseen enemy. A score of dark men dressed in turbans and silks suddenly appeared over the railing, bristling with weapons. A dozen more came from the other side of the ship.

"Papa," Ashiana cried in surprise and relief, "it is the Maharaja's men!"

The battle was over almost before it began. The pirates fought savagely, but they were no match for the legendary Rajput warriors. Scimitars and battle-axes flashed, and the few Englishmen left standing were throwing themselves overboard to escape to their own ship. The Rajputs followed to the rail, releasing volley after volley of flaming arrows that soon had the pirate vessel blazing.

Ashiana pillowed her papa's head in her lap and kissed his temple. "You will be all right, now, Papa," she assured him. "You will."

"Never should have . . . kept you with me, *minha cara.*" His eyes drifted open, then closed. "Your mother would have wanted you to be a . . . proper little English lady."

"Never, Papa! I hate the English. I hate them!"

"No, Ashiana, do not—" A spasm seized him and he could not speak for a moment. "Do not . . . hate half of what you are," he finished, grimacing in pain.

Ashiana was about to reply when she became aware of someone else kneeling beside her, felt a gentle hand on her shoulder. Wiping a grimy sleeve across her eyes, she looked up to see the Maharaja's face. He looked impassive as always, his wrinkled brown skin wreathed with hard lines, his dark eyes revealing no emotion.

"Antonio," he said in his deep, calm voice. "We saw the smoke. Our *cata maran* are swift but I fear we are too late to save your ship, my friend."

As if to underscore his words, the *Adiante* shifted suddenly, its oak timbers groaning as the fire devoured the lower decks.

"We shall take you to safety." The Maharaja signaled to his men.

"No, Kalyan," Ashiana's father objected weakly. "It is my time, and I would . . . stay with my ship. But you must . . . you must take Ashiana with you—"

"Papa, no." Ashiana looked back down at her father,

stricken at the idea. For the first time, and with a depth of understanding that went beyond her years, she realized her papa was not going to be all right. He was dying.

She felt as if all the air had just been knocked from her, as if the very sun had been stolen from the sky. Ashiana had been without a mother from the day of her birth, but she had never been apart from her father. She grasped his hand, her small, pale fingers wrapping firmly around his dark, callused palm. "No, Papa." She started crying again. "I will not leave you!"

He closed his eyes, his face etched with pain. "Kalyan, she must . . . h-have a home. Jayne had no family left in England. And I have—" He coughed, gasping for air and finding only smoke. "I have no one in Portugal—"

"She shall be as my own," the Maharaja said simply, laying a hand on Papa's shoulder.

Ashiana, crying so hard she couldn't speak, tore her gaze from her father's face. Despite the Maharaja's emotionless exterior, his eyes were bright with unshed tears.

"Ashiana," her father whispered, drawing her attention immediately back to him. "I love you, my daughter."

Ashiana hugged him fiercely, her tiny frame shaking with sobs. "Papa, don't leave me."

"Remember always . . ." he whispered. "Remember me, *minha cara* . . ."

The *Adiante* shifted again, heeling over on one side, dangerously low in the water.

"It must be now," Papa said weakly, his eyes still closed as if he had no strength to open them again. "Kalyan . . . know that I told them nothing. Your secret . . . it is safe."

"The gods shall bless your next life, Antonio."

The next thing Ashiana knew, the Maharaja had scooped her into his arms. He and his warriors moved quickly across the ravaged deck toward the rail.

"Papa!" Ashiana screamed, reaching back toward her father's still form. *"Papa!"*

The Maharaja held her tightly as the Rajputs slipped over the side and down into their small boats, casting off their lines and pushing away from the sinking merchantman.

Ashiana screamed wordlessly, fighting the Maharaja's hold on her as the ocean gaped wider and wider between her and the *Adiante*. Smoke and flames and the sea consumed the ship until she couldn't see anything but a small speck of it, struggling against the waves.

Then even that disappeared.

She went limp, sobbing into the Maharaja's silk tunic.

"You must not cry so, little one," he said gently, wrapping a protective arm around her. "You are a Rajput princess now."

Chapter 1

1757

Night cloaked the palace as the Ajmir women slept fitfully in the perfumed splendor of the harem. Wives and daughters, aunts and nieces and cousins, maidservants, concubines, and slave girls had curled up on silken pillows and thick carpets, letting the distant sound of the surf lull them, trying to put the tension and anguish of the past days behind them. Even the *rani vadi*, highest of all the Maharaja's queens, had come out of her private apartments, seeking solace among the others.

All had retired early this night. All but one. Ashiana tiptoed through the women's quarters, moving quickly but carefully so she would not disturb anyone. She did not wish to answer questions about what she was doing leaving the harem at this hour, unescorted by the eunuchs who guarded the doors. Rao's terse note had instructed her to tell no one.

Moonlight spilled in through the broad, onion-shaped windows, sparkling on the gold, diamonds, and rubies that adorned her hair and wrists and fingers. Her mango-colored silk *paridhana* skirt swirled about her ankles as she stepped around a plump serving girl. Ashiana was glad she had decided to remove the tinkling anklets she normally wore.

With a last, hasty glance behind her, she pulled herself up onto one of the window ledges and took off her satin slippers. Clutching them in her hand, she wrapped her diaphanous, flowing *dupatta* shawl close about her, took a deep breath, and leaped down into the gardens that surrounded the harem.

Her bare feet made no sound on the dewy grass as she took a few steps, trying to feel her way in the darkness. The women's quarters sat on the crest of a hill, protected by a maze of walls and hedges and gardens that terraced down the slopes, meant to confound any who did not know the way in. The scents of patchouli and roses and rarer flowers wafted up the hillside on the humid breeze.

Moving toward the innermost wall, Ashiana crept up the makeshift steps the women had put together from ornate caskets that normally held jewels and cosmetics. Despite the warnings of their men, they had wanted to see what happened below.

Peering over the wall, Ashiana could make out the ramparts far down the slope, where the palace grounds met the beach. Warriors still patrolled, their sharp steel *tabars* flashing in the moonlight. Drifts of smoke rose from some of the smoldering outer buildings of the palace, damaged in the battle that had raged there three days ago.

A curse upon all Englishmen, Ashiana swore helplessly, feeling a renewed surge of hatred for the intruders who had caused this. The thieves had come seeking that which their kind had always sought, since the day they set foot in India more than a hundred and fifty years ago: the Nine Sapphires of Kashmir, the legendary gems supposedly protected by her clan for centuries.

How could these English be so foolish—and so savage? With a shiver of fear for her clan, Ashiana turned away from the sight of the ruins below and leaped down from the little staircase. She moved through the damp grass with quick, gliding steps, depending on her bare feet to find the familiar marble-paved path that led to the garden's center, where she was to meet Rao.

If Englishmen would apply a speck of the intelligence Vishnu had blessed all men with, they would stop chasing a myth and instead seek to understand the Hindu way of life, which was far more peaceful—and far superior, Ashiana thought—to theirs.

But these arrogant invaders were not interested in learning. The years had taught them nothing. One would think they would accept what the other Europeans in India knew: the sapphires did not exist. The jewels were no more than a tale, a fantasy invented by an explorer in the time when Alexander the Great ruled this land. Her clan, the Ajmir, were a proud band of Rajput warriors, but they guarded no magical treasure.

Time and again, the Ajmir had been forced to move from one home to the next, trying to escape the sapphire legend and the destruction it brought down upon them, to no avail. They had thought this island inaccessible, and had lived here happily for almost thirty years, but now the English had managed to find them again.

The men who had attacked three days ago were sailors of the East India Company. No better than pirates, to Ashiana's mind. As relentless and cruel as any buccaneers in their efforts to get what they wanted. More than a score of Ajmir warriors had been killed in the battle, according to the eunuchs who guarded the harem. She whispered a fervent prayer to Vishnu the Preserver for the safety of her people.

Ashiana's emotions had not cooled by the time she reached the sculpted center of the harem gardens. She approached the white marble pavilion, ringed with trickling fountains, where Rao had said to wait for him.

Normally, this was a place of peace and serenity for her; she had spent many afternoons here, alone, meditating or stretching in her yoga *asanas* while the other women sought refuge from the sun's heat. Other times she would come here at night to practice the dances she loved to perform, often with Rao and a few peacocks as her only audience.

Now, with the gleaming marble silvered by the full moon, the empty pavilion seemed ghostly, as if it were haunted by the spirits of those who had fallen on the ramparts three days ago. Blinking away frightened tears,

Ashiana cast a curse upon those who had brought violence and death to her clan.

The fact that she was cursing half her own blood did not escape her. If there were some way to open herself up and purge the English taint from her veins, she would. She wondered for the thousandth time what had made her kindhearted father take an English woman for his wife.

She leaned down to put her slippers back on, then rested against one of the elaborately carved pillars, forcing the vexing question aside. Whatever his reasons, the fact that Ashiana was half English was not her own fault. Nor was it her fault that she so strongly resembled the mother she had never known.

Her thoughts and her anger both stilled at once, replaced by anxiety. Was that why Rao had wished a secret meeting with her tonight? Was she to be banished at last?

Ashiana shivered with a sudden chill. From the day she had arrived here, the Maharaja and his people had been kind, adopting her as one of their own. But the fact that she had been presented as a princess did not sit well with everyone in the clan.

She had heard the word whispered in the harem: *feringi.* Outsider. Foreigner.

And the other name, the one she hated most of all. *Angrez.* English.

And now that the despised Englishmen had located the Ajmir clan once more, old wounds had been reopened. She knew that to some, she must be as salt to those wounds.

Perhaps they could no longer tolerate her presence. Perhaps even the love of the Maharaja and his son would no longer be protection enough.

Ashiana's heart lurched as a feeling of loss seized her. She had already had one home and family torn from her. Where could she possibly go if forced to leave this one?

Fighting the panic that rose in her throat, she turned toward one of the fountains that splashed in the silence, slipped off her veil, and wet her face with cool water. *No.* She could not survive losing her clan. She loved the

Ajmir. Memories of her childhood aboard the *Adiante* were little more than shadows now. Sometimes it seemed she had only dreamed it all. Except when she looked at the long scar on her left arm.

A few years ago, one of the Maharaja's talented artists had turned it into a tattoo, a long-stemmed rose of a deep henna color. That gentle disguise, though, could not hide the mark completely. Nor did it make her forget the violence of the Englishmen who had given it to her.

And now that same violence was about to rip her from her home and family a second time.

Ashiana gripped the cool edge of the stone basin and tried to calm herself. Rao would never let it happen. He loved her. Soon she would be his wife; he would order the disgruntled ones in the clan to accept her, and they would. One did not refuse the crown prince.

But she knew that Rao's order could not change what was truly in his people's hearts, any more than it could change the color of the sky . . . or the color of her skin.

Ashiana waited for the surface of the fountain to calm and stared at her reflection. The moonlight and the rippling water obscured her image slightly. If she did not look too closely, it was almost possible to believe for a moment that she truly was an Ajmir princess. She had strong features and ebony hair, inherited from her father, which looked enough like those of a Hindu girl.

The heartfelt wish lasted only a moment, as she sadly admitted all she lacked. She lacked the lushly rounded body. She lacked the rich brown skin. She lacked the dark, mysterious gaze.

Ashiana's slimness, her clear blue eyes, and, most of all, her pallor marked her as her mother's daughter.

She ran her hand through the water, destroying her image and wishing it were equally simple to wipe away her English appearance. She slipped her veil back into place. The only women Ashiana had ever known were those of the Maharaja's harem, and she knew she would never be as beautiful as the plainest maidservant among them.

When Rao had offered marriage last year, she had

thought it the most wonderful, generous thing anyone had ever done for her. He would be a kind husband, and of much higher rank than a *feringi* girl could ever hope for. Ashiana could not be his *vadi*, his first wife, for she had not been born Hindu; he would marry another before her, but he had always assured her that she would be the favorite among all his wives.

Now she felt as if that dream were slipping through her pale fingers. She turned away from the fountain, wondering again why Rao's note had been so terse, dreading the meeting she had been looking forward to all day.

Her mind was so preoccupied, she nearly leaped out of her slippers when she felt something brush against her leg.

"Nicobar!" she said in a hushed tone, kneeling to pet her six-month-old tiger. "Have you no better prey than I tonight, brave hunter?" she whispered in fluent Hindi.

He allowed her to ruffle his fur only a moment before he growled and knocked her hand away with one gangly paw. Nicobar had been a betrothal gift from Rao, one that pleased Ashiana far more than any bauble could have. Rao understood her *so* well.

The tiger cub was at an awkward stage, still half playful kitten, but rapidly becoming a dangerous predator. Flopping onto the grass at her feet, Nicobar blinked sleepily and flicked the tip of his tail. His amber eyes reflected the moonlight, as did the jewels on his elaborate, padded leather collar.

"Shall you keep me company then," she whispered, "until our prince comes to keep his appointment?"

Nicobar yawned ferociously and rolled onto his side, halfheartedly batting at a red frangipani blossom that bobbed in the sultry breeze.

Ashiana started to sit beside him when Nicobar leaped to his feet, crouching low to the ground, his gaze locked on something in the shadows.

Ashiana stared in the same direction, her heart pounding. She had to grab Nicobar's collar to keep him from pouncing on the man coming down the path.

She started to call Rao's name, but the word caught in

her throat when she realized it was not him, but one of the eunuchs.

The man held a small oil lamp which he kept shaded with one hand. By the flickering light, she could see that his expression was grave.

"You are to come with me, Princess Ashiana."

Deep inside the palace, through sinuous corridors Ashiana had never seen before, Rao awaited them in a small chamber lit by candles. He looked tired. More than tired, haggard, as if he had not slept in some time. His gauzy blue *jama* and *shilwar* were rumpled, his dark cheeks stubbled with beard, his brow creased with deep lines.

He was speaking with someone—a woman—and Ashiana and her escort waited a respectful distance away until he finished. Ashiana had to fight an urge to throw herself into Rao's arms and deluge him with a monsoon of questions; such behavior would be improper, verging on scandalous.

When he had finished, Rao addressed them at last. "Ashiana, there was no time to fetch you myself," he said without greeting. *"Mere saath aao.* Come with me. My father awaits."

The woman he had been speaking to turned and raised her head, and Ashiana felt a stab of surprise. It was her maidservant and friend, Padmini, eyes bright with tears.

Padmini rushed over and fell at her mistress's feet, taking Ashiana's hand and squeezing tight as if afraid to let go. "O my mistress!" A sob escaped her and she could say no more.

"Hasin," Rao said to the eunuch, "you may escort Padmini back to the harem."

Padmini rose shakily, her soft brown eyes filled with such sadness, it robbed Ashiana of both breath and voice. Never had she seen her friend so upset—not when Ashiana had broken her leg falling from a tree when they were ten years old, not all the times the Maharaja had chastised Padmini for encouraging Ashiana's unruly nature, not even when the battle had broken out three days ago. The fate that awaited must be truly terrible to bring Padmini to tears.

Her friend had departed with the eunuch before Ashiana could even find the strength to blink. Anguished, she turned toward Rao. "I am . . . to be sent away?" she asked haltingly.

His eyes were impassive, like his father's, his voice abrupt. "This is a time of difficult decisions—"

"*Krupiya*. Please, Rao," she said, so panicked she interrupted. "Please, you must tell me."

He softened slightly and touched her arm, an expression of great intimacy even though they were alone. "There is little time for explanations. But you must believe that no matter what occurs this night, my feelings for you will never change, *premika*."

Despite his endearment, Ashiana felt a sense of inescapable doom. So she *was* to be sent away! The thing she most feared was coming true. She would never have the dreams she craved: marriage to Rao, a sense of belonging, a home among the Ajmir for now and forever. She felt all those hopes wither and fall like petals from a dying jasmine flower.

"Oh, Rao . . ." She started to slump forward weakly but Rao grasped her by the arms and forced her to remain standing.

"Ashiana, you have always been strong, for a woman, and you must be so now. *Tez*. Hurry. My father awaits us."

That news only frightened Ashiana more. Was she to be not only banished, but publicly denounced as well? The pain of loss made her light-headed as Rao led her toward a door and into an adjoining chamber.

This room, much larger than the other, was brightly lit with oil lamps. It took Ashiana's eyes a moment to adjust. The lavish tapestries, jewel-encrusted ceiling, and cotton carpets that decorated the chamber were magnificent even by the Maharaja's standards.

Her heart thudded unevenly as she looked to the far end of the room, where a half-dozen men sat on plump *musnads;* each appeared just as tense and fatigued as Rao. Ashiana guessed, with a fresh jolt of surprise, that she must be in the *durbar* hall—the secret meeting chamber where the Maharaja met with his advisors and the *raj guru,* the high priest. She had no doubt that she was the first woman ever to set foot here.

Ashiana realized Rao was no longer holding her arm and quickly remembered her own manners, modestly lowering her gaze and bowing her head.

"Sit there," Rao whispered, pointing toward a carpet that faced the semicircle of men. Her legs shaking, Ashiana did as he bade, kneeling with her hands folded in her lap. Rao came to stand beside her, then leaned down, keeping his voice low.

"Remove your veil and raise your eyes, *premika.*"

Ashiana started at the unusual command. It was most improper for a woman to appear unveiled in front of men—but then nothing about this night had been normal. Perhaps this was part of some punishment she must suffer. She unknotted her *dupatta* and let it fall, raising her head. Whatever she must face, she would face it with the dignity she had learned among the Ajmir these last fourteen years. Nothing could take that from her.

The council members stared at her for a long time, their expressions harsh and probing. Then, oddly, they all began nodding and murmuring among themselves. Ashiana could not hear their words, but there seemed to be an air of approval among them. It confused her more than ever.

Without another word, Rao went to his seat beside the *gaddi* throne in the center of the half-circle. He seemed more distressed than before.

Ashiana watched him, silently pleading for some sort of explanation, but he would not meet her gaze. She started to glance at the other council members, then felt warmth burning her cheeks. It was unbearably bold to keep returning their looks this way. Ashiana fell into an almost unconscious habit learned long ago: she lowered her eyes and held her head at a slight angle, so that her hair fell like a black curtain to conceal her English appearance.

The men fell silent suddenly, and Ashiana looked up from beneath her lashes to see the Maharaja entering.

He looked older than she had ever seen him, his face drawn and strained beneath his jeweled turban, his shoulders slightly stooped in a way that even his majestic silk robes could not disguise. The sight of him pained her and she felt a fresh wave of anger toward the Englishmen who had attacked the island, and worry for her clan. The past few days had obviously taken a great toll on the Maharaja's spirit. The situation must be even more grave than she had feared.

It took him a long time to move from a passage at the rear of the chamber to his *gaddi.* He settled himself with the help of the *raj guru,* and acknowledged each of his councillors in turn. Then his gaze fell on her.

He began to speak in a solemn tone. "Before we begin, Ashiana, we must know one thing of you." He paused, adding weight to his next words. "Are you English, or are you Rajput?"

"I am Rajput," she replied without hesitation.

"My *beti,* this is not a thing to be taken lightly. Measure your words carefully. Search your heart before you answer."

Ashiana felt a wave of emotion when he called her daughter; she did not need to measure her words, for she knew her heart. Struggling to keep the calm, dignified exterior that was the hallmark of her clan, she repeated her declaration. "I am a Rajput princess of the clan Ajmir." She spoke each word distinctly and firmly. "Nothing shall ever change that."

The Maharaja seemed to relax slightly. He glanced at his advisors with an expression that held both satisfaction and a bit of reproach. The council members whispered and nodded to each other once more.

Silence fell, and the Maharaja sat still for a long time, concern again furrowing his brow. When he spoke at last, he addressed his men, but his eyes never left Ashiana.

"For more than three hundred years," he began, "we the Ajmir have been the defenders of the defenders of India."

There were murmurs of agreement and pride among the council members. The formal words puzzled Ashiana—but the Maharaja's next declaration shook her like a tremor of the earth.

"The sacred stones, the Nine Sapphires of Kashmir, were entrusted into our care long before the first foreign intruders came to our land. Legend foretells that if they be taken from India, our clan shall fall into chaos and ruin, as befell the ancient civilization that once possessed them."

Incredulous, Ashiana could only sit in shock, her fingers gripping the thick carpet she sat on. Questions tumbled through her mind. The sapphires were *real?* How could this be? How was it that this had never even been whispered of in the gossip of the harem?

The Maharaja answered her questions before she could ask. "The sacred gems are of such surpassing beauty, that if their true value were known, all the world's kings would clash to possess them. We have kept the secret, even from our own women, passing it down only from maharaja to crown prince, from council to council, hiding it beneath myths and legends.

"After centuries of such tales, the world no longer believes the sapphires exist." He paused, shaking his head. "All but the English. They are not like the other Europeans. The others came as traders, but these men would strip our land of all its treasures. They proved their savagery on our ramparts three days past."

Ashiana felt her stomach clench. The Maharaja had been merely explaining to her why she must be banished. Now it would come—her denouncement and exile.

The Maharaja's voice took on an edge of criticism, aimed not at her, but at himself. "It is my fault that the English know the sapphires exist. Thirty years past, I was chosen protector, entrusted with the task of moving the stones to a new hiding place. Because I was young and arrogant, I was not careful enough, and one was stolen during the journey. By an Englishman. Despite all our efforts and many Ajmir lives, we have been unable to reclaim it.

We know only that when the thief died, he passed it on to his son."

Ashiana braced herself, poised at the edge of her endurance, waiting for the dreaded words that had not yet come.

"Now the remaining eight are threatened as well. We defeated the attackers three days past, but more Englishmen will come. Many more. I fear they would slaughter every Ajmir warrior, woman, and child to possess the stones. They must be lured away from this island."

This brought louder mutters of assent and urgency from the council members. The Maharaja rose with great dignity from his *gaddi*. "It is time for the sacred stones to be reunited. A protector must be chosen from among us, to reclaim the sapphire stolen by this Englishman and move all nine to a new hiding place. A final resting place, where they will be beyond the reach of thieves forever."

Rao stood and addressed the council, his voice strained. "I still say the task should be mine—"

"The decision has been made," the Maharaja said flatly.

Rao would not be silenced. "This *angrez* is not an ordinary enemy. He has ridden in Kashmir with a band of Maratha tribesmen. He knows the Hindu language, our weapons, our ways. They say the sapphire he possesses has driven him mad to have the other eight. He wears it like a trophy about his neck. Many Rajputs have died—"

"*Chuppi!* Silence, Rao Chand Ajmir!" The Maharaja proved he was yet young and strong enough to make an entire chamber quake with his voice.

Rao immediately knelt down and touched his forehead to the floor. "*Maf kijiye.* I beg forgiveness, Maharaja," he said humbly, though his jaw was clenched.

Ashiana's stomach churned. Never had she seen Rao in such a passion! She could barely follow all that was being said, much less understand what any of it had to do with her banishment.

The Maharaja resumed speaking, calmly, as if he had already forgotten his son's transgression. "The Emperor is to meet with many European traders at his summer palace in Daman, during the festival of *holi*. We shall let it be known that the Maharaja of the Ajmir will be there, and this Englishman will surely come. The protector must get close enough to take the sapphire from him. There will be ample time to do this and kill him before the meeting is complete."

Here he paused, and Ashiana looked from one council member to another, wondering who had been chosen for such a dangerous and important task.

It took her a moment to realize *that they were all looking at her.*

She felt stunned, as if the jeweled ceiling had just fallen down upon her. "M-m-me?" she stuttered. "But . . ." She could not form a coherent thought, much less a sentence. "But I am a woman. How shall I be able to overcome this Englishman when so many warriors have failed?"

When the Maharaja seemed reluctant to reply, Rao answered her question, his voice tinged with bitter irony. "Women are his one weakness."

Ashiana swallowed hard, seeing the logic in her being chosen. A woman would be able to get close to him. If she succeeded, the sapphires and the clan would be saved. If she failed . . . there were many who considered her expendable.

The Maharaja said firmly, "The decision is yours, Ashiana."

Her first impulse was denial. But then a much stronger feeling overcame her, a mixture of hatred for the English and love for her clan. She had stepped into this chamber thinking she was about to be cast out; instead she was being offered a great responsibility.

How could she let the greed and cruelty that had killed her papa and destroyed her childhood home also destroy the Maharaja and the Ajmir?

Still she hesitated, remembering what had been said of this Englishman. Like all his people, he sounded savage, violent—but he was quick-witted as well, a fearsome enemy for even the strongest Ajmir warrior. She had no training in weapons. And she spoke not a word of the English tongue. How could she hope to overcome him?

The Maharaja and his council seemed confident that she could. And if she succeeded ... she would return a heroine. She would marry Rao and at last be finally, truly Ajmir, forever.

As if sensing her thoughts, the Maharaja urged with quiet pride, "They will sing songs of you, Ashiana of the Ajmir. In the histories of the Rajputs, your name shall be written in gold letters."

Ashiana of the Ajmir. It was the first time anyone had called her that. She also saw the concern and protectiveness that filled the Maharaja's gaze. He would not let anything happen to her. And she owed him so much. "I vow by all the gods, my father," she said with a flood of pride and fierce determination, "I will not fail you."

He nodded solemnly, accepting her pledge, his eyes reflecting his admiration, and his love. "We shall leave for Daman tonight. There are a great many preparations to be made. And you must adopt your new identity."

"Identity?" Ashiana asked, her head swirling with the enormity of the challenge she had just taken on.

The Maharaja nodded. "A ruse, to allow you close enough to this Englishman to carry out your task. You shall be presented to him as a gift ... as a slave girl."

Chapter 2

"It is time, D'Avenant."

The Maratha warrior held the torch aloft and repeated himself twice more before Lord Saxon D'Avenant responded. Kneeling in the grass, his entire body rigid, Saxon didn't even look up. Somewhere in a distant corner of his mind, he realized it was his friend Bihar addressing him, but the emotions clouding his thoughts wouldn't let him accept what was being said.

When Saxon finally spoke, it was a single word, the same one he had been repeating all afternoon. The same word that had been screeching through his brain since morning.

"No."

Bihar hesitated, until Saxon slowly raised his head. That single glance made the warrior turn and move away with haste. Saxon returned his gaze to the beautiful woman who lay before him. Mandara.

His legs had gone numb long ago. His white *gharara* breeches, once wet with dew, had dried in the sun until they clung to his heavily muscled thighs. He wasn't ready yet.

After several days of rain, their wedding day had dawned clear, the sky a perfect blue. Through shimmering waves of late-afternoon heat, he could make out the Himalayas breaking into the horizon, their white peaks embraced by clouds. A hot wind tangled his long, loose blond hair against his tanned cheeks, and teased the fields of

23

saffron that stretched for miles across the Kashmir plains. Two men using scythes had cleared a wide circle for the ceremony.

Saxon ignored the crowd of tribespeople that waited uneasily several yards away. He wasn't ready yet. Mandara was almost too beautiful, possessing an unearthly radiance, her dark skin glistening with fragrant oils, her lips reddened with vermilion, her wrists and fingers sparkling with bangles and jewelry, her hair brushed to glossy black perfection. She lay before him veiled in her brilliant wedding silks, as if awaiting his kiss, his touch, the long-awaited consummation of their love.

Saxon stared blankly at the garlands of yellow and red flowers around her neck. They draped across her breasts, over her arms.

And down the sides of her funeral bier.

No, no, no. Screaming it a hundred times in as many languages would not change what had happened. Nothing could erase that gut-wrenching moment this morning, just after they had spoken their vows. They had been walking through the village toward the feast that awaited, surrounded by a boisterous crowd of well-wishers.

She had given him a shy smile. Their gazes had met, held, shared a private message: she no longer belonged with her father and sisters, but with him. She was his wife, ready to share his life and his bed at last. *His wife.*

Then, without warning, out of nowhere, it struck—an arrow no larger than a dart. Struck her so lightly she thought at first it was but an insect. Minutes later, she lay dying in his arms, biting her tongue to hold back screams of agony. With her last breath, she had whispered his name.

"D'Avenant?" Bihar had returned, standing a few feet away this time.

Saxon ground one fist against his palm. Even in the sweltering sun, he could feel the heat of the funeral torch, like a blast from hell aimed straight at his back.

Like a curse. His hand moved to the pouch he wore around his neck, gripping it as if he could crush the gem within. The Maratha villagers had begun a furious search for Mandara's killer, but Saxon knew who it was, and knew they would not find him.

Greyslake. Murdering son of a hell-hound. Poisonous and treacherous, silent as a cobra, he had struck an unexpected target. Saxon hadn't needed to see the engraved gold *G* on the poison-tipped arrow. The cruelty of the act itself was signature enough. *Bastard.* But Greyslake would not have done the deed himself; he would have hired an assassin, someone familiar with Kashmir, someone who could fade away into the fields in minutes.

The most hellish part was that Greyslake must have been in the area for days, lurking, watching Saxon—then instead choosing Mandara as his victim. Contemplating the most vicious moment to strike. Slipping away to let his hireling do the rest.

Saxon felt the edges of the sapphire digging into his palm even through the leather that concealed it. Vengeful blood lust roared through him, but so did fury at himself. He never should have stayed here this long. Rested. Allowed himself to think that his life could be different than it was—

"D'Avenant."

Bihar's voice was gently insistent this time. Saxon quelled the rage that seethed within him. He rose, slowly, his eyes never leaving his wife's still form. His numb legs refused to hold him at first, but Bihar knew better than to offer assistance. Saxon forced his muscles to respond, depending on the long months he had spent training with *moghdurs* to get him to his feet.

Mandara. Every memory had her name attached, even that one. She had shown him the Maratha custom of training with the heavy weights. When he had crawled out of the desert to the peasant village, half-dead from wounds that should have killed him, she had nursed him back to health, using her healing skills and the *moghdurs* to help him regain the use of his arms and legs.

Of all the women he had known, she was the only one who had ever made him think of marriage. There had not been lust between them, but sweetness, quiet gentleness. Even when he thoughtlessly took out his frustrations with harsh words during his long months of recovery, she had responded only with kindness and encouragement, as good and giving as a Hindu goddess of peace come to earth from paradise.

But Saxon had tainted her. Brought down his quest and the curse and Greyslake and death upon her. Because of her help, he was now stronger and healthier than he had been in all his thirty years—but she was gone.

His wife. Gone.

He stood, towering over the warrior who came to stand by his side. He wasn't ready, he never would be. But it was time.

He turned to look at Bihar, at the torch. The orange-and-yellow flame licked at the wind.

"A moment," Saxon said, his voice sounding distant and hollow even to his own ears.

Walking to the far side of the bier, he knelt and lifted Mandara's left hand, willing his fingers not to shake. The gold wedding band she wore felt so delicate beneath his broad fingers, and cold. Unearthly cold. The ring was an English custom, not Hindu, but Mandara had been willing to accept it, knowing how important his people and their ways were to him.

He bent his head, closed his eyes, pressed her hand to his rough cheek, his mind refusing to acknowledge that her skin felt as cold as the ring. He had known such warmth, such gentleness in her touch.

Emotions raked through him, soft words he had never been able to say aloud. Words she would now never hear.

I love you, my Mandara. I am your husband and you are my wife, and I swear to you that no other will take your place. My soul shall seek yours in the next life, my love.

Forcing himself to let go, he laid her hand back upon her breast, covering it with one of the brightly colored garlands.

He missed his footing as he stepped back, and Bihar

came to stand next to him. Saxon held out his hand. His friend gave him the torch without a word.

For one agonizing moment, Saxon remained frozen, his arm rigid, his fingers bloodless. Then a strangled roar began deep in his chest. It came out as Mandara's name. He jammed the torch into the bier, setting the wood and rushes ablaze. Within minutes, the fire leaped into the sky. The women in the crowd fell to their knees, crying and tearing at their hair.

Saxon felt as if he'd just sliced out his own heart with a hot saber.

He turned and walked away, the flames searing him inside until nothing was left but black ashes, until he could no longer feel grief or rage, or even pain anymore.

Saxon blinked rapidly, squinting in the darkness. His head ached. His mouth felt as dry as cotton. How many days had passed? He couldn't remember. He knew only that there had been a large span of time between the moment he had seen Mandara's body consumed by fire, and the realization that he had just heard a sound.

It took another full minute to remember where he was. The same place he had been since walking blindly away from the funeral: the hut he occupied at the eastern side of the village. He sat on the dirt floor amid a clutter of broken earthenware, shattered oil lamps, torn strips that had once been a *dhurrie*, remnants of a woven screen, and bits of a carved stool that had been snapped like a twig. He barely remembered doing it, except that he had cuts and splinters on his hands.

He stared out the hut's one window, in the direction of the stream, into the night.

The sound came again. A knock. It barely registered. Saxon's mind, awakened now from its dazed paralysis, had returned to its last conscious thought: cursing every god that anyone had ever believed in.

He wondered how he could get his hands on a bottle of rum or illicit *tadi* palm wine or anything that would make him pass out. Liquor was forbidden among the Hindu

Marathas. Sleep would not come. So he sat and stared into the darkness.

The knock invaded his consciousness a third time, and the door creaked open. Light flickered tentatively into the shadows.

"I have a message for D'Avenant." A man's voice squeaked in high-pitched, fluent Hindi, mispronouncing the name. "From England."

For the first time in days, Saxon felt something. He resented the hell out of it, but there was no stopping the familiar tension that flooded his veins. Too many years on the edge, years spent watching for Ajmir warriors or Greyslake around every turn, had made the aggressive response involuntary.

No one in England knew he was here. Not even his family, except for his brother Julian, who didn't speak Hindi.

And Julian would know better than to trust a messenger with Saxon's location.

"*Nikal jao,*" Saxon said with soft malice. "Get out."

Perhaps, he thought calmly, Greyslake had returned. Perhaps he had finally grown bored of subterfuge and cat-and-mouse games and decided on a direct confrontation. Without conscious effort, Saxon had already mentally reviewed the array of weapons that hung on the wall behind him and selected one.

"I am to deliver a message to Saxon D'Avenant," the man insisted, his voice rising as he again mangled the family name.

The too-familiar killing instinct had taken full control now. Saxon rose casually, as if to lean out the window, not yet turning around. "It's not *dee*-avinant," he said lightly. "It's *dahv*-inant."

In the next second, Saxon whirled and snatched a *khan-jar* dagger from the wall. Like fluid lightning, he slammed the messenger up against the doorjamb and had the blade at his throat all in the space of one breath.

"Bloody Christ. Julian!" Only his razor-honed reflexes saved his brother from the sharp edge of honed steel.

"Damnation!" Julian's gray eyes, wide with fear and surprise, were locked on the knife. "That's one fine welcome, Sax! I see being on extended holiday hasn't improved your sense of humor any." His face regained its color as his expression shifted easily to amusement. "But let's use the full family name, shall we? We're not just the *Dahv*-inants, we're the 'world-wandering, seafaring, scandalous, depraved *Dahv*-inants.' How the devil are you?"

"Since when do you know Hindi?" Saxon belatedly threw the *khanjar* aside and let his brother down from the doorjamb.

"The *Rising Star*'s been up in the stocks at Bombay for repairs and refitting since Christmas." Julian adjusted his East India Company captain's uniform, meticulously straightening the medals clustered on the lapel. "I sought comfort with this charming little courtesan. You wouldn't believe what else she—"

"Never mind." Saxon stepped back and glowered at him. "You complete idiot, your sense of humor is going to be the death of you someday."

"Good to see you too, Sax." Julian picked up the primitive lantern he had dropped. "The locals warned me you were in a foul mood, but they wouldn't elaborate. I assured them I had seen it all before."

Saxon frowned in irritation. No one could get a response out of him faster than his irresponsible younger brother with his penchant for practical jokes. Despite being as opposite as a bowsprit from a sternpost, the two of them were only a year apart, and had always been the closest of the four D'Avenant brothers.

"What the hell brings you all the way out here?"

Julian looked startled at the surly question. He regarded Saxon with raised eyebrows, holding the lantern higher, then noticed the clutter strewn across the floor on the far side of the hut. His lighthearted air instantly turned serious. "Sax, what the devil happened? What's wrong with—"

"Say what you came to say." Saxon turned on his heel and stalked back to the window.

Julian persisted. "When you wrote a few weeks ago," he said slowly, "you said you weren't well enough to travel yet. Sax, you look healthy as a horse. Why haven't you come back to Bombay?"

Saxon remained mute.

"You know, the Company hasn't exactly been happy about one of its captains taking a year-long unannounced holiday. Not that you don't deserve one. It's just so unlike you. The *Valor*'s sitting there with her cargo holds empty. And that pack of smugglers you call a crew are as loyal as bull terriers, but they're getting itchy. They've become a bit of a menace."

No reply.

"Let me guess. Some pretty little *larki* caught your eye, and you—"

"Stow it, Julian."

The clipped warning was enough. If Julian was still curious about the subject, he kept it to himself and didn't attempt to bring it up again. He fell into an uncharacteristic silence.

Saxon released a harsh breath. His head throbbed with the force of two warships pounding each other with cannon fire. He didn't want to snap at his brother, but he didn't want him here, either. He didn't want anyone here. "Tell me whatever the devil you came here to tell me and leave me *alone,* damn it."

Instead of replying in kind, Julian kept his tone mild and shifted to small talk. "Mother said to send you her regards, last time I saw her. She's still flitting around London redefining the term 'eccentric.' Would you believe she's actually applied to lecture in history at the University?"

"What does that—"

"She would, of course, appreciate a visit from you."

Saxon didn't respond to his goading. "I can't go home. You know why." It had been years since he had ridden up the long drive to the door of Silverton Park in Kent; but when there were people in the world who wanted to cut one's throat, it was wisest to stay out of sight, on the move, and away from home and loved ones. Saxon abruptly changed the subject away from himself. "How is Max?"

"Still sick." Julian sighed heavily. "Still confined to bed and having trouble breathing, but it doesn't seem to be getting worse."

Saxon shook his head wearily. He added regret to the knot of useless, discarded feelings that filled him inside like a clump of melted lead. Here among the Marathas—for how long? Had it really been a year?—he had almost allowed himself to forget his family, his responsibility to Max, his quest. It was a moment before he realized that Julian had fallen silent again.

Saxon turned slowly to face him.

"You're not even going to ask about Dalton, are you?" Julian said, his disappointment clear.

Leaning against the thatched wall, Saxon folded his arms over his chest. He didn't bother to shake his head. It was a stupid question. He regarded his brother with an impatient, silent glower.

"You can't hate him forever."

"Whom I choose to hate is my own business," Saxon said tightly. "And I surmise he is at least still alive, because if his high-and-mightiness were dead, it would make me the Duke of Silverton, and you, in your inimitable way, wouldn't be able to resist calling me 'your grace.' Now what are you—"

"Dalton's still in Russia, aboard the *Prince of Malabar.*" Julian answered the question that Saxon hadn't asked. "But I only know that through a friend. We've had no word from him."

Saxon digested the news about the eldest D'Avenant without reaction and returned to his original question. "So if the family are all more or less the same, what the devil brings you here?"

Julian folded his arms in imitation of the brother he so resembled. He smiled, the slow, satisfied smile of one about to bestow a much-wanted gift. "The sapphires."

Saxon came away from the wall with a jerk, every nerve and sinew instantly on edge.

"The Ajmir have been located. Less than a fortnight ago. I knew you would want to know right away, so I came as fast as I could . . ."

Awash in a painful flash of memories, Saxon didn't hear the rest of what his brother was saying. For ten years, he had sought the missing Sapphires of Kashmir, and his father had searched for uncountable years before him; on his deathbed, he had pressed the egg-sized gem into Saxon's palm and made him swear not to rest until he had taken the other eight.

Brandon D'Avenant had been a notorious black sheep who overindulged in gambling and drink, and couldn't resist the enormous wager that challenged him to steal one of the sapphires. Too late he discovered the consequences of his actions. Not all the legends that surrounded the gems were mere myth: the curse, the one rumored to have haunted the stones from ancient times before they passed into Ajmir hands, was real.

Saxon had watched his father slowly die of a strange illness that stole the very breath from his lungs. Within days of his death, the same illness had suddenly struck Max—not Dalton, his father's eldest and best-loved son; not Saxon, who now possessed the sapphire; not Julian—just gentle, studious Max, the youngest of the four brothers. That was when Saxon had left to seek the jewels, on that first ill-fated voyage with his friend Greyslake.

According to the ancient curse, only one thing could save his brother's life: all nine sapphires had to be reunited in the hands of the thief or one of his blood heirs. Simple.

The only problem was that the Ajmir weren't about to just hand the other jewels over. On the contrary, they preferred to leave the thief's family cursed forever. Three Ajmir warriors had taunted Saxon about that when they captured and tortured him in the desert, before he managed to kill them and escape.

He realized Julian was still speaking.

". . . on some godforsaken islands in the Bay of Bengal.

Called the Andamans. But the Maharaja himself will attend this meeting at the Emperor's summer palace in Daman."

"They're moving the stones." Saxon's mind was already working.

"Exactly what I thought. Which is why I polished a little brass at Company headquarters to get our names on the list for this palaver." Julian came to stand directly in front of him, his gaze full of concern. "So what say you, Sax? Are you going to stay out here among the natives and the pretty *larkis* forever, or shall we pack up these—" He nodded to the array of weapons on the far wall. "—charming souvenirs of yours and get ourselves to Daman?"

Pretty larkis. Julian couldn't know how much that might have hurt.

But it didn't.

Saxon acknowledged, without struggle, that the part of him that could feel hurt, or anything else, the part that belonged to Mandara, had died with her.

It was time to finish what had started ten years ago. He had been a fool to think he could put it aside for a life of peace and pastoral innocence, even for a short while.

This was what he was. The familiar, powerful, urgent sensation replaced the numbing pall that had hung over him. It sizzled through him, like hot sunlight on churning seas.

The killing instinct.

Where he found the sapphires, he would also find Greyslake—and whatever dark deeds Saxon had committed in the name of this quest would pale next to what he would do when he found him.

Moving around his brother, he picked up the *khanjar* he had dropped on the floor. He twirled it deftly. The blade flashed in the lamplight, a lethal silver blur.

This was what he was.

"To Daman."

Chapter 3

Ashiana took one look at her intended target and nearly lost her nerve.

"*He* is the one?" she whispered, her throat suddenly dry. Standing behind a lattice screen in the Emperor's palace at Daman, she peered into the *diwan-i-khas,* the grand audience chamber, her gaze fastened on the Englishman.

Her heartbeat unsteady, she turned wide eyes to the Maharaja, who had just pointed out Saxon D'Avenant.

The Maharaja nodded. "*Han.* Yes. He is the one."

Ashiana couldn't hear anything else for a moment, except her blood rushing in her ears. Clustered around her in the shadows, musicians, fakirs, and three score of slave girls whispered excitedly among themselves, waiting for the Emperor's command to enter and perform for his important visitors. On the other side of the screen, nearly fifty emissaries from the Dutch, Portuguese, and English trading companies sat listening to Emperor Alamgir the Second speak.

Ashiana looked through the intricately carved lattice again. "Not the other one?" she asked hopefully, pointing to another blond man, sitting beside the first. He looked similar but younger, not so powerfully muscled ... less dangerous.

The Maharaja, who wore simple robes and carried a small *tabla* drum to blend in with the crowd of entertainers, shook his head. "No, not him. Do not allow the physical appearance of this Saxon D'Avenant to daunt your

34

courage, Ashiana of the Ajmir. He is only a man. He has weaknesses. You will find them."

Swallowing hard, Ashiana studied her enemy, who sat a few feet away. *Weaknesses?* Saxon D'Avenant looked as solid and unconquerable as a fortress, his craggy features like stone chiseled by a sculptor who lacked an eye for elegance. He was all angles and sharp lines, broad jaw and prominent cheekbones. His nose had clearly been broken at least once, for it had a pronounced kink in the middle. He did not wear a wig like the other Europeans, but even his blond hair, hanging loose to his shoulders, did not soften his appearance.

The Englishman's obvious strength made Ashiana's every instinct urge her to turn and flee. His British East India Company uniform strained across his chest and shoulders, the embroidered blue coat much too small, the gold buttons on his snug white waistcoat ready to tear free if he but took a deep breath. It was as if the gods had tried to pack too much physical prowess into this one man.

And she was to be made his slave girl.

Her legs went weak and she laced her fingers through the lattice screen to steady herself. Her fear only worsened when he shifted uncomfortably and Ashiana noticed something else he wore: the Englishman's right hand rested on a sword, a weapon unlike the ceremonial blades carried by the other European traders. She recognized it as a *shamshir,* the light, curved, deadly saber favored by Hindu warriors.

It reminded her that he knew a great deal about her people and their ways. And their weapons.

Seized by sheer panic, she closed her eyes to shut him out. Only years of yoga practice helped her bring both breath and heartbeat under control.

After a moment, she forced her fear aside, reminding herself that the Maharaja had trained her well. They had gone over every detail of their plan a hundred times since arriving in Daman. The Emperor himself had agreed to assist them; an old ally and friend of the Maharaja, he put his resources at their disposal without probing too deeply for explanations. He would even play a small role in their ruse this afternoon.

This Saxon D'Avenant might be expert with sword, knife, and pistol, but she had less obvious weapons at her command, things he couldn't dream of.

As for being his slave, it was only playacting—something she had always been good at. She would have the sapphire and be gone before he had the chance to do anything more than kiss her.

She opened her eyes, studying his face, his mouth. One kiss, she told herself. She could survive one kiss. Besides, now was no time for second thoughts. Even as she watched, the Emperor made an impatient motion, interrupting a Dutchman who had been speaking of a new shipping route.

"I weary of this," Alamgir the Second said loftily. "The day's discussions are done. We shall continue tomorrow." Reaching for a jewel-encrusted gold hookah beside him, he inhaled deeply then exhaled, tobacco smoke curling around his moustache and beard. He nodded to one of his guards, who dashed toward the rear of the hall.

The guard stuck his head around the corner of the lattice screen. "The fakirs. Quickly."

Ashiana swallowed the lump of fear that had knotted in her throat. The musicians and slave girls would be summoned next.

The women giggled nervously, making last-minute adjustments to their provocative costumes as they traded opinions about the more handsome men among the Emperor's visitors.

The Maharaja touched Ashiana's arm. "Durga, goddess of battle, shall see you safely through this task, *beti.*"

Turning, Ashiana looked up at him and her nervousness ebbed. Still, she had the vague feeling that the Maharaja had not told her everything he knew about this Englishman. There was something he was purposely leaving unsaid—perhaps something so terrifying, it would make her turn back.

She pushed her doubts aside, letting her mind flood with

memories of the many Ajmir who had died at Saxon D'Avenant's hands. She remembered that he was a thief and son of a thief, greedy, ruthless, a man completely lacking in honor. An Englishman.

She remembered her papa dying on the deck of the *Adiante*.

Her hatred kindled and seared away the last of her hesitation. "I am ready, Maharaja."

He touched her cheek, a gesture of such tenderness, it nearly brought most unseemly tears to her eyes. "Within days, you shall be home," he whispered, "and your brave deed shall be made known to all the clan."

Ashiana smiled tremulously, clinging to that thought. The Ajmir, even her friend Padmini, had been told that Ashiana was being sent away to live in the Emperor's harem. The secret of the sapphires would be kept until the stones were safely hidden once and for all.

And if she failed . . . another protector would have to be chosen to finish her task. The clan would never know the truth of the risk she had agreed to take.

"I will not fail you," she said fiercely.

From the other side of the screen, they could hear the Europeans applaud as the fakirs ended their brief display of magical feats. The Emperor clapped his hands and called for the slave girls. The musicians went in first, to tune their instruments.

"Remember," the Maharaja whispered, stepping back into the shadows, "as soon as you have the sacred stone, make your way to the chamber of the winds. The eunuch Hasin shall meet you there. He will accompany you while you take the sapphires to their new hiding place."

"*Han*, Maharaja." Ashiana had gone over every step that led from the Emperor's *preet chatra*, the pavilion of pleasure, to the underground chamber, a dozen times. She would stop on the way to get the other eight sapphires from their hiding place in her room. She could walk the entire path in total darkness if need be.

The sounds of flutes and drums and sitars filled the scented air as the musicians began to play.

"You will be the most celebrated heroine the Aj-mir have ever known, my daughter," the Maharaja said proudly, before he turned and slipped away into the palace corridors.

Ashiana watched him go, feeling a sharp, painful echo of another time when she had been separated from the only family she had known, from the father she loved.

She was completely alone now.

But then the silk-swathed girls began to move forward, and there was no more time for thinking.

They lined up at the entrance to the audience chamber, where a eunuch held a gold tray bearing dozens of tiny sil-ver carafes, and a second servant held an armful of flower garlands. Each girl took a carafe and a garland before glid-ing gracefully inside.

Waiting her turn at the end of the line, Ashiana felt awe at the riot of color that greeted her eyes. The Emperor's *diwan-i-khas* had been built to dazzle and overwhelm, its ceilings of solid gold, its walls gleaming with inlaid ivory and mother-of-pearl, its massive marble pillars wrapped with lavish lengths of red-and-gold brocade.

A canopy of red silk billowed over the entire hall, fas-tened with red silken cords and huge tassels. Enamel lamps burned precious oils that scented the air with jas-mine and the essence of the rare flower called "queen of the night." Everywhere silver trays laden with mangos, guavas, pomegranates, and grapes sat ready to appease the guests' hunger.

Reclining on his quilted satin *musnad*, the Emperor smoked his hookah and smiled as he watched the slave girls file in. "The most beautiful women in all my empire have been selected to entertain you." His gaze flicked up to meet Ashiana's as she came to the front of the line. "But first they shall honor you with proper greetings."

At his signal, each girl went to kneel before one of the European guests. The Emperor had let it be known that the burly-looking Englishman was to be left alone. No doubt the slave girls were quite happy to comply with that command, Ashiana thought as she moved toward Saxon D'Avenant.

D'Avenant did not even glance at her as she knelt at his feet, the silver carafe clutched in her hand; he was conversing in low tones with the blond man who sat beside him—who in turn had his eyes on an African slave girl kneeling before him. She flashed Ashiana a wide-eyed look of sympathy.

This close to D'Avenant, Ashiana felt renewed awe at his physical size, but also noticed the tension in him; while the other Europeans freely partook of the fruit, *tadi* wine, hookahs, and chewing betels heaped around them, D'Avenant had not touched any of the pleasures offered him. He looked as stiff and tense and out of place as a panther dropped into a gathering of lions.

No, not a panther, Ashiana decided as she knelt there, willing her heart to slow down. A caracal. That was what he reminded her of: the honey-colored hunting cats that prowled the rain forests of her island home, hungry for prey yet so wary of other predators that they never relaxed the merest muscle.

As yet, he had not noticed her.

"It is the greatest of honors to be anointed with the precious balm known as attar of roses," the Emperor explained for the benefit of those unfamiliar with the custom. "And so shall you be welcomed this night, my estimable guests. The first anointment shall be upon the forehead, to honor your wisdom."

Ashiana sprinkled some of the scented oil on her fingertips. As she raised her hand to dab the Englishman's forehead, he turned to face her at last.

His gaze locked with hers. Ashiana froze in mid-motion.

His eyes gleamed an uncannily bright silver-gray, sharp and cold. Like diamonds. Like *tabar* blades. They captured her with an expression that sent a shiver through her veins. There was no warmth in that gaze. No mercy. His golden brows, slashing downward toward the inner corners of his eyes, only added to his harsh, angry look.

This will be over soon, she admonished herself. *You are an Ajmir princess. Act with the bravery of your clan!*

To him, she said in soft Hindi, "I mean no harm, sahib."

It irked her to call him "sir," but her soothing words were a lie in any event.

He didn't reply or indicate that he understood, only kept his eyes steadily upon hers while she dabbed his forehead with the attar. The scent of roses perfumed the air between them.

His skin felt warm, like smooth, dark sand heated by the sun; Ashiana's stomach made an odd little leap. Confused by the unfamiliar sensation, she looked away, bending her head as she tipped the carafe a second time.

"The second anointment shall be upon the lips, my guests," the Emperor said, "to honor the truth of the words you have spoken this day."

Wetting her fingers again, Ashiana looked up and repeated the motion. She touched his lips with just one fingertip, but their softness took her by surprise—as did the quick, subtle shift in D'Avenant's gaze.

His eyes flicked from her veiled face to her barely clad breasts and back again. The silvery color darkened; they seemed no less cold, but now held a look unlike any she had seen directed toward her before. She withdrew her hand, trembling despite herself.

In the Maharaja's harem, Ashiana had heard countless frank discussions of men, and physical appetites, and the act that took place between man and woman . . . but never had she pictured herself in any such interlude. Until now. Until she saw the unmistakable hunger in Saxon D'Avenant's eyes.

More startling than the arousal she saw reflected there was the tingling sensation she felt in her own body, beginning at her very center and flowing outward in little shivers. It unnerved her. D'Avenant's interest was exactly what she had hoped for, what she had intended, so why did she feel so . . . strange?

She decided it must be nervousness, though it was unlike any nervousness she had felt before.

He kept looking at her, as if in his mind he were peeling away her veil, her *choli* bodice, every bit of iridescent silk that covered her pale skin.

The younger man at D'Avenant's side glanced her way and muttered something in English. A humorless smile quirked at the corner of D'Avenant's rigid mouth, and he translated for her in low, fluent Hindi. "My brother says he wishes you were not already a woman of the Emperor's harem, for you and your friend here would make an excellent start to a harem of his own."

Ashiana lowered her gaze, feeling embarrassment warm her cheeks. It was unacceptably bold to speak so to a woman—even a slave girl. *Unmannered curs,* she thought. *Both of them.*

She had almost forgotten the carafe in her hand until the Emperor spoke again. "The final anointment shall be over the heart, my guests, to honor your courage."

Remembering the role she was supposed to be playing, Ashiana reached up to unbutton the Englishman's ruffled white shirt. Without warning, he knocked her hand away. She inhaled in surprise. His expression had lost any hint of humor; he stared down at her with suspicion, every muscle taut.

"*Maf kijiye,*" she apologized. "I meant no offense, sahib."

He did not relax, nor did he say a word to explain why he had stopped her when he had not objected to her other touches.

Finally Ashiana set the carafe down, her pulse pounding. She would do well to remember that D'Avenant could be as unpredictable as he was strong.

Lifting the garland of red blossoms that was the final step in the customary greeting, she started to raise it toward him, but he jerked aside as if it were made of fire rather than flowers.

"*Nahin.* No," he growled, adding something in English that sounded like a curse.

Puzzled, Ashiana placed the garland at his feet instead.

It did not matter; she had gained his notice, and that was all she had wished to do, for the moment.

They stared at one another, silver eyes locked with sapphire, until the Emperor's voice broke the spell.

"And now that you have been properly greeted and honored, my guests, you shall be entertained, with a dance that shall linger in your memory long after you have departed my palace."

Saxon resented the familiar hunger that seethed in him as he watched the pale beauty join the other slave girls in the center of the hall, her tinkling anklets and bracelets making music as she walked. She was dressed like all the others, and she spoke fluent Hindi, but she was clearly European. Saxon wondered how she had come to be here—and why she affected him so powerfully.

He blamed his almost painful state of arousal on a year of celibate living, not to mention complete exhaustion. He and Julian had all but raced here from Kashmir, stopping only to get Saxon's uniform from aboard the *Valor.*

That had been a waste of time, he grimaced, shifting uncomfortably in the too-tight frock coat and breeches. He hadn't realized just how much the *moghdurs* had increased his muscle size until he tried on his old uniform. He would have to order a new one from Company headquarters.

For now, he had more pressing problems. He had endured an entire day of endless trade discussions, and so far the Maharaja of the Ajmir was nowhere to be seen. It seemed every other *nawab,* prince, and potentate in ten provinces was here, each introduced to the Europeans in wearisome detail.

The day had been spent in bowing and complimenting and exchanging gifts, each more elaborate than the last, from turbans and robes in silver cloth, to jewel-encrusted daggers, to a matched pair of trained elephants with gold fetters, presented to the leader of the Dutch trading company.

But no representative from the clan Ajmir had appeared. In fact, Saxon thought in annoyance, he had yet to hear a single mention of the clan. He was getting impatient. The sapphires seemed no closer than they had yesterday, or last month, or ten years ago. The Emperor's legendary hospitality was beginning to wear on him.

Except, he had to admit, for this particular entertainment. He tried not to look at the European slave as the women began their dance—but failed. In this sultry, perfume-laden palace, she was like a breath of cool air off the Dover cliffs, a pale rose plucked fresh from a Covent Square garden.

How the devil had she come to be in the Emperor's harem? Kidnapped in childhood, perhaps? Her touch still glistened on his mouth; he wiped away the rose-scented oil, but could not wipe away the memory of her fingertip brushing lightly, wetly over his bottom lip.

A thought of Mandara flashed into his head, but this girl was nothing like his wife. Mandara had been sweet as a goddess of peace and innocence; this slave was bold as a bacchanalian nymph, inviting chase and conquest. She made him think of old, bad habits, pleasures he had not partaken of in a long time.

He found himself wondering how her hand might have felt on his bare chest, then shoved the image aside, irritated.

Of course he had stopped her from completing the anointment ceremony—he couldn't risk exposing the pouch around his neck.

The slave girls began their dance, and Saxon tried to observe with casual disinterest. Instead, he found his attention locked on the English-looking girl as she swirled and dipped into one erotic pose after another. Her sultry blue eyes burned with sensual promise.

Saxon felt heat surge through him, every drop of blood in his body pounding toward his groin. He cursed his weakness. But what man wouldn't respond to her? She had the pale elegance of a duchess combined with the wanton nature of a harem girl.

Bending backwards, she threw her arms over her head

in the heat of the dance, her breasts nearly thrusting free of their scant covering.

"Jesus," he whispered under his breath.

He heard Julian chuckle beside him. "Easy, Sax," he admonished, though his dry voice reflected his own strain. "Remember why we're here."

Scowling at his brother, Saxon tried to do just that. He was grateful for the ceremonial *kamarband* that had been presented to him earlier; without the embroidered blue cloth draped over his lap, his interest in the little slave would be obvious for all to see.

She and the others now moved in a circle, turning and swaying to the exotic sounds of the musicians' pipes and drums, faster and faster as the dance built toward a climax. The rings on their fingers flashed as their hands swirled in elaborate, hypnotic movements. Every few steps, they froze in intricate poses, like statues, only to sweep into motion a second later.

Golden chains about the pale girl's bare waist shifted with every subtle thrust of her hips. Her graceful, undulating spins made the weighted hem of her sheer *peshwaz* cloak wrap and unwrap provocatively around her slim ankles.

Saxon's heart took up the beat of the drum.

Perhaps it was mere arrogance, but she seemed to be dancing for him alone. She glided about the chamber with the other women, but always when they stopped she seemed to be in front of him, here giving him a flash of creamy thigh, a moment later skipping near so that her flowing skirts brushed against him, her perfume wafting after her. Once she flashed him a smile as bewitching as it was inviting.

Perhaps she considered her brazen behavior mere flirting, but its effect on Saxon was dangerous. He did not feel the least bit playful. He wanted her—but if he dared so much as touch her, it would cost him a hand.

He was damn close to not caring. It had been too long since he had buried himself in the soft recesses of a woman. In the span of the last ten minutes, the need in his body had built to an explosive level.

The dancers threw themselves into the final rhythms of the performance with abandon. She moved close to him again, eyes closed, lips parted.

Her body quivered with what looked for all the world like the last throes of sexual pleasure.

Saxon forgot how to breathe. Overpowering lust seized him, burned through his veins, arrowed straight into every bit of bone and sinew. When he felt certain he couldn't stand it a second longer, the dance ended abruptly.

The slave girls spun in one final, dramatic pose, then the music stopped and they fell at the feet of the Emperor's guests.

The men sat in collective, lustful silence for a full minute before they managed a polite, civilized applause.

Saxon didn't join in, feeling neither polite nor civilized. She knelt before him, head bent, breath rasping out in little panting sounds, back and shoulders rising and falling rapidly. Saxon had to stifle an urge to grab her, yank her against his body, and ravish her thoroughly. A carafe of cool water sat beside him and he fought another impulse, to pick it up and douse his lap.

Slowly, she raised her eyes to meet his.

To say he felt as if he were drowning didn't begin to describe the sensation. It was like standing on the deck of the *Valor*, watching the midday sun strike facets of dazzling turquoise and opal from the jewel-blue waves of the Indian Ocean. She kept her lids half-lowered, which only enhanced her languorous, sensual appearance.

Her skin, though flushed from her exertion, put him in mind of the fine silk the Hindus called "white of the clouds when the rain is spent."

And her lips . . . full, red petals that beckoned for the touch of his mouth, his tongue . . .

"Does she please you, Englishman?" the Emperor said lightly.

Saxon counted three breaths before he could tear his gaze from the woman at his feet. He quickly reminded himself of the manners required in the Indian court, where flattery was a subtle and refined art. "She is a beauty beyond compare, great Emperor. Surely, the flower of your harem."

The Emperor waved his hand dismissingly. "A passingly able dancer, but pale for my taste. A gift from the clan Ajmir many years ago, when she was yet a child. She has long been in my harem, but she has never caught my fancy."

Saxon felt his heart thud against his ribs at the news that this girl had once lived among the Ajmir. It was the first time he had even heard the clan mentioned since he arrived in Daman. "Truly, she does not have the look of a Hindu," he said deftly. "She is, perhaps, English?"

"*Han,* English and Portuguese. Daughter of a sea captain," the Emperor replied in a bored tone. "He traded her in exchange for treasure, and the Ajmir gave her to me. They could not abide an English girl among them. I understand there is little love lost between that clan and your people." He picked up a slice of melon from the tray beside him and bit into it.

"Indeed, great Emperor, there is truth in what you say."

Alamgir the Second spat out a seed. "Would you like her, Englishman? She is yours."

Saxon was stunned at the casual gift. "Emperor . . . I am without words. I am unworthy of—"

"Sax." Julian nudged him in the ribs, whispering harshly. "Refusing a gift is an unpardonable insult. Let's leave here with our heads still attached to our necks, shall we?"

Saxon looked down at the girl, who remained frozen at his feet, eyes wide. He could see that she was trembling.

The Emperor dismissed the musicians and other slave girls with a clap of his hands. "She has been trained most thoroughly in the ways of love. I am sure she will please you," he said, as if the matter were already closed. "And she is yet a virgin."

That last bit of information aroused Saxon to an almost painful level. Damnation, he didn't know what to say that wouldn't get his head lopped off. He could not refuse a gift from the Emperor, but the last thing he needed right now was to be saddled with a woman.

When he didn't speak, Julian whispered urgently, "Say something, Sax. Hell, if you don't want her, I'll be glad to take her."

Saxon was too busy thinking to reply. It was impossible. Yet . . . she just might know something useful about the Ajmir, something that could help him get the sapphires.

And God knew he needed physical release. He could at least use her for that. She appeared amply qualified to satisfy a man. A girl with a mixture of delicate English blood, fiery Portuguese temperament, and harem training—sweet Jesus, why not? She would be completely his to do with as he pleased.

And when he was done with her, he could leave her behind or give her away.

When he did not speak, Julian addressed the Emperor. "Great and wise Emperor, I—"

"I thank you for the generous gift," Saxon broke in. "I accept with much gratitude."

He reached down and touched her, as he had been longing to, cupping her chin, caressing her bottom lip with his thumb through the silk of her veil.

"Koi bat nahin," the Emperor replied. "You are welcome." Smiling, he summoned one of his eunuchs. "I shall have her made ready for you. She will await you in the pavilion of pleasure."

Chapter 4

Her stomach knotted with nervousness, her heart thrumming a rapid beat, Ashiana followed the eunuch who led her out of the harem, her slippers silent in the hushed corridors. He guided her toward the *preet chatra,* the pavilion of pleasure, where she would await her new . . .

Master.

She swallowed hard, her pulse pounding even as she thought the word. Her confidence and courage had started to waver the moment D'Avenant touched her, his fingers cupping her chin possessively, his thumb brushing over her lower lip, his gray eyes ablaze with desire.

The sensations he had ignited within her were far different from the tingling she had experienced when *she* touched *him.* During the greeting ceremony, she had been the one in control, protected from him by the distance that custom and etiquette demanded. Now everything was different.

Now there would be no distance.

With trembling fingers, she wiped away the beads of perspiration that dotted her upper lip. For the past hour, the women of the harem had worked efficiently to prepare her for a night of passion, bathing her, massaging the stiffness from her muscles, burning sandalwood incense so that her hair absorbed the fragrance as it dried. Then they had rubbed herbal essences into her skin until it glowed with the pale luster of pearls, all the while offering tidbits of advice on how to enslave a man's heart.

The entire time, Ashiana had clung to one thought: she was not being prepared for a night of lovemaking, but for a deception. Dawn would find Saxon D'Avenant bereft of seduction, slave girl—and sapphire.

She had repeated that thought like a mantra while the women rubbed beeswax onto her lips to make her mouth look moist and full, and emphasized the shape of her eyes with black collyrium, painted on with a paper-thin brush. She had actually started to feel calm by the time they dusted henna powder over her pale cheeks to add much-needed color, and used more henna, mixed with a drop of patchouli oil, to create intricate patterns on her palms and the soles of her feet.

But her resolve had fled when they whisked the red tint over the tips of her breasts, to deepen the color of the rosy peaks. Panic and bravery had battled within her while the women dressed her in *salwar* pantaloons of iridescent purple fabric, layers of sheer skirts, and a sleeveless bodice, tight-fitting and low-cut; her darkened nipples showed through the lavender silk.

Even the familiar, weighted *peshwaz* cloak she wore did not make her feel better. As she took the final few steps toward the pavilion of pleasure, panic was winning. She ran her thumb over the onyx ring she wore on her right hand, and tried to remember that she and the Maharaja had gone over this plan in every detail.

But the Englishman's scorching expression had left no doubt as to *his* plans for *her.* How could she hope to hold him at bay long enough to take the sapphire and escape? Vishnu help her!

Her thoughts were so filled with D'Avenant that she nearly collided with the eunuch's back when he stopped before the *preet chatra* doors. He pushed open the massive gem-encrusted portal.

Her throat constricted. "One . . . one of the guards will bring my . . . —" She forced the word out. "—master, as

... as soon as the Emperor and his guests have finished their evening meal in the audience hall?"

She already knew the answer, but the question let her delay going into that chamber for one more moment.

"*Han.* Yes, mistress." The eunuch bowed and moved aside. "Pray call for me, if you require assistance before then. No one will disturb you once your master arrives."

"*Dhanyavad,*" she managed to say in a small, choked voice. "Thank you."

She stepped inside, and he closed the door behind her.

Saxon noted that he was not the only European being led through the darkened palace corridors to one diversion or another. Emperor Alamgir the Second certainly seemed to be generous with his hospitality. Too generous, Saxon thought irritably; the blasted feast had been interminable. He had been forced to sit through three hours of endless courses of kebabs and tandoori, overlong toasts to the guests' good health, and a terminally dull discussion of trade tariffs.

The entire time, all he could think about was a pair of ocean-blue eyes, mist-pale skin, and a lithe, soft body that begged to be unveiled.

Only one fact dampened his eagerness as he followed a guard to the *preet chatra*: he would have little time to spend with his slave girl. Talking to one of the other English delegates during the meal, he had learned a piece of information that would make lingering here impossible.

Greyslake was on his way to the Andaman Islands with all speed.

Hatred had rivered through him, cold and deep, upon hearing the name. Saxon could not pass up a chance to have his vengeance for Mandara's death *and* get the sapphires. Greyslake was a Royal Navy officer with access to spies in all the corners of the East—and he could very well know something Saxon did not. Perhaps there was a reason the Ajmir had not been seen or heard from here in Daman. Perhaps this meeting was only intended as a diversion, and the sapphires were yet on the islands.

Saxon had dispatched Julian to ready the *Valor* for an immediate departure. His light, fast Indiaman could outpace Greyslake's man-of-war, but Greyslake had a head start. Saxon intended to sail with the dawn tide.

Which gave him only a few hours to enjoy his slave girl. After tonight he would never see her again. He intended to put her sensual talents to good use, perhaps see if she knew anything helpful about the Ajmir—but he had no intention of taking her with him. He would have to devise some way to leave her behind without insulting the Emperor.

His guide left him at the entrance of the *preet chatra* with a bow and a smile. "All that you have need of, you will find inside, sahib."

Left alone in the darkened corridor, Saxon let those words sink in for a moment, his blood pumping, his body tense. Then he thrust open the door and strode inside.

The scent of pungent incense and the sound of trickling water hit him first, only to be forgotten upon seeing the beauty who stood in the center of the pavilion, hands clasped, gaze lowered.

She had been prepared for him, as promised: garbed in sheer layers of lavender silk, her skin glistening like new morning sunlight, her hair a black cascade beneath her diaphanous veil.

He belatedly remembered to close the door behind him. By habit, he evaluated the security of his surroundings in one glance. Two entrances: the door he had just come in and an open terrace on the far side of the chamber. No closets, no trunks where assailants might conceal themselves. There was a knife, six inches long, on a platter of fruit in one corner.

Satisfied that the *shamshir* sword at his waist would be equal to any threat that might arise, he moved into the chamber and indulged himself in a slower perusal of the pavilion's other attributes.

Flickering oil lamps in sconces about the room cast a low, dusky light, reflected a hundred times over in mirrors of various sizes imbedded in the walls and ceiling. An enormous mattress on a raised platform, curtained with gauze, took up one wall; a hammock swung in the breeze on the adjacent terrace; pillows had been strewn about in inviting disarray.

What most caught his imagination was a shallow bathing pool of pure gold, just large enough for two, that filled another side of the chamber, fed by a fountain in the shape of the fertility god Nandi. Lotus blossoms floated on the water's surface.

Saxon's gaze drifted back to the woman. She did not speak, did not look at him, but he could see her barely clad breasts moving rapidly with her every nervous breath. Not saying a word, he stole closer, silently.

He came to stand directly in front of her and she stopped breathing altogether. He could smell the scent of her hair—warm sandalwood—and the perfumed lotions they had rubbed into her pearlescent skin. She had flowers, tiny white rosebuds, plaited into her hair.

"Look at me," he ordered.

Her only response was to flinch, and Saxon had to remind himself that, though she appeared English, she did not understand his language. He tried again. *"Mujhe dekho."*

She hesitantly raised her head, and Saxon again experienced that jarring sensation of diving over the edge of a waterfall into a bottomless sea of blue.

They stared into one another's eyes, only inches of space between their bodies. Saxon felt a tantalizing anticipation, enduring and savoring those last taut seconds between not yet touching and skin against skin. He couldn't stand it any longer than that.

He reached out with one hand and unfastened her veil, slipped the silk covering from her hair, and let both float to the floor. She trembled. Raising his other hand, he ran his fingers through her black tresses, plucking loose the flowers and sending them tumbling. Free of the Hindu trappings, she looked more European, and that pleased him.

He did not want any reminders this night of another

woman, another place. His presence here had nothing to do with any of that; this was lust, pure and raw and powerful. This delectable creature would satisfy him, the way food satisfied his hunger or water slaked his thirst. He needed her for that, would use her for that, nothing more.

He caressed her blushing, petal-soft cheeks, then ran his hands down her throat, over her shoulders, along her slim arms. Just the feel of her made his body take fire. The patter of the fountain was the only sound in the silence in the room.

"Is it true what the Emperor said?" Saxon asked in low, fluent Hindi, his eyes traveling from her thick-lashed eyes to her full, perfectly shaped lips.

She turned pale and looked at him in confusion.

"That you are yet a virgin?" Saxon clarified.

Her gaze dipped to the floor again, and a flush suffused her cheeks, reddening them a shade deeper than the rouge she wore. *"Han,* sahib," she affirmed softly.

Whether it was the husky caress of her voice or the confirmation, Saxon wasn't sure, but he felt every drop of blood in his body surge into his loins. He would be the first man to benefit from her years in the harem—but he did not have time for more than a brief taste. He felt regret, and something more: her shyness touched him. It was unexpected in a well-trained slave girl.

Both emotions made him angry at himself. He hadn't intended the wench to arouse anything but his manhood. He wasn't here to feel anything for her; he was here to enjoy her, and he had precious few hours in which to do so.

He stepped away, turned his back, and yanked off the frock coat that had been binding his shoulders all day. "I shall remedy your maidenly condition posthaste," he said coldly. He started unbuttoning his waistcoat. "In fairness, I should tell you that I know your game."

"G-game?" she asked with breathless innocence. "I play no game, sahib."

He snapped around and choked out a sarcastic laugh. "I have crossed the ocean from Madagascar to Ceylon and Madeira to Canton." Tossing his waistcoat to the floor, he started untying his ruffled cravat. "I have tasted every temptation the world has to offer, and I know the foolish wish every harem girl like you lives by. The *Kama Sutra* command that you all commit to heart: 'You must fetter his soul before you bind your body to his in lovemaking.' "

Saxon dropped his shirt into the pile of clothing on the floor. Naked to the waist but for the leather pouch around his neck, he moved toward her, circled her like a hunter. Then he stepped up behind her and lowered his lips to her ear. "I assure you that you will never fetter my soul." Circling her bare waist with one arm, he pulled her hips against him, nestling his arousal against her softness. "So let's just get on with the binding of bodies."

Ashiana's reason scattered in a rain of sensations. With D'Avenant's arm locked about her, she couldn't think, couldn't move, couldn't even take a breath. She could only feel. The hardness of his muscles. The vast size of his body. The way he held her, making her seem small and frail by comparison. The bristly hair of his arm against the tender skin of her waist. The cold hilt of his *shamshir* nudging her hip.

And the low rasp of his voice, so close to her ear, his words struck like thunderclaps. He spoke in a husky growl, more to himself than to her. "Where shall I take you first? The pool. Or perhaps the bed."

She stiffened in his embrace, fighting sheer terror. "*Krupiya,* sahib. Please, I—I thought—"

"You are not here to think." He buried his face in her hair, trailed his lips down the nape of her neck with quick, hungry nips. A hail of icy-hot shivers danced down her back, making her gasp in surprise.

His hand shifted upward to cup her breast, his thumb and forefinger finding her nipple and teasing it to hardness. Ashiana felt an unfamiliar, dizzying tightness in her midsection. Flinching away from his roaming hand, she choked out a plea of denial, unsure whether she was denying his aggressiveness or her unexpected reaction.

He turned her suddenly, yanking her up against him. The forceful impact knocked the breath from her. His broad hands shaped her buttocks, lifting her to him, molding her softness against the straining juncture of his breeches.

The startling contact shredded Ashiana's courage. This was happening too fast! She struggled, pressing her fists against his shoulders. "*Ruko!* Wait! I have—"

"—a body created by the devil himself," he finished for her. "And every inch of it is mine." He raised one hand to bury his fingers in her hair. Tilting her head back, he captured her mouth.

Captured—and conquered. His lips melded, parted, opened hers in one deft movement. It wasn't a kiss; it was pure ravishment, his heat and his power pounding through her. His tongue slid forward, thrusting against hers, and a cascade of flame flared through Ashiana, surging toward the center of her being. He tasted of potent spices and forbidden *tadi* wine as he crushed her to him. Consumed her. Surrounded her with the smells of hookah smoke and his own masculine, salty tang.

He sent her thoughts spinning. Confused and frightened, she tried to pull away, but his rock-hard arm easily held her still while he fully explored her. Ashiana was helpless against his rough possessiveness, his almost savage fervor. The searing brand of his mouth on hers burned with a wildness beyond imagining, lit a dozen fires inside her.

He slid his hand between their bodies, seeking and finding, boldly caressing the tender center of her womanhood through the silky layers of her skirts and *salwar.*

Shock exploded inside Ashiana. Her whirling thoughts jolted back to why she was here and who this man was. Enemy! Thief! *Englishman!*

That fact above all others filled her with hatred and shame. She must not allow this. She must not let D'Avenant make her helpless. She was an Ajmir princess! For the honor of her duty and her clan, she must defeat him.

She fought desperately, breaking the kiss. "Please, I—"

"What is this resistance, woman?" He wrapped both arms around her waist, refusing to let her go. His eyes had darkened to the color of stone.

Ashiana tried to remember the arguments she had prepared for this moment. "I—I am sorry, sahib . . . I did not . . ." It was very difficult to think when he was holding her so tightly and glaring at her that way. "I did not expect—"

"I will not tolerate defiance. Not from a slave." His arm flexed, drawing her closer against his chest, flattening her breasts against the wall of muscle. "*My* slave."

"*Maf kijiye.* It is . . . I—I—"

"I told you, woman, I have no patience for games."

"It . . ." Ashiana ducked her head. "It is my first time and I am afraid," she blurted.

That bit of honesty appeared to have some effect. Frowning, D'Avenant loosened his hold, enough so she could at least take a breath. A second later he released her, though his next words belied his action. "I don't care a blasted fig whether it is your first time. Before this night is over you will have your second. And your third."

Heart hammering, Ashiana backed away from him, grateful for whatever distance she could get. "Of . . . of course. I—it is my only wish to please you, sahib."

The sight of him standing there, angry and aroused, naked but for his breeches and the sword, made her lightheaded with fear. She had never seen a man like him: he was so powerfully built that his skin was stretched taut, everywhere, from the swaths of muscle over his shoulders and chest to the iron-hard sinews girding his ribs. Long, angry scars striped his arms. Ashiana knew from experience that even his hands and fingers held incredible strength.

If he chose to use force he could take her in a heartbeat, and they both knew it.

She lowered her eyes. "You are m-most patient. I am unworthy of so understanding a master. It is not right for me to fight you, and I—I should not feel so afraid."

"The Emperor said you have been trained thoroughly in the ways of love," D'Avenant said gruffly. "Did he lie?"

"Nahin. No, he did not lie—"

"Then it is time for you to make good on the promise your body made to me earlier." He advanced on her. "You were not so reluctant when you danced."

Ashiana evaded him and launched into her prepared explanation, while she had the chance. "I have been taught many ways to please a man, many steps a slave girl may use to take her master to the highest pinnacle of bliss, but they require that we proceed slowly. But of course, we do not have to think of such pleasure, if it is not what you wish."

He stopped a few steps away from her. Peeking up from beneath her lashes, Ashiana could see that he was scowling at her.

"I doubt very much," he said with a cynical bite to his voice, "that you could teach me anything new."

"Nahin, of course not, you are right. You said you have experienced all the world has to offer." She hung her head dejectedly. "I should be beaten for daring to suggest I could pleasure you, sahib."

With an air of surrender, Ashiana walked over to stand before him. She raised her face to his, tears pooling in her eyes. "As you wish. Take me quickly."

Perhaps it was the resignation in her voice, perhaps the tears, but something won her the desired result.

A host of emotions crossed D'Avenant's features, first surprise then anger then frustration. "I would prefer that you fight me like a she-cat than act like a sacrifice being led to slaughter!"

A tear slipped onto her cheek and she winced away from his wrath. "I w-will do whatever you command, master."

D'Avenant's lips thinned to a taut line. He reached out and grasped her chin . . . but his touch held just a bit less forcefulness than it had before. He tilted her head up, making her meet his gaze. "I suppose," he ground out, "that it would not kill me to do this slowly. The first time."

"It would be best—for you," she promised, half-lowering her lashes to give him a pleading gaze.

Indecision flickered in his eyes. Ashiana's heart slowed its frantic beat imperceptibly. In that instant, she knew she had learned something important about this Englishman. Something she hadn't expected.

Beneath his ruthless exterior, he was not all storm and steel.

"And what would be the first of these steps you would pleasure me with?" he asked darkly.

She nodded toward the pool.

That seemed to interest him, at least for the moment. He grabbed her hand and led her over to the water's edge, then let her go. Folding his thick-hewn arms over his broad chest, he stared at her challengingly, his eyes a smoldering smoke-gray.

"Show me."

Ashiana's throat went dry. The veins on his arms stood out in sharp relief, as if there were no room for them amid all that muscle. Beneath the tinkling sound of the fountain that fed the pool, she could hear his breathing, deep, heavy, hungry. Still, she felt a flutter in her chest, her anxiety now mixed with hope. Her plan was once more on course. If she could just distract him in an endless, drawn-out—

His impatient, growled command cut short her thoughts. "Begin."

Chapter 5

⌒⌒⌒☙❍❍☙⌒⌒⌒

Saxon found himself struggling for control as the girl stepped away from him a few paces and started to disrobe. Their single kiss already had him violently aroused—and cursing his own honor, the soul-deep sense of right and wrong that prevented him from taking her as forcefully as his body demanded.

Heat and hunger condensed inside him as he watched her remove her skirts: one after another sliding downward until a shimmering lake of lavender silk lapped about her ankles. The ravenous sexual longing he felt was familiar, yet far more intense than any he had known before; it was almost as if he were experiencing her excitement blended with his own. As if this was his first time as well as hers. The sensation startled him.

He had been celibate too damned long.

She slipped her sheer *peshwaz* cloak from her shoulders, letting it drop slowly to the floor. Wearing only her *choli* bodice and *salwar* now, she walked back to him, her hips swaying in a motion that locked his eyes and his thoughts on her lower body. She came to his side, knelt at his feet, head bowed, and took off her bracelets, one at a time, then her rings. She placed them all on one of the silver platters, heaped with small sweets called *qandi,* that lined the pool's edge.

Her hands and arms bare, she raised her eyes to his, her face at the level of his thigh, her air submissive, her red lips full and bruised from his kiss. The thought that those

59

lips might be as responsive to his manhood as they had been to his mouth nearly proved his undoing.

Jaw clenched, he stared down at her, burning. His hand strayed through her hair. He very nearly decided to make the fantasy come true, but didn't trust himself. Never had he felt this close to totally losing control over his own strength; if he didn't get his lust back on a leash, he was going to hurt her.

She smiled tremulously, whispering, "And now you must get into the pool, sahib."

He tried to focus on her eyes—instead of her mouth and the almost palpable warmth of her breath fanning over his groin. He forcibly reminded himself that despite her harem training, she was yet new to this. She was also small and damnably fragile in comparison to him.

Unstrapping his *shamshir*, he laid it close at hand on the pool's edge, then stripped out of his breeches. She turned her head, cheeks aflame, averting her eyes as he stepped down into the water.

The pool was about six feet square and four deep, with a broad, smooth ledge on all four sides that served as a seat. He settled himself on that, but the cool water swirling about his ribs had absolutely no effect on his raging arousal. If anything, the wetness redoubled his desire. The surface was so crystalline-clear that he knew the girl could see every inch of him. She kept her gaze on his face.

He leaned back, resting his arms along the edge. "And now you will join me."

"I—in a moment, my master," she demurred.

He almost insisted, then didn't. *Control,* he rebuked himself fiercely. It had become almost a test. Mind over matter. This slip of a girl did *not* have the power to scuttle his self-discipline. "A *short* moment."

She picked up one of the dozens of flasks that lined the pool's edge—a small bottle made of blue glass—and pulled out the stopper. A warm, fruity fragrance spiced the air.

Watching her every move, he raised one eyebrow, fighting his own impatience. She tilted the bottle and poured a line of thick white liquid along his left arm and shoulder, then rubbed it in. It felt cool and wet at first, but warmed with the contact of her skin against his.

When she moved on to his right arm, he leaned his head back and looked up at her skeptically. "I have been massaged by courtesans with far more skill than that. I thought you were going to show me something new. If you cannot—"

She leaned forward and blew on his arm, her breath turning the warm ointment into sizzling heat. His entire body jerked, splashing a wave over the edge of the pool.

"What kind of fakir's trick is this? It feels like liquid fire!"

"It is not a trick, but the Emperor's own secret, sahib," she explained. "This unguent was created by one of the palace physicians. I do not know how it is made."

Saxon fell silent, the potion's heat glittering through him. He cared less about its contents than the intriguing possibilities of how they might use it. This maddening test of his discipline might prove worth the endurance after all.

He shifted sideways in the water, stretching out along the seat to allow her access to all of him. "Continue," he ordered.

Trying to look pleased instead of terrified, Ashiana reclined by the side of the pool, bringing her face closer to his. She desperately tried to ignore the frantic tension in her stomach. Touching him so intimately was almost beyond bearing.

He was her enemy, a killer who had taken the lives of many Ajmir warriors. An English marauder. She hated him, with all the hatred she had been nursing in her soul since that day on the blood-washed deck of the *Adiante* fourteen years ago.

Yet every brush of her fingers against his skin, every clash of their eyes, every time she felt the size and power of his muscles, some unknown, unnamed, un*wanted* stirring sprang to life within her. It was shameful, unthinkable.

Thank Vishnu she only had to play the role of his slave girl for this short time.

The fact that her plan was not working added to her anxiety. He was too wary, too careful, always keeping his weapon close at hand and his eyes flicking from her to his surroundings. She could not get him to relax. To catch him off guard, to trap him, she would have to work harder. *That* was what she had to think about, she reminded herself. She must forget about her own reactions and focus on his.

Placing one fingertip under his rough, stubbled chin, she urged him to tip his head back. He did so, half-closing his eyes to keep watching her.

She poured more of the ointment, then rubbed her moistened fingers along his throat, feeling the throbbing of his pulse, and the deeper vibration of his voice when he made a low sound of pleasure. Carefully avoiding the leather pouch about his neck, she slid her hand across the broad, wet planes of his chest, spreading the liquid everywhere before she bent her head to torment him with her breath.

He groaned and captured her hand when she would have pulled away, sitting up suddenly, sloshing water over the side of the pool.

"Enough of this. You . . ." His voice trailed off as he looked closely at the tattoo that ran from her wrist to her elbow. He ran his thumb over the delicate red rose. "What is that? A scar from a whip?"

Ashiana stiffened. "F-from childhood."

"You must have been no more cooperative with your Ajmir master than you have been with me," he said with dry humor.

"It . . . it was a long time ago." Only with great effort did she keep her voice steady. How she longed to shout the truth! *It was not the Ajmir that did this to me, but your kind! English pirates who tortured and killed my father!*

He looked up, but kept running his thumb over the scar, back and forth. "I suppose you must despise the Ajmir.

I'm sure they mistreated you badly. They hate the English, you know."

A heartbeat passed. Another.

"Yes," Ashiana said slowly, her eyes locked on his. "I know."

His expression softened a bit and he laced his fingers through hers, with new gentleness.

Ashiana knew he was only trying to trick her. That was not caring she saw in his eyes—it was cunning. She itched to tear her hand from his, but did not dare anger him.

"I don't suppose you remember any of their legends?" he asked lightly.

"*Nahin,* sahib. I only lived among them when I was very young."

"Yes, so the Emperor said. But surely you know the tale of the Nine Sapphires of Kashmir."

He massaged her fingers, playfully. Ashiana shrugged. "I—I have heard the myth. Everyone has."

"But do you remember anything more, from when you were a child?" He planted a kiss where the scar ended at the base of her palm. "Perhaps rumors of where the stones are hidden?"

Here! In the palace! In my room! Ashiana wanted to boast. She stifled that mad impulse and instead replied in a bewildered tone. "Hidden? The sapphires are only a myth."

Tingling heat radiated like sunstreaks from the play of his lips along the sensitive skin of her wrist.

She stifled that feeling as well.

"A myth, yes," he said finally.

"And we have strayed from our purpose, my master." Ashiana pulled her hand away. She sat up and reached for a towel.

D'Avenant glowered at her. "We have not finished with the pool yet," he said in a deep tone.

"There are many more steps for us to climb, my master, if I am to take you to the pinnacle—"

"The devil take the pinnacle." He caught her arm and pulled her back down until she lay beside him again.

Grabbing the blue bottle, he wet his own finger with the liquid, then slid it over her lips.

Ashiana inhaled sharply at the cool, wet sensation. He circled the nape of her neck with one hand, pulled her close, and blew softly, igniting sparks that sizzled along her mouth. Drawing her closer still, he kissed her again and the sparks flared into a blaze. She had thought his ardor cooled by the distraction of their conversation—but she could not have been more wrong!

Breaking the kiss, he poured another splash of ointment over her fingers and raised himself partway out of the water. He took her hand, pressing it against his wet ribs. Fear and shock and the dizzying contrast of his muscular body and the fiery potion spun wildly together inside Ashiana. Sealing his mouth over hers again, he slid her hand down into the water, over his belly, lower.

She tried to pull away but he held her fast and kept urging her hand further—and then she could *feel* his aroused member, smooth and veined and large as the rest of his powerfully built body. She made a sound of protest deep in her throat but he swallowed her objections and curved her fingers around his throbbing length.

Ashiana thought she would faint. She could feel him growing harder as he thrust against her fingers. Groaning into her mouth, he held her there.

Without warning, he suddenly broke the kiss and stood up, like a sea-god bursting from the ocean. Before she could utter an objection, he swept her into his arms, soaking her thin garments.

"Enough of these tortures, woman." He yanked her to a sitting position at the edge of the pool. Her hennaed feet dangled, tinting the water red. He reached for the waist of her *salwar.* Ashiana couldn't catch her breath. Fear made her numb.

He growled what sounded like an English curse at encountering the elaborate knots.

"M-merely one more of the steps, my master." She managed a husky tone. Her time had run out. His patience was at an end—and so was her bravery. She had to put the final part of her plan into action while she still had the chance. She reached for the silver platter heaped with *qandi*.

She must win at all costs, and quickly. Picking up one of the sugary sweets, she adopted a teasing tone. "While you unfasten the knots, my master, you might allow me one more kiss."

Opening her mouth, she slowly, purposefully extended her tongue and placed the treat on the tip.

She saw him hesitate and struggle in a mind-battering war of male lust against caution and control.

To prove she meant no harm, she swallowed the candy, licked her lips and picked up another. "Please," she whispered, placing it on her tongue. Lowering her lashes, tilting up her chin, she opened her mouth to receive him.

A low growl tore from him. He took the bait so forcefully that he would have knocked her over if he hadn't been holding on to her. He ripped at the knots with his hands while he ravaged her mouth in a deep kiss.

Ashiana reached behind her, found the platter. She flicked open her onyx ring, spilling out a *qandi* that looked as ordinary as all the others.

The Englishman had two knots undone, and to Ashiana's horror, his fingers were proving nimble even with the distraction of the kissing game.

With a quick, cheating nip, she won the first round. She pulled free of his mouth, bit down on the sweet to release its liquid center and licked her lips as she swallowed it.

"A second try, sahib?" She held up the new piece of *qandi* teasingly before popping it in her mouth. She intended to let the Englishman win this round—and he would not find this treat so sweet.

But she was so focused on what she had to do that she was completely unprepared for what he did.

He sat back in the pool, pulling her with him.

She hit the water with a gasp and would have choked on the candy but, incredibly, he saved her. His tongue found it and stole it from her with a deep kiss that threatened to rob her very breath. He bit down on it and swallowed—

and unfastened the last of the knots that bound her *salwar.*
The silk slid down over her hips.

She cried out in panic. *"Ruko—"*

"No," he said roughly, hauling her against him as he
settled himself on the underwater bench. "No more waiting."

The purple silk tangled about her legs. He held her tight
while he pushed it out of the way. He pressed her hips to
his.

Ashiana sobbed, trying to twist away from him.
"Krupiya—"

The rest of the plea was lost when his mouth found the
peak of her breast and suckled it through the soaked fabric
of her bodice. Ashiana cried out at the sharp sensation—
and the knowledge that she was lost. His hands maneu-
vered her into position. She could feel his heat against the
softness between her thighs.

But then, as suddenly as a candle being extinguished,
his hold on her changed.

His arms started to shake. Letting her go, he raised his
hands and stared at them in confusion.

Ashiana pushed away from him, splashing to the edge
of the pool. D'Avenant had only time to flash her one accusing, furious look before the drug took him completely.

He slumped backward, falling like a giant *sal* tree cut
from its roots. His head hit the edge of the pool. Blood
stained the water crimson.

Ashiana leaped forward to grab him before he could
sink beneath the surface completely. With his weight
buoyed, she managed to lift him upward so that he was sitting more securely on the wide seat.

A second later she let go and leaped back as if he had
burned her hands. She didn't know why she had just done
that. She should have let him drown!

She scrambled up out of the pool, trembling. Her
clothes were soaked, the bottom half of her hair wet. She
re-knotted her *salwar* and backed away from the Englishman, her eyes on the blood in his blond hair.

By all that was right, she *should* kill him. She knew that. It was part of the reason she had been sent here.

But now, looking at him, she found she could not. She was not capable of killing. Ashiana cursed her weakness. Truly, she was not worthy of this task! Rao would not have hesitated. Nor, she knew, would the Englishman have hesitated to take her life, had he realized she was an Ajmir spy sent to steal the sapphire—

The sapphire!

Ashiana forced her shaking legs to move. She ran to the corner and grabbed the little knife from the platter of fruit, then cautiously edged back toward the Englishman. Reaching down, she cut the pouch from around his neck, half-afraid he would come awake and grab her.

She dashed back across the chamber and tore open the strings. There was only one item inside. Holding her breath, she clutched the hard, oval object in her fist and took it out.

She opened her hand. The ninth sapphire of Kashmir sparkled with azure splendor in her palm.

Lamplight struck the stone and sent rays of silver-blue spiraling over her hand, across the floor, reflecting from the pavilion's mirrored walls. Perfectly faceted by ancient, expert hands, the egg-sized gem felt warm against her skin, its color a deep, fathomless blue unmatched by ocean depths, midnight sky, or poet's dream. Closing her eyes, Ashiana clasped the sapphire against her pounding heart.

Elation swept through her. No warrior had been able to do this, but she, Ashiana of the Ajmir, had overcome the Englishman and reclaimed the sacred stone!

She looked down at D'Avenant again. With his head thrown back over the edge of the pool, he was completely vulnerable. She could kill him with a single stroke of his own sword.

But she *couldn't*.

She turned away from him, deeply vexed by her hesitation.

The sapphires were what was important, she reasoned. If the gods demanded D'Avenant's life, perhaps he would slide back down into that pool and drown. Perhaps he would die from the blow to his head. Let it be in their hands. Ashiana didn't have time to debate with herself any longer.

She concealed the sapphire and the leather pouch in the deep pockets of her *salwar,* picked up a towel, and rubbed herself and her clothes dry as best she could. Then she donned her skirts and *peshwaz* and snatched up her jewelry.

Not daring to linger a second beyond that, she hurried toward the door and peeked out into the corridor. There was no one around. As the eunuch had said, no one ventured near the Emperor's *preet chatra.* Pausing, she darted one last look back at the Englishman.

He would be furious when he awoke, but she and the sapphires would be safe by then, miles away.

"If it is the gods' will that you live, I give you your life, Englishman," she said quietly, feeling magnanimous now that she had won victory over him. "Use your remaining years to change your ways."

With that, she slipped into the darkened corridor.

Quick, quiet steps carried Ashiana to the harem, through the shadowed chamber where many of the women were asleep, toward the private apartments occupied by the Emperor's wives and favorites. She had her hand on the door to the connecting corridor when a voice stopped her.

"Ashiana-ji," a maidservant called in a friendly whisper, "some gifts arrived for you this evening. One of the eunuchs put them in your chamber."

Ashiana tensed with surprise and worry. "Gifts?"

"We thought they were from the Emperor," the girl explained. "You are yet new, and already he has given you a private apartment—we thought him most taken with you." Her voice turned sad. "You must have offended him greatly for him to give you away."

"*Han,* I fear it is so," Ashiana said, affecting a disconsolate air. "My new master has sent me to gather my things before he takes me away with him. I must hurry.

My thanks for the news." She touched her head and heart in farewell, and stepped through the door, her pulse hammering.

She hurried down the corridor as fast as her bare feet would carry her. She was not expecting any "gifts." Who had been in her room? Reaching her quarters, she slipped inside, not even pausing to light the oil lamps.

Moonlight filtered in through the woven screens. Ashiana breathed a sigh of relief: her other *peshwaz* cloak—the twin of the one she had on—lay where she had left it atop her satin mattress.

She ran over and picked it up, reverently fingering the rounded, lapis-inlaid ornaments that decorated the hem. They looked for all the world like the normal decorations one would find on any dancer's *peshwaz*—but nine of them had been carefully hollowed out by the Maharaja's most skilled craftsman. Touching one, Ashiana tripped the almost-invisible hinge. One of the Nine Sapphires of Kashmir fell into her palm.

Releasing a shaky breath, she put it back in place and hurriedly checked the rest of the lapis "shells." All eight jewels were there.

Trembling, she withdrew the ninth sapphire from the pocket of her *salwar* and placed it inside the ninth container. Snapping it shut, she felt so overcome with joy and relief she almost cried.

She discarded the *peshwaz* she had on and donned the one that contained the sapphires, her heart soaring. Letting herself indulge her happiness for just a moment, she swirled and stopped in a dancing pose, thrilling to the feel of the weighted hem wrapping around her legs.

"Thanks be to Vishnu," she said aloud.

A sound from beside the door made Ashiana freeze, then turn. In her concern for the stones, she had almost forgotten the gifts the maidservant had mentioned. To the right of the door sat a large, ornate box, beside a basket heaped with fabric-wrapped parcels. Ashiana ran over, her *peshwaz* swishing about her ankles, and knelt before the lumpy assortment. She lit one of the oil lamps that flanked the entrance.

"What by Hanuman's tail is all this?"

A low caterwaul emanated from the box.

Ashiana gasped. "Oh, *no*. Nico!"

Her tiger's familiar *puh-puh-puh* sound came in reply.

Ashiana didn't dare let him out; she didn't have time! She rifled through the other parcels, seeking some explanation of how Nicobar had come to be here. To her surprise, she found her belongings from home: her clothes, her jewelry, the Christian cross she had worn as a child. One box held food for Nicobar. At the bottom of another was a note, tied with ribbon.

She knew who had sent all this even before she read it: Padmini! "O my friend, what have you done?" Ashiana cried softly. She skimmed the letter: Padmini had cajoled one of her many male admirers into bringing Ashiana's things to her new home, to give her comfort.

Ashiana closed her eyes. It was kind for Padmini to go to such trouble, but completely unnecessary. As soon as her mission was done in a few days, Ashiana would be returning home to the Andamans with the Maharaja.

But what was she to do with her skittish tiger until then? She could not take him along while she hid the jewels. Nor could she leave him here; the lightly woven screens over the windows would never hold him. And if she left him in his box, he would be yowling the palace down before long. He couldn't help but attract attention she didn't need.

She decided quickly, for she had no time to delay; Hasin was waiting for her at the cave of the winds. She ran to her mattress and took out the small cloth bag she had hidden underneath; inside was the potent sleeping potion she had used to taint the *qandi* earlier.

Returning to the door, she opened the box of food Padmini had sent and put a few drops of the drug on some of Nico's favorite dried meat. She loosened the leather strap on the crate, opening it just a crack, and dropped in a generous portion of the food. Poor Nico was so hungry, he didn't even try to escape, but quickly turned his attention to his meal, eating noisily.

"*Maf kijiye,* my Nico." Ashiana refastened the strap, stroking the crate. "I am sorry to leave you this way, but I cannot let you out. I must send Hasin back for you. You and I and the Maharaja will all leave together, just as soon as I have hidden the stones. I promise."

Her tiger made a rather sleepy growl. She could not stay and calm him further. Precious seconds were slipping by.

She rose with a last apologetic look at her pet and hurried to the door, eager to rendezvous with Hasin and complete her mission.

Chapter 6

$\sim\sim$

J ulian's boots echoed like whip cracks as he strode through the palace, following one of the Emperor's guards toward the *preet chatra*. The well-armed men at the palace entrance had made him wait while they verified that he was indeed one of the trade-meeting guests, then they let him pass when he explained his purpose.

Trailing the red-turbaned guard, Julian wore an uncharacteristic scowl. He didn't relish having to interrupt his brother. Saxon would be angry, but there was no helping it; if he wanted to sail with the morning tide, he would have to come back to the *Valor* now.

As soon as Julian had informed Saxon's crew that the ship would put to sea at dawn, they had snapped into action. With the zeal of sailors landlocked too long, they fitted out the sails and rigging, loaded supplies, began the sweaty, time-consuming task of weighing anchor, and rounded up crewmen from their seats in local punchhouses and dalliances with local women.

A routine check of the hull, however, had revealed damage to the keelson, the large timber that gave the ship's keel added strength. The damage had gone unnoticed on the short trip up the coast from Bombay, but could prove troublesome on the five-week voyage to the Andaman Islands. Saxon would have to make the decision whether to delay and fix it or set out after Greyslake at dawn and hope for the best.

As the guard led the way through one lavish corridor

after another, a more pleasant thought eased Julian's scowl a bit. He took it as an encouraging sign that Saxon had lingered this long with the pretty little slave girl. If ever there was a man who needed a few hours of self-indulgence and relaxation, it was his brother. His crew would think it a welcome change to encounter him in any mood other than surly.

Saxon hadn't always been that way, Julian thought, his frown returning. In younger, happier days, they had been two of a kind, the gleeful rapscallions of county Kent.

But then their brother Dalton deserted the family, their father died, and Saxon's transformation had taken place. He had been only twenty when it all fell on his shoulders: the quest for the sapphires *and* all the responsibilities for the D'Avenant shipping interests, estates, tenants, and investments. Saxon's sense of humor and gentle nature quickly gave way to rigid seriousness and a tyrannical streak.

He seemed determined not only to lift the curse and save young Max's life, but to make up for the sins of their black-sheep father—and he no longer made time for anything so frivolous as fun or relaxation. Julian had thought the year with the Marathas might have done Sax some good, but if anything, he seemed worse than before, wound up tighter than a ship's windlass. He refused to even talk about his extended holiday.

Julian couldn't help but sigh wearily as his escort turned down another long, dark hallway. He hoped that Saxon had changed his mind about leaving the slave girl here. A woman underfoot—especially this fetching harem dancer— might be just the thing to shake Saxon out of his black mood. A good bottle of Madeira and the attentions of an enthusiastic lady could solve most of life's difficulties, at least in Julian's opinion.

The guard stopped at a crossing of three corridors and Julian waited impatiently. The passages, lit only by oil lamps on the walls every few yards, all looked the same to him. He caught the feminine scent of mingled perfumes to the left and guessed the harem and *preet chatra* must lay in that direction. He was about to suggest following their noses when the guard turned down the left hallway.

They hadn't taken two steps when they almost collided with Saxon's slave girl, hurrying in their direction, looking behind her instead of where she was going. She spun to a stop, an exclamation escaping her lips.

"Good God, woman," Julian cried. "Where are you running to?"

Eyes wide, she only gaped at him. Remembering that she did not understand English, Julian repeated himself in Hindi. *"Kahan bhag rahi ho?"*

"I—I . . ." She looked from him to the guard, blinking, apparently so stunned she couldn't answer.

From her appearance, Julian realized she must have just had a most unsettling encounter with the legendary D'Avenant charm: her veil was missing, her hair tumbled loose about her shoulders, and her cosmetics were kissed away.

"It's all right," Julian soothed, unable to suppress a grin. "I'm not going to bite you. Where is my brother?"

At last she snapped out of her stupor. She dropped her gaze, and in a shy effort to cover herself, gathered her sheer *peshwaz* closer, the weighted hem wrapping about her ankles. "My . . . my master finished with me some time ago," she said softly, her words quick and tremulous. "He left and said for me to pack my belongings, that he would come back to fetch me."

"He already left for his ship?"

"Han." She nodded.

"But I have been at his ship all night and have not yet seen him."

"P-perhaps you and he passed on your journey to the palace."

"Perhaps." Julian studied the girl for a moment; Saxon probably planned to "forget" to come back for her, thus ridding himself of the Emperor's unwanted gift.

But there was something else here that wasn't quite right. The guard posed the question before Julian could think to ask it.

"If you are supposed to be gathering your things, woman, then why are you wandering the corridors unescorted?"

Cringing at his severe tone, she raised her head, her blue eyes filled with pleading. *"Krupiya,* please do not tell anyone. I was going to say my farewells to my . . . my friends. They are cooks who work in the kitchens."

"Your secret is safe," Julian promised, still looking at her with curiosity. She seemed edgy, as if she wanted to turn and run from them. "Perhaps I should go to the pavilion and see if Saxon might not have returned to look for you there."

"Nahin, no, you musn't," she cried. "The . . . the Emperor is already using the *preet chatra."*

The guard confirmed what she said with a nod. "The Emperor does use it each night, sahib."

"And my . . . my master said for me to await him at the harem," the girl put in. She turned back the way she had come. "And I shall be late meeting him if I do not—"

"Wait." Julian stopped her, taking her by the elbow. "I can guess what has happened."

The girl stiffened.

Julian grinned at her, a new and mischievous idea forming in his mind; he wasn't going to let Sax discard this pretty gift so easily. "My brother has probably been delayed at the *Valor,* but I'm *sure* he wouldn't want you to be left behind. Let's go and see if he has indeed arrived there in my absence."

All color fled her cheeks. "B-but my master told me to wait here for him!"

"But now that I am here, I can escort you to the ship and save him a trip back." Julian kept a firm grip on her arm, tugging her along beside him as the guard turned to lead the way back toward the palace entrance.

"Krupiya, what of my belongings? I cannot leave without them." She tried to dig in her heels on the slippery marble floor. "If you will only allow me to—"

"I shall have someone fetch your things." Julian would not slow down, making her keep up with his long-legged stride. He knew his brother would be furious at this unwelcome interference. Eventually though, he thought confidently, his grin widening, Saxon would thank him for it.

Ashiana sat trembling on the rickety seat of the horse-drawn *ghari* cart, clinging to the side with one hand, her mind working desperately fast. She thought of yelling for help, but the night air was already filled with the cries of the noisy crowd celebrating the festival of *holi*: a melee of people thronged the streets, marking the end of winter with songs and dances and bonfires, tossing handfuls of colored powders made from crushed flowers at one another. Scores of European sailors had joined in as well, singing and shouting, clutching cups of coconut liqueur.

She kept darting looks at the ground jouncing past, but the Englishman's brother—he had said his name, something like "Lorjulian"—had a manacle-hold on her wrist.

"Please don't try jumping out again," he warned beside her. "You were lucky you didn't break your neck!"

She didn't reply, only sat tense and terrified, the breeze tangling her hair and fluttering through her *peshwaz*. Her attempt to leap into the crowd had failed. So had her appeal to the guards at the palace entrance; she could say little without giving herself away. The story of her being given to the Englishman had already spread through the palace. The guards had barely spared a glance for a mere slave girl, saying they must obey the Emperor's wishes. They had already verified who Lorjulian was when he came in, so they did not interfere.

She had tried a different approach, objecting that she had no slippers or veil and must be allowed to return to the harem to get some. Lorjulian had paused just long enough to ask the guards to send her belongings to the quay—then he simply picked her up, ignoring her yelp of protest, and carried her.

The cart-boy, paid a generous handful of rupees, eagerly led the horse through the twisting, crowded streets. Ashiana's heart was beating so hard, she felt light-headed. She experimentally tried to free her arm from Lorjulian's grip, but he possessed the same easy strength as his brother.

He kept looking at her, his expression puzzled. "Surely my brother is not so terrible a master that you wish to kill yourself by jumping from the cart rather than return to him."

Ashiana gulped for air and for courage. "Please, sahib, will you not allow me to go back to the palace and say farewell to my friends? They are the only family I have known—"

"I don't think there is enough time." He shook his head. "But when we reach the ship, you can ask Saxon."

Ashiana fought rising panic. When they reached the ship, she would be finished! "H-he will never let me return to the palace," she pleaded, the quiver in her voice real. "He will be angry that I disobeyed his orders by leaving without him—"

"If he is angry, the blame shall be mine, not yours," Lorjulian said firmly. "I'm sure he will be quick to forgive you."

Forgive her? He would kill her! Ashiana drew a shaking breath. Letting her fright and her desperation show in her eyes, she tried a more emotional appeal. "I have not been entirely honest, O honorable sahib."

"How so?" His eyes narrowed in an expression that made him look disturbingly like his brother. It nearly unnerved her.

"It . . . it is my freedom I seek," she said softly. "Can you not let me go? I have been a slave all my life. It has always been my dream to be free, since I was a child. This is the only chance I have ever had. Please, *please* let me be free."

His features softened. For a moment she dared hope that she had hit upon the right tactic—but then he looked away and focused on the road before them. "I am sure it must be frightening for you, the idea of leaving here," he said gently. "But I honestly believe you will make Saxon happy. And I think you will find he is not so bad, after a time. Have you ever been on a European ship before?"

Cold desperation rained down on Ashiana. Nothing she could say would persuade him to let her go! She found herself replying to his question, numbly. "Only when I was very young."

"You'll be comfortable aboard the *Valor*. She's an India-man." He glanced at her. "Do you know what that is?"

Ashiana dazedly shook her head.

"Indiamen are called 'the aristocrats of the oceans.' Armed like warships but with plenty of cargo holds below the gun deck, and the hull is more slender, for speed. Five hundred tons, thirty guns, and a crew of ninety, all hand-picked. The Company pays the best wages, so we get the best men. And I think you'll be surprised at how luxurious the captain's cabin is . . ."

Ashiana barely heard anything more he said or the sounds of the festival around them. She just stared into the firelit night, frozen with fear for the sapphires—and herself.

The cart jounced off the dirt road and onto the wooden slats that formed the quay. She spun to face the stark forest of masts that loomed out of the darkness. The scent of the sea hung thick in the air. As the boy slowed the horse, Lorjulian leaned forward to give him directions, still keeping a firm hold on her. She was shaking so hard now, her bracelets jangled.

He turned back toward her and frowned. "I wish that you would stop looking as if you were being taken to your execution. If my brother is angry, it will be with me, not you. And if he *is* angry at you, I promise you my protection."

Ashiana swallowed hard, surprised by his noble offer—but it didn't relieve her anxiety. Her voice felt dry and thin when she answered. "*Dhanyavad.* Thank you."

The *ghari* cart jolted to a stop before one of the largest of the huge foreign ships.

Julian tossed the boy a generous tip, then hopped down and lifted the girl to the ground. She tried to break and run the instant her bare toes touched wood, but he caught her effortlessly.

"You have nothing to fear," he said patiently. "No one is going to hurt you. Saxon might even agree to grant you your freedom."

She didn't seem to believe that. In fact, she looked like she might cry. She was so beautiful and small and vulnerable, he felt the urge to hold her close, to reassure her, to . . .

He tried to scuttle those thoughts. Circling her waist with one arm—purely to keep her from running, he told himself—he turned his attention to the *Valor,* moored a short distance out in the harbor.

The Indiaman's size and magnificence made her instantly recognizable, even among the ships of the other European traders. The white, red, and blue East India Company ensign snapped in the wind at her stern. Lamps hung from the masts and yards lit the deck as the crew scrambled to prepare for departure. One of the small boats called *masulahs,* used to carry crew and cargo back and forth to the quay, came away from the ship's side and started toward them, carrying a single man.

Julian smiled. It was probably Saxon, wondering what the hell his brother was doing.

Turning his smile on the girl, Julian nodded to the *Valor.* "Let me be the first to welcome you aboard. This will be your new home for the next few weeks."

She looked like she was going to faint. Before he had the chance to say anything more, the *masulah* drew near—and to his surprise, it was the ship's first mate, Wesley Wodeford Wyatt, who leaped out and came up onto the quay. Lanky as a mainmast and thin as a belaying-pin, Wyatt normally went about his duties with jovial efficiency, but at the moment his deeply tanned face was taut with concern. "Have ye found the cap'n?"

Julian let loose an oath of surprise and alarm. He shifted to speaking English. "Saxon hasn't returned yet?"

"No, he hasn't." Wyatt ran a hand through his gray-peppered brown hair. "There's been no sign of him, an' the tide will be in before ye know it. I thought ye were bringin' him back. An' who by the Blessed Mother would this little peach in the harem silks be?"

"A gift to Saxon from the Emperor," Julian said distractedly, looking down at her with new uncertainty. Something was definitely wrong here. "She said Saxon left for the ship some time ago."

Eyes wide, she looked from one man to another, apparently not understanding a word of their conversation.

Julian addressed her in Hindi. "My brother has not arrived yet."

"I—I do not understand why."

"You're sure you don't know where he might be?"

"Perhaps he was waylaid," she said weakly. "Or decided to take part in the festival."

Julian didn't believe that for a moment and his expression said as much. She tried to wrench free of him but Julian caught her wrists, suddenly filled with suspicion. The fear she had shown all night took on a new meaning; perhaps there was a reason she didn't want to meet up with Saxon again.

Wyatt fixed a glare on her. "Ye think she has somethin' to do with the cap'n's disappearance?"

"I'm afraid that's a possibility." Julian handed her over to the first mate. "Wyatt, I want you to escort this girl to Saxon's cabin and see that she stays there."

"Aye, sir." The mate's sea-hardened fingers fastened about her arm as firmly as they would about a slippery halyard.

Ashiana shrank from him, trying frantically to get free. *Nahin, krupiya,* please, there has been a mistake—"

"Yes, but I think I'm the one who made it," Julian said. "Make sure she doesn't leave, Wyatt. I'm going back to the palace and this time I'm not leaving until I find out what the devil happened to my brother."

With that, he turned and stalked back toward the road, his steps thunderous on the wooden quay.

* * *

Pain throbbed in Saxon's head with relentless, hammer-hard blows. Voices, a jumbled, distant hum of sound, intruded and receded. Then the sharp scent of something being waved under his nose forced him upward through the darkness—only to experience more pain as something smacked against his face. An open hand.

The residue of fury at the edges of his consciousness finally brought him awake.

He forced his eyes open, then swore and shut them just as quickly against the glare of light that reflected off the mirrored ceiling.

"Come *on,* Sax." The hand slapped his face again. "Come out of it!"

Angry at his tormentor and angrier at his own weakness, Saxon opened his eyes again, ignoring the light that assaulted him. A half-dozen faces floated in his line of vision, then merged and resolved into two: Julian, leaning over him, and a palace guard.

Awareness flooded in. Saxon realized he was lying on the cold marble floor in the *preet chatra,* in a puddle of water. He was naked but for a towel they had thrown over him. He tried to raise his head, but agony splintered through his temples. Gritting his teeth, he cursed again, falling back on a coat folded beneath his head.

"Thank God," Julian said. "I thought you had really furled your jibs for good this time."

Saxon could hardly make out the words over the buzz of pain and an unfamiliar grogginess that made everything seem slow and muffled.

"Was there an accident, sahib?" the guard asked with concern. "Did you slip in the pool?"

"Are you all right, Sax? How do you feel?"

Saxon felt like he had just been scraped up from the floor of a tavern after three days of drinking. The muddled sensation was like being foxed, but somehow different. The last thing he remembered was a flood of pure rage—then nothing, blackness.

As he came awake, from years of habit, he reached for the leather pouch he wore around his neck.

It was missing.

"Christ!" He tried to sit up. "Jesus almighty Christ!"

Julian and the guard fell back in surprise.

"Easy, Sax. You've got a nasty bump on the head—"

"That *bitch!*" Saxon snarled. He pushed himself to one elbow and shoved Julian's hand away when his brother tried to get him to lie down again. "Where are my clothes?"

His words sounded thick and garbled, and he wasn't sure the two men understood. Not waiting for assistance, Saxon struggled to sit up, forced his muscles to respond, and made it to one knee.

"Sax, I don't think you should be moving around just yet—"

"That thieving little *bitch!*" Saxon's thoughts cleared as murderous rage pumped through his veins. Half-leaning on Julian, he stumbled to his feet. "How long have I been out?"

"If you'll just wait a—"

"We'll have to stay in Daman until we find her." He grabbed his breeches from beside the pool, swaying badly as he bent to put them on. He snatched up his boots and shirt. "We're going to miss the bloody tide, but—"

"I know where she is," Julian interrupted.

Saxon froze.

"She's on the *Valor,*" Julian explained. "In your cabin—"

Saxon didn't hear the rest of the sentence. Jamming on his boots, he stormed out of the *preet chatra,* every fiber of his being ready to explode with Satan's own wrath.

Chapter 7

The Englishman would kill her.

If he still lived, if he hadn't drowned or died from the blow to his head, his brother would find him in the *preet chatra* and bring him straight here to his cabin.

And then he would kill her.

The image of D'Avenant throttling her with his bare hands flashed over and over through Ashiana's mind until she was half-paralyzed with terror. Never in her young life had she confronted her own death with such heart-clenching certainty. She pounded her fists against the door until her hands were numb . . . and knew it would avail her nothing.

The sailor named Wyatt took his orders most seriously. He had marched her straight to his captain's cabin, thrust her inside then posted himself outside the door, deaf to her tears.

Gulping in harsh sobs of the salty, stuffy air, Ashiana finally leaned her forehead against the smooth wood and let her hands fall to her sides, despair draining her strength. She had already tried to open the thick mullioned windows that looked out over the stern of the ship, but they wouldn't budge. She had no way out and no one to blame but herself. The rocking motion of the waves and an overwhelming sense of helplessness made her feel ill.

If only she hadn't been so pleased with herself for reuniting the jewels! If only she hadn't been so confident, so filled with foolish pride! Instead of congratulating herself, she should have been concentrating on the dangers that lay ahead. Now she would pay with her life for the lesson.

And when she was gone ... the most painful punishment was that all nine sapphires would be in the Englishman's hands. Not only had she failed in her mission, failed the Maharaja, failed her clan—she had delivered her people's most sacred treasure directly into the hands of the enemy!

It was too much to bear. Ashiana felt a fresh moan of anguish rise in her throat, but forced it down. By all that was holy, she must not allow this to happen!

Bracing her hands against the door, she pushed herself away, forcing herself to stand up straight. She was an Ajmir princess. She could not admit defeat, not while there was so much as a whisper of life left in her body. Nor could she waste precious time on self-pity.

D'Avenant might choke the breath from her with his bare hands, but somehow she must keep the stones from him. She had taken a sacred vow to safeguard them, and by Vishnu the Preserver, she would do so!

She whirled and surveyed her prison with wild eyes. How much time did she have? How long would it take Lorjulian to find his brother? An hour? Half that? Minutes?

With shaking hands, Ashiana removed her *peshwaz* and clutched it to her breast. The secret compartments had safely hidden the jewels until now, but subjected to the Englishman's search ... in his violent mood, he could very well break one of the finely wrought clasps. She could picture the sapphires falling at his feet.

Shuddering at the image, she paced the cabin, looking for a hiding place. The bookcase? Beneath the bed? The writing desk? The battered sea chest? The cabin was luxurious, as Lorjulian had said, but none of its furnishings would conceal the sapphires from D'Avenant's eyes for long.

At that thought, despair struck again: Lorjulian and Wyatt had both seen her *wearing* the *peshwaz* when she was taken aboard! If she hid it, how could she explain its

sudden disappearance during her imprisonment in the
cabin?

Raising a trembling hand to her forehead, Ashiana could
think of only one thing to do. It would be risky, but it
might work. Displayed on the far wall was a vast collection of weapons—*shamshirs, katars,* pistols, and many
lethal-looking axes and blades completely unfamiliar to
her. Renewed terror sliced through her at the reminder of
D'Avenant's reputation for violence, but she pushed it to a
distant corner of her mind.

She knew she could not hope to use the weapons against
the Englishman; half of them looked too heavy for her to
lift, and besides, he would give her no chance. No, she
could not use them for their intended purpose, but as
tools . . .

Once decided, she acted quickly. She chose a broad, flat
bhuj and an odd little forked weapon from the wall and
dashed to the darkest corner of the cabin. Slipping off one
of her layered lavender skirts, she spread it on the floor
beside her.

Then she emptied the *peshwaz* of its precious contents,
one by one.

Less than half an hour later, she stood beside the writing
desk opposite the door, rested one hand on the smooth top,
and told herself it was best to meet the Englishman
bravely, not cowering at his feet. Her gaze darted to the
corner beside the bookcase.

She had hidden the sapphires in the wall, securely bundled in one of her skirts, tucked into the shallow space between the timbers that formed the skeleton of the ship.

At first, she had thought of hiding the gems in the floor,
but the floor planking was too thick; the panels used on
the walls were thinner, enough so that she had been able
to loosen one with her makeshift tools. She had eased it
open, stuffed the jewels inside, closed it and tapped the
nails back into place, weeping loudly the entire time to
cover the sounds. As before, Wyatt had ignored her sobs.

When the Maharaja learned of her failure, he would

choose a new protector to complete her mission. The thought made her blink back tears: he would know nothing of her fate, only that she had failed him. She could only hope that whoever came after D'Avenant would find the jewels somehow.

If she had to die, at least she had the satisfaction of having accomplished one thing: the Nine Sapphires of Kashmir were reunited, and would stay that way. Somehow the new protector would find them. She didn't dare leave behind any clues or a note.

She didn't have the chance to think about it further.

The door flew open in a blur of speed. It hit the wall with such force that several of the weapons on display clattered to the floor with a metallic crash. A cry tore from Ashiana's throat despite her resolve to show courage.

D'Avenant filled the portal, one fist still planted against the door, the ends of his open shirt fluttering, his blond hair stained with crimson at the temple, his lips twisted into a snarl.

Ashiana felt all the blood drain from her face. Perhaps the gods would look kindly upon her in her next life.

"You thieving little bitch!"

He crossed the cabin in two steps, grabbed her by the arms, and jerked her up against his bare chest. "Where is it?" He shook her, his eyes boring into her. *"Where in the bloody blazing hell is it?"*

Ashiana stared up at him mutely. Her throat had closed off. She couldn't speak, couldn't make a sound, couldn't even take a breath.

He shoved her back against the wall, knocking the air from her. Ruthlessly, his hands roved over her body, into her bodice, the pockets of her *salwar,* tearing the fabric. Ashiana cried out in wordless terror. What he had shown her before had been unfeeling lust, but this coldness went far beyond that. His fingers grabbed and delved and ripped, handling her with pure, icy rage.

When he did not find what he sought, he wrapped one hand through her hair and pulled her head back. "Damn you to hell! What have you done with my sapphire?"

"I do not have it!" she gasped, finding her voice at last.

"I can tell that!" He spun her about and suddenly let go. Ashiana stumbled, almost falling. She backed away, but two steps brought her up against the bookcase.

He stood where he was, fists clenched, every muscle rigid. He took several fast, deep breaths and his voice shifted to a cool, deadly tone. "If you value your life, you will tell me where it is. *Now.*"

"I swear by all the gods, I do not want to die! If I had it, I would return it to you!"

"Then tell me where it is."

"I—I did not want to steal it! I was forced into it! By a stranger. He said he would kill me if I did not get it for him."

D'Avenant snatched up one of the massive swords that had fallen from the wall and whirled it toward her in an expert arc.

Ashiana screamed—but he did not kill her.

Not yet. The point poised just at the base of her throat.

"By whatever gods you claim to hold dear," he said in that taut, deceptively soft voice, "you will pay with your life if you lie."

"I swear it!" Ashiana closed her eyes, shuddering at the touch of the cold, sharp steel against her skin. "I—I am but a slave girl. I knew nothing of your jewel. Th-this man was the one who told me. He was waiting in the *preet chatra* when I arrived there. He threatened me with a pistol. He told me what I must do and he said he would kill me and my friends in the harem if I failed!" She opened her eyes, crying now. "I am sorry—"

At that moment, Lorjulian came running through the door. "Sax, Jesus—"

"Stay out of this, Julian," the Englishman snapped, his eyes never leaving Ashiana. "Who was this 'stranger'?" he asked sarcastically. "What did he look like?"

Ashiana thought quickly, trying to decide what would sound even remotely believable. "One of the Europeans. He w-was dressed as all the others were. Dark clothes, and a hat with three corners. And the white false hair."

Saxon scowled, feeling a fresh surge of fury. He should kill her right now and be done with it. The girl had already proved herself a dangerous, deceitful little wench. She had drugged him, taken his jewel, almost killed him. Her story was probably entirely false; she was only trying to save her pretty little neck.

Yet . . . there was the name that kept pounding through Saxon's head with every painful throb of his temple. The name that had been gnawing at him since supper. It got stronger upon hearing that this supposed "stranger" was European.

Greyslake. Or one of his minions.

He swore viciously. "Tell me more about this stranger," he demanded, trying to sort truth from lie. "What color were his eyes? What did his face look like?"

She shook her head, gingerly, for he kept the sword point balanced at her throat. Tears ran down her cheeks and into the black hair that had tumbled about her shoulders. "He would not let me see his face. He looked like any other European. And I was too frightened to think! He was pointing a pistol at me."

"What about his voice—his accent?"

"He spoke Hindi. And I do not know one European accent from another. I am only a slave girl!"

Frustration and fury roiling inside him, Saxon pressed the blade closer against her tender skin. "If you are lying to me, woman—"

"I swear it is true. *He* told me of the jewel. *He* gave me the drug and instructed me how to use it. I would not know of such things. I only did as he told me!"

Saxon kept the sword at her throat. He could not believe her the innocent she painted herself to be, yet all of this *did* have Greyslake's mark stamped on it. Treachery. Poison. Hiring—or blackmailing—someone else to do the deed. If this girl were in league with his enemies, she could have finished him; she could have used his own *shamshir,* or easier yet, pushed him beneath the water and let him drown. Instead she had run.

He couldn't trust half of what she said, but what if even

part of it were true? What if one of Greyslake's men was spiriting the sapphire out of Daman at this very moment—while they stood there arguing?

He turned and addressed Julian, shifting to English so that she wouldn't understand. "Tell me what happened, Julian. Where did you find her after she left me?"

"She was in the corridor, not far from the harem," Julian said, a bit sheepishly. He looked from his brother to Ashiana and back with an expression of vexation. "She seemed nervous, and fearful of going back to you. I should have suspected something."

"Yes, you should have," Saxon said tightly. "She was alone? She didn't have my leather pouch?"

"I didn't search her, but she wasn't carrying anything, and yes, she was alone. I didn't see or hear anyone else. She said she was supposed to gather her things, that you had left and were going to return for her."

Saxon pinned Ashiana with another probing gaze, shifting back to Hindi. "You have lied to me. My brother says that you had my leather pouch when he met you in the corridor."

She blinked at Julian in clear astonishment. "But that is not true! The European stranger was waiting just outside the *preet chatra*. He took the pouch from me and ran without a word." She looked at Saxon again, her expression pleading. "I was so grateful for my life, I couldn't think of what to do. But I knew you would be furious if you found me. My only thought was to get away!"

Saxon swore vividly and threw the sword aside. This was pointless. He could question her all day and it wouldn't get him his sapphire back. They were wasting precious time.

Julian spoke softly, in English. "Her story fits with her actions when I found her, Sax. Her only thought *was* to get away. She tried several times. It sounds like she might be telling the truth."

"*Might* is one hell of a big word." Saxon glared at the trembling girl.

"Whoever this stranger was, he can't have gotten far. We could search—"

"We don't have bloody time to search," Saxon snapped. "We have to sail in less than an hour if we're going to catch the tide and make it to the Andamans before Greyslake. If he's the one who's got my sapphire, I'll be damned to the devil and back again before I let him have the other eight!"

"Uh, Sax," Julian said slowly. "About that—there's something I didn't have a chance to tell you."

Saxon shot him an irritated glance, gritting his teeth, certain his mood was about to get worse. "What?"

"We discovered damage to the keelson when we were preparing to sail. It wasn't serious enough to cause trouble on the coast, but I'm not sure it'll hold up for weeks on the open sea. You'd better take a look at it."

"Bloody blue blazing hell." Saxon turned and fixed a stare on the girl. He didn't have time for this. She shrank from him when he stepped toward her, but he grabbed her by the arms and hauled her up against him. His hands circled her wrists with expertly applied pressure. "Tell me again what this accomplice of yours looked like."

"He was not my accomplice! He forced—"

"Then you will not mind telling me what I want to know."

"*Krupiya,* I told you, he looked like the other Europeans—"

He tightened his grip and she immediately supplied more details.

"H-his clothes were dark blue, and he was tall, and rather heavy. That is all I know!"

Saxon held her a moment longer, his body taut, his mind racing ahead to what he must do. With Julian's help, he could launch a search here in Daman while he sailed to the Andamans.

The question was, what to do with the girl? He knew what he *should* do. Sell her. Hell, give her away. At the very least, put her off his ship and get her as bloody far away from him as possible.

But even as he weighed those alternatives, he knew he wouldn't choose any of them. He had the unpleasant suspicion that if he let her out of his sight, she would only cause him worse trouble than she already had.

She either had his sapphire or knew who did. Either way, she was his only link to it now, and he wasn't going to let her go. Whether she was a pawn or part of some plot, she knew more than she was telling—and he meant to get the truth out of her. However long it took. Whatever means he had to use.

He finally let go of her and spoke softly to his brother. "Wait for me on deck, Julian. And send Wyatt back down here."

With one last, strangely unhappy look at the girl, Julian left without argument.

Rubbing her wrists, the girl watched Julian leave, then slowly returned her gaze to Saxon's, her eyes reflecting desperate fear. Probably the first honest feeling she had shown him all day, he thought derisively.

"I—I see now that I have done a grievous wrong," she said. "I could go with you back to the city and help—"

Saxon silenced her with a harsh bark of laughter. *"Thank you* for the offer of assistance, but I am not going back to the city. And neither are you."

"Krupiya, I do not understand—"

"Then let me make it clear for you," he said coldly. "You have cost me a great deal, you lying little *chokri.* Until I get that sapphire back, I am not letting you out of my sight. Sooner or later you are going to tell me the truth." His eyes burned hers. "I haven't finished with you yet. I haven't even begun."

Before she could do more than gape at him, Wyatt arrived in the doorway.

"Sir?" The mate darted a wary, suspicious glance toward the girl.

"Wyatt, I want you to fasten a bolt to this door so I can lock it from the outside. But first take every single weapon out of here—and anything that could be used as a weapon—and stow them somewhere."

"Aye, sir." He started picking up the knives that had fallen on the floor.

Saxon gave his slave girl a cool, emotionless smile. "I will return in a few hours. I suggest you sleep until then. It's the last rest you'll have for a while."

He turned and slammed the door behind him, his back rigid. Seething, Saxon moved down the cramped corridor and took the steps at the far end two at a time. Julian was waiting for him on deck.

"I'm sorry, Sax. I should have—"

"Stow it, Julian. It's too late for hindsight now."

They walked to the rail together, threading their way among sailors who were preparing the *Valor* for departure; the sky in the east had lightened to gray.

Julian hung his head. "She just seemed so . . . so—"

"Innocent?" Saxon said with mocking accusation. "Your problem is that you are far too easily taken in by a pretty face."

Julian's head snapped up. "And you weren't?"

"*I* knew her for what she was from the start. It doesn't matter if she's called slave or courtesan or dancing girl— she's got a whore's training and a thief's heart. I'll not turn my back on her for a second, but I fully intend to get the truth out of her. When I'm finished with her, I'll sell her."

Julian looked distressed. "Sax, go easy—"

"*Easy?*" Saxon eyed his brother with disbelief. "She'll get what she deserves. No more, no less."

Still looking pained, Julian changed the subject. "A servant brought her belongings down from the palace. One of the men said they arrived while we were gone. They stowed them below—"

"Fine," Saxon interrupted, his mind still on his sapphire. "I want you to do something, Julian—"

"You want me to see if I can track down this mysterious 'stranger.' "

"If he exists, if there's even a chance—we have to have that jewel back."

Julian nodded. "The *Rising Star* is still in Bombay for

repairs for three more weeks. I had planned to sail home, but I'll stay until I can find out something."

"I don't care what you have to do or who you have to bribe. If it's here, find it and get it back."

"I'll do what I can."

They stood awkwardly for a moment, neither reaching out to shake hands or embrace as they usually did when parting for an extended time. Some barrier had sprung up between them, and Saxon knew with irritating certainty that it had to do with the girl. His brother didn't approve of what he planned to do with her.

Too bloody bad, he thought stubbornly. Julian had always been too blasted naive and softhearted, always trying to see the good in people, always eager to find the bright side in any situation. Well, there was no good in this girl and there sure as hell was no bright side to this accursed mess.

Saxon turned and glared into the line of blue that rimmed the rapidly brightening horizon. "I have to take a look at that keelson." His voice hardened. "See you when we return, Julian."

He turned without another word and strode across the deck.

Chapter 8

Trapped.

Her heart pounding, her back pressed against the locked door, Ashiana looked from the unyielding windows to the wall picked clean of weapons. From somewhere below her feet, she heard and felt a heavy, metallic clanking. A long-forgotten memory stirred, from her days aboard the *Adiante*: the anchor was being hauled aboard. They were leaving already!

Her stomach squeezed into a knot. She was still alive, but the reprieve was only temporary; D'Avenant would no doubt kill her after he had interrogated her—and perhaps meted out an even worse fate.

Her gaze was pulled unwillingly to the thick-hewn bed, the white sheets and fat pillows and the geometric designs stamped in white on the dark-blue Tijara coverlet. She couldn't move or blink or even breathe.

In the epic tales told by Ajmir storytellers, this was the point at which the brave princess usually threw herself into a pyre to avoid being defiled by the enemy.

Ashiana closed her eyes and bit her lower lip. She had never understood why the women of the clan always applauded that ending or why a princess would do such a thing. Once, she had asked it aloud: as long as one had life, did not one also have hope? The women had turned and stared at her, their eyes expressing their disapproval: *feringi*. Outsider.

Ashiana had instantly regretted her boldness and

94

withdrawn the question, wanting so badly to be one of them. Over the years, she had become accomplished at suppressing her unruly nature, keeping her true self and her true feelings hidden.

She was about to face the ultimate test of that skill. Opening her eyes, she summoned her courage as dawn's first rays shimmered through the windows, onto the bed. She must not let the Englishman suspect her true identity; if he discovered that she was an Ajmir spy, her mission and her life would be over.

Perhaps, just perhaps, he might be merciful—if she could keep him wondering. Keep him thinking, even a little bit, that she had been only a pawn in all this, a simple slave girl who had lived her entire life in the Emperor's harem, threatened and blackmailed by this "European stranger." D'Avenant *had* seemed to latch on to that part of her story.

A tiny bud of hope bloomed through the wintry terror that had gripped her.

There was no pyre conveniently at hand—and she knew she had already made her choice, despite the epic tales. As long as she still lived, she was still the sworn protector of the Nine Sapphires of Kashmir. Never would she willingly desert them or her duty. Never.

No matter what the Englishman meted out.

The bright sun of full morning blazed on the quarterdeck. Along the distant shoreline, the spires of Daman stretched into the sky, no larger than needles at this distance.

Saxon took off his shirt to mop the sweat from his chest and shoulders. Inspecting the damaged keelson and working alongside his men to shore it up had taken longer than expected, but he felt satisfied that it no longer posed a danger.

The exertion had taken the edge off his anger, leaving behind a slow, cold burn. He leaned on the rail, his jaw set. He found no pleasure in the familiar rhythms of the open sea, the brilliant sun and crashing waves and foamy white spray cresting along the hull. His crew was in a jovial mood, but they kept their high spirits tamped down while in his vicinity.

It had been a year since Saxon had stood on this deck and seen nothing but blue in every direction.

A year that had changed everything.

His temple still throbbed. He bent his head, rubbing at it. The *Valor* had always been his one haven from the quest he lived with, the one place he could let down his guard and trust everyone around him. But he would find no peace, no escape on the ocean. Not this voyage.

From the age of fourteen, Saxon had known the movement of a deck beneath his feet and the sound of the surf in the darkness as he went to sleep at night. Back in London, it was said that D'Avenant's were born with salt water instead of blood in their veins; his family had sailed for the East India Company since it was chartered over a hundred and fifty years ago.

He himself had navigated through gales that tried to slam him permanently into the deep, fallen prey to scurvy and fevers, wielded pistol and saber against pirates, and eaten more hardtack, sour grog, and salt pork than he cared to remember.

But always, beneath it all, had been a soul-felt love of the sea . . . and he couldn't feel it anymore.

He raised his head, every muscle aching with the movement, and glared at the expanse of water. *He couldn't feel it.*

Even that had been seared away, with everything else in his heart, in the funeral pyre that day on the Kashmir plain.

He looked at the churning waters and saw only another adversary to be conquered. He thought only of the distance to be crossed, sapphires to be found, enemies to be overcome . . . vengeance to be taken.

He straightened with a jerk and pushed himself away from the rail. Tupper was at the wheel, his most experienced helmsman, while Simmons, the third mate, kept a keen eye on their latitude with a backstaff. The crew was ably handling the complicated tracery of spars and halyards that controlled the sails and drew power from the wind. The *Valor* wouldn't vary a degree off course; there was no need for him to be here. His men parted to let him pass.

"South by southeast, Tupper. Hold her steady."

"Aye, sir."

Saxon swung down the steps to the main deck, still holding his damp shirt in one fist. He kept his anger in check as he went through the aft hatch and down the companionway, into the darkness belowdecks. He meant to have the truth from the maddening little *chokri* waiting in his cabin, but he could afford to go about it coolly and slowly now. Time and the sea were on his side; she had nowhere to run.

Reaching his cabin, he looked at the lock with approval. Wyatt had done well. Not even his wily little slave would be able to trick her way past that. He slid the bolt and pushed the door open cautiously, half-expecting to be greeted with either a desperate attack or an equally desperate volley of tears.

Instead, she was standing calmly at the windows beside the bed, hands clasped, eyes dry. She looked at him warily, as if she thought he might throw her against the wall that very second and beat the truth out of her.

Saxon held her gaze for a long, intimidating moment, letting her worry. Then he shut the door behind him and went to the washbasin in the corner, dropping his shirt on the floor.

Despite her outward show of calm, he could hear her breath coming short and shallow. The tension of awaiting his return had obviously frayed her nerves. Good.

He poured a small amount of water and, speaking Hindi, sprang a question on her. "This 'stranger' in the *preet chatra*—was his hair brown or black?"

"Neither, sahib," she said, quickly, tremulously. "As I told you before, he wore the white false hair."

Saxon splashed his face and chest and ran his wet hands through his hair. He had hoped to catch her off guard with that trick question, trip her up. He tried another. "You said he threatened you with a knife. What was it like?"

"*Nahin.* No, not a knife. A pistol. It was small, so that it just fit in his hand, and plated with silver metal."

It sounded like a dueling pistol—but she still could be lying. She might have seen a European pistol somewhere before. He gingerly dabbed at the cut on his temple. The pain hadn't lessened, but the bleeding had stopped. Taking a towel from its peg on the wall, he turned toward her again. She kept her attention on his face as he dried his chest and arms.

He let the silence stretch taut.

She snapped in a little less than three minutes. "A-are you not going to ask me any more questions?"

"No."

She blinked. "Why not?"

"Because you expect me to. You've obviously had time to think about your story and anticipate what I might ask."

She looked startled—then panic suddenly welled in her blue eyes. "Are you going to kill me?" she whispered.

He folded the towel, set it aside, and leaned back against the bulkhead. "Killing you now would be a waste of a perfectly useful slave girl."

He emphasized the *now* and did not say whether he might kill her later. He saw the question in her eyes, and deliberately let it linger in her mind. It would play havoc with her nerves—and leave her unprepared when he chose a more unexpected moment to question her.

He could think of many ways to fill the moments until then. Hunger suddenly heated his body as they stood there, staring warily at one another.

His gaze left hers to trace over the alabaster perfection of her breasts, the slender curve of her waist, the silk-veiled secrets below. Against his better judgment, against all reason, he still wanted her. The chit's treachery did nothing to diminish the memories of her lithe body curving into his, those thinly clad breasts filling his hands so perfectly. Desire curled in his gut. Even standing still, neither moving nor making a sound, she still had the power to torture him.

And he had had more than enough torture for one day.

He came away from the bulkhead and stepped toward her, slow and purposeful. "I am obviously not going to get any information out of you at the moment, but I can wait. Eventually, *chokri,*" he said with low promise, "you will tell me everything."

She shivered when he reached out and tilted her chin up on the edge of his fist.

"In the meantime," he continued in that same tone, "you can make yourself useful in other ways."

"*Han,* I . . . I . . . can be most useful to you, sahib. I am a passable storyteller. And I shall keep the cabin clean. And I can sing—"

He laughed. "This ship has a crew of ninety and every one of them has a station and a duty. There are no unnecessary hands on an Indiaman." Withdrawing his hand, he turned away and started to take off his boots, letting each drop with a *thwack.*

She flinched as they struck the floor.

He straightened, now wearing nothing but his breeches. "Your station will be there." He pointed toward the bed. "And your duty will be to please me. And I don't intend for you to use your mouth for any idiotic singing."

What little color was left in her cheeks fled. Her lower lip started to tremble. Saxon ignored both, flatly refusing to let himself acknowledge her fear. She had tricked him before; he would not be taken in again by her feigned innocence. He knew this wench for what she was.

"And do not think you have escaped punishment," he said coldly. "If I decide to spare you—*if*—then I shall rid myself of you when we arrive at our destination. We are sailing for the Andaman Islands, so perhaps I shall sell you—" He paused to add impact to his next words. "—to the Ajmir."

She gave a quick, wide-eyed gasp and lowered her gaze to the floor. "But—"

"Do not bother to remind me that you lived among

them as a child, or that they gave you to the Emperor because they couldn't stand the sight of you. I'm sure there will be a cart-maker or a goatherd somewhere among them who could use the services of a whore and won't mind your English looks. Or the fact that you're also a liar and a thief."

When she raised her face to his, slowly, her expression had changed to one of complete anguish. "*Krupiya,* not the Ajmir," she pleaded, her eyes shining with tears. "I—I would go gladly to a new master anywhere else, but not there!"

"They deserve you. But first you are going to satisfy this master."

A flicker of emotion appeared in her eyes, just for a second. It might have been hatred—for him, for them. It might have been something else. He didn't care. He welcomed her hatred; her meek passivity, so utterly, clearly false, irked him. The fire in his gut demanded conquest, not tenderness.

He folded his arms over his chest. "Now stop bothering me with questions and come here. That tearful performance might have impressed my brother, but it's a waste of time on me."

Her eyes blazed again before her expression went completely flat, emotionless. She came toward him, a single, hesitant step.

Saxon closed the distance between them. His impatient hands took her by her bare waist and pressed her hips to his. He was already aroused, but the feel of her skin beneath his fingers, her femininity pressing against his breeches with only bits of cloth between them, made him rock-hard.

A tremor shuddered through her. He ignored it. He raised one hand to steal through her hair, tilting her head back, holding her still while he lowered his mouth to the shadowy cleft between her breasts. His lips and tongue and teeth played over the soft, silk-clad mounds; her body jerked once, but she did not try to resist.

She still smelled of sandalwood and patchouli oil. He

drank in the scent, and with it the memory of her betrayal in the *preet chatra* . . . his thwarted desire.

Not this time.

He slid her *peshwaz* from her shoulders and let it fall to the floor. She remained stiff in his embrace.

"Where have all your harem tricks fled?" he mocked, raising his head to look down at her. His thumb found her nipple and circled it, urging it to fullness. She bit her lip to stifle a cry and lowered her lashes.

"You can stop the blushing-virgin performance. That was probably a lie as well, wasn't it? Just one more trick to slow me down so you would have time to poison me."

With one sweep of his hand, her silk *choli* bodice drifted after the *peshwaz,* baring her breasts to his gaze and his touch.

She kept her eyes squeezed shut. He ran his hands downward until he was cupping a single perfect, soft globe in each hand. He kneaded and caressed, letting himself fully enjoy every tender curve. Her nipples beaded against his palms. God, she was beautiful—

He stifled that thought, not intending to let himself feel anything for her, not even appreciation. *Treacherous,* he reminded himself. *Deceitful. Dangerous.*

But the other word wouldn't leave his mind. *Beautiful.* The most desirable slip of pale feminine flesh he had ever seen. A siren that even the sailors of legend could never have resisted.

And he was no legend.

He held her closer, his hands moving lower to shape the curves of her buttocks. His arousal thrust rampantly against her belly. He buried his face in her hair, his breath coming hard and fast against the slim column of her throat. He could feel her warm, pounding pulse, a gentler echo of his own.

"Stop pretending, little *chokri,* " he urged suddenly. "We've weeks alone together and you've nowhere to run from me but the ocean. Why not make our time together pleasant?"

She remained frozen against him, yielding and yet not

yielding some inner part of herself. Her eyes remained shut, her scented, lush, pampered body unbending.

"No matter." He instantly regretted his gentle entreaty. "I've no need for your talents. We'll do this my way."

He took the waist of her *salwar* in both hands, and the purple silk, already torn during his search for the sapphire, gave way with little effort. She was now nude but for her bracelets and rings and earrings, and the layers of sheer skirts that tantalizingly veiled her most feminine treasure.

Sheer perfection greeted his eyes in her every line, from her rose-tipped breasts to her tiny waist to her long, long slender legs. Even her feet looked delicate and small. Her only blemish was the scar on her left arm, and even that had been transformed into a work of art, the exquisitely drawn flower adding to her exotic allure.

His gaze rose to lock with hers. His body would not let him hesitate a second longer.

To hell with the skirts. She could leave them on.

He scooped her into his arms and deposited her on the bed, pulled back the covers, and shifted her onto the sheets. Primitive need ripped through him, filling him with the urgency to possess, to mate. He stripped off his breeches and positioned himself above her in a single fluid movement. His weight balanced on his arms, he pinned her down with his hips, his rigid shaft pressing against her thigh.

Ashiana cried out, desperately frightened now that the moment was at hand. She tried to shut down every bit of feeling inside her, to lie still and lifeless beneath him. But her senses seemed to conspire against her, coming vibrantly to life with awareness of him: the friction of his sun-heated skin against hers, the weight of his hard-muscled body, the coaxing, seductive touch of his hands. His lips were suddenly at her ear, nibbling at her lobe, at her earring, his beard abrading the delicate skin of her jaw.

Shivers danced down the back of her neck to meet with the sparks that sizzled up from below, where he rubbed himself against her soft mound in a way that made her feel singed, branded, burned, melting.

He tried to nudge her legs apart with one knee. "Open for me, *chokri*," he commanded in a low, tight voice.

Ashiana had resolved to endure whatever he meted out—but she was afraid to obey. Afraid of the strange, wanton sensations he made her feel ... the languid heat, the tightening ache in her belly, the warm dampness between her thighs. He nuzzled her neck, but she clung to her hatred, loathing him with every fiber of her being. She would not help him. Her resistance apparently made him lose the last of his control. He reached down with one strong hand and opened her legs.

Then, without warning, he filled her in a single surging stroke.

Ashiana didn't realize she had cried out, only felt a sharp, burning pain and heard the sound of her voice hanging in the silence the next second. He stilled, holding himself suspended above her.

She thought for a second she might pass out from the shock of his sudden invasion, but she remained all too conscious, her cry dissolving into a thready sob that echoed up from the depths of her. He was too large, much too large for the delicate passage he had thrust himself into!

He muttered what sounded like a rough curse in English.

But he didn't stop.

No, that was the most hateful thing of all. He had to know he had caused her pain, but he did not stop.

He only pulled out of her a little way, then moved forward again, though more slowly this time.

Ashiana dug her nails into his back. She would not beg him to stop, but by all the gods ... She tensed as he tried to sheath himself to the hilt again, her body tightening at the unfamiliar intrusion, making his goal impossible unless he used brute force.

"Relax," he ordered in a strained voice.

She would not open her eyes. She would not look at him. She would most certainly not obey.

When she didn't move a muscle, he slid a hand between

their bodies and touched her, touched a part of her that even he had never touched before.

Ashiana gasped as the tip of his finger found a sensitive spot at the center of her downy triangle. He just grazed it, moving in a tiny circle. Unimaginable, icy-hot bolts shimmered through her every nerve ending, making her feel flushed, breathless, aching.

When she tried to catch her breath, it came out as a moan. He held himself utterly still within her and kept brushing that swollen nubbin, teasing it, searing her with a heat she had never known before, hotter than a tandoor oven.

"Nahin! No!" Ashiana gasped. Curse him, this was far more nefarious than resorting to force! An unfurling bloom of bright fire spread through her, seized her attention. It was as overpowering as it was unexpected, tingling, building, sweeping through her with soft tendrils of flame and pleasure. It stole her breath, made her heart race—made her forget to resist him.

He withdrew his hand after a moment, but her traitorous body had already softened enough to accommodate his. With a groan, he sheathed himself, withdrew, then pushed forward again.

Ashiana caught her breath, but not in pain this time. The pain faded with his every slow stroke, replaced by a feeling of fullness . . . sliding, pulsing fullness. Against her will, the bloom of pleasure stretched its fire-tipped petals inside her again, straining, reaching, filling her with an aching restlessness.

Her lips parted. D'Avenant took her face between his broad hands, lowering his mouth to hers—but stopped short before their lips met.

"No," he ground out, turning his face away. "I'll not trust those treacherous lips again." He pressed his cheek against hers, his breath rasping hot through her tangled hair as his thrusts gathered force and speed.

Ashiana cried out in astonishment as he stroked into her so deeply that her hips rose up to meet his. All pretense at passiveness had disappeared; there was only her body and his, blazing together with shuddering strain. She arched into him, needing, wanting ... she did not know what, only that she would die if the swirling tension inside her did not end.

The movement of her hips seemed to enflame him. He raised himself above her, taking her faster, harder. Suddenly his whole body went rigid, his teeth clenched as a low groan escaped from deep in his chest. Ashiana felt him move inside her, once, twice, again, and then he collapsed atop her, pressing her back into the sheets, surrounding her with his scent and a muskiness that she knew was a blend of them both.

As her heartbeat slowed, reason returned. She thought she would die of shame. She wished she could, right then, right at that moment, so that she would never have to look at him again.

Her wish was not to come true, for he levered himself up on one elbow, looking down at her with an unfamiliar expression swirling in his silver eyes, a look that was at once distant and intimate. She was astonished to see emotion there, almost like ... regret.

He brushed his fingers over her cheek, wiping away her tears. "Are you—"

He froze, his expression hardening, his eyes turning frosty. Ashiana didn't know what he had been going to say or what she had done to make him angry. He left her body and got up from the bed, turning his back on her, snatching up his breeches and jamming his legs into them.

Without a single word, he dressed and left the cabin, slamming the door behind him. Ashiana heard the bolt flung into place.

She was left alone in the tangled sheets and her torn skirts, alone with her mortification, her hatred ... and the far deeper shame of what he had made her feel.

Chapter 9

*L*ungs burning, muscles aching, legs pumping, he ran. He could not get enough air but he kept running, flattening stalks of saffron beneath his boots, pushing himself harder. The faster he raced, the further away she seemed, standing beside the stream . . . alone, so utterly alone. Deserted.

She huddled into herself, one hand over her eyes, the cascade of black hair half-obscuring her face as if she could not bear to look at him.

Straining, reaching toward her, he threw himself against the wind, wind that stole his voice, filled his mouth, choked out sound when he tried to call her name.

"M—"

Wind that fluttered the petals of the yellow and red flowers draped about her neck.

"Man—"

Wind that carried one word to him, her sweet voice heavy with a whisper of sorrow that was his name.
"Saxon."

An arrow hissed past him—

Saxon wrenched awake and upright all at once. "Mandara!"

The phantom arrow still whistled through his mind as he realized where he was. No reply came from the darkness surrounding him, the star-pricked sky above, the hard English oak of the deck beneath him.

There was no sound at all but the snap of the East India

Company ensign over his head and the lap of the waves along the *Valor*'s hull. The night air that filled the sails ruffled his hair with icy fingers and chilled the sweat from his forehead.

He was on the aft deck, had sat down only moments ago after pacing the ship for hours.

The dream drained away, slowly, twining downward like thorned tendrils that tore him inside. He tensed against the memory, against the pain of it, against the frustrated urge to strike out, to slam his fist on the deck until he couldn't feel anything but blood and numbness.

Forcibly relaxing his clenched hands, he drew in a long breath. Slowly the impulse faded, leaving only an ache behind, an ache and the emptiness.

Closing his eyes, he let himself fall back against the taffrail. He had not dreamed of Mandara before this. Two score nights had passed since her death and he had never once dreamed of her. He had thought that part of himself closed off forever.

It was almost as if she were haunting him. Damning him for what had taken place hours before in his cabin . . . for the fact that the little English wench in harem silks had comandeered his thoughts from the moment he had joined his body to hers.

Swearing, he rubbed his hands over his face. He couldn't stop thinking about the chit. Or feeling—an infuriating mix of desire and remorse and exhilaration and guilt. Damn him, in that moment before he left her, he had almost asked whether she was all right. He had wanted to hold her in his arms and soothe her!

Saxon pushed himself to his feet, prowling about the aft deck until he found himself at the far rail. He had spent the entire day trying to exhaust himself with physical labor, doing everything he could to distract himself from the image of that delicate little rose curled in his bed and her silent tears.

What the hell was wrong with him? She was a slave and he was her master. He had done nothing that wasn't his right. Perhaps he had been a bit rough in taking her innocence—

Innocence. That was the thing. He never would have thought to associate the word "innocence" with his slave girl, but she had told the truth on that point: the Emperor had never taken a fancy to her in all the years she had spent in his harem. Saxon gritted his teeth, feeling that somehow, this girl was not at all what he thought she was.

Innocence and treachery. Truth and lies. Pleasure and guilt. It was enough to drive a man mad.

From amidships came the sound of the *Valor*'s bell, rung three times by one of the crewmen on night watch. It would be daylight in a few hours. Saxon again ran a weary hand over his eyes. He knew he needed sleep, but didn't want to let himself doze off again. Not now, not knowing what awaited him in his dreams.

He couldn't rest, couldn't concentrate enough to go below and work at his charts or his logbook . . . and the last thing he could do was go back to his cabin, to his little slave.

Because that was the one thing he wanted to do.

Wanted it so badly it unnerved him.

Saxon hung his head, leaning out over the rail, letting the wind tear through his hair and rip at the open neck of his shirt. The cold blasted at him as he cursed at himself.

By hell's fire, he could not understand why this woman should have such a hold on his thoughts. Her body was feminine perfection, true, but he had known other temptresses of equal beauty. A girl in Marseilles by the name of Colette leaped to mind. Then there was one in the bordello at Buenos Aires whose name escaped him, but whose talents were permanently imprinted on his memory. And of course Chu Hua, the Cantonese courtesan who had initiated him into the ways of lovemaking when he had been but sixteen.

Was this wench really so different?

He had been celibate too long, he decided. That was the cause of his confusion. He turned the idea over and over in his head as the wind-gathered spray stung his face.

That had to be it. He had kept his physical appetites bottled up for over a year, and now he was overreacting.

Saxon straightened, feeling somewhat better. He had taken entirely the wrong tack here. Denial only made his hunger more acute, made this slave girl seem somehow exceptional. What he needed to do was go below and sate himself completely.

Once he had taken her a few more times, he would see how ordinary she truly was. His interest would turn to indifference.

And indifference was what he must have. Saxon stared out across the waves that he could hear but not see in the darkness. He could allow himself a man's unavoidable physical instincts, but he could not forgive feelings of any sort. Not even guilt, for it bespoke something deeper underneath.

Experiencing anything—*anything*—other than simple lust was a betrayal of his vow to Mandara, and that he would not do. That vow was one of the last scraps of honor in his life, one of the last . . . anchors he had in this sea of darkness and treachery that threatened to pull him down once and for all.

He would do what he must to get this girl off his mind. He would, eventually, get the truth from her. And when they reached the Andamans, he would get her off his ship and out of his life.

By the time Saxon opened the door to his cabin, he felt in command of himself once again, and ready to take his seductive problem in hand. Late-morning sunlight streamed through the mullioned windows, warming the room and tracing a latticework of shadows over the freshly made bed. He had thought to find her there—either asleep or crying and accusing—but once again she wasn't where he expected her to be.

She was, in fact, balanced against the wall that used to play host to his collection of weapons, upside down, her limbs tangled into an elaborate yoga pose, her eyes closed.

And she was wearing a sheet.

She had folded and knotted it around her to form a sort of sari and leggings.

He halted in the doorway and stared. "What the devil are you doing?"

Her eyes flew open, but she didn't lose her balance. Saxon realized he had spoken in English and repeated his question in Hindi. Without responding, she gracefully unfolded herself, lowering her feet to the floor and standing upright. She backed against the wall and kept her gaze lowered.

"*Maf kijiye.* Pardon, sahib," she said in a thready whisper. "I . . . I was meditating."

"Upside down?" He shut the door.

She blushed, moving her head in that odd little way that made her hair fall forward to partially mask her pale features. "It . . . it is . . ."

"Say it, woman. If you have strange habits, I would know."

"It was a pose for the relief of . . . for pain."

She shifted her weight uncomfortably, and Saxon suddenly understood: she was still suffering not just soreness but pain from the day before. He must have hurt her worse than he thought. He felt a wave of guilt and fought it off, telling himself he didn't care.

"I see," he said gruffly. "And what the devil are you wearing?"

She looked down at her makeshift garment, adjusting the knot at her bodice.

That simple motion of her hand flooded his senses. All at once Saxon was aware of the throb of her pulse at the base of her throat, the smooth ivory of her skin against the white sheet, the lush swell of her breasts that the plain cotton fabric only emphasized. In a heartbeat, he was aroused, ready for her, aching to have her.

Her voice was very small when she finally replied. "Your *naukar*-man, Nickerson, when he came with the washing-water and the food—I asked him to dispose of my clothes. I could not wear the *salwar* again. They were too . . . badly torn."

Saxon felt fresh guilt surge through him. He ruthlessly throttled it. "I see," he repeated tightly.

Turning away from her, he stalked to his sea chest, stripping off his shirt and taking out a fresh one. He had sent Nickerson, the ship's steward, down with a change of linens and food and water for her. He hadn't thought about the fact that her garments would be unwearable.

After what he had done to them.

That didn't matter either, he told himself, letting the lid of the sea chest fall with a resounding *thwack*; for his purposes, she didn't need clothes. Holding the fresh shirt in one fist, he slid his gaze back to hers.

She kept her back firmly to the wall and watched him with wide eyes. When he stepped toward her, not putting on the shirt, her lower lip began to tremble. Again she tilted her head downward in that gesture that hid her face behind a cascade of black hair.

"Stop it," he ordered abruptly.

"S-sahib?" Her voice wasn't even a whisper. "What is it you wish me to stop?"

Stop acting modest and innocent, he wanted to shout. *Stop blushing. Stop hiding your eyes and your face. Stop falling into that pose that makes you look more Hindu than European. Stop looking like my—*

"I wish you to look at me when I am speaking to you." He crossed to her and placed a firm hand under her chin, tipping her head up.

A violent, visible shiver ran through her entire body. *"Krupiya!* Please!" she cried. "Don't . . . don't hurt me again."

Startled, Saxon withdrew his hand. The girl's eyes had gone vacant, flat with a look he had seen only once before, in the gaze of a man who had surrendered to madness after months at sea—just before he threw himself over the rail to his death.

Saxon felt something twist inside him at the thought that his merest touch tormented her. The feeling only made him angry at himself. "It would not hurt so badly the second time," he assured her.

A spark of unmistakable anger shimmered to life in her blue eyes. "Even so," she said, breathing rapidly. "I—I could not bear it."

Saxon gritted his teeth. Her fear was understandable, yet it irked him beyond reason that she should find him unbearable. "I suppose until you have recovered I would get no pleasure in taking you."

She started to duck her head again, then caught herself. She brought her gaze back up to hold his, but didn't reply, except for a blush that thoroughly rouged her cheeks.

He muttered a vivid, salty oath, then jerked away from her and put on his shirt, pacing from the end of the bed to his bookcase as he buttoned it. He would give her time, then, damn it—but he was only thinking of himself. Taking her now would make everything worse; he wanted to get the most physical pleasure out of her that he could. It was the only way to be done with her.

"I will grant you two days' rest." He stopped his pacing and scowled at her, fastening the last button at his throat. "I wouldn't want to exhaust you, woman, any more than I would overwork a prized horse."

Her eyes still glittered, but she didn't express anger, or relief, as he might expect. Instead, her response took him by surprise.

"I have a name," she said, quietly but firmly. "I am called Ashiana."

He fixed her with a glare. Why the devil did she have to tell him that? *Ashiana*. A name to attach to all the images that tortured him. A name that flowed like the sea-blue of her eyes, like a warm Bengal wind, like—

"Your name does not matter, *chokri*. I will call you whatever I choose to call you. And you will do whatever I say you will do. Because it is what I wish."

Not trusting himself to stay one second longer or say one more word, he turned and left, slamming the door behind him. There was something satisfying in the sound and feel of wood striking wood, something solid.

Unlike his control, he thought ruefully, which seemed to

be slipping through his hands even as he tried to get a tighter grip on it.

He headed below to find Fergus MacNeil, the purser in charge of the ship's stores. He would have to get the wench something to wear, if he wasn't going to bed her for two days.

Something much more substantial than a sheet.

"Lusting *bandar.* Back end of an *unt. Suar. Angrez!*"

Shaking, Ashiana stared at the spot where D'Avenant had last stood and vented all the insults she could think of. Comparing him to an ape, the back end of a camel, and a pig wasn't quite adequate, but the last word seemed to sum it up.

Angrez. English!

How could any man be so cold? How could he have hurt her, then tell her he meant to do it again? And to compare her to a beast of burden! Truly, this D'Avenant was a shining example of his kind.

Trembling, she went to the door, walking gingerly; she was still tender where he had joined his body to hers. Trying the latch, she found it locked.

Of course. He had thought of that. He wouldn't want to take any chance of her getting away. He wouldn't want to deny himself pleasure.

Refusing to give in to tears, Ashiana went back to her place by the wall and settled herself into the lotus pose, closing her eyes. She had spent four hours this morning in meditation, yet in the span of a few minutes, D'Avenant had shredded her calm. She kept waiting for him to pounce on her—either with lust or with questions—and the tension was starting to drive her completely *paagal.*

Which was no doubt what he wanted. She could not believe she had insisted on being called by name. What foolish impulse had made her blurt that out?

All her years of studying the ways of mental peace and serenity availed her nothing; he seemed to have the power to provoke her with a single word or look. Every time he came near her, she could feel an indefinable energy sizzling between them that made her pulse beat faster. She couldn't stop herself from noticing the chiseled, muscular angles of his chest and arms, or the way his light hair made his skin seem so dark. She couldn't even seem to *breathe* properly in his presence, which left her feeling all tingly and strange. It was not an unpleasant sensation, and that only unnerved and dismayed her all the more.

And his touch . . .

Nahin. She wouldn't let herself think about that. Even the brief, firm contact of his hand on her chin just now . . . the memory made her shiver.

Worse, she knew her reactions didn't come from fear, but from something else. Something she didn't understand.

Disgust, she tried to tell herself. *Revulsion.*

Ashiana had the deeply unsettling feeling that neither of those words was accurate. Whatever the feeling was, she did not want to experience it with him again. Ever.

As she tried to meditate, another worry troubled her as well. She hadn't thought of it until late in the night, as she lay awake. The nagging question refused to go away.

Would Rao, her betrothed, the Maharaja's son, still accept her as a wife?

Losing her innocence had truly *not* been her choice. Her only concern had been for the sapphires, for her duty. But would Rao understand?

She firmly set the question aside and began humming a low mantra. She could not afford to let herself worry about the future; she must keep her mind focused on getting through each day, each moment, until the ship reached the Andamans.

Ashiana slanted a look at the section of the wall where the sapphires were hidden. If D'Avenant guessed that she was in truth an Ajmir spy, that she had not only *his* missing sapphire, but all *nine*, right here beneath his very nose . . .

She shivered again and closed her eyes, working a deep *pranayama* breath. She had just begun to calm and focus her thoughts when D'Avenant returned.

Startled when the door opened, she rose warily. She

wished he were more predictable; she could never tell when he left whether he would return in hours or minutes.

He regarded her with a stern expression, holding an armful of clothing which he dropped on the bed.

"I won't have you distracting my crew by going about in a sheet," he said by way of explanation.

Ashiana almost asked how that would be possible, since she was kept locked in his cabin at all times, then thought better of it. If she could not get her unruly nature under control, he might begin to guess that she had not been raised as a slave girl at all.

"I am ... grateful, sahib," she forced herself to say, stepping closer to the bed to see what he had brought.

There was a long, heavy garment made of scratchy, gray fabric—like a *choli* bodice and *paridhana* skirt, but all in one piece, with long, very uncomfortable-looking sleeves. Tangled up with it were two other skirts, plain white, edged with flounces and frills; and an odd-shaped piece that was very stiff when she poked at it. It seemed to be made of flat pieces of bamboo!

She sifted among the rest of the pile, finding a pair of long silk tubes—the purpose of which she could only guess at—various ribbons and fastenings, and a pair of very plain leather slippers.

There were no ornaments, no veils, no jewelry—not so much as a single bracelet. Not even the meanest slave in the harem of the most impoverished raja would be asked to wear such as this. Did the Englishman mean to humiliate her?

"I—I am grateful, sahib, but might I humbly ask whether you have anything else? If you've fabric aboard, I might fashion myself something more suitable. I have never worn *angrez* clothes before—"

"You will grow used to it," he said flatly. "We've samples from European and Oriental textile mills aboard, but this is what I prefer you to wear."

"But—"

"And I am going to teach you English as well."

Ashiana stared at him in openmouthed, speechless surprise.

He held up a warning hand, cutting off her question before she could ask it. *"Because* it is what I wish."

It was several seconds before Ashiana realized her mouth was still open. She closed it, biting down hard to stop a storm of confused questions. Why would he object to her wearing Hindu clothes? They were far more pleasing to the eye—and he said that what he wanted of her was pleasure. And why would he not want her to speak Hindi?

He was either being purposely cruel, or he had such deep hatred for Hindu ways, he found them offensive. Ashiana wrestled with simmering pride. How could he be so prejudiced against her people, after he had lived among Hindus?

But of course: he was English. Prejudiced, arrogant, cruel—

"You will get dressed now," he commanded in a deep, unyielding tone.

Ashiana let herself hold his stare defiantly for just a moment. His eyes glittered cold silver. He exuded icy cool. She adjusted the knotted sheet she wore and he clenched his fists.

Tread most carefully, she reminded herself, instantly lowering her gaze, remembering how unpredictable he could be. If she wanted to live long enough to carry out her duty, she had best start acting like a proper slave girl.

"Maf kijiye, sahib," she said softly, submissively, waving a hand over the garments. "Which would you like me to wear?"

"*All* of it."

Her head came up. She couldn't help it. "*All* of it?" she sputtered. "I . . ." She choked back a protest and lowered her chin a notch. "I—I will do as you say. *Han,* sahib."

He folded his arms over his chest. "We will start your English lessons with that. The word for *han* is 'yes.' The opposite of 'yes' is 'no'—but that's not a word I expect to hear from you."

Ashiana held her tongue in check.

"And instead of calling me *sahib*, you may call me 'master' or 'my lord.'"

Her eyes on the pile of clothing, Ashiana told herself she must think of her duty. She dared not give D'Avenant any reason to end her life. On the contrary, she wanted to give him every reason to spare her—and make good his threat to sell her to the Ajmir.

"Yes, my lord," she said, twisting her tongue around the strange sounds, her first words of English. She looked up at him from beneath her lashes.

Though it was difficult to measure his feelings, he seemed pleased. There was just the slightest softening of his granite features.

Relieved to have at least a brief truce, Ashiana started sorting through the garments, trying to decide which of the graceless items she was supposed to put on first.

She started to remove the sheet she wore, when, to her surprise, D'Avenant turned his back.

The man was utterly impossible to figure out. How could he be so hateful one moment, only to be thoughtful of her modesty the next? If he was trying to drive her *paagal*, he was off to an excellent start.

Ashiana thought of asking for the English word for *paagal*, but squelched the impulse.

Dropping the sheet, she quickly picked up one of the white skirts, examining it with a frown. Did this go on top of the gray *choli-paridhana*, or beneath? She didn't have even the most distant idea.

It rustled as she put it on. She started to tie it about her waist, but it seemed much too long, dragging on the floor behind her.

D'Avenant kept pacing back and forth in front of his bookcase. She wished he would stop. The tools she had used to hide the gems had left tiny scrape marks on the wall panel; every time he went near that corner, she feared he might notice.

Her stomach in knots, Ashiana struggled with the overly long skirt. Perhaps it was meant to be worn higher. She moved it up and settled it beneath her arms, tying it in place over her breasts. It fell to just below her knees.

She picked up the other white skirt. This one was a bit shorter, so she pulled it on overtop the first and fastened it about her hips.

She frowned. That couldn't be right. She looked as big and billowy as a festival tent.

"Sah—my lord?"

D'Avenant stilled his pacing and turned slowly around.

Ashiana looked down at herself and back up at him, raising her hands helplessly. "I do not think this is right."

His eyebrows arched. The corners of his mouth quirked upward into what was almost a smile. After fighting it for a moment, he laughed. "No." He shook his head. "It's not."

Ashiana blushed furiously, feeling foolish. "I've never seen an *angrez* woman."

"No, it's rather obvious that you haven't. Here." He came over and scooped the clothing on the bed out of the way and pushed her downward, gently. "Sit."

She did as he ordered, the contact of his hand on her bare shoulder rendering her momentarily breathless.

He knelt in front of her. "You might as well learn the words for what it is you're wearing." He picked up one of the silk tubes from the bed and held it up. " 'Stocking,' " he pronounced.

Ashiana imitated the strange, harsh-sounding word. "Stok-eeng."

He took her foot, resting it on his knee. He went still.

His fingers touched her toes, the smooth arch, her ankle. His voice sounded dry when he spoke again. " 'Foot.' "

Ashiana had to struggle with the strange sound that began the word—and she did not like the warmth of his hand, the strong, firm way he held her, the uncomfortable shivery sensations in her stomach. "F-foot," she repeated at last.

He slipped the *stok-eeng* over her *foot,* quickly, as if he didn't want to be doing it, then moved it up over her knee, where he fastened it into place by tying one of the ribbons snugly around the top.

His fingertips lingered there, at the soft spot at the back of her knee. The swirls in Ashiana's middle converged into a warm tightness and suddenly she couldn't catch her breath.

His hand moved downward, slowly, over her calf, warming the silk and her skin. He didn't say a word. Ashiana didn't—couldn't—speak. Or move. Or do anything but look down at his tousled hair and think of how it looked like sunlight.

" 'Leg,' " he said at last, his voice so low she had to strain to hear it.

When she did not repeat the word, he raised his head. Their gazes locked. For just an instant Ashiana saw—*felt*—the heat in his eyes.

"Leg," she whispered.

As if her breath had blown out a flame, the warmth in his eyes vanished. The more familiar coldness slid back into place and he nudged her foot from his knee. He fitted out her other *leg* with a *stok-eeng*, his movements brisk, then bid her to rise.

"Turn around," he said roughly.

When she was slow to move, he turned her about, then untied the white skirt Ashiana had placed around her breasts, settling it at her waist. She gasped, but his hands were so quick, she didn't even have time to feel his touch. He took the bamboo-stiff garment and wrapped it around her.

"Ai-*ee!*" she protested with an indrawn breath as he laced it tightly.

"It's supposed to fit that way."

He told her the name of the torturous device—*kor-set*—and the name for the skirts, an enormously long word which she could not pronounce if her life depended on it, though it was something like *pet-ee-koots*.

When he had finished strapping her into the *kor-set*, she walked about experimentally, stiffly, looking down in dismay at her new clothes. "I feel like an elephant armored for battle."

"Perhaps I should start calling you Ganesha."

Ashiana glanced up and saw that he was grinning. Ganesha was the Hindu god of luck, the elephant god. "I only wish I had Ganesha's trunk," she gasped. "It might be easier to breathe."

"Be careful what you ask for," he advised. "I understand he grants wishes."

"You do not think it would be an improvement?" She extended one arm in front of her nose like a trunk and improvised a trumpeting noise.

His grin gave way to a soft laugh. "No. I prefer you and your nose tiny. Come here, little Ganesha."

He lifted the gray thing—a *gow-oon,* he said—over her head; Ashiana thought for a moment she would suffocate, it was so heavy, but then he pulled it down into place and began to work at the scores of little fastenings up the back.

"Now I am truly an elephant," she muttered, frowning at the unattractive color. She fidgeted, already hot and uncomfortable. "Surely, sah—" She struggled to remember the name she was supposed to call him. "—my lord, not all *angrez* women wear this sort of *gow-oon* all of the time?"

"This is not even a formal ensemble, little Ganesha. You've no hoop or pannier."

Ashiana did not ask what either of those were. She did not want to know. The *kor-set* was painful enough.

"Lift your hair out of the way."

Ashiana did as he ordered, piling her hair atop her head and holding it there with both hands.

His thumb brushed the bare nape of her neck. It was not a caress, not done on purpose, but that didn't change Ashiana's reaction. A shudder went through her entire body, straight from the touch of his thumb to her very depths.

She knew he could feel it. He went still. He didn't say or do anything, just stood there, his breath warm and tickling against the dusting of hair on the nape of her neck.

A moment later his hands settled on her shoulders, firm but not forceful. He took a half-step forward, bringing his body into full contact with hers. She gasped but couldn't make herself move, couldn't even drop her hands.

He leaned down, brushing his lips over that spot his thumb had just grazed. Ashiana made a small cry, confusion and fear and that other, unnamed feeling all flowing up from inside her.

The Englishman went rigid. He suddenly let go and backed away with a low, frustrated sound, leaving the last few fastenings at the top of her gown undone.

Ashiana let her hair fall, pulling it around her like she would a *peshwaz,* crossing her arms over herself, her hands touching her shoulders where his hands had just been. She bent her head. She felt like crying.

Not because he had touched her, but because she hadn't protested, hadn't tried to stop him.

Hadn't wanted to stop him.

From behind her, she heard his voice, rougher now, as cold as it had been earlier. "Why did you not eat the food I had Nickerson bring down for you?"

Ashiana turned to face him, taken aback at the abrupt change of subject. She took refuge from her feelings in pride, casting a disdainful look at the plate of food she had left untouched on his writing desk. "I do not eat meat."

He looked at her through narrowed eyes. "You are Hindu?"

She shook her head. "No, my lord," she said in English. "Christian then?"

That question touched a very old and very painful place within her. She threaded her fingers together and started to tilt her head downward from habit.

"Look at me," he warned.

She raised her head, her temper flaring anew. Why did he seem determined to eradicate all of her Hindu ways? "I am not a Hindu by birth, so I cannot claim to be truly Hindu, but I was raised in their traditions." She lifted her chin higher and spoke before she could stop herself. "You may clothe me however you wish, my lord, and force me to speak whatever language you wish, but I will *never* be one of your kind."

"What do you mean 'your kind'?" he tossed back. "You are of the same 'kind' as I. You are English."

Aghast, Ashiana backed up a step and choked out a denial. "No! I am a—" She barely managed to stop, a heartbeat from declaring herself an Ajmir princess.

"Well?" D'Avenant demanded. "If you are not English, then what exactly are you?"

Ashiana shrugged. "I am ... I am a slave girl. I do not have a home or people." She did not have to force the sadness that lay beneath those words. "Except what my master chooses to give me."

D'Avenant looked as if what she had said surprised him. A second later, though, he shifted back to his previous expression, a tight-lipped, stiff-jawed scowl. "It is well that you understand that," he said. "Because *I* am your master and what *I* choose is that you will look and speak English."

Ashiana didn't flinch this time when he slammed the door behind him. She was getting used to it. The man didn't seem capable of leaving a room quietly.

Returning to the wall, she let herself sink slowly to the floor. She tried to fold herself into a familiar, comforting yoga pose, but D'Avenant had robbed her of even that; the *kor-set* made stretching—even breathing—impossible.

She sat with her back ramrod-straight and picked at the uncomfortable dress, hating it, hating every moment she was forced to spend on this ship filled with enemies.

She told herself it didn't matter. Let him take away the clothes, the language, the traditions she had learned to cherish among the Ajmir all these years. It didn't matter how much he tried to change her.

He could never touch her heart, and in her heart, she was an Ajmir princess. Forever.

Chapter 10

 ∼∽Ꝺ∽∼

With the sun beating down mercilessly, the fickle
wind stilled, and the *Valor* becalmed, Saxon was
not in the best of moods this morning. His crew manned
the yards, trimming the sails to catch every chance breeze
so that the ship could inch forward. A few of the men not
on watch trailed bait astern, fishing for sharks; according
to an old sailors' superstition, the wind would pick up if
they caught one.

Sitting on the binnacle box in front of the ship's wheel,
frowning, Saxon fiddled with a brass Hadley quadrant he
had bought on his last visit to Fort William in Calcutta.
He was starting to think a shark might be more help than
the expensive, newfangled navigational instrument.

The fact that he had not slept last night did little to
improve his humor. He'd gotten what rest he could, but
only in ten- or fifteen-minute snatches, on deck. As soon
as he let himself drift off longer than that, he slipped into
the dream again, into the nightmare images that lurked at
the edge of his consciousness ... Mandara's tears, the
arrow—

He cut his finger on the sharp metal edge of the Hadley
and muttered a curse.

"Cap'n? There's a wee bit of a problem below, sir."

It took a moment for Fergus MacNeil's brogue to pen-
etrate Saxon's thoughts. Setting aside the Hadley, he
looked up at the young purser, who stood at rigid attention
a yard away. His fresh-scrubbed face was a bit pale, his

123

black hair mussed and his hat missing. "Problem, MacNeil?"

"Aye, sir. I didna wish to disturb ye, Cap'n, but I think this requires your personal attention. 'Tis no' like anything I've encountered before. I know I'm no' quite so experienced as most, but if there is one thing I know, sir, 'tis cargo. I *am* the one charged with keeping it all in order, and though I may spend more time on my account books than—"

"Is there a point here somewhere, MacNeil?" If Saxon let the talkative young officer go on, they would be here until supper.

"Yes, sir. Sorry, sir. There's a problem with the lass's belongings in the hold."

Saxon squinted into the sun, wondering whether fatigue was playing tricks with his hearing, or if perhaps MacNeil was the one confused. "*What* belongings? Make yourself clear, man."

"The ones Lord Julian ordered us to stow below, sir— the lass's things. He had them brought up from the palace when we left morning before last."

Saxon frowned. He vaguely remembered Julian saying something about the slave girl's belongings being brought aboard, but had been too concerned about his missing sapphire at the time to care. "And what is the problem? Haven't we room aboard for a few perfumes and silks?"

" 'Tis no' that, Cap'n. They've been fine since we left port. But this morning . . . uh, there's a box, sir, and 'tis . . . well, 'tis making an odd noise."

Saxon wondered again whether he was fully awake. "A box making a *noise?*" he repeated incredulously.

" 'Tis no' like anything I've ever heard, sir. I thought you'd best look at it, Cap'n."

Saxon stood, exhaling slowly. His slave girl seemed to be a source of an endless variety of trouble. "Lead on, MacNeil."

The young officer hastened across the deck toward the main hatch that led to the cargo holds below. They lowered themselves down the ladder, their eyes adjusting to the darkness. Carefully placed lanterns provided scant light, enough for them to chart a course through the piles of casks, crates, and sacks. The hold smelled of wood and packing straw and the spicy-sweet odor of tea.

MacNeil went all the way to the rear of the main chamber, where a small bundle of clothing, wrapped and tied with a length of silk, had been deposited beside a basket and a small crate, bound with a leather strap. He stopped a few feet away, seeming reluctant to get any closer; he picked up his hat from where it had apparently fallen earlier.

"Well?" Saxon surveyed the seemingly harmless collection of goods. "What noise is it you were speaking of?"

MacNeil leaned forward, head cocked, and listened for a moment. "I dinna hear it now, Cap'n, but I tell ye, that crate there—" he pointed a wary finger. "—'twas makin' odd sounds like a banshee were in it. And it moved, sir."

Saxon looked skeptically at the box in question, walked over, and crouched down to examine it. It looked utterly ordinary. "I don't think we've any spirits to worry about, MacNeil." A hint of a smile tugged at his mouth; sailors tended to be a superstitious lot, and Scotsmen more than most. "But I would like to know what the devil she's got here." He peeked into the basket, which contained nothing more interesting than cosmetics and other feminine frippery. He reached for the crate.

"Cap'n, take care, sir! 'Tis a demon beastie!"

"MacNeil," Saxon said patiently, untying the leather strap, "I'm sure there's nothing more dangerous in here than slippers and—"

The lid burst open. A snarling blur of orange and white exploded past him and what felt like a dozen knife blades slashed his right arm. Saxon fell on his back with a vicious oath.

MacNeil ran to his side. "God's mercy, sir, what *is* that?"

"It's a tiger!" Saxon bellowed, holding his bleeding arm. The growling animal—a small one, perhaps only half-grown—ran as far as it could, then turned and gave them a flat-eared, fang-baring hiss that made MacNeil go pale.

"Get me a pistol!" Saxon shoved himself to his feet, trying to ignore the fiery pain in his forearm. The tiger turned and leaped onto a stack of crates, bounding over the top and down the other side. They could hear it snarling and hissing. "And get Wyatt and tell him to bring the girl down here!"

MacNeil ran to carry out his orders, skirting the crates by a wide berth as he made his way through the hold. Saxon was left to keep an eye—or rather, an ear—on the dangerous little creature. It kept prowling back and forth on the far side of the boxes, alternating between a coughing, spitting sound and a fierce growl.

Saxon tore off what was left of his sleeve and did his best to bind up the deep slashes on his arm. Why the hell hadn't the treacherous little *chokri* warned him she had a bloody tiger among her things? It might have killed one of his crew.

Minutes later, he heard voices on the far side of the hold, as his men came down the ladder and quickly made their way forward. MacNeil was first, armed to the teeth with pistols, swords, and knives. Then Wyatt stepped into the light, holding firmly to Ashiana's arm.

Saxon met them in the middle of the chamber, greeting his slave girl with an accusing glare. "Would you like to explain what in blazes that animal is doing on my ship?"

Her wide-eyed gaze went from his bloodied arm to the stack of boxes on the other side of the hold—from whence a thoroughly displeased roar reverberated through the small chamber.

"Nico?" she whispered, covering her mouth with one hand as if in disbelief. "Oh, no!"

"You mean to tell me you didn't know about this?"

"I swear it! I cannot—it must have been when Lorjulian asked someone to send my things to the ship. The servants must have sent *everything* that was in my rooms!"

MacNeil handed Saxon one of the pistols he had

brought down and tried to hand him a sword as well, but Saxon waved it away.

The girl fell silent, her eyes on the weapons, then started fighting Wyatt's hold on her. "*Krupiya!* Please! You must not! He will not hurt anyone."

His arm throbbing, Saxon gave her a dry look. Another ferocious snarl rose from behind the piles of cargo. He loaded the pistol. "What is a slave girl doing with a tiger in the first place?"

"He is a pet. He was a gift—from the Emperor, earlier this year, be-before I fell from favor."

Saxon couldn't tell whether she was telling the truth and didn't care. He cocked the pistol and warily moved forward.

Wyatt had to hold the girl by both arms. She struggled desperately, as if she would throw herself in the path of the bullet. "*Nahin*, please! Oh, don't! He is only a cub!"

"Lass, that 'cub' near took the cap'n's arm off," MacNeil informed her in thickly accented Hindi.

"*Krupiya*, it is not his fault! He is only hungry. I tell you he is tame. I have trained him myself. If we feed him—"

"I am not going to take food out of the mouths of my crew and give it to a bloody animal!" Saxon didn't take his attention from his search.

"Take food from me, then! Give him the meat I will not be eating." She started sobbing. "He is so small. And it is only a few weeks to the islands. You can put him off the ship with me."

"I haven't decided to spare your life yet," Saxon reminded her with a sharp look. "If I had any sense, I would throw you *both* overboard right now!"

She sank to her knees at Wyatt's feet, raising her tear-streaked face. "Please, I will do anything."

As Saxon gazed down at her, he realized that the moment he had been waiting for had just presented itself. Now was the time to strike, while she was emotional and unprepared. "Try telling me what I want to know," he demanded silkily.

He didn't have to be any more specific than that; she clearly knew what he wanted, but her shoulders slumped and she hung her head. "I have already *told* you everything," she whispered. "I swear upon my life, I swear by all the gods, that what I told you before was the truth. If . . . if you cannot believe me, then kill me if you must, but I beg you, do not kill Nicobar to punish me—" She sobbed so hard, she could not continue.

Saxon gritted his teeth, and not because of the pain in his arm. The defeat and resignation in her voice were almost convincing; she was either telling the truth, or she was the most incredibly gifted liar he had ever met. Her vulnerability brought an unwanted surge of protectiveness from deep inside him—and struck him with a disturbing flash of insight: he was tired of threatening her. *He wanted to believe her.*

No! He ruthlessly forced himself to turn back toward the crates.

"Please don't," she begged softly. "Please don't hurt him."

Saxon froze, the pistol in his hand suddenly feeling cold and heavy. Those were the words she had spoken to him the day before, when he had been about to bed her again— and he felt the same drowning wave of guilt.

Damn her, shooting the beast was the only sensible choice! Couldn't she understand that? He couldn't have the blasted thing roaming his ship for five weeks or even *one* week.

But as he looked at her, kneeling there, crying her heart out for the sake of a blasted animal, the sensible thing suddenly seemed so distasteful, he couldn't do it. He couldn't hunt down her beloved tiger and kill it.

He lowered the weapon, before he had even made a conscious decision to do so, cursing himself, cursing her for having the power to make him feel what he did not want to feel.

"How do you propose to get him out of my cargo hold?" he asked tightly. "I'm not going to let your blasted 'pet' destroy all the valuable goods in here."

His men looked at him in surprise. Ashiana slumped forward in relief. "*Dhanyavad*. Thank you, my lord. Thank you."

MacNeil blinked in disbelief a couple of times before he recovered enough to nod at the port side of the ship. "Some of the private bays are still empty, sir."

Saxon jammed the pistol into his belt. "Fine. Put him in one of those, then."

As Wyatt helped Ashiana to her feet, she smiled at him, her face aglow with relief and pleasure. "Show me where to take him. He will come to me."

The three men stepped back to let her lure the tiger from his hiding place; she strode confidently toward the stack of crates, utterly fearless.

Saxon felt his stomach clench and kept his hand poised over his gun, ignoring the fiery pain in his arm. The animal might be 'tame,' but it was also hungry and frightened. If it looked like the little beast was going to so much as lay a claw on her—

The sudden, forceful thought took him by surprise. When had her life, her safety, become important to him? Only days ago he had been ready to throttle her himself.

He forced the question aside. She was the only link to his missing sapphire. And he wanted her around to warm his bed for the next few weeks. That was all. It wouldn't do him any good to let her get damaged.

Still, he had to choke back an exclamation when she bent down and peeked between a pair of boxes.

"Nico," she said soothingly, coaxingly. "Nico . . ."

The low, round sound of her voice rolling over the vowel in that hypnotic tone did strange things to Saxon's nerve endings.

Then she started a series of purring, feline sounds in the back of her throat, and every muscle in his body went taut. His thoughts instantly flooded with an image of Ashiana's lithe body beneath him, curving naked into his, while she wrapped her arms around his neck and made those pleasured little murmurs against his cheek, her breath warm as she sighed them in his ear.

He forced himself back to reality, unnerved by the vividness of the fantasy. The tiger had stopped growling and hissing. A second later there was the click of claws striking wood and it jumped lightly to the top of the stack—directly above her. From that position, the animal could take out her throat with one quick slash. A deep rumble came from its chest, somewhere between a growl and a purr.

"Careful," Saxon warned, stepping forward, his hand firm on the pistol.

"Shhh," she whispered, whether to him or her pet he couldn't tell. She raised one hand and let the tiger sniff the backs of her fingers, speaking to him all the while in soft Hindi. "I am here, Nicobar, it is all right. Nothing will hurt you. I promise, my *premi.*"

To his profound irritation, Saxon found himself wondering why the tiger merited such tender attention and gentle nothings from her lips. *He* was the one bleeding, after all.

She had never used such a soft tone with him. Not once.

He shook off the irksome thought. A second later there was a mutual intake of breath from all three men in the hold when the tiger leaped down . . .

. . . and landed gently at her feet.

They all exhaled shakily while she scratched the top of Nicobar's head. They tensed when the animal batted her with one paw, but she knelt and started to wrestle with him, tussling vigorously, playfully. "Hello, my Nico." She smiled, laughing. "Yes, I am glad to see you too!"

Saxon glanced at his men, who were watching the unfolding scene with equal variations of his own stupor.

The girl patted the tiger's belly, rubbed between its shoulder blades until he purred, then carefully took him by the collar. "Nico will not cause any more trouble now," she said matter-of-factly.

Watching her ease with the beast, it took Saxon a moment to find his voice. "Wyatt, MacNeil, let's open up one of those private bays."

The two men snapped into action, moving aside a pile of particularly heavy cargo. Behind it was one of the secret storage compartments that Saxon used to hide smuggled goods from the prying eyes of customs officials.

"Bring him over here," he called to Ashiana, snapping his fingers.

When there was no reply, he turned toward her. She stared at him, then at the compartment, then back again, her expression changing to one of horror, as if he had just sprouted horns and a tail. "You are a *pirate!*" she cried.

"A smuggler," he corrected.

Holding the tiger with one hand, she pointed at the secret cargo bay. "Only a pirate would have such as this on his ship!"

Saxon exhaled between his teeth. His patience had been taxed as far as it would go this day. "I'm not of a mind to argue it with you at the moment. I've more important things to attend to." His arm stung like hell and the makeshift bandage was already soaked with blood. "Wyatt!"

"Sir?"

"Since no one else can get near that blasted little beast, she'll have to take care of it—but you will accompany her from my cabin and back again. Once a day. And no side trips in between."

"Aye, sir."

Saxon settled a heated gaze on Ashiana. "I will *see* you later. I think you understand my meaning."

He pivoted on his heel and left her in the company of her precious tiger, feeling her glare burning into his back.

Chapter 11

*P*irate. The word seared itself into Ashiana's mind, sent her spinning downward into a whirlpool of memories as she glared at D'Avenant's retreating back. The cargo hold of the Englishman's ship faded and she was once again on the deck of the *Adiante,* her eyes stinging with tears and smoke, the scent of cannon shot and scattered spices overwhelming her—and the clamor of the pirates' laughter, the crack of the lash and her father's screams crowding out all other sound.

She could hear the weakness of Papa's voice as he lay dying. *"Remember me, minha cara . . ."*

Breathing hard, Ashiana squeezed her eyes shut, then blinked to clear her vision, unable to tell for a dizzying moment whether her tears were remembered or real. Her left arm stung. She stared down at it. No, it could not be; the wound had healed years ago. She inhaled a steadying breath, tasting not smoke and spices but the dry mustiness of the Englishman's cargo hold.

Pirate. The word and the memories it brought choked out all reason, all feeling except for hate. But . . . that wasn't true. Other emotions mingled with it as well.

Hurt and betrayal.

Why did it hurt her so to discover that D'Avenant was a pirate?

She rubbed at the tip of the henna rose that peeked out from the sleeve of her gray *angrez* gown. Like her memories, the tattoo and the scar could not be soothed away.

The tall young officer said something to her.

Ashiana raised her head to look at him, trying to shake off the images that had seized her. He stood at one side of the empty cargo bay—the secret compartment that had been concealed behind a hidden hatch.

She shook her head, not understanding a word of the strange-sounding English the man spoke. He repeated himself in stilted, thickly accented Hindi. "The tiger? Shall we put him inside, miss?"

She looked down at Nicobar, who sat still and docile at her feet. The other officer, Wyatt, had already covered the floor of the secret compartment with packing straw. They were waiting impatiently for her to coax her pet inside. Nico bared his teeth and spat when Wyatt reached toward him.

Turning to his companion, who still held an array of weapons, Wyatt said something in English. Giving Ashiana a disapproving look, he stalked away, leaving the two of them to wrestle with the problem of getting Nico into his new home.

"He is going to get something for your pet to eat," the other man explained in his odd, lilting accent.

Ashiana nodded, still feeling dazed by her memories.

"My name is MacNeil," the young officer said, putting the weapons down, except for a knife that he tucked into his belt. He gave her an embarrassed smile. "I know you say he is tame, miss, but he looks like he might not mind munching on a Scot until his supper arrives."

"A Scot?" Ashiana repeated the odd word that he had said in English.

"A person from Scotland, miss, like myself." He doffed his hat and bowed slightly. "It is a land to the north of England, a wee bit colder and wilder, but we like it that way."

He grinned as he said it and Ashiana found herself returning his smile. She decided that she liked this MacNeil. He was certainly the kindest person she'd yet encountered aboard the Englishman's ship. Her smile faded as she realized that he must be a pirate as well.

MacNeil had already turned his attention to Nico, who had flopped on the floor at Ashiana's feet as she absently scratched the white fur of his stomach with her bare toes. "The tiger, miss? Might we put him inside?"

Realizing the man was still a bit afraid of her pet, Ashiana coaxed Nico to his feet and led him forward. He balked at the opening to the small enclosure, until Ashiana crawled in ahead of him and sat down on the straw. The compartment was just tall enough for her to sit upright, but it was quite wide and long. Nico followed her in and began exploring his new surroundings.

"You have a wonderful way with him, miss," MacNeil said, crouching beside the open hatch, still looking a little uneasy as Nico dashed from one side of his enclosure to the other. "It is generous of the captain to let you keep him."

Ashiana wrinkled her nose. "Indeed, one would not expect generosity from a—" She cut herself off and looked away, reminding herself of her place.

"A pirate?" MacNeil finished for her. He laughed, sitting down just outside the compartment. "I am afraid you have it wrong, miss. The *Valor* sails under the Company ensign, not the Jolly Roger."

Ashiana gave him a perplexed frown, not understanding that last reference. "You are very honorable to defend your captain."

His grin faded. "Here now, miss. I won't have you thinking ill of the captain. He's no pirate."

Ashiana kept her attention on Nicobar, trying to persuade him to calm down and stop running about and scattering his straw.

MacNeil was insistent. "The captain might be a bit . . . well, a bit sharp round the edges, but he's an honest sort. And I should know. I keep his accounts."

Ashiana could not listen to any more. "If he is honest, why would he have something such as this built into his ship?" She raised both hands to indicate the compartment she was sitting in.

"The private bays are for smuggling, not piracy. The

Valor pays for every bit of cargo she takes aboard. The captain insists on that."

Ashiana shook her head. "I do not understand. There is a difference between pirates and smugglers?"

MacNeil looked surprised and affronted. "Pirates steal. And they murder and pillage. Smugglers just . . . well, they just prefer not to let customs officials see every bit of what they've got. Customs officials," he explained before she could ask, "are the men back in England—government men—who decide what goods English ships may and may not trade. Some captains don't like rules." He grinned again. "And they don't like paying a tax on every tea leaf and china plate they take aboard. So they carry on a bit of smuggling on the side."

Ashiana lifted an eyebrow. "So a smuggler is not a pirate, but he is a man who does not deal honestly."

"No, no, that's not it at all." MacNeil's face flushed with vexation. "The D'Avenant ships are the most successful in the Company. They make thousands of pounds every year, every shilling of it honest. But the captain, he receives but a wee bit of that. The Company pays him a wage—and takes the biggest share of the *Valor*'s profits. The rest goes to the captain's older brother, the Duke of Silverton. The Duke's the one who owns all the family ships."

Nicobar at last tired of his rambles and came to lie beside Ashiana, flicking the tip of his tail as he began washing himself. Ashiana ran a hand through his striped fur, still unable to make sense of the jumble of information and feelings inside her. "I do not understand how that makes smuggling an honest endeavor."

"It . . . well . . ." The young man sighed in exasperation. "I don't suppose that it does. Still, it—don't you see? The money earned by the *Valor* is Company money and *family* money. The captain wouldn't think of skimming any of it for himself, even though he's the one who earns it. But he's a younger son, like me. Like a lot of us on the Company ships. And he has to look to his own future. The cargo he stows here—" He indicated the little room that was now Nico's home. "—and in the other private bays, that's his. He'll be a wealthy man in a few more years . . ."

Ashiana's thoughts drifted as the talkative Scot went on into a discussion of the unfairness of the English system of inheritance. She rested her hand on Nico's broad, furry head. It was strange, but she understood, in a way, what MacNeil had told her. She had jumped to entirely the wrong conclusion; D'Avenant was not a pirate. In fact, he could not even bring himself to take money earned by his own ship. Because the money belonged to someone else.

His smuggling was, in an odd way . . . honorable. Which was difficult for her to grasp. She had believed him completely lacking in honor.

Just as she had believed him completely merciless, heartless. But then why was he letting her keep Nicobar, instead of shooting him? She still didn't quite understand why he had changed his mind about that.

It was all too perplexing to think about, so Ashiana resolved not to. Nor would she think about the way her heart had leaped into her throat when she had seen his badly slashed arm. The thought of him being hurt—

No. She could not allow herself to think about it! None of those thoughts or feelings were important. None of them changed the fact that Saxon D'Avenant was her enemy. Or excused his trying to steal the sapphires. Or made up for the way he had hurt her.

At least she understood *why* he wanted the gems now: they would bring him wealth beyond his dreams, more than he could make in a lifetime of smuggling. He would have riches that would put his brother the Duke to shame.

Ashiana let her fingers trail through Nicobar's black stripes, feeling inexplicably disappointed, almost sad. D'Avenant was simply greedy. Perhaps he was not a pirate, but he was still a thief, ruthless in his quest. And arrogant, too, to risk death for mere riches. And so deeply prejudiced against her people that he could not stand to let her wear Hindu clothes or speak her native tongue.

She realized that MacNeil was still talking. ". . . And

then there are the expenses in building one's own estate—"

"MacNeil," Wyatt's voice said, his tone warning.

Ashiana looked up to see the older man standing just behind MacNeil. He said something in English, and the Scot promptly stood up and saluted. While Ashiana could not understand the words they exchanged, she could tell that Wyatt was not happy about his officer being in any way friendly to her; Wyatt had not liked her from the start, and Nico's arrival apparently did not improve his opinion of her.

Wyatt turned, said something to her in clipped English, and placed a wooden bucket filled with water and a platter of meat just inside the door. Nicobar jerked from Ashiana's grasp and bounded toward the food.

The two men jumped back, but Nicobar was more interested in the meal than in them. Wyatt called to Ashiana and motioned that she should step out.

She appealed to the young Scot. "Could I not stay with him a while longer? Just until he has finished eating?"

MacNeil translated her request to Wyatt, who looked displeased but issued a curt order, then turned and stalked off to sit on a crate a short distance away.

MacNeil, with his back to his superior, smiled down at her. "He says five minutes, miss, but I'll see if I can keep him busy long enough to give you a little more time. We'll wait for you out here. Mr. Wyatt says the captain has ordered that we leave the hatch open, whenever you're in there with the beastie. Wouldn't want anything to happen to you."

Ashiana's heart gave a startled skip. Was that what D'Avenant had *said*—that he wouldn't want anything to happen to her? Or was it only what MacNeil inferred? She almost asked, then choked back the question.

It was not possible that the Englishman could be concerned about her. It seemed unlikely that he still meant to kill her, since he was letting her keep Nico, but he might just be playing games, trying to lull her into unwariness and trick her into admitting the truth.

Weary at trying to puzzle it all out, she smiled up at MacNeil. "I thank you for the extra time with Nico."

Flashing his easy grin, MacNeil went to take a seat beside Wyatt, and started doing what he did best: talking. Ashiana felt pleased and again perplexed by the young man's kind nature. Perhaps Scots were quite different from the English.

As she knelt there in the straw, watching Nicobar noisily enjoy his meal, an idea began to form in Ashiana's mind. It came to her like a stroke of light from the sky, bright as the jewels on Nico's collar, sparkling in the lantern light. She wondered why she had not thought of it earlier. But of course, she had been thinking of . . .

She frowned and forced thoughts of D'Avenant to the back of her mind, letting her idea take hold and become a plan. It made her feel relieved, excited, frightened, and hopeful all at once: Nicobar's collar! It was thick, padded, just the right size—the perfect hiding place for the sapphires!

She would no longer have to worry about the Englishman accidentally discovering the gems in his cabin. He certainly wouldn't go near Nico again. And he had ordered that she look after her tiger once a day.

Her heart and mind raced. Tomorrow, when Wyatt brought her back to see to Nico, she would have to bring the sapphires with her. It would be risky, but not overly difficult—not with the bulky, layered English skirts D'Avenant had ordered her to wear. He had thought he was punishing her, but instead he had unwittingly helped her!

When they reached the Andamans, when D'Avenant sold her to the Ajmir . . . she would walk off his ship with Nicobar and the sapphires, and he would be none the wiser.

That night, Ashiana got almost no sleep. She kept waiting for the Englishman to come to her as he had threatened. But he never entered his cabin.

An unsettling thought plagued her: perhaps Nico had injured him worse than she had realized.

Vexed to find herself concerned about it, she resolutely told herself she was being ridiculous. D'Avenant was probably doing this to torment her. Still, she could not close her eyes; she lay awake, staring at the ceiling of his cabin. When she finally fell into an exhausted, fitful slumber, she was haunted by images of pirates and fire and her papa, and the sea consuming the *Adiante*.

She awoke trembling, well before dawn the next morning. Tired but eager to get on with her plan, she searched through D'Avenant's chest of clothing until she found something she could use as a tool to pry open the wall panel: a thick length of leather with a large, square piece of metal attached to one end.

Before long, she was tying the silk bundle of sapphires to her thigh with the ribbon fastenings from her *stokeengs*. The multiple layers of *pet-ee-koots* and her heavy gray skirt concealed it well enough.

But Wyatt did not come to fetch her.

Something was wrong. She waited, paced, meditated, and finally in frustration, pounded on the door, but no one came.

Fear settled over her shoulders and chilled its way down her back. Usually by now Wyatt or the steward, Nickerson, would have brought her morning meal. It was almost as if everyone had deserted the ship and left her behind.

Now that she noticed it, she did not hear the usual sounds of the crew working. She didn't hear anyone at all.

She tried to calm herself; perhaps this all had to do with some aspect of running an English ship that she wasn't familiar with.

Morning passed and faded into afternoon, and her stomach began growling. Ashiana was debating whether she should put the sapphires back into the wall, when suddenly the door opened.

She whirled, her heart in her throat, expecting D'Avenant, come to make good his threat at last.

Wyatt stood in the portal, carrying a bucket of water and food for Nico.

Ashiana exhaled in relief and smiled at him. "I was afraid you were not coming."

Obviously not understanding her Hindi, he curtly gestured for her to preceed him into the corridor. Ashiana did so, following him up to the deck, then down to the dark cargo holds below. The crew looked to be going about their normal tasks. Ashiana felt frustrated that she and Wyatt could not understand one another; she could not ask him what had gone wrong.

Or whether his captain was well.

Below, he showed her where to find fresh straw, then opened the hatch to Nico's enclosure for her, retreating to sit on a crate a good distance away.

Her heart pounding and her mouth dry, Ashiana replaced Nico's straw with fresh bedding and gave him the food and water—placing them well away from the entrance so she and her tiger were out of Wyatt's sight.

Nicobar, unfortunately, was in a playful mood. As soon as he had eaten, he rolled over and batted at Ashiana's hands, nipping at her.

"*Nahin*, Nico. Stop," she whispered. "I do not wish to play."

To placate him, she rubbed beneath his chin with one hand. He stretched out, paws in the air, and purred, a deep rumble that echoed off the walls.

She could hear Wyatt mutter something; from his tone, it sounded like he thought she was taking too long. Ashiana tried to hurry. Taking Nico's paw, she coaxed him, carefully, into extending his claws. She managed to angle one of the knife-sharp little talons just enough to cut the leather lacing that held his collar shut. He snarled and twisted away, and she had to wrestle him a bit before he would calm down again. She quickly unlaced the collar, just a few stitches, her fingers shaking.

She tore out the padding, then reached under her skirt and unwrapped the sapphires, leaving the silk tied to her thigh. Quickly, quietly, trying to keep Nico still, she pushed the gems, one by one, through the opening in his collar.

She had almost all of them in when Wyatt apparently lost patience. He came to stand just outside Nico's enclosure.

"Enough time," he said in barely understandable Hindi. "Come now."

Ashiana froze, holding Nicobar down. Looking over her shoulder, she could see Wyatt's legs from where she sat. If he bent down . . .

Her fingers forced the last two sapphires into the collar. "I am sorry, I do not understand. What was that you said? Did you mean to say that I have spent enough time? But of course, you are right. You have been most generous in allowing me to stay this long, and I—"

"Enough time," he repeated, bending down and scowling at her. He motioned for her to come out.

Barely breathing, Ashiana forced a smile to her lips. The stones were hidden, but she would not have the chance to re-lace Nico's collar. Not with Wyatt glaring at her.

Still kneeling, she bent down to give her tiger one last hug. He growled and squirmed but she managed to wrap the ends of the laces twice around the collar and knot them underneath. At least they would not be left dangling; it would have to do until she could return and finish it properly tomorrow. None of the crew would get close enough to him to notice. She hoped.

"Come now," Wyatt said impatiently.

Keeping her smile firmly in place, Ashiana turned and moved in a slow crouch to the entrance, scattering the white cotton stuffing into Nicobar's bedding with her toes.

When she was out, Wyatt put the hatch back in place. As he slid it shut, Ashiana bent down to look at her pet. She could see nothing different about his collar from here.

Relieved, she offered up a little prayer of thanks and gave her pet a genuine smile. "I will see you tomorrow, my Nico."

She turned to follow Wyatt back to the cabin, feeling better and happier than she had in days.

MacNeil made sure he had a knife in his belt, a sword at his side, and a pistol in his hand before he decided it was safe enough to take a closer look at the lass's pet. The beastie had been making distressed noises all evening, but MacNeil wanted to check for himself before bothering the captain about it.

Slipping the hatch to one side, just a few inches, he held his lantern close and peered inside.

"What be the trouble, ye demon beastie? The lassie will be back t' tend ye tomorrow."

The tiger snarled and a razor-edged paw darted through the opening. MacNeil jumped back, almost dropping the lantern, and quickly replaced the hatch. "Well, if that be your humor, ye can just wait, then."

He turned and started to walk away, but a curious realization tickled his mind. He would swear he had seen something, just for a second, in the lantern light.

A flash reflecting from the animal's straw, a brilliant blue flash.

Turning back toward the hatch, MacNeil pursed his lips and considered taking a closer look. He just as quickly shook his head and discarded the daft notion. It had probably only been a trick of the light, shining off the animal's jewel-studded collar.

Still, it *was* odd, he decided as he went back to his account books. And anything odd aboard the *Valor* was worth mentioning to the captain.

He would do so as soon as he saw him in the morning.

Chapter 12

The unmoving sea reflected pinpricks of starlight along its glassy obsidian surface. The wind barely teased the limp sails, a puff of air that wouldn't move a leaf on a tree, much less a five-hundred-ton ship on the ocean. Frustration and unease knotted Saxon's gut. It seemed the closer he got to finding the sapphires and finished his quest, the more nature and the gods conspired to keep him from it.

He paused amidships, glaring down at the mirror-smooth waters that he could hear gently lapping about the hull in the darkness. His only consolation was that Greyslake, wherever the bastard was out here, would be equally becalmed aboard his Royal Navy man-of-war. The race to the Andamans was moving forward by inches instead of miles, but it was still a race.

"Evening, Captain."

"Hamilton." Saxon nodded in acknowledgment of the helmsman's salute. His crew was getting used to seeing their captain on deck during the midnight watch; they no longer acted nervous in his presence, afraid he was checking up on them. After three nights, they seemed to understand that he was there for his own reasons.

Saxon wearily acknowledged that he had more than enough to keep any man awake. The sapphires. Greyslake. A becalmed ship.

A tiger in his cargo hold. A maddeningly attractive woman who utterly despised him.

And the nightmare. That more than anything kept him from closing his eyes for more than a catnap.

He stepped down from the quarterdeck, jarring his bandaged right arm. He muttered an oath through gritted teeth and continued his slow walk along the rail, hooking his thumb in the waistband of his breeches to try and keep the arm still. It stung as if the devil himself were stabbing at it with a pitchfork.

Working on the damaged keelson had only made the pain worse—and kept him from his promised visit to his slave girl. The keelson was chief among the concerns weighing on his mind at the moment: it had started leaking again. He had joined his men in shoring it up, unable to just stand by and give orders and pray the blasted thing would hold.

Finally, about an hour ago, all appeared secure, but Saxon was still concerned that it had given way in such calm seas. Never in nine years of voyages had the *Valor* failed him, but the season of *varsha* was drawing near, the time of the summer monsoons. If they chanced to be caught in an early storm before reaching the islands—

"Good evenin' t' ye Cap'n."

Saxon nodded in response to the port watchman's salute, not stopping to discuss the ship's progress with the older man as he sometimes did.

Along with his worry about the keelson, his throbbing arm also brought back the memory of the last heated exchange he'd had with Ashiana. He hadn't had time to think about it. Nor had he wanted to, he added ruefully.

The ice-blue loathing in her eyes when she called him a pirate had struck him harder than a slap—and he still felt the sting. He had let her keep the tiger, he had stood there bleeding, and all she could show him was defiance and anger and hatred. That was his thanks.

It didn't matter, he told himself coldly. Let her believe what she wanted. And let her shower her tenderness on that blasted animal. He hadn't relented about shooting the beast because he wanted her gratitude. He had done it because . . .

He stopped to lean on the starboard rail, on his good arm. It annoyed him thoroughly to realize he couldn't think of a single rational, sensible reason. Perhaps he *had* done it because he sought to win some softening in her attitude toward him.

But if she wouldn't give an inch, so be it. He didn't need her gratitude. Or her concern. Or her smiles and her sweetness. He didn't care if the ice never melted from her eyes.

He had weakened once; he would guard against it more carefully in the future. There was only one thing that he wanted from Ashiana now. And *that* didn't require anything but her physical participation.

He turned and leaned back against the rail, imagining what he would do if he had her here, right now. His body stirred as the image took hold: Ashiana naked beneath him on the deck.

He had often fantasized about making love in the open air aboard ship, amid the wind and seas and other forces that were untamed and untamable. Lack of privacy and lack of a daring lady had always kept him from making the fantasy come true.

A slow smile curved his mouth. Having one's own slave girl made all things possible.

Barely completing the thought, he called the starboard watchman. "Elliott!"

Lantern in hand, the man appeared out of the darkness. "Sir?"

"The *Valor* won't move until the wind picks up, so there's no point in you and Foxworthy and Hamilton being out here tonight. Get them and go below. And see that no one else comes abovedecks until I personally summon the next watch."

The sailor looked at him with a curious expression but clearly knew better than to question the order. "Aye, sir."

Saxon waited at the rail as the men went below, his pulse already pounding in anticipation. He had given

Ashiana the two days he had promised—more than that, three. He had been far too generous with her.

It was time to show her who was the master here.

Ashiana sat down on the bed, stood up, then forced herself to sit back down again. D'Avenant had not come to her last night as he had threatened, nor had he yet put in an appearance this night.

She did not know which worried her more: the fact that he might come, or the fact that he had not.

She could not shrug off the uneasiness that had settled on her shoulders, the sinking feeling that his injured arm must be serious after all. If Nicobar's claws had struck deeply, or if the wound had become infected . . . but surely Wyatt would have said something.

But what could Wyatt say? They could not speak one another's languages. All the officer had done was look at her with a stern and disapproving expression.

Ashiana began pacing again, telling herself that was the way Wyatt always looked at her. He was not angry over her having caused some terrible fate to befall his captain.

And what matter to her if something *had* happened to D'Avenant? It would be to her benefit. She could carry out her mission more easily. She should be pleased.

But she was not.

Vishnu help her, she knew she should not care . . . but she did. The thought of him being badly hurt gave her no pleasure. In fact, it made unexpected tears well in her eyes.

Perhaps he simply had more pressing matters to attend to. Or perhaps he was so angry about Nico that he wanted nothing more to do with her. In any event, if he intended to come to her tonight, he surely would have done so by now.

Ashiana rubbed her eyes. Exhausted with unanswered questions and wildly tangled emotions, she went back to the bed, struggled with the buttons on the back of her *gow-oon,* and let it slide to the floor. She untied her *kor-set* and tossed the despised thing aside, along with the rest of her *angrez* garb.

She blew out the lantern and slipped beneath the covers, holding them up to her chin, her stare fixed on the door.

After a time, her eyelids began to feel heavy. She blinked, trying to stay awake, but a late supper and an evening spent worrying took their toll. Her gaze slid to the corner. At least she had that to be thankful for, she thought sleepily. At least the nine sapphires were safe below with Nicobar.

That was all that really mattered ... her duty ... her clan ... all else was unimportant ...

She did not remember falling asleep. She wasn't sure whether minutes or hours had passed when she awakened to a noise at the door. She sat up with a start, clutching the sheet.

The portal swung open, silently. There was no mistaking the tall, broad-shouldered silhouette that filled the doorway, framed by light from the corridor beyond.

The first thing Ashiana felt was relief—oh, Vishnu, *such* relief that he had not been badly hurt after all.

Uncertainty followed hard and fast. D'Avenant had come for her, as he had threatened. Oddly, she realized that the quivery sensation in her stomach had nothing to do with fear.

She could not make out his expression in the darkness, though he must be able to see her quite clearly. Light spilled in behind him, falling across the bed to cloak her in his shadow.

He didn't move for a long moment, didn't even appear to be breathing. When he finally stepped inside, he did not slam the door as she had expected.

Instead he crossed the cabin in three strides and scooped her into his arms, covers and all. Ashiana started to cry out but her breath caught in her throat when he winced, pausing for a second to shift her weight off his wounded arm.

Remorse and concern stole her outraged words—and in that instant, she could see his expression clearly in the light. His silvered gaze shone like a blade, sharp with desire and determination. But beneath the hard edge, she saw something else, a feeling she had not seen there before. Almost like . . . an ache, a pain that she somehow sensed had nothing to do with his injury.

It made her forget to struggle or even protest. She was completely nude in his arms but for the bedclothes, yet she could not find her voice until he was halfway into the corridor.

"Sahib!" she cried, sudden panic making her forget the English word she was supposed to call him. "Your crew! You cannot mean to go—*nahin!*"

By the time she had uttered that stunned denial, it was too late. He had moved swiftly through the cramped passageway and mounted the steps, carrying her on deck. As he walked confidently forward in the starlit darkness, she could see that the deck was deserted. They were alone but for a few gulls diving about the masts.

She had feared he meant to humiliate her before his crew—but that wasn't his intent at all!

Moving to a sheltered corner of the bow, he laid her on the deck, still tangled in the blanket and sheets, and knelt beside her, stripping off his shirt.

Summer's heat thickened the air but Ashiana began to shake, chilled by the memory of how he had hurt her before. "*Krupiya.* Please, sah—my . . . lord. D-do not—"

He laid a finger on her lips to silence her. Ashiana's lower lip quivered beneath his touch. The fierce energy in his gaze told her that nothing she could say would stop him. Her words could no more hold him back than they could hold back the lightning and thunder of a storm.

His expression unyielding, he kicked off the rest of his clothes. Moonlight cast sharp shadows along the muscular angles of his body as he braced one arm across her, cutting off any chance of flight. Then he was beside her, disentangling her from the sheet, his arms circling her to pull her close.

Ashiana trembled as his hard form molded to hers, the bristly hair of his chest and legs rasping her tender skin, his broad hands sure and strong on her back. He bent his head and almost kissed her, but turned aside at the last moment, a breath away from joining their mouths, as if to remind her that he still did not trust her.

Ashiana could barely breathe, not because of his hold on her, but because her entire body had gone rigid with fear of what was to come. Even her hands were balled into tense fists. She could feel the full measure of his arousal, thrusting against her belly. A ragged sob escaped through her clamped teeth.

He ignored it, shifting her beneath him, one hand urging her hips up to meet his. She whimpered a wordless plea. Nothing stopped him.

Desperate, she wrenched her arm free of his embrace, thinking to push him away, to offer some reason why he must not do this, why he must give her more time. But when she flailed out, her hand struck his bandaged wound.

He flinched. They both stilled.

She withdrew her hand instantly, her only thought of his pain. Surprise and confusion tumbled through her; his being hurt was the last thing she should be concerned about at the moment, but she could not deny what she felt. She wanted to apologize—for hurting him just now, for what Nico had done, for all of it.

As she looked up at him, the apology stuck in her throat; he would think she was only trying to save herself.

Unable to say it, she cautiously touched him, letting her hand rest gently on his injured arm. Under the probing intensity of his gaze, she lowered her lashes; when she raised them again, his quicksilver eyes had darkened. She sensed—she wasn't sure how—that he knew what she meant to say: that she hadn't meant for him to be hurt. Didn't want him to be hurt.

She expected him to chastise her again about Nico, or say something angry or sarcastic. Instead, he lowered his lips to her ear, and whispered only three words.

"Koi bat nahin. It is nothing."

He held himself above her for a second, his weight balanced on his forearms, the breezeless, sultry air heavy with the scent of the sea and the sound of their unsteady breathing.

In that moment, it seemed as if some of the raging fire in him had been extinguished, his forcefulness loosening and shifting along with his hold on her. He lay beside her again, still holding her close, but it was no longer the grasp of a man who meant to take, to conquer. He nuzzled the edge of her jaw, her throat, her hair. He stroked her back with one hand.

As his blunt fingers trailed lightly down her spine, Ashiana could not remember the protests she had been about to utter.

His mouth kissed, caressed, whispered over the taut peak of one breast. His tongue touched her. She arched her back instinctively, without thinking. Her hands found his shoulders but only fluttered there; she did not push him away.

She remembered then the words of protest she had been about to say, remembered all the reasons why he must not do this, but she did not voice a single one. As he held her, caressed her, aroused her, the new gentleness in him defeated her as no amount of force could have.

She felt as if the deck had suddenly shifted out from under her, the night sky and glassy sea spinning out of place. What was happening? Where was her anger, her outrage, the hatred she had felt for this man only days ago?

The fear was still there, fear of his strength and his power, fear of what his body could do to hers. But the rest . . .

She could not find the other feelings. She sought them desperately but could not summon them forth. She could only tremble against him, afraid of him and—now—afraid of herself.

His hand skimmed along the curve of her waist, over her belly, lower. Ashiana clamped her thighs together, her breath coming in little terrified gulps.

He didn't force her to allow him access to the softness between her thighs, but before she could draw her knees up protectively, he covered her legs with one of his own. His fingers traced swirls at the upper edge of the downy triangle.

He lowered his roughened cheek to hers, his long hair tickling her face, his lips again at her ear. "*Vaada kartha hun*. I promise," he whispered. "I promise, Ashiana. I will not hurt you."

A tiny sob welled up from within her. She did not know which surprised and touched her more—his promise, or the fact that he had just called her by name.

But she could not bring herself to relax, could not yet trust his words. She knew what it felt like to have him inside her, how much it would hurt. She squeezed her eyes shut, her body still braced for the pain.

He did not hurry her, but neither did he let her go. He held her still, his leg across hers, and captured her wrists with one hand. He stretched her arms up over her head and began a leisurely siege, kissing the scar on her wrist, finding a sensitive, ticklish spot on the inside of her elbow, nuzzling her breast, the masculine stubble of his beard abrading the feminine curve.

With the deck at her back and his grasp unyielding, Ashiana was his prisoner as he found and aroused every secret, tender place. The attentions of his lips and tongue sent hot shivers trailing after his kisses. The wet heat of his mouth brought her nipple to an impudent peak, then he coaxed the other to pebble-hardness. He nipped her, his teeth just grazing her. She bit her lower lip to stop a cry, and heard herself moan anyway.

This was nothing like what she had experienced with him before. Nothing at all. He wasn't forcing and overpowering, but giving . . . pleasing.

Ashiana tried again to pull away, not wanting the sensations that sparked and flared within her, not wanting to feel what he was making her feel. She tossed her head and tried to wriggle out from beneath him, but her movements only brought her more fully into his mouth.

He held her down, lingering over her breasts, cupping one soft globe as he suckled. His low sound of pleasure reverberated through his chest and into her. A melting warmth began between her thighs, an unsettling heat that cascaded upward and downward, until she felt as if she were made entirely of flame.

She opened her mouth in a soundless plea, but wasn't sure whether she meant to beg him to stop or continue. Her back arched off the deck as unfamiliar, restless tremors fluttered to life within her.

A tiny cry of longing escaped her.

He slid his hand over her ribs, down to the intimate center that she had denied him moments before. She tensed, but then ... then she felt his touch, seeking and finding and parting her, so sure, so gentle.

The pad of his thumb brushed against that nubbin that felt swollen and aching, and her whimper ebbed into a low moan. He touched her again, just teasing her at first, then more firmly. He stroked her feminine softness, slowly, almost lazily.

She could feel the dampness there, knew he could feel it as well, but she could find no shame in it. He gently moved his thumb in agonizingly slow circles, and she caught the scent of her own desire and heard the rumble of pleasure in his chest as he did too. Her body responded to his, just as surely as his responded to hers—as each of them had responded to the other, in so many ways, from the moment they met.

He eased a finger inside of her, then another, moving in and out in a deliberate way that shocked and pleasured and made her blood pound in her veins. Her sharp breaths and soft cries mingled with the warm night air around them. He held his gaze locked on hers and moved his hand in that suggestive motion, faster now.

Her body arched and undulated at his every touch, flickers of fire racing through her. She gave herself over to the heat of the night and the scents of the sea and the ship and the heady tang of their mutual desire.

As she looked up at him through half-closed eyes, her heart told her that more than their bodies intertwined there on the tangle of blankets, more than their gazes, more than their thoughts.

And when he moved his hand away and lowered himself against her, this time she did not tense or pull away. This time—she did not know how, did not let herself question why—she believed him; she knew, just as she knew the stars above shone in the darkness, that he would not hurt her.

The pelt of golden hair on his chest felt rough against her breasts. The heat of his muscular body covering hers, the hardness, the rampant maleness of him intoxicated her. She gasped as he moved his hips, and she felt just the tip of him touch her, the swollen, velvety head of his manhood, pressing into her, separating her soft cleft.

And then he was there, inside her, so smoothly and easily that it whisked away all memory of what had happened between them before. She felt him push forward, heard their voices mingling and straining together, and then they were one, embedded and surrounding and part of one another.

And the feeling was not painful, but exquisite.

He shut his eyes, his features etched with an intense pleasure that seemed on the edge of pain. He buried his face in her tangled hair and she could feel his breath coming harsh and fast against her throat.

He began moving his hips, thrusting in long, deep strokes that sent delicious explosions dancing through Ashiana. She felt stretched and filled, astonished and soaring. Heat and tension built from deep inside her with every arc of his body into hers, like a shimmering wave of sun-warmed water, rising and flowing with the power and force of the entire sea.

She closed her eyes and held on to him, reaching for heights she had never known existed. Fire-tipped wings unfurled and swept her with him into the moonlit sky, through darkness toward light. Together they strained upward, higher, faster. Her hips lifted to meet his, her arms clutching him closer, her fingers kneading the corded muscles of his back and neck.

Breath, scent, thought, movement all merged and joined, becoming one, until it was no longer possible to tell which was hers and which his. They were no longer apart, no longer alone on the deck in the night; something had bloomed and taken life between them, leaving both gasping and shuddering as they held on, straining together, closer, higher.

He clasped her against his hard form, his thrusts taking on speed and force. She moaned wordlessly at the sensation of his male muscle and strength and hardness sinking into her soft feminine curves again and again. The passion sizzling between them shone with a light unmatched by flame or sun.

Then a sudden, unexpected, blinding flash of pure ecstasy ripped through Ashiana, as if they had ignited a new star. She cried out at the intense sensation—a dazzling shower of sunfire bursting all at once within her. She clung to him, half-afraid she was dying, tumbling through clouds, her body washed by light and heat.

Wave after wave broke and crashed over her, a shimmering tide that ebbed and returned, on and on, rippling through her, leaving her shivering, shattered, yet utterly whole and replete.

An instant later he matched her cry, thrusting deeply, flowing into her as if his strength, his force, his determination had become part of her, and her release had released something in him. His power had become hers—hers to share, hers to take and give back tenfold. Chest heaving, he slowed and came to rest atop her, his weight crushing and yet welcome.

Bodies spent, limbs tangled, muscles limp, they lay in each other's arms, still joined, breathing hard. Ashiana trembled, but not from fear this time. The last of her fear of him had vanished, like darkness chased by dawn.

No, this time she trembled with the knowledge that something between them had just changed. Something she could not yet name.

But something, she knew, that she could not change back.

* * *

The wind woke him. Not the cowardly puff of air that had barely ruffled the sails for the past days, but a true wind. He felt it on his face, in his hair, against his bare chest, and realized that Ashiana no longer lay curled against him.

He came slowly to awareness, floating upward on pleasant memories of her passionate response to him. He had made love to her twice more, the second time turning on his back to draw her astride him; her initial surprise at finding herself on top had quickly vanished, when he sank deeply into her and showed her with his hands on her hips how to move. Her excitement had sharpened his, driving them both to wild abandon, leaving them shuddering in each other's arms with the force of their climax. Afterward, they had lain side by side for a long, silent time, neither speaking, neither pulling away. They must have drifted asleep.

Saxon sat up in the tangle of sheets, feeling a lurch of unease until he saw her only a few feet away, a sheet clutched about her. She leaned against the rail, looking down at the waves below, her slim, pale form languishing in a pose that bespoke sadness.

A sadness that sparked an instant response in him, a concern as unexpected as it was deep.

"Ashiana?"

She turned toward him, startled from her reverie, then quickly ducked her head—but not before he had seen the tears on her cheeks.

He went to her side and lifted her chin, bringing her face to his with a gentleness that surprised them both.

"I didn't . . . hurt you." He practically had to tear the unwelcome words from his throat.

"Nahin, sah—my lord. No."

Her reply was so soft, he had to lean closer to hear it over the gathering wind. "Then what has made you weep?"

She turned away from his touch and huddled into

herself, looking uncomfortable and reluctant. "It was nothing that you did, my lord."

He felt relief but was still not satisfied. He rested his hand lightly on her bare shoulder and spoke without thinking, as if his reason had detached from his control. "Tell me."

When she did not respond, he took her in his arms, pulling her against his chest and leaning into the rail beside her.

"Tell me," he commanded softly. "What were you thinking?"

She swallowed hard, twice, before speaking. She kept staring down at the water. "I was thinking of . . . forgetting."

He found the response odd, and his own curiosity about it odder still. Rather than question himself, he questioned her. "Forgetting what?"

"The sea."

The word was so simple, yet so heavy with pain, with memory and regret, that it started an ache right in the center of his chest. "Why," he asked in a tone barely above a whisper, "would you forget the sea?"

She tried to pull out of his embrace then, but he held her fast. She turned her face up to his and smiled. "I am foolish. A foolish woman. I—"

"How is it that the sea causes you such pain?"

She seemed vexed that she could not stir him from the subject. Turning her face back to the waves, she spoke hesitantly at first, then more quickly. "I was born at sea. I spent my first years traveling with my father on his ship, and I loved it so. The waves and the wind. The sound of it at night. I even loved the storms. But all that was before my father—" She stopped herself suddenly. "Before he . . . before he sold me to the Ajmir."

Almost without thinking, Saxon tightened his arm around her. He understood now; being aboard ship reminded her of her father's rejection. "The sea causes you pain because you remember him."

She kept her gaze downcast, but the wind played in her

hair, lifting it from her cheek, and he could see that she was blinking back tears. She nodded.

Again he felt that unfamiliar ache. To Saxon's distinct vexation, he realized that he was experiencing her pain. Just as he had felt her excitement during their lovemaking, he felt her sadness now. It was as if they shared some strange connection of words and touch that captured feelings, the way sails connected to rigging captured the wind.

He, too, had once loved the sea. Looking down at it with her in his arms, he could almost feel it again.

The onslaught of emotions stunned him. He had convinced himself that all he wanted of the woman in his arms was physical release, had told himself she was nothing more than a treacherous, lying slave girl with a whore's training and a thief's cunning heart. But every moment he spent with her proved to him how wrong he had been—and every moment made him want another moment.

Ashiana. Even her name was warm and elusive, like the wind. He couldn't keep his eyes, his mind, or his hands from her. Her innocent sensuality astonished and captivated him, as had her daring with the tiger earlier ... as had her tender apology when she so gently laid her hand on his arm.

He was just as hungry for that tenderness as he was for the curves and pleasures of her body. It was time he admitted that, though admitting it was one of the hardest things he had ever done.

"The wind is up," he said abruptly. "It is time to summon the next watch."

She didn't reply or even protest when he picked her up in his arms. Her expression of sadness didn't change when he carried her below and deposited her in his bed.

He dressed quickly, eager to be once again in command of his thoughts and feel more like himself. He went to fetch the watchmen from below, and soon the ship was picking up speed under the helmsman's hand.

But Saxon still felt ... off balance somehow. He stood on the deck, knowing he should stay and monitor the

Valor's progress, but all he could think about was that there were yet a few hours of darkness.

And he did not want to spend them here.

It took him only moments to get back to his cabin, but she was asleep when he arrived. He shut the door quietly behind him, already aroused even before he had stripped off his clothing and slipped into bed beside her, taking her in his arms.

She slumbered deeply, as if she had not rested in some time. He wondered what it was that had kept her awake, and found himself loathe to disturb her.

He brushed a tendril of hair from her forehead; she looked so vulnerable, so small. Delicate. Soft little tiger-tamer. He felt again that surge of protectiveness he had experienced before.

Carefully wrapping one muscled arm about her waist, he tucked her closer against his chest. Within minutes, he joined her in a deep, full, much-needed sleep.

And for the first time in many nights, he did not dream.

Chapter 13

Ashiana awoke gradually, reluctantly, not wanting to leave behind the feeling of being safe and protected that had seeped into her dreams. As she slipped upward to awareness, she wondered where the pleasant feeling had come from; she had felt very much alone when she had fallen asleep.

She thought she was still alone, but as she opened her eyes, a candle's glow and the gray half-light sifting through the mullioned windows illuminated him.

Him.

Wearing only a pair of breeches, he sat at his writing desk, leaning to the side, his head resting on one fist. Brow furrowed, he stared down at the large, leather-bound book he often wrote in, his pen unmoving on the page.

Not making a sound, Ashiana studied him through her lashes. She wondered when he had returned to the cabin, and if he had slept. He looked tired. The lines about his mouth and eyes were more pronounced than usual.

Instantly she chastised herself for being concerned about him. She should not be aware of what was usual or unusual in his expression. She should not feel worry or anything else for this man.

Just as she should not have felt such glorious pleasure hours ago on the deck, when his body cleaved into hers with such heat and passion while the sea winds caressed them both.

Burning with shame, she closed her eyes. Sadness

flooded in again—just as it had when she had stood at the rail and looked down at the sea, remembering her papa and his last words.

Words that now tore at her heart: *"Remember me, minha cara."*

She had not remembered him. She had forgotten. Her papa had been tortured and died at the hands of English pirates, and it was *not* an honor to his memory to . . . to . . .

To share her body with an Englishman and find such pleasure in it!

She was unworthy. She was weak. Rao had once called her strong, but he didn't know her as well as he thought. By Lakshmi's mercy, she didn't know herself! Not anymore. Her body still felt warm and sensitive from D'Avenant's lovemaking, felt so . . . so . . .

Vibrant. Wonderful. Oh, Vishnu help her, she was weak!

Helpless against the force that had taken hold of her, Ashiana could not stop herself from opening her eyes to look upon him again. He still sat at his desk, writing now, his plume bobbing and scratching across the page.

Saxon D'Avenant. Englishman. Smuggler. Thief. The man who was her people's worst enemy.

And the man who had given her soaring joy unlike any she had known.

The candlelight gilded his skin with a warm glow and shone on his tangled hair. The tracery of scars up and down his arms stood out in sharp relief, except where the bandage on his right forearm hid Nicobar's recent contribution.

Flickering shadows accented the line of his jaw, the breadth of his shoulders, the muscles that molded bone and sinew into power and strength. She vividly recalled every moment of his hard, angular form melding with hers, briefly becoming part of her in that mysterious, ancient way.

As she watched him, thought of him, thought of them together, she felt a swift response—tingling along her limbs, a tightening in her belly, soft warmth between her thighs.

And an ache that she could only call . . . desire.

"Good morning," he said quietly.

Startled, Ashiana gasped and shut her eyes, then realized she could no longer feign sleep. Chagrined, she lifted her lashes again, her cheeks flushed.

He had not stopped writing or even looked her way, but a grin quirked at one corner of his mouth. She wondered how long he had known she was watching him—and if he had guessed the direction of her thoughts.

"I—I—" she stuttered, "I did not wish to disturb you, my lord."

"You did not." He laid down his plume and slanted her a look. "Except for one rather small sigh."

"I . . . it . . . that was a yawn," Ashiana insisted, not even realizing she had made a sound. Her blush deepened. Both of them had spoken in whispers, as if reluctant to rouse the anger that had so recently been put to rest between them.

He studied her the same way she had looked at him, and she saw her own desire reflected tenfold. Then, slowly, he smiled, with such warmth it made Ashiana feel as if she were melting. His smile dazzled her, showing off his even white teeth, softening his features until he looked so very . . .

So very what? Handsome? *Nahin!* She must not let herself think this way! Handsome was Rao, her betrothed. Dark face, dark eyes, dark hair. Not this bright-haired, silver-eyed Englishman.

He leaned back in his chair, his fingers toying with the pen, that grin still playing about his mouth . . . and it was then she noticed it did not truly reach his eyes. No, mingled with the hunger in his eyes was that ache she had seen in them earlier, when he first came to the cabin and swept her into his arms.

She had to fight back an urge to get out of the bed and go to him, wanting to ask what it was that pained him, wanting to touch him, wanting to soothe away the hurt.

Inwardly, she cursed herself. She was weak. And dishonorable. Shameful!

But none of it took away the wanting.

He nodded to the small table on the other side of the bed. "There is food, if you are hungry."

Grateful for the distraction, she turned away from him and discovered a plate of fruits. He had already cut them into slices.

"Fruit is usually a luxury on a ship," he explained, turning back to his work, "but we're only a few days out of port."

Ashiana knew that the delicacies heaped on the plate would be a luxury to his crew at any time; he was being kind in giving her so much. He simply would not admit it.

His thoughtfulness touched her. And confused her. And increased her sadness all the more. This gentle truce between them felt so wonderful ... and so utterly, awfully wrong.

Unable to grapple with questions of virtue and sin at the moment, she focused on something more easily understandable: her growling stomach. Wrapping the sheet about her, she sat up and balanced the plate of mangoes, tamarinds, grapes, and plantains on her lap.

"Thank you, my lord," she said in English, biting into a piece of tamarind. The sweet, tart juice made her eyes water as it tingled on her tongue and slid down her throat. She ate in silence, watching him write.

It wasn't until she had nearly finished that she realized he hadn't had a bite. She held out the plate toward him. "Will you not have any?"

He shook his head.

Ashiana left a few slices anyway, in case he changed his mind. She set the plate on the table, then drew her legs up, wrapping her arms about them, resting her head on her knees. She kept her face turned toward him. He kept working, seeming determined not to look at her again.

"Have you slept?" she asked impulsively, her voice soft with concern.

His head swiveled toward her. Their gazes met and

locked. Just for a moment, the pain lifted from his eyes, leaving behind warm silver. "Beside you," he replied, his voice as soft as hers. "For several hours."

The next instant, the discomfort returned to his gaze, intensified now. Ashiana did not understand why a good night's sleep should upset him.

She realized then that *he* had been the source of her contentment last night, that feeling of being safe and protected. She did not remember him sleeping beside her, yet she knew. The knowledge made her feel warm all over, not with shame or embarrassment but with . . . pleasure.

The candle had burned low and started to flicker out. Neither of them noticed until the flame extinguished in a puff of smoke, leaving the cabin swathed only in fog-colored light from the windows over Ashiana's head.

He muttered an oath. Ashiana's eyes traced his silhouette as he opened the desk drawer and looked for a fresh candle. She wished he would leave them in darkness; the shadows of night made the cabin and everything in it seem unreal, dreamlike, suspended in time.

Light made it all too sharp and real and glaring with questions she could not face or answer.

He found a candle. She almost asked him not to light it. She stopped herself a breath away from doing so. Some part of her held back, unable to voice her unspoken wantings, unable to admit, even to herself, how much her attitude toward him had changed.

The candle flared in the darkness.

He set the wooden sconce beside his book, picked up his pen, but sat looking down without writing. It seemed a very long time before either of them moved.

When he finally glanced toward her again, Ashiana felt her stomach give a little jump. His expression had returned to the cool, harsh lines she was familiar with, all trace of vulnerability gone.

She disliked that look. She hadn't realized how much until now. It reminded her of all the anger and distrust and arguments they had had before, all the unpleasantness between them. She found she was not yet ready to end their brief, sweet peace. To keep him from retreating further behind that mask of control, she recklessly stepped into uncertain territory.

"How did you come to have those scars on your arms?" she asked, then added, lightly, "Surely you have not encountered Nicobar somewhere before?"

He seemed to take a dim view of her humor, his lips thinning. "No, I am fortunate to have made the personal acquaintance of only one tiger in my lifetime."

"Then what sort of animal was it that wounded you so badly?"

He did not speak for a moment, and when he did, his voice was very low. "It was not an animal at all." He looked down at his unbandaged arm. "Though I suppose that depends on your opinion of the Ajmir. I had the misfortune to be caught by one of their raiding bands, in the north." His gaze flicked toward her. "They are no more fond of me than they were of you, or any other English."

Ashiana was speechless; his story wasn't what she had expected at all.

He continued, his tone casual. "Three of them dragged me a few miles into the Thar Desert and almost made ribbons of me, with very small and very deadly knives. They were quite good at it—keeping me alive while inflicting the greatest amount of damage possible."

She inhaled sharply, shocked at the thought that her own people . . . that they were capable of . . . that they would carry out such horrific torture! *Nahin,* it was not possible!

"I'm afraid they underestimated me, however," he said with an undertone of satisfaction. "I had a small explosive device that I used to carry with me, an ingenious little invention I picked up in Canton. When I managed to get my hands on my coat, I tripped it. Killed them all and almost did myself in in the process."

Ashiana could not say a word. She felt light-headed. She had always believed in Ajmir warriors as paragons of courage and virtue! Her people were good and honorable and merciful—even to their enemies. Never had she heard of a member of her clan doing something so savage.

But Saxon had no reason to lie to her: he thought she hated the Ajmir as much as he did.

Swallowing on a dry throat, she choked out one word. "But ... b-but ..."

What she wanted to ask was *why*. Why hadn't they simply taken the sapphire and killed him? Why had they been so cruel, so arrogant as to linger to torture him to death?

She forced down those questions and asked the obvious one instead. "But ... how did you survive such wounds?"

He set his jaw. "I almost didn't. I was half-dead, alone in the desert. But I ..." He paused. "I still had enough strength to crawl. It was only sheer luck that I made it to a village."

A shadow of agony passed over his face. "No one had ever survived the Thar before. The villagers thought it was a miracle. Thought I was some kind of god." He paused again, closing his eyes. "They healed me," he finished simply, clenching his jaw, clearly determined to say no more.

Silence hung between them, heavy with all that had been said, and all that had not.

Ashiana lowered her forehead to her knees, fighting a sudden wave of dizziness. She felt sick, dazed, as if she had just been told that the sky was not blue, that the sun did not rise in the east and set in the west.

What he had told her about the Ajmir was unimaginable—yet she did not doubt that it had happened. If his scars were not evidence enough, there was the raw pain on his face as he recounted the story, so overpowering he was not able to hide it.

The Ajmir had tortured him ... just as the English had tortured her father.

Every fiber of Ashiana's being screamed in denial. It felt like she was being torn in two.

Before she could gather her senses enough to form any more questions, Saxon suddenly dropped his pen on the desk and left. She raised her head just in time to see the door shut behind him. The bolt slid into place.

And Ashiana had never felt so utterly alone.

* * *

She had fallen asleep with tears on her cheeks.

Sitting beside her on the bed, Saxon could see the damp lines clearly on her fair skin. Morning light poured through the windows over her head, warming the cabin and casting shadows over her slender form.

Certain that she was truly asleep this time, he indulged himself in the impulse to stay there, beside her.

Her tears made him feel something very much like wonder. Had she experienced his pain so vividly that she would cry for him? How was it that they were so attuned to one another that they could feel each other's emotions?

And what the devil had possessed him to spill out the truth about what had happened to him in the Thar?

He stood and moved away from her, running a hand through his hair. He had explained more to her than he had to Julian, for God's sake. What lunacy drove him to expose something so personal?

And what drew him back to her side now?

He turned and looked at her again, desire and reason warring within him. The sensible thing to do about the girl was to get away from her and stay away from her. He had already let her become far too important to him. He knew that. It was why he had stalked out of the cabin two hours ago.

But here he was again.

With a frustrated exhalation, he picked up his ship's log from the desk and put it back in the small trunk underneath. Walking to the washstand in the far corner, he performed his morning ablutions, then took fresh clothes from his sea chest and began to dress.

He found no reassurance in the familiar routine. His gaze kept straying back to Ashiana's sleeping form.

He would have to get his passions under control, he warned himself, pulling on a shirt.

He was not a callow youth. And she was not his first mistress.

Saxon D'Avenant knew better than to let a beautiful girl and a few tumbles turn his mind into so much mush. He could not allow himself to forget that Ashiana had lied to him, tricked him, almost killed him.

He could not allow himself to forget his vow to Mandara.

Saxon's hands stilled at his collar. He felt a sudden wave of anger at himself, remembering that he had slept without dreaming last night.

Had he forgotten his wife so easily? Forgotten that he was to blame for her death? Put aside all that she had meant to him?

He finished buttoning his shirt with quick, savage movements. There was no comparison between the two women. None at all. Ashiana could not hold a candle to his Mandara. Mandara was sweetness, innocence, purity, goodness. Ashiana was . . .

He paused, thinking, then yanked on his boots. He wasn't sure just yet how to classify her. She wasn't the opposite of those qualities, not exactly. She ably filled his desires for a bed partner, for someone to listen, for a little feminine tenderness now and then. She was proving to be the most engaging mistress he'd ever had.

But she was also a deceitful, treacherous little chit, far too quick-witted for her own good—or his. He could not trust her. Not when her allure was so dangerously laced with deception. She could never be to him what Mandara had been.

So there was no reason to feel guilty.

Fully dressed, Saxon sat on the bed again, satisfied that he finally had everything sorted out. He ran his fingers through Ashiana's silken black hair, untangling the strands.

She satisfied him for now. That was all. That was enough. It would last only a short time longer. After all, he would be putting her off his ship at the Andamans.

Ashiana stirred and stretched, yawning.

Opening her eyes, she stilled in mid-stretch, looking amazed to see him there.

Saxon withdrew his hand from her tresses. "It's morning."

He stood and stepped away, feeling foolish for stating

the obvious, yet pleased with himself for keeping his topic and his tone cool and dispassionate. He paced about the bed, settling on the chair at his desk.

"Yes," she replied at last, squinting into the bright sunlight that streamed in over her head. "It is morning."

"As long as we are both awake, and you've already had your breakfast, I suppose this would be a good opportunity to work on your English?"

She blinked a few times, looking confused, but for once, she did not argue with him. Perhaps because he had not phrased it as an order.

Or perhaps she welcomed the distraction as much as he did. She seemed no more eager than he to reopen their previous conversation.

Better, he thought, to keep everything between them mundane. Impersonal.

Safe.

"Yes, my lord," she replied in soft English. "I suppose it would."

"Very well," he said, all business. This—" He picked up the pen from his desk. "— is a *pen.*"

"Pen," Ashiana repeated dutifully.

More than an hour slipped by as he taught her the words for the furniture and other items in the cabin, along with a few simple verbs. Ashiana proved an able pupil, but after a while it seemed she found the lessons tiring. Her pronunciation began to slip.

"Let's go back to the beginning." Saxon picked up the plume and moved it to the window. "Where is the pen?"

Head resting on her knees, Ashiana responded tiredly. "The pen is on the wallow."

He raised an eyebrow. "The what?"

"The wallow," she repeated, yawning.

He looked from her to the pen and back, comprehension dawning. "No," he corrected. "This is a wall." He thumped the wood with one hand. "This is a window." He tapped the glass.

"And together they are a wallow."

"No, a window and a wall do not make a wallow." He

kept his tone brisk. "Now where is the pen?" He got up and went to the door.

"The pen is beside the walldoor."

He looked her way, frowning.

Her expression was earnest, but a smile crept across her features for a second before she quelled it. She looked adorably sleepy and rumpled, sitting in his bed, wrapped in a sheet, trying to feign seriousness.

"Hmmm," Saxon grumbled, trying to look stern and reproachful. Instead, he found himself fighting a smile as well. It was obvious she had lost interest in learning for the day. He walked back to the bed and held the pen beneath the table beside it. "And what about now?"

Her grin reappeared. "The pen is under the tabledeck."

"Try again," he advised dryly.

She did. Ashiana tried every word he had taught her—more or less. She "forgot" all she had learned, in the span of a few minutes. *Chair* and *bureau* became *chaireau, water* and *fish* twisted into *wafishter,* and the *bay* sound in *basin* somehow lost its "sin" and got mangled up with the tamarind she had eaten earlier to create *bearfruit.*

Saxon stood looking down at her with one eyebrow lifted. "Bearfruit?"

She frowned. *"Tamarsin?"*

He lost all hope of continuing.

"Mangobay?"

A chuckle escaped him and he gave up, tossing the pen over his shoulder. "You are either tired or the most singularly disastrous student I have ever met."

"I am a *singlestew?*"

"A disastrous singlestew."

Ashiana folded her arms indignantly, but after a second she dissolved in giggles. He sat on the bed beside her, chuckling with a full, deep humor he didn't even try to hold in. Ashiana laughed so hard she hiccuped and fell back on the pillows, trying to catch her breath. When she reached up to dab at her eyes, the sheet slipped aside, exposing one rose-tipped breast.

She didn't seem to notice. Saxon went still.

After a moment of his silence, she stopped laughing, her face still flushed, her eyes shining.

He reached out and stroked her cheek, not knowing why, not knowing anything but that he wanted to.

She seemed to realize only then that she was naked to his gaze, but she did not cover herself. Her hand came up to touch his, and rested there. Her smile wavered, then held, taking on a new warmth that radiated into him.

She turned her face into his palm, her lashes lowering to dust her cheeks. Suddenly the cabin seemed very quiet, the air too hot to breathe.

In the next second, the sheet that covered her was on the floor. His hand sought her, touched, quested, and found. She was already damp. One finger delved into her. A throaty, feminine cry of wanting tore from her parted lips. Her hips arched off the bed.

After just that one teasing touch, he rolled her onto her stomach. Her moan dissolved into a questioning murmur, muffled by the pillows—but it just as quickly became a gasp when he drew her to her knees. There was no time to take off his clothes, no time for anything but their urgent need. With a quick unfastening of his breeches, he sank into her feminine heat from behind, sheathing his hard length within her, driving home, sliding out, plunging again. Again, oh God, again.

His thrusts brought husky, wordless cries from her lips, rich with pleasure, with wonder and welcome. The position allowed him full access to the swollen nubbin hidden in the nest of her dark, damp curls. Balancing his weight on one arm, he stroked her while his hips ground against hers, burying him to the hilt inside her.

His wet fingers whisked and tormented until her head thrashed on the pillows and her hands gripped fistfuls of bedding. Her throbbing heat and moist tightness grasped and held him within. Their low groans tangled around one another.

His mouth found the nape of her neck, his tongue tracing the delicate dusting of hair, his teeth nibbling at her exposed earlobes. As their bodies moved together in that primitive dance, he existed with her in a place beyond reason, beyond control, a paradise where he died and was remade of need and hunger and passion and utterly unknown, new emotions. He shifted his arm, crushed her to him, took her fast and hard. Pressure, pleasure, ecstasy built within.

Too quickly, it exploded, searing out of him in a rush. *"Ashiana!"*

He breathed her name again, pumping his seed into her. Her body arched upward into his and she threw her head back, crying out with her own release, the tiny muscle spasms caressing his length exquisitely.

Reluctantly sliding out of her, he rolled onto his side and gathered her to him, caressing the hot, perspiration-sheened skin of her back. He whispered her name again. "Ashiana."

But this time words tumbled out after it. "I'll not sell you. To the Ajmir or anyone else."

Hell, hell, hell. Hellfire and damnation.

Bloody blazing hell.

The afternoon sun beat down on the quarterdeck; the entire day had almost slipped past before Saxon managed to tear himself away from his cabin, to make an appearance on deck. Only after many more hours with her. Hours of long, silent, gentle lovemaking to make up for his quick ravishment.

Each time, she responded to him with complete trust and passion. They had already gone through a good portion of the *Kama Sutra,* from what he remembered of the erotic guide. In fact, they could add a few chapters of their own. Never had a woman given herself to him, and to her own sensuality, so fully.

He absently touched the knotted cravat he wore. It wasn't something he usually bothered with at sea, but he needed it to cover the passionate little bite-marks on his neck and chest. It was only fair, he supposed; he had left her with whisker burns on her inner thighs.

He subdued a wicked grin and tried to force his

thoughts back to the present. The wind had strengthened, driving the *Valor* over the white-cresting waves. He stood beside the helmsman, went about his normal routine, but his mind was not on his work at all today.

Hell, he didn't know why he had made that impulsive promise to Ashiana. But he *did* know—had known as soon as the words were out—that he meant it.

He was not going to sell her. Certainly not to the Ajmir. He would not do to her what her father had done. She deserved better.

She had only clung to him after he had spoken the words, trembling in his arms, not making any reply. She must have felt inexpressible relief; he had felt her heart pounding against her chest, so fast he thought it would give out.

He realized the unexpected words had not come entirely out of concern for Ashiana, but for himself. The idea of her with another man—any other man—sent a fierce surge of jealousy through his veins. He could not tolerate the feeling.

She was his to do with as he chose, and if he chose not to give her up yet, so be it. He could at least keep her until they returned to Daman.

What harm was there in keeping her for just a few more weeks?

"Cap'n, begging your pardon, sir?"

Saxon turned to find the young Scotsman beside him, hat in hand. "What is it now, MacNeil?"

" 'Tis the beastie again, sir—"

"I thought I asked you to take care of whatever the animal needed."

"Aye, sir, that you did. But 'tis something I saw. In the tiger's bedding, I most definitely saw a—"

"Ahoy! Ship ahoy on the port beam!"

The startling cry came from the crow's nest far overhead. Every man on deck looked upward. Suspense crackled through the air as they waited for word on whether it was friend or foe.

"What flag does she fly?" Saxon called through cupped hands.

"English, sir." There was a pause. "Royal Navy."

"Your problem will have to wait, MacNeil." Saxon vaulted down the steps that led from the quarterdeck to the main deck and ran toward the bow. The forward watchman already had a spyglass trained on the approaching vessel.

"She's coming full out, sir, straight toward us," he said with trepidation.

Saxon took the glass. Royal Navy ships often gained crewman by taking sailors off merchant vessels in a ruthless but legal act known as "press-ganging." That, however, wasn't the most urgent thought on his mind at the moment.

He trained the glass on the intruder's bow, searching for the ship's name. Fury exploded through him when he found it, a blood lust that blinded out all else but vengeance and violence. He grated out a curse, low and vicious.

"Greyslake."

Chapter 14

S axon gripped the spyglass so tightly his fingers nearly left dents in the brass. Under normal conditions, his light, fast Indiaman might outrun Greyslake's man-of-war, but Saxon didn't dare order his crew to make full sail; the damaged keelson would never stand up to the pounding it would take at top speed. If it gave way, they would founder.

Blast it to hell, it wasn't like Greyslake to come out in the open like this. Treachery and subterfuge were more his style. Trying to tamp down his sizzling fury, Saxon raised the glass again. H.M.S. *Phoenix*. There was no mistaking it.

Whatever the reason for this sudden appearance, Greyslake was neatly robbing him of the chance to take vengeance for Mandara's murder. He could hardly kill a Royal Navy captain in full view of a shipful of Royal Navy officers. Saxon's personal grudge would have to wait.

He turned to the men who had gathered around him and began barking orders.

"Man the battle stations. Muster all hands. Find Wyatt and tell him the Navy is paying us a call. And Beckford and Mullins. Tell them to stay out of the cargo bays. That's the first place they'll look."

"Aye, sir." The men ran to carry out their orders.

Saxon glanced up to the quarterdeck, where MacNeil

was among those scrambling to ready the ship's defenses. "And tell MacNeil to get the hell out of here too."

The young Scotsman, Wyatt, and the other crewmen Saxon had named had all served in His Majesty's Navy—and left without permission. Deserters could be hanged without trial. He couldn't take the chance that Greyslake's officers might have seen one of them before.

The boatswain's whistle repeated the signal for all hands on deck. Within minutes, the men had assembled and manned their stations. The *Phoenix* was overhauling them rapidly; they could now make out her two gun decks, bristling with cannon.

Like the experienced fighters they were, the *Valor*'s crew faced the oncoming man-of-war without flinching—despite the fact that they were outgunned, and outmanned ten to one. Weapons were brought up from below and passed around. Saxon tied a belt around his waist and hung his *shamshir* sword from it, leaving the blade unsheathed. He shoved a pistol into his waistband.

His Majesty's Navy and the East India Company were supposedly on the same side, but in reality their rivalry was old and deep and often erupted into unpleasantness. Saxon didn't know what Greyslake's game was, but he wasn't going to give up ship, men, or cargo without a fight.

Sweeping toward them at top speed, His Majesty's sloop *Phoenix* sliced through the surf, fast and deadly as a harpoon. The *Phoenix* was a massive third-rate ship of the line—swift and powerful enough to battle a much larger French or Spanish warship and emerge victorious. As she drew near, they could see her crewmen thronging the rigging, ready to sweep over the gunwales at their captain's command. Saxon forbade his men to make any moves that might be seen as hostile.

It was more difficult to keep the peace when the warship came alongside. Her crew used grappling hooks and ropes to bind the two vessels together. Only a few feet separated them now.

"Steady, men," Saxon warned. He wasn't going to take

the chance of anyone being shot on a trumped-up charge of treason against His Majesty's officers. Standing amidships, he allowed the *Valor*'s entry port to be opened to allow for the gangway that the Navy men sent across.

The cold, familiar weight of the *shamshir* felt good against Saxon's palm. He felt an odd eagerness to see his old nemesis again, along with a fierce urge to bury the blade in Greyslake's gut on sight.

Saxon scanned the gathering company of *Phoenix* officers, all blue-and-white uniforms with their freshly polished buttons and ruffles and gold braid and flashing steel sabers. They waited on their side of the gangway.

And then he saw Greyslake.

Had it really been eight years? Eight? Greyslake glided among his milling crewmen like a shark, cold and deadly, not a medal out of place on his uniform, not a waver in the smile he always wore, not a speck of dirt on the perfectly tailored white gloves that he rarely removed in public.

He stepped up onto the gangway, towering above the assembled ships' companies, surveying all with a critical, superior air.

A tidal wave of fury came crashing down on Saxon— and with it, years of memories. The two of them were the same age. Both came from seafaring families. Both were second sons. Both had gotten their first taste of the sea's beauty and cruelty on the same East India Company ship at fourteen. They had been best friends once.

Until one tragic incident made them enemies forever.

Greyslake lowered his gaze until his brown eyes settled on Saxon.

All thought of the past, all long-ago wishes for peace fled Saxon's mind. Looking at that face, he saw only images of Mandara: her limp body in his arms. The poison-tipped gold arrow engraved with a *G*. The screams she struggled to hold back as she died an agonizing death. Hatred and rage and lethal urgency seared away all else.

One shot could kill him at this range.

One clean shot and it would all be over.

Greyslake's smile widened imperceptibly, as if he had

read Saxon's thought. Without fear, he crossed the slim plank that linked the pitching vessels, slowly, deliberately, without misstep. Not requesting permission to come aboard, he leaped down onto the *Valor*'s deck. A score of his officers followed.

Deliberately ignoring protocol, Saxon stood where he was and made them come to him. The blue-and-white flotilla stalked over.

Greyslake came to a halt with only inches of deck between them. "D'Avenant." He said it in a cold, brisk tone, all the more chilling for its lack of threat.

"Greyslake." Saxon hid neither his hatred nor his contempt.

"What purpose finds you in these waters?"

"The usual." They both knew he wasn't referring to trade.

"And what cargo do you carry?"

He sounded for all the world like a customs official making an inspection. Saxon replied with soft, sharp menace. "Silk, muslin, indigo. Let's get to the point."

"Still haven't acquired any patience, I see." Surprisingly, Greyslake obliged and ended the small talk. "I require a few of your men."

Saxon smiled without humor. He had anticipated that particular demand. "Afraid I can't spare any."

"It's not a request," one of the Naval officers said belligerently.

Greyslake cut the man off with a flick of his white-gloved hand. "I will be taking twenty-five, D'Avenant."

Saxon's smile disappeared. "That's a quarter of my crew."

Greyslake nodded. "Yes. It is."

The violence crackling in the scant air between them suddenly intensified into almost-visible lightning. Losing a quarter of the crew would leave the *Valor* dangerously short-handed—and make it impossible for Saxon to reach the Andamans first. It would virtually guarantee Greyslake the best chance at the sapphires.

"I can't offer you more than a half-dozen," Saxon said tightly.

"The *Phoenix* requires twenty-five able-bodied men," Greyslake stated. "And my officers are ready to enforce the King's law. Are you ready to comply?"

"Perhaps you weren't aware that Indiamen are exempt from press-ganging, Greyslake. The Admiralty signed an agreement with the East India Company directors. You won't be taking a single man off my ship."

The Naval officers chuckled.

"Perhaps *you* weren't aware," Greyslake countered, "that the agreement you refer to does not apply in time of war."

"England is not at war."

"You've been sadly out of touch, Captain. Some new little quarrel with France has broken out. My ship may be recalled to England to fight at any time, and I need more men. Matters of state come before commerce, D'Avenant."

Saxon could hear his crew turning restless. Not one of them relished the idea of serving on one of His Majesty's overcrowded warships, where rations and pay ran poor to none and disease and brutality were common. Worse, men gathered by press-gangs were never allowed to set foot on shore again, but passed from ship to ship to ensure they did not desert. Freedom came only with death or desertion.

Saxon knew that Greyslake didn't need or want the men. What he wanted was the sapphires—to keep Saxon from getting them . . . to leave the D'Avenant family forever cursed.

Because he held Saxon responsible for the loss of his own family.

"Why waste your time on this?" Saxon said in a low tone for Greyslake's ears only. "You might slow me down but nothing you can do will stop me. Nothing."

They stared at one another, eyes bright and sharp as knives with the intensity of their mutual hatred. Saxon heard the unmistakable soft scrape of a blade being slipped from its scabbard. Hands drifted toward triggers and sword hilts.

"If there is trouble," Greyslake warned in the same low tone, "I'll see every one of these outlaws you call a crew hanged from the *Phoenix* yardarms before nightfall."

Saxon's hand hovered near his pistol. "If you're still alive to give the order."

Greyslake's face took on a strange, detached expression. "I can't be killed. You know that better than anyone."

"You're as mortal as the next man. I could prove it. Right now."

"You already proved that I'm not. Eight years ago."

"It was an *accident,* damn it."

"It was *planned,* you murdering son of a bitch." The veneer of civility slipped. Greyslake's white-gloved hands shook violently.

One of the Naval lieutenants looked at his captain with concern. "Sir?"

Greyslake shook off the man's hand, his stare never leaving Saxon's face. "Give me twenty-five men or you and everyone aboard will hang for treason!"

"You'll not take one sailor off this ship."

Scores of men from the *Phoenix* swept over the gunwales at a whistle from one of their officers. The two crews separated, the Navy troops in their striped shirts and white breeches facing the *Valor*'s rough-hewn sailors.

Greyslake raised one hand, ready to signal his men to take what they sought by force. "D'Avenant . . ." he said warningly.

They glared at one another.

Saxon clenched his fists, knowing he had already made his decision and hating it. He couldn't let this turn into open warfare between the two crews. He could not throw away his men's lives for his own personal vengeance. Greyslake might, but he couldn't.

Damn it, he couldn't. "Palmer! Thorpe!"

The two men appeared at his side and saluted.

Gritting his teeth, Saxon grated out the hardest order he had ever given. "Assist His Majesty's Navy while they select twenty-five men." Saxon felt disgust at Greyslake's look of triumph.

"Cap'n?"

"Do it."

"My officers shall need no help, D'Avenant." Greyslake ordered his lieutenants to go about the business of selecting the best from among the *Valor*'s crew. "They've a good eye for strong seafarers. Not that we'll find any aboard this scow."

Saxon didn't reply to the cheap insult. Greyslake seemed disappointed that he had been robbed of the legal chance to hang every man aboard.

Greyslake composed himself. His smile slid back into place. "Have you mustered *all* your crew on deck?"

"Every man."

"You wouldn't be harboring any deserters from His Majesty's service?"

"Of course not. That's illegal."

"Yes," Greyslake said dryly. He stepped away to confer with two of his officers, then returned. "Just to make sure, my lieutenants and I will search the rest of your ship personally."

Saxon gritted back a protest; it would be useless. He could only hope that Wyatt, MacNeil, and the rest were well hidden by now. The party of Navy men went to the aft hatch that led below. Saxon followed. Greyslake turned and held up a hand.

"Your assistance is not required. I suggest you stay here and see that your men remain orderly. Anyone attempting to interfere with His Majesty's officers will be shot for treason." His dark eyes blazed eagerly. *"Any*one."

Greyslake turned and disappeared below. Saxon stood at the hatch, clenching and unclenching his fists, wanting nothing more in that moment than to fasten his hands around Greyslake's throat and squeeze. No doubt the royally-protected thieves planned to help themselves to a bit of his cargo as well as twenty-five of his men.

Saxon was so filled with frustrated rage and vengeance, he did not remember that he had something much more precious than men and cargo below—until he heard a scream from the direction of his cabin.

Ashiana!

He ignored the risk of taking a bullet in the back. He ignored the shouts behind him. One jump carried him down the companionway and he ran through the passage. Three of Greyslake's men raced after him.

"Stop!" one of them shouted. "I order you to stop!"

Saxon didn't heed. He didn't stop until he had thrown open the door to his cabin.

Greyslake had Ashiana against the wall, one hand wrapped in her black hair. Her eyes were wide with terror. He had taken off one glove to stroke her cheek with his bare hand . . . that horrifying hand that fire had scarred and twisted.

"Let her go!" Saxon drew his pistol. One of the officers tried to grab it. He sent the man sprawling with a well-placed kick. His *shamshir* was enough to hold the others at bay. "I said *let her go.*"

Greyslake ignored him, his attention on Ashiana. "You lied, D'Avenant. You said you had assembled everyone on deck."

"Every *man* is on deck. The girl is of no interest to you."

"I must disagree. Oh, I certainly must. She's on your ship. I could take her with me and let you argue your case before the Lord High Admiral back in London. When you get there. Months from now." He ran his hand over Ashiana's porcelain skin. She shuddered and squeezed her eyes shut.

Saxon aimed the pistol at Greyslake's head. "You know you don't have to give me any more reasons to kill you."

"You're not that stupid."

"Neither are you."

"Give me the girl and you can keep your twenty-five men."

"You have three seconds to let her go." Saxon cocked the weapon, ready to fire.

"You haven't considered my offer."

"One."

"Kill me and you'll never leave this cabin alive."

"Two."

"I'll hang every man aboard. I swear it."

Saxon couldn't hear anything but Ashiana's terrified little gasps. "Three."

His finger tightened on the trigger. Greyslake released her; he stepped away a few inches, but kept looking her up and down hungrily. She remained flattened against the wall, trembling, looking wildly from Saxon to the Navy men and back again. She clearly didn't understand what was happening or a word of what had been said.

Greyslake turned toward Saxon. "You always were a lunatic when it came to women. They're your one weakness." His smile returned as he put his glove back on. He shook his head. "Your one weakness."

"Stow it and get out. You'll not find any crewmen in here." Saxon kept the pistol aimed at Greyslake's head.

"You're an idiot to risk everything you have for a female." He stared at Ashiana again, and his voice turned taunting. "Though I can see how a man might be willing to die for a few hours between her legs."

Saxon launched himself forward in a mindless haze of fury. The side of his pistol caught Greyslake right across the face before any of the officers could stop him. They dragged him off their captain, but not before he landed a kick that connected solidly with Greyslake's midsection.

They wrested the weapons from Saxon's hands and held him by the arms. Greyslake shook off his men as they tried to help him to his feet. He wiped the blood from his mouth with the back of one hand, crimson staining his white glove. "You *will* pay for that," he snapped.

"Add it to my account," Saxon fired back, trying to wrest from the officers' grip.

"Release him," Greyslake ordered. "Get on with it. Find me every deserter he's hiding on this bloody barge!"

The officers let Saxon go and left with his weapons.

Greyslake followed them to the door, then turned, his dark gaze lingering over Ashiana. His features had settled into that eerie mask again, his swollen, bloody lip making it all the more macabre. "You never learn, D'Avenant. I will exact tenfold whatever you may do to me."

"It is you who owe me, and I plan to collect. Soon."

Greyslake didn't seem to hear him. His smile turned mysterious. "The girl would have been better off with me. You will understand that before long."

He turned with a military snap and strode out, leaving the door open behind him, calling back over his shoulder, "Do not interfere with us any further."

Saxon glared at his retreating back, feeling only slightly better for having drawn blood. Then he heard a sob behind him and all thought of Greyslake faded.

He spun around. Ashiana's knees buckled and she began to slump to the floor. He caught her before she could fall and held her against him. "Are you all right?" he asked in urgent Hindi.

She didn't say anything for a moment, simply letting him hold her, trembling in his arms.

"Did he hurt you?" Saxon took her face between his hands.

"No," she said, gasping for breath. "He . . . they burst in without any warning . . . I . . ." She turned to look down at the bed. "Mr. Wyatt?"

To Saxon's surprise, Wyatt appeared from under the bed.

"I'm sorry, sir," the first mate said. "Sorry I didn't help when the trouble started."

"I didn't need any help," Saxon demurred, still holding Ashiana. "Why the devil did you hide in *here?*"

"I didn't intend to, sir. I was hid below, but I came up to fetch the girl. I thought you—I thought I should hide her as well, sir. Didn't think you'd want Captain Greyslake to get ahold of her."

Saxon nodded grimly. Wyatt knew of the enmity between him and Greyslake; the first mate had been with him since that first ill-fated voyage on which Greyslake and his family had been passengers. "Good thinking, Wyatt."

"It is my fault that Mr. Wyatt was almost captured,"

Ashiana said in Hindi. "He came to the door and I did not understand what he was saying. He seemed angry and I thought . . . I thought something had happened to you. I wanted to go and see you, but he was trying to get me to go below—and then we heard the men coming down the corridor."

Wyatt let Ashiana finish her rapid Hindi before he continued. "I don't know what she's telling you sir, but I have to say . . ." He looked at Ashiana, and there was a new respect in his eyes. "She protected me, sir. I ducked under the bed when I heard those Navy blighters coming down the hall. Instead of making a fuss or getting hysterical, she kept her head, she did. Seemed to understand I didn't want to be found. She distracted them to keep them from looking for me."

Saxon gave Ashiana a squeeze, looking at her with pride. He spoke in soft Hindi. "What made you take on all those armed Navy officers to protect Wyatt? He's never exactly been pleasant toward you."

She lowered her lashes than looked up again. "It was the honorable thing to do," she said simply. "He seemed very afraid that these men would find him."

Holding her, Saxon felt warm admiration—and something much stronger that he didn't have time to think about. "Wyatt." He addressed his man in English. "It looks like they've gone down to the holds, but I suggest you get yourself back under the bed for now. I'll send someone with word as soon as they're gone."

"Aye, sir." Wyatt saluted. "And sir?"

Leading Ashiana to the door, Saxon stopped. "Yes?"

"Please tell the . . . lady that I thank her for her bravery."

Saxon translated the message to Ashiana.

She turned and smiled at the first mate. "You are welcome," she said in English.

Wyatt shrugged, but beneath his gruff expression and his stubbly beard, he was blushing. He returned to his hiding place.

Saxon knew he'd better get back to his crew before

anything else went wrong, but he lingered at the door, so many feelings and questions and concerns knotted up inside him, he didn't know where to begin. "You are sure he didn't hurt you?"

She shook her head. "He only frightened me."

"Ashiana, you have to tell me—was he the one who ordered you to take the jewel?"

"The one who . . . Oh! Oh, no, I do not think . . . no, he was not the one," she finished. "The man was shorter. And heavier. I have never seen this man before."

Saxon pulled her into his arms. "And you'll never see him again," he said firmly.

She tilted her head up. "Who—"

He kissed her before she could finish the question.

Kissed her.

After he had sworn to never again trust those treacherous lips, Saxon molded his mouth to hers and kissed her warmly, deeply, possessively. His tongue slid over hers, filled her mouth, retreated then plunged forth again greedily. He forgot vows and vengeance and hatred and anything but the need to meld with her for even that brief moment, to know that she was still here. Still his. No other's.

When he finally lifted his head, he could see by her eyes that he had left her dazed as well as breathless.

After a moment—he wasn't sure how—he managed to let her go. "I don't think they'll come back here, but Wyatt will stay here with you until they've left the ship," he said abruptly.

He turned and closed the door behind him without another word.

Ashiana noticed that this time, he did not lock it.

She leaned against the door, shaken by all that had taken place in the span of minutes—the appearance of the strange Englishmen, Saxon defending her, and then . . .

His kiss. That wonderful, melting, ungentle joining that was in every way as intimate, almost more so, than the way their bodies had joined hours before.

Cheeks hot, she wrapped her trembling arms about

herself. Everything was shifting between the two of them. Like dark storm clouds giving way before the wind, their anger and hatred had been replaced by . . .

By emotions she didn't want to think about. *Couldn't* think about. She knew only one thing, and she knew it with every ounce of her mind, heart and soul: she was not supposed to feel this way about the enemy.

But even the word "enemy" itself no longer seemed to apply to him.

How, oh, Vishnu, *how* was she going to find the strength to do what she must once they reached the Andamans? He no longer planned to sell her—which left her only one choice.

Escape. Leave him. Take Nicobar and the jewels and escape. And never see him again. He trusted her more now; it would be easier to get away.

Hot tears burned behind her tightly closed eyes, and Ashiana knew they did not come from concern about completing her mission.

Lanterns illuminated the darkness of the cargo hold. The *Phoenix* had departed an hour ago, but Saxon would not rest until he had personally checked every inch of his ship to make sure Greyslake and his minions hadn't added sabotage to press-ganging and thievery today.

Wyatt kept repeating the number with disbelief. "Sixty-five, sir. How is the *Valor* going to get on with only sixty-five hands?"

"We'll all put in double hours, double work. Every man will have to do more than his share."

"And if we get caught in one of the summer monsoons, sir?" MacNeil asked from beside Wyatt.

Saxon exhaled slowly. The picture would be grim if a storm caught them when they were this short-handed. He thought again of Greyslake's mysterious comment: *The girl would be better off with me . . .*

He shook off the uneasy feeling; Greyslake couldn't control the weather, for God's sake.

Working in silence, the three of them made a thorough

inspection of the holds. It looked as if some small items of cargo were missing, but they had expected that. They examined the hull at and below the waterline. They checked the shored-up keelson. They found no sign that anything vital had been tampered with.

"It all looks good, sir," Wyatt said with relief.

"Yes," Saxon agreed, though he still felt uneasy about Greyslake's strange comment concerning Ashiana. Probably just one more barb meant to irritate him. He'd be better off putting it out of his mind, now that he had gone over the *Valor* from stem to stern.

Besides, he could think of a much better way to spend his evening.

"The two of you had better get yourselves to the officers' mess for supper. I'll see you in the morning."

"Thank you, sir." Wyatt saluted and started back toward the hatch.

MacNeil lingered behind. "Sir . . ." he began tentatively.

"What is it, MacNeil?" Saxon said impatiently. "Out with it."

"There is that matter I spoke to you about this morning—the beastie?"

Saxon sighed in frustration. He obviously wasn't going to hear the end of the blasted tiger's trivial problems until he checked on it himself. "Yes, of course. Let's have a look at him, then. You said you saw something?"

MacNeil led the way back through the cargo hold, toward Nicobar's private bay. "A blue flash, sir, in his straw. Wondrous strange it was. A bright sapphire-blue."

Saxon had so much on his mind, it took a second for the significance of that particular color to sink in.

"*Sapphire*-blue?"

"Aye, sir." MacNeil cautiously opened Nicobar's pen, sliding the hatch aside.

Holding his lantern aloft, Saxon knelt down and stared inside. He saw exactly what MacNeil had described—an unmistakable flash of light, bright sapphire-blue *light*. Coming from the animal's bedding.

His heart began to pound against his ribs.

Nicobar was in a far corner of the enclosure, rubbing his neck against a broken nail that jutted out of the wall. Saxon moved inside. The animal growled.

"Sir . . ." MacNeil warned.

"The tiger's not that dangerous, MacNeil. Ashiana wrestled with it, for God's sake." Saxon reached out to touch whatever it was in the straw. He picked it up.

Even as he held it in his hand, his mind could not accept what it was. Then the truth ripped through him—and rage right along with it. Blinding, seething, soul-deep rage. His missing sapphire! *She had had it all along!*

Nicobar snarled. Saxon tore his gaze from the Sapphire of Kashmir sparkling in his palm and glanced up. The tiger kept shaking its head uncomfortably. It looked as if the animal had been trying to get its collar off by rubbing against the nail. The jagged bit of iron had slashed the leather.

Saxon hung his lantern on a peg, awash in disbelief. For shining through the cuts, unmistakable in the light, he could see *similar flashes of sapphire blue.*

Heedless of claws and fangs, he crept forward and grabbed Nicobar by the collar.

"Sir?" MacNeil queried with concern.

Saxon didn't even hear him. He wrestled with the tiger and held it down by brute force. There were more sapphires stuffed inside the collar!

He touched the jeweled leather and suddenly a strange energy, like heat and light from the sun itself, seemed to radiate out of the stones. It ran up his arm, through his chest, and down into his other hand, where he still gripped the other sapphire in his fist. His body jerked with the force of it.

"Jesus!" he cried, stunned by the unnatural sensation, dazed by the knowledge of what he was holding in his hands—and what it meant about Ashiana. *"Jesus Holy Christ!"*

"Sir?" MacNeil asked. "I don't think 'tis a good idea—"

An explosion ripped through the hold.

Chapter 15

❧❦

The deafening roar from below shattered the evening's silence and jolted the ship. Ashiana tumbled from her yoga position, falling headlong across the cabin. Her shoulder struck the corner of the bookshelf. She cried out at the pain that tore down her arm.

Vishnu's mercy! What was happening?

Sinking to the floor, she could feel the entire ship shudder beneath her. A second explosion shook the *Valor*. This one shattered the mullioned windows over the bed. Caught in a spray of flying glass, Ashiana covered her head, screaming. The shards cut into her back and arms like a hundred tiny knives.

Sheer heart-thundering panic held her frozen, hunched into a small ball. Were they under attack? The other English ship had departed an hour ago!

The acrid scents of fire and smoke and burning gunpowder assailed her. For a moment she thought she had been knocked unconscious. That she was dreaming of that horrible long-ago day aboard her father's merchantman.

She raised her head. The agony in her shoulder and dozens of bleeding cuts from the glass told her she was very much awake.

Terror seized her. The door hung at a crazy angle, half blasted off its hinges. Part of the ceiling—above the spot where she had stood seconds before—had caved in. The doorway was completely blocked with smoldering timbers. She could hear screams from the other side.

Ashiana struggled to her knees. She must get to Nicobar—the sapphires—

Saxon!

Please, by all the gods, she prayed, *let him be alive!* The thought brought her to her feet despite the pain in her limp arm. She clung to the corner of the bookshelf with her good hand, forced herself to remain standing.

Glass glittered all across the floor. Her feet were bare. Quickly, desperately, she grabbed books that had fallen from the shelf and tossed them down in front of her. Using them as stepping stones, she picked her way toward the blocked exit, her heart hammering.

She gasped for air, for relief against the bursts of agony that threatened to pull her down into blackness. She wrapped her good hand in the folds of her thick gray skirt and, using all her strength, pushed against the heavy, charred beams and pieces of broken wood crisscrossed over the doorway.

She could not move any of them. And there was no opening large enough for her to squeeze through.

Icy fear chased down her spine. She was trapped.

The fire billowed closer. It licked at the timbers with crackling orange tongues.

"*Bachao!* Help!" she shouted. "Please!"

She could hear no more screams from the other side. The blaze danced upward along the pile of wood, pouring smoke into the cabin. Coughing, Ashiana shouted again. She could not draw a breath for a third cry.

Air. She needed air. She fell back from the fire, stumbling toward the shattered windows, blinded by the sooty gray cloud that clogged the room. She could barely feel the glass that slashed her feet. She felt dizzy, hot, her lungs seared, consciousness slipping.

She made it to the window and clung there. The ash-laden smoke devoured what little fresh air came in through the broken panes. Ashiana fell to her knees, gasping for breath, for life.

"Saxon," she sobbed. It was prayer, plea, farewell, regret. "Saxon, *bachao.*"

He had never taught her the English word for help.

In the next instant the *Valor* heaved over onto one side with a creaking, straining thunder. Ashiana raised her good arm to protect herself as she was thrown against the far wall—with the books, table, bed, glass and everything in the cabin.

A sharp wooden edge struck her head and snuffed out her dry-throated scream. Darkness engulfed her.

"Abandon ship!"

Seething rage kept Saxon on his feet as he shouted the order again and again, struggling upward through the blazing decks of the capsizing *Valor*, his shirt and breeches soaked from swimming his way out of the flooded hold.

He had no business being alive. The first blast would have killed him—if he hadn't been in that pen with the tiger. The explosion had knocked him flat and blown out one wall of the hidden cargo bay.

And killed MacNeil.

Saxon tried to forget the image of the young Scotsman's broken body.

Tried to forget the sapphires, now lost forever.

The tiger had run snarling from one wall of flames to another—before leaping out a gaping hole that had been blown in the side of the stern. Into the sea. Still wearing the sapphires in its tattered collar.

Except for the one that Saxon, miraculously, still had. He had been holding it so tightly, even the explosion hadn't knocked it from him. He had stuffed the stone into his pocket.

"Abandon ship!" he shouted hoarsely. He couldn't think of anything now but saving those left alive.

He pulled himself upward, hand over hand on the ladder, toward the main hatch. There was no light above, only thick black smoke that blocked out the setting sun.

He had to use every bit of his strength to lever himself out and onto the deck. The ship was tilted at a wild angle, the mainmast snapped like a branch, sails and rigging dragging in the water. She was sinking fast.

The few crewmen left alive had obeyed the order to abandon ship; most of the boats were down and away. Heading for the *Phoenix*. He could see her in the distance, coming about in the blood-red blaze of sunset.

Unbelievable rage snapped through him. Greyslake was going to play the hero and rescue the survivors of this "unfortunate accident." *Bastard.* Taking vengeance by fire. An eye for an eye. *He should have guessed.*

But Saxon had no time for memories or wrath. He ran toward the stern, leaning forward to make up for the steep slope of the deck, toward a group of sailors helping the wounded into one of the last boats.

Toward the companionway that led to the cabins below.

He stopped, turned. Indecision seized him. Chest heaving, he cursed. All he could feel was overpowering fury at the loss of his ship, at Greyslake.

At Ashiana.

What idiocy to have ever trusted her! She was the enemy—at the very least in league with the Ajmir, if not Greyslake. The thieving, lying, deceitful little bitch had easily distracted him in bed while she kept the sapphires hidden. *Damn* her!

She might have even taken part in this murderous sabotage. Perhaps the entire scene in his cabin had been a diversion—to keep him occupied while Greyslake's minions planted explosives. Greyslake had been insistent on taking her with him. It all added up.

Saxon stood frozen at the top of the stairs. He should leave her behind. Leave her to die.

If she wasn't dead already.

Two steps carried him down the companionway and then he was running for his cabin through a choking, blinding fog of smoke.

There wasn't time to question what he was doing. Flames and a pile of timber—he didn't know how thick—completely blocked the door. He heard no screams from inside. She could be dead already.

Shielding his face with one arm, he crouched low and threw himself into the wall of fire. It sizzled on his wet clothes. He grabbed the nearest beam and pulled. It burned his hands but didn't budge.

One thick plank supported all the rest. He bent down and threw his shoulder against it. He put every ounce of his strength into the exertion, shouting and snarling with it. Sweat poured down his face, stung his eyes. It felt like the muscles in his back would tear apart. He could smell his singed hair and clothes.

At last the wood, already damaged, snapped in half. The others balanced atop it fell. Saxon jumped back and barely avoided being crushed.

It cleared just enough of an opening at the top for him to squeeze through. Coughing on smoke that scalded his mouth and throat, he climbed onto the flaming timbers, ignoring the heat, the pain from dozens of burns. He made it up and over and leaped down into his cabin.

The room was black with smoke. He gripped the edge of the broken door to keep himself upright on the sharply angled deck, crouching low so he could breathe and see.

Everything had crashed into a broken heap against the far wall. His heart clenched: he could make out the edge of Ashiana's gray woolen gown beneath the crush. She wasn't moving.

He shouted her name and let go of the door before he had time to draw a breath or even think of how little time was left.

Before the smoke consumed the last of the air.

Before the fire made escape impossible.

Before the sea swallowed the *Valor* and him with it.

Instinct and brute strength took over. He tore into the pile, shoving aside tables, broken pieces of wood, smashed furnishings. He cut his hands on shards of glass that covered everything and never felt the pain.

The ash became so thick that he breathed more soot than air. It nearly made him black out. He held his breath. Smoke made vision impossible, but he kept digging. His starved, seared lungs felt like they would burst.

Finally he uncovered her. She had somehow fallen between the bed and the wall. The mattress, wedged against her, had protected her from the worst of it—but she had dozens of cuts and was bleeding badly from a wound in her scalp. He pulled her free. She was barely breathing. It felt like her left arm was broken.

Lifting her from the rubble, holding her in his arms, he turned toward the doorway.

It was too late.

The fire had blown back in their direction. It blazed up the entire wall, crackled along the ceiling, blasted the cabin with killing heat. They were both dead if they didn't get out *now*.

He shifted Ashiana onto his shoulder and climbed over the debris toward the smashed windows. He gripped the ledge and chopped wildly at the twisted bits of wood that had held the panes, breaking an opening large enough. Outside, night had fallen.

The furniture was in flames now, the bedclothes, his books. The hem of Ashiana's skirt caught fire. He smothered it with his bare hand.

There was no time left. He lifted Ashiana onto his back, wrapped her good arm around his neck, and held her tightly. He levered himself up onto the ledge and squeezed through the opening. Bits of glass ripped at his belly and legs.

He balanced on the edge for a second, kicked free, and they both fell.

There wasn't even time for a deep breath. They smashed into the water. The impact wrenched Ashiana from his hands. Sinking with her, he grabbed for her and missed.

He was buoyed upward, but her woolen dress pulled her under. Diving, he tried again, catching her wrist, but the waves and the pull of the sinking ship dragged her away.

His tortured lungs demanded air. Saxon kicked upward. He broke the surface amid a tossing, floating chaos of planks and rigging and debris. Taking a great heaving gasp, he choked on a mouthful of salt water and smoke.

He dove again—and could not find her.

The *Valor* was almost entirely under water, five hundred

tons sinking like a stone, pulling everything in its wake with it. The ship bled great black billows of smoke that turned the sea into pitch. Saxon dove and turned and swam through the night-dark water and found nothing.

His meager gasp of air had run out. Consciousness wavered. If he took the time to swim for the surface again, she would be dead.

It was his life or hers.

Chapter 16

Shafts of sunlight gleamed through the shifting fronds far overhead. Ashiana squeezed her eyes shut to block out the brightness and winced at the throbbing in her temple. The pain brought a shock of awareness.

She was alive.

And on *land*.

Her heart hammered as everything came flooding back: the explosions, the fire, the *Valor* tossing onto one side . . . and then blackness.

How had she escaped the ship? How had she come to be here—and where exactly was she?

The raucous twittering of birds, the low buzz of insects, and the scent of the sea all competed in the humid air. She could feel sandy ground beneath her. Slowly, carefully, she opened her eyes again, shading them with one hand. A hundred hot pinpricks from the bits of glass in her back and arms made the movement painful. She could feel dried blood on her forehead. Her hair was damp and matted.

Giant *sal* trees towered around her, enormous gray sentinels wrapped with vines. Turning her head, she could see that she was in a forest clearing. A jungle of cool green leaves thwarted the sun's heat. The thick undergrowth reflected every shade of shadowed emerald, a tangle of broad, flat leaves rioting with wild orchids in brilliant reds and purples. From somewhere overhead she could hear the screech of a monkey.

It almost looked like . . . home, like the Andamans. But that could not be.

She tried to sit up. Her left shoulder still hurt like Shiva the Destroyer's vengeance, but she found she could move her arm; it no longer hung limp. As she lifted herself to one elbow, her head pounded fiercely.

Her groan choked into a fit of coughing. Her throat felt as if it had been rasped by a file. She could taste the sooty, salty bitterness of smoke and seawater. Her mouth felt burned. She would have given anything in that moment for the smallest sip of something cool to soothe the painful dryness.

Shaking and weak, she managed to sit up. It was then that she noticed her clothes—her *gow-oon* was gone! She wore only her *kor-set* and the tattered remnants of her *petti-koot*, one edge of it singed.

Another coughing spasm seized her and suddenly her stomach heaved. Falling to her side, she retched, choking up salt water. She wiped her mouth with one trembling hand.

Food and the bleeding cut on her forehead could wait, but she must have water. Perhaps whoever had brought her here had gone to find some.

Pray Vishnu, had it been Saxon who had saved her? Was he alive? Was he all right?

Trembling, Ashiana sat up again, more slowly this time. She carefully picked bits of glass out of her feet, biting her lip against the pain; her soles were badly cut. Leaning against a tree for support, she stood. Lush green undergrowth carpeted parts of the forest floor. She gingerly took a step toward a patch.

"Saxon?" she called. Another fit of coughing shook her. Feeling dizzy, she bent her head.

Only then did she see the footprints in the sandy soil. Deep, large prints made by a man.

Feeling a surge of hope, she started to follow them, supporting herself on trees and vines as she went, wincing with each step. Someone had cleared a path through the tangled plants. She tried to call out again, but decided she had best save her voice.

She had only gone a short distance into the trees when she saw him, coming through the forest toward her.

"Saxon!" Ashiana felt such heart-soaring relief that she would have thrown herself into his arms, but her feet hurt so terribly she couldn't take another step.

Saxon stopped in his tracks.

He wore only his breeches. He had jagged cuts on his legs and stomach, and burns all over his shoulders and arms. And he was covered with dirt, especially his hands. But it was his expression that stole the joy from her heart and struck dread in its place.

He stared at her with that icy, angry glare she disliked so much. He didn't say a word.

"A-are you all right?" she asked, confused. "What hap—"

"Sabotage." He fired it at her like a shot.

Ashiana shivered. His anger over the loss of his ship was understandable, but she didn't know why it seemed directed at her. "Your crew?" she whispered.

"A few escaped in the boats," he said tightly, still not moving a single rigid muscle.

Ashiana hung her head, unable to bear the thought of any of the men she had grown to like—MacNeil, Wyatt, all of them—dying so horribly. Her own pain was so little compared to that. "But how did you . . . how did we—"

"*We* almost didn't escape. I got you out of the cabin and went over the side but the pull of the ship separated us. It was only pure luck I found you again before we both drowned. I tore that damned dress off you and grabbed onto a chunk of planking and started swimming. When the sun came up, I saw this island."

Ashiana flinched at his rapid-fire explanation but she raised her head and held his gaze, letting her thanks shine through in her eyes. Swimming all night with those wounds must have tested the limits of his strength and endurance. He had risked his life to save her; it made his attitude that much more confusing. "But no one . . . you haven't seen anyone else?"

"Bits and pieces of my ship have been washing up on shore all day." His jaw clenched. "But no one *alive.*"

Ashiana shuddered at his meaning. That must be why he was covered with dirt; she remembered hearing once that Europeans buried their dead.

Horror at it all overwhelmed her, but beneath it she felt an even stronger gratitude to the gods for sparing his life.

"D-did you mend my shoulder somehow?" She moved her left arm experimentally. "I thought it was broken."

"Your arm was pulled from the socket. I snapped it back in. You should be fine."

"Thank you," she said tentatively. "H-how did you know to do that?"

He went still. The entire forest around them seemed to go silent. His eyes iced over completely. "I knew a healer once."

As suddenly as he had appeared, he turned and walked back the way he had come, saying curtly, "I have things to attend to."

Perplexed, Ashiana watched him, then followed, wincing at each painful step. "Have you found any fresh water? Do you think we might be rescued?"

"No, I haven't and no, I don't." He kept walking, not slowing his long-legged stride. "The ship wasn't expected back at Daman for weeks. By the time anyone even notices it's missing, we could be here a very long time."

"But won't the—" She struggled to remember the word. "—the *Na-vee* ship send out men to search?"

He made a rude sound. "The *Na-vee* already picked up the survivors. They probably think I went down with the *Valor.* My men saw me go below just before she sank."

"Is it not possible that someone on another ship saw the fire?"

"We're in one of the main trade routes but there aren't many ships at sea this time of year," he snapped. "Now leave me alone."

Ashiana stopped trying to keep up with him. Breathing

hard from the exertion, she leaned against a tree. The cut on her forehead had started bleeding again and her feet were too painful to walk any further.

She could not understand his surly attitude toward her. It was as if . . . as if the tenderness they had shared in his cabin had never taken place. As if he were once more the harsh, ruthless Englishman who didn't care whether she lived or died. Why, then, had he risked himself to save her?

Her relief at being alive and on land dwindled. She didn't have to ask why few ships traveled at this time of year. It was *varsha*—season of the monsoons. And the two of them were alone on a small island. When the storms hit . . .

She blinked back tears that suddenly pooled in her eyes. She had been so focused on Saxon that she hadn't realized, until now, how much she had lost when the *Valor* went down.

Nicobar. Her shoulders started to shake as her tears spilled. He must have perished, trapped in the ship and drowned at the bottom of the sea. Desolation swept over her as the truth struck home.

Nico was gone—and the sapphires with him.

Everything she had done had been for nothing. The Nine Sapphires of Kashmir were lost, forever. All the lives spent, all the efforts wasted, all her people had endured . . .

Ashiana covered her face with her hands and wept.

Only one thought consoled her: the sacred stones were beyond the reach of thieves. And all nine were together; she had accomplished that. She raised her head, listening to the distant sound of the surf. The bottom of the sea was not the planned hiding place, but there was nothing anyone could do to retrieve them now.

Her mission was finished.

That thought gave her some comfort. The sapphires were gone, her duty over . . . and that meant she no longer had to consider Saxon her enemy.

The idea settled through her warmly. Squaring her shoulders, she started down the path he had taken, ignoring her physical pain. It was time for both of them to begin healing.

Together, they would find some way to survive. He was understandably angry about what had happened to his ship and crew; he was merely taking it out on her because she was the only person around.

But he had risked his life for her. And before that, on his ship, he had been wondrously gentle and sweet and caring with her. She felt certain that those feelings were still there, hidden beneath his unyielding exterior.

She walked faster and caught up with him near the beach. "Saxon?" she called after him.

She could see him ahead, but he did not slow down.

"My lord?" she tried again. "I think you should let me look at your cuts. And those burns."

He jerked to a halt and turned on her. "I do not require a healer!"

Ashiana stopped, taken aback. "But you should rest—"

"*You,*" he said in a low, warning tone, "should leave me alone. Leave me *alone,* damn you."

Ashiana stared at him, startled and hurt. Cautiously, she closed the distance between them, softening her tone. "I—I know it is a terrible loss, your ship and your men." She reached out to touch him.

He snatched his arm away as if she would burn him. His eyes glittered and his voice sharpened. "You do not know a bloody thing about what I have lost."

He stalked away from her again.

Ashiana stopped trying to follow him. Folding her arms over her chest, she frowned at his bare, tanned back as he disappeared down the path.

Why did he have to be so insistent about being left alone in his anger and grief? He had rescued her, but he would not let her do the slightest thing to help him. Infuriating man!

With a sigh, she turned and started back into the forest. He would need her to survive, even if he wouldn't admit it; their refuge was very much like her home in the Andamans, and there were things she knew about these islands that he might not. Where to find food. Which plants were edible and which poisonous. How very dangerous the small *caracal* wildcats could be.

Years ago, she and her friend Padmini used to spend whole days roaming the forests, before Ashiana realized that acceptance among the Ajmir meant giving up the boyish ways she had learned aboard her father's ship. She was certain she could remember many of the skills her maidservant had taught her.

Saxon was being foolishly, stubbornly male about refusing to accept her help, but she hoped a few days' time would start to heal his pain. At least enough for him to allow her near without snarling at her.

He seemed a bit like Nico in that way. A sad smile curved her lips. It was all a matter of knowing when and how to approach him.

He would need her. They would need each other. But for now she would do as he asked and leave him alone.

At least, she thought with a sigh, things could not get any worse between them.

For the next three days, Ashiana kept her mind on practical matters and made good use of her time. Following a band of furry gray langur monkeys, she let them lead her to a freshwater spring. She drank deeply, washed herself, and cleaned her cuts as best she could, picking every splinter of glass from her skin, except for some on her back that she could not reach.

Gathering fallen *padauk* fronds, she cut them into strips, using the sharp edge of a shell found on the beach, then wove the strips into mats. On high ground in the center of the island, she constructed a little shelter for herself, beside a dense stand of trees that would provide some protection against the wind. Green bamboo made solid, flexible poles, lashed together with vines. She laced the *padauk* mats to the poles in overlapping layers, forming a peaked roof. It should keep her dry even in a monsoon, she thought with pride.

She discovered that the island offered a variety of

familiar foods, and soon collected a respectable cache of coconuts, papayas, *sapota* fruit, and crabs picked from the beach when the tide went out in the evening.

She even put together a sort of signaling device. She gathered every bit of shiny metal that washed up from the *Valor*—eating utensils, mostly—and tied them to one of her mats. It wasn't quite as bright as a mirror might have been, but it flashed in the sun. They could use it to draw the attention of a ship, if they saw one.

In three days, she did not see a sign of Saxon.

Except for the graves down on the shore, six of them.

He was either busy with some task of his own, or purposely avoiding her. She had been all over the island and had never come across him.

Last night, she had awakened to a sound very near her shelter. Lifting her head, she saw a shadow, just beyond the light of the fire she kept burning to scare predators away. But when she called out, there was no reply. The next instant, the shadow had vanished.

In the light of day it seemed clear that it had only been an overly bold animal. Ashiana put it out of her mind.

She stirred the salve she was making, in a broad, flat shell over heated rocks; she had used the ointment on her feet, wrapping them in soft leaves, and her cuts were healing well already. She intended to use this new supply on Saxon's burns. Even if she had to ambush him to do so.

The salve appeared to be the right thickness now. She put the stick aside and wrapped her hand in a length of cloth, torn from her singed *pet-ti-koot*, before picking up the hot shell.

Standing, she wiped her perspiration-beaded brow, then on impulse, ducked into her shelter. She picked up a hollowed-out pineapple filled with a sweet drink she had made earlier from fruit juice, water, and coconut milk. She took it with her as a peace offering.

Now then, where best to start looking for him?

She started down the path she had cleared to the beach. She would follow his footprints from there and hope they led somewhere. Saxon might try to keep his pain hidden, but she knew the burns must hurt him terribly; she was at least going to tend his injuries before he went prowling off alone again.

But it was not footprints she saw when she arrived on the shore. It was an animal, stalking along the water's edge.

She froze, not even breathing, only a few feet beyond the trees. But it was much too large and too dark to be a *caracal.*

A chill ran through her. It almost looked like—

"Nicobar!"

The shell and the drink dropped unnoticed from her hands. She ran toward him, oblivious to the pain as her feet pounded into the sand. He stumbled and fell and she called his name again. Nico raised his head, panting. She dropped to her knees and caught him up in her arms, tears blurring her vision.

He made a watery, weak growl of protest. His fur was soaked and matted. "Oh, Nico!" Ashiana ran her hands over him but could not feel any broken bones. He was exhausted but unhurt. "Nico, you are all right!" she cried gratefully, burying her face in his ruff.

It was only then that she noticed his torn collar. Ashiana went still. She wiped the tears from her eyes. The sapphires! How could she have forgotten?

Her stomach twisted painfully. She darted a look over her shoulder, searching all along the shoreline, peering into the trees. Saxon, as usual, was nowhere near her.

She turned her back anyway, blocking any view of what she was doing. She unfastened Nico's collar, removed it, and lay it on the sand, her hands trembling.

"Nico, what happened to your collar?" she whispered in astonishment, carefully opening the slashed leather. Her heart was in her throat as she counted the stones. It would be a miracle if all nine were there after Nico's time in the sea.

Six . . . seven . . . eight.

Eight.

One was missing. Ashiana sat back on her heels, staring

in dismay at the brilliant blue gems. She raised her head, looking at the crashing surf. One must have fallen out. It was lost at sea. Lost, and she could never get it back.

Her shoulders sank. The Nine Sapphires of Kashmir were separated again.

She sat for a long time looking down at the eight that were left, thinking of all that had been done to possess these jewels. She thought of the Ajmir lives lost at the hands of the English.

And of the Ajmir warriors who had tortured Saxon.

Of all that had happened to her since she first agreed to become protector of the sacred stones. So little made sense anymore; the clear certainty she had once had, that her people, her clan, were all-virtuous and the English all-evil, no longer burned within her.

Gone, like her innocence.

Nicobar lay his head in her lap with a weary sound. She stroked his striped fur. "It is all right, my Nico," she whispered, resting her forehead against his. "Or it will be."

If she admitted the truth, she had felt relief that her mission was done, that the sapphires had been taken out of her hands; now the gods had given them back to her.

And her sworn duty—as long as she could draw breath, no matter what troubling questions swirled in her head— was to keep the Nine Sapphires of Kashmir out of the hands of the English.

The enemy.

She glanced over her shoulder again, still seeing only trees. She no longer thought of Saxon as her enemy, but neither could she let him get his hands on the stones. She must hide them.

But where? The island was too small, and he was too unpredictable. No matter where she hid them, he might find them. If not him, then some future travelers who happened upon this place.

She turned back to the waves that crashed upon the shore.

The sea. It was the best solution. With one sapphire lost out there somewhere, they would be reunited, in a way.

Working quickly once she had decided, she stuffed the sapphires back into Nicobar's collar. She could not simply fling them into the waves and chance that they might wash ashore, like the rocks and shells that lined the beach.

"Stay here, Nico." Standing, she took off her clothes and left them on the sand, not so much because she didn't want to get them wet, but because they made it so difficult to breathe properly. She tore a strip of cloth from her *pet-ti-koot*. With that and the collar grasped in one fist, she strode into the surf. The warm, salty water stung her feet and the dozens of cuts on her back and arms, but the pain faded after a moment.

Ashiana had always been a strong swimmer; she and Padmini often liked to evade the harem eunuchs and escape the heat of the palace for a midnight swim. Walking into the water until she could not stand upright anymore, she took a breath and dove into the waves, straight and strong as an arrow.

The water sparkled clear as glass, dancing with beams of sunlight that struck flashes of turquoise and azure from the depths. Schools of black-and-white-striped fish with speckled tails darted around her. Below, great reefs of flame-colored coral teemed with undulating yellow ferns and small sea creatures.

Ashiana swam straight out from shore, returning to the surface for a breath whenever she needed one; years of yoga practice made her breathing slow and easy, and holding it in the warm water felt quite comfortable.

She selected a hiding place she could find again if need be: a long, sinuous reef of bright orange, shaped like an elephant's trunk. When she was able to leave the island and return to the Maharaja, she would tell him what had happened, and exactly where the stones were. He would decide what must be done.

And if she never left this place, the secret would die with her.

Rising to the surface, she turned toward shore to find a landmark. She decided on a clump of three trees that towered above the others, about an arrow's flight away. She positioned herself so that they were straight ahead, then took a huge breath and dove deep, toward the reef.

She found a hole about the size and depth of her arm and stuffed the collar inside. After another breath, she dove again, picking up rocks from the sea floor. Using all her strength, she shoved them into place, squeezing them in tight to block the hole. She tied the strip of white cloth from her *pet-ti-koot* to an undulating frond of seaweed in the middle of the reef.

Ashiana rose to the surface. Taking a gasp of air, she slicked her hair back, treading water. She could see nothing on shore but Nico, now washing himself.

Swimming back to the island, she felt a sense of peace. She had sworn to reunite the sapphires and move them to a new hiding place; she had done that, at least as best she could. Her duty was finished. She was the only one who knew where the sapphires were, and she would never tell anyone but the Maharaja.

Reaching shore, she dressed quickly and coaxed Nicobar to his feet. Together, they walked back to where she had dropped the salve and the drink. Both had soaked into the sand. Frowning, she picked up the shell and the empty pineapple.

She started back toward her little encampment. "Come, Nico. I will make more and then we will go find Saxon." Her heart lightened and she smiled down at her tiger. "Perhaps it will cheer him to see that you have survived."

Chapter 17

Saxon banked the last of his signal fires for the day. He kept several burning on the island each night, hoping to attract any ship that might come within range. He had yet to see so much as a speck on the horizon.

The past three days and nights had been a blur of oppressive, mind-numbing heat, pain from his wounds—and slow-burning fury that would not be quelled.

He turned from the fire-pit and moved down the beach, his temples throbbing and his already-raw hands and arms stinging. He headed for the makeshift lean-to of leaves and branches he had made to keep out the sun's heat.

At least Ashiana had done as he demanded and stayed the bloody hell away from him. The memory of their first encounter in the forest made his anger simmer. How dare she keep up her act, following him with her tremulous smiles and her eye-batting inquiries after his health. *God*, he could have throttled the life from her right then. Right there in the jungle like one of the beasts that prowled through the trees.

What made him even angrier was that he couldn't answer her question about why he had saved her. He didn't know why.

Nor did he know why he had tracked her to her shelter the other night. Why he had thought it important to check on her.

Why he had lingered, long after she had settled back to sleep.

He couldn't answer any of the dozens of *whys* that ricocheted through his head. He kept trudging down the beach as the morning sun sizzled higher. The glare struck the sugar-white sand and rose in ribbons of heat.

He would grant her her life, nothing more. He tried to put thoughts of the wench out of his mind . . . and failed.

Because of her treachery, he was right back where he had started ten years ago. He possessed one sapphire, but the other eight were beyond his reach.

All *nine* had been within his grasp—right on his own *ship,* for God's sake—and he had never suspected. She had played him like a fish on a line, reeled him in with her lush body, her laughter, her sensual response, her sweet feminine tenderness. All false.

He had allowed himself to forget Mandara, and for what?

For a female spy who was only doing her job.

The anger he felt at himself was almost equal to that he felt for Ashiana. It was not only the pain from his burns and cuts that kept him from sleeping at night. The nightmare had returned, more forceful than before; every time he closed his eyes, he could see Mandara twisting in agony, trying so bravely to hold back her screams, going limp and lifeless in his arms—

"My lord?"

Saxon stopped in his tracks.

He heard the call again, from far behind him, but almost thought the heat had addled his head. Did the blasted woman have no sense at all?

Turning, he saw her coming toward him, walking quickly, a smile on her face.

And her tiger beside her!

Astonishment sliced through him, followed by a jolt of suspicion that made him keep still and clamp down an outraged exclamation.

How long had the tiger been here?

And *where* was its collar?

Was that the reason she had decided to keep up her

feigned concern that day in the forest? Was she once again hiding the sapphires?

He kept his expression neutral and his questions to himself as she approached, the great cat slinking along by her side.

She looked well—he cursed himself for noticing—with her glossy black hair tumbling about her pale corset-cinched curves. The sun had brought out a sprinkling of very English-looking freckles on her cheeks and the bridge of her nose.

She held a pineapple in one hand and a shell filled with a brownish, sticky-looking substance in the other.

"I am so glad to finally find you," she said as she stopped a few paces away, her smile widening tentatively. "Are you all right?"

Lying, deceitful wench. "Well enough." He tore his gaze from her long enough to look down at the tiger.

"I found Nico walking on the beach this morning. Isn't it wonderful?"

"Wonderful," he echoed.

"It seems his collar came off in the sea, but he is unhurt. Tigers are very strong swimmers, you know. They often swim from one island to another in search of prey."

"How interesting." Saxon felt his gut clench as his suspicion strengthened. He glared into the animal's golden eyes. The collar had been damaged; it seemed unlikely that it had stayed on.

But it was equally unlikely that she was telling the truth.

And the tiger wasn't talking. The beast rolled over and stretched out on the sand, panting in the sultry heat.

Saxon slid his gaze back to Ashiana's, noticing now that her pale skin bore shades of pink, especially the delicate upper curves of her breasts. "You should stay out of the sun."

He cursed himself silently as soon as he said it. What did it matter to him if she fried?

And as soon as he had glanced at the swell of her breasts, bound by the corset, his eyes took in a dozen other details: the edging of lace that just hid her nipples, the pounding of her pulse at her throat, the wisps of silky black hair curling damply about her neck . . . and lower, the damaged petticoat that exposed one slender, feminine leg.

His body responded so swiftly it nearly wrenched a groan from his dry throat; he managed to get himself under control and return his gaze to hers.

Her smile had fled and her cheeks had flushed with color that came not from the sun. She stuttered, "I—I have not. B-b-been in the sun, I mean." She gestured toward the center of the island. "I built a shelter up—"

"I know where it is."

Her gaze snapped back to his. He didn't bother to explain his comment; he saw by her surprised expression and the deepened color in her cheeks that she knew it had been him, that night in the shadows.

She glanced down at the sand, then back up, and after an uncomfortable moment, she held out the pineapple, her voice dropping to a whisper. "I made this for you."

Still the consummate actress. Whoever she was working for, they had chosen their spy well.

That sharp, cynical, bitter thought blinded him for a second. But he knew her game now. The advantage was his. He could turn the tables on her . . . all he needed to do was play along.

He forced a smile to his lips. "What is it?"

Looking relieved, she took a step closer. "It is made of fruit juice and coconut milk. I think you will like it."

As she held it out, another image assaulted him. Paradise. This was like paradise and she was like Eve with the fated apple. Offering him sin cloaked in sweetness. One taste would be damnation.

It might even be poisoned. Would she kill him, after everything that had happened between them?

He reached out so fast he startled her. He grabbed the pineapple, tilted his head back, and drained the contents in one long draught.

It tasted cool and sweet, soothing on his painful throat.

He wiped his mouth with the back of one hand and passed the emptied pineapple back to her. "Thank you."

She seemed pleased. "I made this, too." She indicated the seashell full of brown paste. "For your burns. They don't seem to be healing well."

Saxon stiffened, barely subduing an oath. Mandara had been a healer. For this lying wench to usurp such an honorable role—that he could not accept.

But the closer he got to Ashiana, the easier it would be to discover where she had hidden the sapphires.

Saxon turned his blistered palms up and she gasped.

"Oh, please, you must let me help you," she said in a small voice.

Help me, he thought bitterly. He buried the sarcasm beneath a pleasant facade and gave her a nod. "Very well."

Walking to the edge of the forest with her at his heels, he sat in the shade beneath a tree. "Go ahead."

She settled herself in front of him, cross-legged, then set the empty pineapple aside and placed the seashell in the sand next to her. The tiger prowled over to them and lay in the shade a few yards away, flicking its tail.

She took his hand gently in both of hers.

Saxon tried to shut down all feeling inside him . . . but the heat of her touch felt more intense than the sun, and the softness of her skin, the nearness of her body, gave him pleasure he did not want. He kept his face a mask of indifference.

At the first touch of her fingers coated with the cool, wet salve, he flinched.

Her gaze flew to his. "I'm sorry. Am I hurting you?"

"No," he ground out.

"I don't mean to. I'm sorry."

She sounded so blasted sincere. He had to bite down hard to stop a sarcastic retort.

Working carefully, delicately, she spread the salve over one wounded hand, then the other. She bent her head and her hair wafted down from her shoulder to tease his bare feet. He tensed. She didn't seem to notice.

Nor did she notice that her position gave him a full

view of her breasts, dangerously close to spilling over the edge of their lacy wrappings.

He squeezed his eyes shut. She knew exactly what she was doing, he reminded himself viciously. She was merely playing her role, the one she had perfected aboard his ship.

But knowing her for a spy didn't abate the desire that pumped through him. She was still the most luscious sample of feminine flesh he had ever seen.

Having her this close, barely clothed, touching him—it all stirred memories of the time on deck, the nights in his bed. The mornings. The hours in between. Her soft nakedness clasping his body as her tight, wet sheath caressed his shaft.

He could not force aside the images fast enough; his manhood pulsed to full arousal. He gritted his teeth and stared down at her silky dark head, bent over him. He could not believe she didn't notice the effect she was having on him.

Taking a deep breath, he looked upward, focusing on the cool green leaves laced overhead. He was not going to be drawn into her trap this time. He would not let her use her body to distract him from the truth of who and what she was—and what he needed to get from her.

The sapphires. He repeated it in his mind like a religious chant. The *sapphires*.

"There," she pronounced, straightening. She placed his hands, palms up, on his knees. "Try not to touch anything for an hour or so."

She moved to his side, apparently missing the scorching reply in his eyes: if he touched anything, she would be the first to know.

She tended his arms, shoulders, and back, humming now. She seemed pleased with herself.

Probably congratulating herself, he thought darkly, on having snared him in her web once again. She would soon discover precisely who was the spider and who the fly in this situation.

Every whisk of her fingers over his skin was torture. He much preferred the physical pain of his injuries. When she had finished with the burns, she came around to sit facing him again, her expression earnest.

"Is that better?"

"Yes," he lied. His wounds hurt less, but he most definitely did not feel better.

She dipped a finger in the salve and nodded toward his stomach. "This worked very well on the cuts on my feet. May I . . . ?"

Saxon worked very hard to remain still and keep his breathing even. "Yes."

The first touch of her fingertips, cool and wet and so close to that part of him that was already throbbing and aroused, nearly proved his undoing. The fact that he *knew* she must be doing it on purpose only made him more determined not to be lured into her seductive games.

He kept his gaze fixed on a point at sea above her head—and tried not to think of tearing off his breeches and pinning her down in the sand.

Her fingers trembled. Suddenly she went still.

He looked down just as she looked up. Both froze. Only inches separated their mouths.

Their breath mingled. Her wide blue eyes glistened with an expression that was as soft as it was surprised. He could smell the warm, clean scent of her hair. Her lips parted, so near to touching his that if he just . . .

She jerked back so quickly that she almost fell over. "I—I think you should finish this." She dropped the shell, her entire body flushed, her breathing fast and shallow.

Before he could say anything, she stood up and stepped away. "I . . . it . . . I'm feeling dizzy. I think it would be best if I got out of the sun. As you said."

"Ashiana!" He didn't have the chance to point out that they had been sitting in the shade. She fled so fast that she left both her pineapple and her tiger behind. Nicobar rose and stretched and trotted after her.

"Damn." Saxon scowled in the direction she had disappeared. He didn't understand the wench at all. One minute she played the seductress; the next, she ran from him as if she hadn't realized, until that moment, the potent effect she had on him.

His mouth curved into a cynical smile. He knew her game. She was baiting him, purposely trying to encourage him to pursue.

And he was ready and willing to comply.

He finished applying the salve to the rest of the cuts on his belly and legs. If there was one thing he had in abundance at the moment, it was time. Time to watch her carefully, time to follow her every movement—time to discover where she had hidden the jewels.

Standing, he picked up the seashell and the empty pineapple. He headed down the path she had taken, toward her little shelter.

Men, Ashiana had decided four days later, were unfathomable creatures put on earth by Vishnu for the sole purpose of driving women mad.

A steady rain had been falling all day, and after less than a minute outside the shelter, her hair and clothes were soaked. It was worth a drenching, though, just to have some time alone. Saxon had disappeared into the forest an hour ago with a stern command that she not leave her—*their*, she corrected herself with a frown—encampment.

She plucked another ripe red fruit from its bush and added it to the newly woven basket balanced on her hip. She had only gone a short distance from the clearing, and besides, she didn't care if he was angry. They were no longer on his ship, and she was tired of following orders.

She supposed she should be pleased by his concern for her safety, but she was not.

Truly, she could not understand him in the least. For the first few days on the island, he had avoided her completely. Now he would not let her out of his sight for a moment. He accompanied her everywhere.

At night, though he refused to share her shelter, he slept beside the fire and watched her until she fell asleep. Whenever she awakened, he was there, on guard.

"I do not need a guard," she had protested after two

days of this. "How do you think I managed on my own before?"

"Quite well," he had replied, eating one of her steamed crabs. "But I want to make up for my earlier behavior."

Ashiana pricked her thumb on a thorn and winced, popping it in her mouth. Make up for his behavior, indeed. It was all most strange. He tended the fire and gathered food, complimented her meals, and let her see to his wounds, which were healing very well. Twice a day, they would walk along the shore, all the way around the island, banking or lighting the signal fires, and looking for ships on the horizon.

He talked with her, smiled now and then when she made a joke, and expressed great concern for her safety.

Not once had he made any physical advances; on the contrary, he flinched away every time they came close to touching.

Something wasn't right and it was making her more nervous every day. She didn't know what to call it, but he seemed different. He wasn't as surly as he had been, but neither was he the gentle, caring man he had been aboard the *Valor.*

The man she missed.

She hadn't realized how much, until these past few days.

Ashiana tipped her chin up and let the rain wash over her face, wishing it could wash away the feelings she had inside. The longing. The loneliness.

That first morning on the beach when she had tended Saxon's injuries, she had wanted *so* very badly to kiss him.

Blushing at the memory, she lowered her head with an unhappy sigh. She could not let herself think such thoughts. It wasn't right. Sooner or later they would be rescued; she felt confident of that now. They would return to the mainland, and from there she would go back to the Maharaja. Back to Rao.

Back to where she belonged. With her clan. Her people. Her betrothed.

She no longer viewed Saxon as the enemy, yet she knew she could not allow herself to wish for . . . for . . .

He was an Englishman. She was an Ajmir princess. Those two simple facts made anything more than a brief, secret truce impossible. They would help one another survive, that was all.

She should be grateful that he no longer desired her. On his ship, it had been too easy to tell herself that she was his prisoner, that she had nowhere to run and no choice in the matter of sharing his bed. She no longer had that excuse.

She went back to picking fruit, letting the warm, steady rain soothe her unease. Their new, chaste relationship made it easier to live with her conscience. She already had enough explaining to do when she returned home.

But, oh, how she had wanted to kiss him.

She pricked her finger on another thorn and muttered an English curse she had heard Saxon use, barely realizing she had said it.

"Not at all suitable language for a lady."

Ashiana whirled, startled. Saxon was only a few feet away and she had never heard him approach. "How long have you been standing there?"

"What are you doing this far from the shelter? In the pouring rain, I might add."

"Gathering fruit." She noticed with annoyance that he had sidestepped her question with a question. He did that often of late. "Where did you go—"

"We should get back." He walked over and took the basket from her hands. "This rain is becoming an official monsoon."

Ashiana had to admit he was right. Already, the downpour had gathered strength until it was almost painful on bare skin. Saxon moved through the trees without giving her a chance to question him further.

As usual. Frowning, Ashiana started after him.

By the time she had followed him back to their encampment, the rain was pounding down so fast and hard it was difficult to stand up. She hunched over against the needle-sharp drops and ran for the shelter.

He held open the woven mat that served as a door, then handed her the basket of fruit after she had ducked inside. Then he let the mat fall shut.

Ashiana stared at the closed entrance dumbfounded, then pushed it open and poked her head out in the rain. "You can't stay outside in the monsoon," she said irritably. "You'll drown. Or at the very least, take ill."

"I'll be fine."

Ashiana had had enough of his annoying attitude. "If you are staying out here, so will I." To prove her point, she stepped out and faced him mutinously.

He glowered at her through the downpour. "Stop being foolish."

"I've every right to be as foolish as you." She folded her arms across her chest.

His gaze dipped to her breasts and Ashiana felt a shaft of heat flash through her, suddenly aware that her wet, thin garments had molded transparently to her body. Perhaps her insistence was not so wise after all—but it was too late to turn back now.

"Get inside," he said roughly.

She opened her mouth to object, but he spun her around, pushed her forward.

And followed her inside.

Ashiana tried to feel pleased with herself instead of nervous. There was just enough room for the two of them sitting down. And Nicobar, of course, though he took up more than his share of space.

"What the devil is he doing in here?" Saxon asked testily.

Ashiana laid a protective hand on Nico's broad, furry head. "I can't make him stay outside in a monsoon."

"I thought you said tigers liked water."

"If he goes, so will I."

"Fine. We'll all stay inside. One big happy family."

He muttered something in English that Ashiana couldn't make out, and tied the mat in place over the opening.

The rain thundered down on the enclosure, but the tightly woven *padauk* mats held. It seemed the three of them would stay reasonably dry. Ashiana toweled herself off with soft leaves from a pile she had collected. She offered a handful to Saxon.

He looked at them dubiously. "You think of everything, don't you." He did not phrase it as a question.

"I am only thinking of your comfort."

"You're very good at that."

It didn't sound like a compliment. Ashiana was growing weary at trying to figure out the hidden layers of meaning that seemed to lace his every sentence. She tossed the leaves to him. "I think you should at least clean off your hands. Your wounds aren't healed yet." In the waning daylight, she looked disapprovingly at the dirt caked on his fingers. "Have you been . . . digging again?"

He picked up the leaves and dried his hands and arms, not looking at her. "Something like that."

He must have been burying another of his crew. Strange, Ashiana didn't remember seeing any . . . anyone during their morning walk on the beach. Perhaps he had noticed the body and avoided drawing her attention to it, not wanting to distress her.

In any event, he didn't seem inclined to discuss it further.

He tossed the crumpled leaves outside. The two of them sat in silence, listening to the increasingly forceful monsoon. They had already eaten their evening meal, and they could not take their usual walk, so there was nothing to do.

Nothing.

Saxon slouched lower against the woven side of the shelter. Ashiana scratched the bridge of Nicobar's nose and wished, for once, that her tiger were a bit smaller. He took up so much of the floor that only inches lay between her and Saxon.

The air felt hot, too, the moisture from the rain misting the air like steam, clinging to her skin.

"Would you like to teach me some more English?"

"No." .

"I only thought that it might make—"

"I said no."

Ashiana stopped trying. If he wanted to return to his surly ways, so be it. That was fine with her. At least it was a familiar mood.

Turning her back on him, she snuggled down into Nicobar's warm, dry fur. Closing her eyes, she listened to the rain pattering on the mats. The steady, rhythmic sound slowly lulled her to sleep.

She awakened some time later when Nicobar moved and her head hit the sandy floor with a thunk. She must have been asleep a long while, for the shelter was now so dark she could not see a hairsbreadth in front of her.

Nico, making small noises, bumped his head against the mat laced over the opening on their side of the shelter.

"Just a moment, Nico," Ashiana whispered, unlacing it to let him out. He slunk into the rain, then sauntered off through the trees. The monsoon still hammered down, making dents in the sandy forest floor. It would be impossible to keep a fire burning tonight to warn predators away, but Nico should be enough. She hoped. Total darkness enveloped the clearing. She let the flap fall back and tied it into place.

Turning, she was surprised to find that Saxon had not awakened. As her eyes adjusted to the pitch blackness, she could just make out his large form sprawled in a rather uncomfortable-looking position on his side. Perhaps it was merely fatigue that had made him irritable. She hoped he would feel better in the morning.

Curling up and pillowing her head on her arm, she started to drift off when a cry from him startled her.

She sat up and looked down at him. "Saxon?"

He seemed to still be asleep, though he was breathing heavily, his chest heaving as though he were running a race. He mumbled something in English, tossing his head.

"Saxon?" She touched his shoulder gently.

Suddenly he cried out as if in pain and sat bolt upright. She gasped but did not move away.

"It is only a nightmare," she whispered soothingly in Hindi.

She had barely finished the sentence when his arms went around her. He embraced her with crushing strength, muttering rapidly in Hindi now, his words slurred as though he were still half-asleep. She could make out only some of what he kept repeating.

"Thank God. You are *alive*. Thank God."

Aware that he was not yet fully awake, Ashiana did not try to pull away. "I . . . I am fine," she whispered.

She wasn't sure he heard her. He stroked her long hair, cupped her face between his hands, fluttered kisses over her forehead, her cheeks. And then his lips found hers.

Longing and heat flooded through her. He kissed her so warmly, so tenderly that she went weak in his arms. This was the man she remembered, the one she had known aboard the *Valor*. The one she had missed so very much.

"Saxon," she sighed as he withdrew his mouth from hers.

He feathered kisses over her nose, her chin, her jaw. He whispered to her in the darkness, his voice husky with an emotion stronger than she had ever heard from him before. *"Meri jaan,* I thought I had lost you."

He had called her "my love."

Ashiana's heart skipped a beat, then raced. She wrapped her arms around his neck and returned his kiss, murmuring against his mouth. "Saxon, yes. Oh, yes. I have missed you so. Ever since we arrived on the island, you have been acting so strangely—"

He made a choked sound and froze.

He snatched his arms away, releasing her so quickly she fell back against the woven side of the shelter.

"Saxon?" she asked softly, confused. "What is wrong? What is it?"

He swore viciously. "What *is* it?" he shouted. "It's enough, that's what it is! *Damn* you!"

Ashiana flinched away from his anger, utterly bewildered. "I do not—"

"Enough of your tricks and your lies!" He grabbed her

by the arms, jerking her up against him. "You are *not* her, do you understand me? You are not!"

"Who?" Ashiana cried. "Who are you talking about?"

"Someone you could *never* measure up to, you lying little wench." His fingers bit into her arms. "I am sick of your deceit! The way you smile so sweetly and offer yourself so freely, when I *know* what you are. It is time for the truth. The *complete* truth."

"I don't understand—"

He shoved her to the ground, so hard it cut off the rest of her sentence. He balanced himself over her and pinned her there, holding her wrists. "Tell me the truth, damn you."

"What truth?" she sobbed. "I don't understand what you are talking about! You are hurting me—"

"The sapphires," he said in a low, dangerous voice. "I want to know who you are and who the hell you're working for and what you've done with the Nine Sapphires of Kashmir."

Chapter 18

Ashiana could not breathe, speak, hear, or even blink in that horrifying moment. The night and the storm closed in around her. Her heart seemed frozen to solid ice. She could only stare up into the darkness, unable to see Saxon's expression—but fully able to feel his fury, as powerful and bruising as his grip on her wrists.

"I—I do not know what you mean!" she sputtered.

"The sapphires," he snarled, leaning closer. "The ones you kept hidden in that blasted tiger's collar."

"You are mad! I do not—"

"Stow it. I've had a bellyful of your lies. I *saw* the jewels. On the ship before the explosion. You had them all along."

Ashiana willed the sandy ground to open up and swallow her. He knew! Vishnu help her, he *knew!* Her mind whirled, trying to think of some way to explain, deny, conceal.

Then a sudden realization struck her: it no longer mattered.

He clearly did not know where she had hidden them. He had no proof that she had them now—only that she had had them before. The sapphires were safe beneath the sea. She had done her duty. She had kept her promise to her clan.

Her heart skipped, fluttered, began to pound, louder than the rain that hammered on the mats. So much suddenly made sense—his changed attitude toward her, his

223

anger, his avoiding her. He was furious because she had tricked him.

In that moment, she wanted but one thing, wanted it with every beat of her racing heart: to be free of it all. Free of her role, free of the deceptions and lies that separated her from Saxon.

Free.

If she could make him understand . . .

"I am sorry." She began quickly, trembling in his grasp. "I never meant for any of this to happen."

He released her suddenly, though he still loomed over her like the storm clouds that loomed over the island. "You are a spy."

He pronounced the word with such contempt, she wanted desperately to deny it. The truth would make him hate her—but a lie would only make everything worse. She squeezed her eyes shut, braced herself, whispered.

"Yes."

With a snarled oath, he backed away. He sat as far from her as was possible in the rain-battered shelter. "Tell me. All of it. And God help me, if you lie—"

"I won't." She shook her head, sitting up gingerly. "I don't have to anymore. The sapphires are gone."

"I warned you, woman—"

"They are *gone,*" she insisted. "I have no reason to lie to you now because I have nothing left to protect! They *were* in Nicobar's collar. You are right about that. But when he came ashore, he was not wearing it. They are lost somewhere at sea."

She vowed to herself that that one lie, utterly necessary, would be the last she ever told him.

He didn't say anything for a moment. She wondered whether he would believe her, and hoped he could not see her shivering in the darkness.

When he spoke again, his voice sounded low and lethally sharp. "Start at the beginning."

Ashiana wrapped her arms around herself, feeling a chill. He sounded so full of anger and outrage . . . and hurt.

For that more than anything, she regretted all that had happened. But wishing would not take back the past weeks. Her only hope in making him understand lay in the truth.

"Part ... part of what you already know is true—"

"Then let's start with whatever the hell your first lie was and work forward from there."

She tried not to feel the sting of his words. "The first truth I must tell you," she said quietly, "is that I am a Rajput princess of the clan Ajmir."

The curse he uttered this time was a particularly short, expressive one she had not heard him use before. "That explains a great deal," he said through clenched teeth. "Knives and torture didn't do the job so they sent a female spy with white skin and blue eyes to lure me into bed."

Ashiana winced; it all sounded so deliberate and ugly put that way. Her role pained her all the more, now that she knew how the Ajmir warriors had tortured him. "I was never—"

"How can you side with the Ajmir when you are English?"

Her temper flared. "I am *not* English! The Ajmir are my people. My clan. My family."

"Your face and your skin tell a different story, *chokri.*"

Ashiana didn't like hearing him call her that; he had not used the word since before ... before their time together on his ship. She must make him understand the perfectly valid reasons for what she had done. Desperation and pride battled within her.

"I *am* an Ajmir princess," she insisted, clenching her fists. "My father was a Portuguese merchant captain. He married an English woman, just as the Emperor told you. That was the true part. But my father did not *sell* me to the Ajmir. They adopted me."

"Ah," Saxon said bitingly. "And there the lies began."

Ashiana shut her eyes as emotion choked up in her throat. "You are not listening! The Ajmir rescued me when my father was murdered by Englishmen. Pirates. I was but six years old and I saw them torture him to death. Heard it and saw it!" Tears, hot and sudden, burned behind her lashes. She opened her eyes and glared into the shadows, thrusting out her left arm, though it was too dark for him to see.

"This tattoo that you have noticed? The scar? It did not come from an Ajmir master. It came from an English whip!"

For once, he remained silent.

"The pirates would have tortured me, too. They wanted to force my father to tell them what he knew about the sapphires. He was an old friend of the Maharaja of the Ajmir. We were near the Andamans and the Maharaja and his men came, b-but . . ." Her voice wavered. The rest of the story spilled out as the tears spilled onto her cheeks. "But they were too late. The English savages killed him and I was left with no one. My mother died on the day of my birth, and when Papa died, I . . ."

She took a breath and forced herself to finish. "I was alone. I had no one. The Maharaja adopted me. The Ajmir gave me everything when I had nothing. They are my *family.*"

"Which explains how you knew so much about these islands. Where to find food. How to make mats from fronds." Saxon struck the side of the shelter with one fist. His voice sounded as harsh as before. "You were never one of the Emperor's slave girls in Daman."

"No, I was not. We only went there to—"

"To get to me," he finished for her.

"To reclaim the sapphire," she corrected. "I never meant harm to you. Please, you must understand, the Maharaja has been as a father to me—"

"So naturally you would do whatever he told you. Lie, steal, poison me—"

"I did *not* poison you! And our cause is honorable! The sapphires are sacred stones. They belong in India. It is the English who are nothing but thieves. You think to come to our land and strip it of all its treasures!"

He still didn't seem to be listening. "So you had this all planned," he said coolly. "The Emperor didn't give you to me by accident. You meant to steal the sapphire and catch a free ride aboard my ship back to the Andamans."

"No," she protested. "I was to take the sacred stone and leave the palace. I never meant for you to fall and hit your head in the pool. And I never meant to go near your ship. Your brother caught me by surprise, and then I was trapped in your cabin, and . . . and . . ."

"And to protect the stones, you gave yourself to me," he said contemptuously. "You used every one of your harem tricks to keep me from asking too many questions about that missing jewel. Well, let me tell you, *chokri*, I've known some whores in my day, but not one of them could match your skill. You kept me hard and kept me from thinking about anything but bedding you."

The insult made her cheeks sting and her jaw drop. "That is not true! I never . . . it was not . . . I was a virgin our first time!" Her anger sizzled to the surface. "And if you will recall, it was *you* who gave me little choice in the matter!"

"The first time," he agreed slowly, grudgingly. "But after that, you made me believe that you wanted me just as much as I wanted you."

Ashiana's face burned with color. How could she deny it? But how could she confirm what he said without proclaiming herself to be the whore he accused her of being?

When she didn't respond, he spoke louder. "And even once we were here, on the island, after the sapphires were 'lost'—"

"They *are* lost," she insisted at the sarcastic way he said it.

"After, as you said, you had nothing left to protect, you *still* kept up the act. Coming to me with your smiles and your fluttering lashes and your blasted pineapple. Wanting me to believe that you cared about me. Why didn't you just stop pretending?"

His booming voice echoed in the humid air. The drumming of the rain sounded deafening on the mats overhead.

Ashiana braced her hands on the dirt floor. Her fingers sank into the sugary sand. "I was not pretending," she said quietly. "Not now, and not before." It was agonizingly difficult to say that aloud, but she could not let him believe that her feelings had merely been part of her plan.

He whistled, low and soft and mocking. "You are even better at this than I thought."

"I am telling you the truth."

"The truth?" he ground out. "The truth is that you are an Ajmir princess. The English killed your father. The English threaten your people and their treasure. The *truth* is that you despise every last one of us."

She ducked her head, feeling an uncomfortable tingling that began at the nape of her neck and danced down her shoulders. "I have learned," she whispered, "not to . . . not to hate *all* the English."

She looked up, wishing fervently that she could see his expression. He remained only a shadow among darker shades of black.

"I let you fool me once," he said coldly. "It won't happen again."

"I have no reason to lie to you anymore. I tended your wounds because I do care. I *care* about what happens to you. And I think . . ." She almost couldn't say it. "I think you care about me."

A strangled laugh choked out of him.

It hurt her worse than anything he had ever said or done to her. Worse than if he had struck her to the ground with his fist.

She blinked back tears. "You do," she insisted. "You risked your life to save me when the ship went down. That was *after* you knew I was a spy."

His laughter stopped.

Her hope strengthened. "Why? Why would you have done that if you truly hated me? And why would you have come to my shelter that night? I think you wanted to see if I was all right."

"I stumbled across the clearing," he snapped. "I had no idea you were there."

Ashiana didn't remind him that she had had a fire burning at the time. "But why—"

"Stow it. Save your bloody *whys*. I don't know why. Reflex. Temporary madness. Sublime stupidity. Why else would I risk my neck for a thieving, deceitful little wench like you? You toss around words like 'honorable' and 'caring' when every second since you met me has been a fraud—"

A bump on the side of the shelter interrupted him. Ashiana recognized the low *puh-puh-puh* sound accompanied by scratching. Grateful for the distraction, she unfastened the mat that covered the opening and let her tiger in, wet fur and all.

"And what about him," Saxon said scathingly. "I suppose he's part of the whole scheme. That story about him being a gift from the Emperor and 'accidentally' on my ship was one more lie."

Ashiana wrapped her arms around Nicobar's neck, protecting and seeking solace. "Nicobar *was* on the ship by accident. But he was not a gift from the Emperor. He was a gift from—" She stopped herself suddenly.

"From whom?"

Frustration and hurt made her blurt out the truth before she could think. "From the Maharaja's eldest son, Prince Rao. My betrothed."

For the span of one heartbeat, Saxon remained mute.

Then he released a breath between his teeth with a low sound from his throat that made Ashiana shiver. When he finally spoke, he used a tone she had never heard from him before, anger and disbelief dangerously laced with something she didn't dare believe was jealousy.

"A gift from your *what?*"

"My betrothed," she repeated, peevishly wanting to hurt him as he had hurt her.

"Really?" he said silkily. "And do you suppose that this future husband of yours is going to be pleased to learn that I've had you? I doubt he'll accept his enemy's leavings."

The crude insult struck home, for she had asked herself that very question and could not answer. "*He* is a prince. A man who honors his word and his people. He has always accepted me for what I am! And he loves me!"

Saxon reached out, so swift and silent she didn't have time to evade him. He ignored Nicobar's growl of warning, grabbed her arm, and yanked her to him.

"How nice for both of you. I'm sure you'll be very happy together. In fact, I'd like to give you a wedding gift. Not that I'm actually going to *give* it to you—it's just something for you to think about." His voice took on an icy edge that terrified her. "I still have one of the sapphires."

Ashiana gaped at him in disbelief. "No. No! How *could* you?"

"It fell out of that blasted tiger's collar and I found it in the straw before the explosion. I've got it and I'm keeping it. Tell *that* to your betrothed while you're busy explaining how you lost your innocence." He shoved her away. "Tell him how you gave all for the cause. Then tell him you're right back where you started from."

"You have to give it back!"

His laugh mocked her. "Why? What does it matter now? The others are gone, lost at sea—aren't they?"

"Yes," she said quickly. "Yes, but you cannot be so stubborn. That sapphire belongs to my people. Please, you must give it up."

"I'm supposed to hand it over to you? You and Prince Accepting? After all the lies and the tricks and the hell you've put me through? *Chokri,* if you haven't figured it out by now, let me spell it out for you: you are the *enemy.*"

"No. Oh, no, no, no . . ." Ashiana hung her head, feeling utterly defeated. She could not make him understand. She had told him the truth, told him of her father's death, of her love for her adopted family, of all the reasons she had done what she had done. None of it mattered to him. And why should it?

She did not matter to him.

"Why?" she sobbed. *"Why* are the sapphires so important to you?"

He went rigid. "I told you to save your questions. You tricked me once. You won't get a second chance."

She could hear him untying the mat that covered the opening on the far side of the shelter.

"You cannot be that greedy and selfish!" she cried.

He stepped outside. She could barely hear his reply over the rain that lashed the forest.

"You have no idea what I can be."

Ashiana felt as if something had just been torn in two within her, ripped asunder to leave behind only emptiness and pain beyond any she had known. "Then you are no better than all the other English! You are nothing but an arrogant, heartless thief, without honor!" Her throat constricted. "You are not the man I thought you were!"

"That makes us even."

He let the mat slap back into place and left her alone in the darkness and the rain and her tears.

Chapter 19

A week in the rains left Saxon feeling thoroughly soaked and thoroughly bad-tempered. Nothing could lighten his mood, not even the fact that this was the first dry day since the monsoon had struck. The clouds abated just enough to let the late-afternoon sun shine through.

The storm had made mincemeat of the lean-to he had built from leaves and branches; it had also made cooking next to impossible, and he was hungry for a hot meal. Deciding to do some fishing, he crafted a pole from bamboo and some line from the fibers of a vine; for a hook, he ripped a nail from a washed-up plank and beat it into shape with a rock. Grasping the makeshift rod in one fist, he strode through the dripping undergrowth toward the beach.

Living alone again after being in Ashiana's encampment had been harder than he would have guessed. And it wasn't just because she was better at finding the choicest edibles and building a bloody perfect, dry little shelter. To his complete self-disgust, he found that he missed her.

Twice he had started toward her encampment, only to turn back a few yards away, her words clawing through him.

"Prince Rao . . . my betrothed . . . he loves me!"

Well, let him have her, Saxon thought viciously, knocking aside a vine that blocked his path. He would have nothing more to do with the wench. She was exactly what he had called her: a whore, sharing herself so freely and eagerly with him when she had already pledged herself to another man.

It was only one more reason to leave her alone—if her treachery wasn't already enough. Which it was.

Did the chit have so little regard for the marriage promise she had made to this bloody prince of hers? Did she *ever* keep her word, to anyone? Did her damned duty mean so much to her that she would do anything for it—even lay with the enemy?

He had no answers. All he had was one gut-clenching certainty: she was not the kind of woman he wanted. She was not innocent and kind and sweet and devoted to one man.

She was not Mandara.

Saxon gripped the bamboo pole and welcomed the sun's stifling heat as he stalked through the forest. None of it mattered, he told himself. Her lies did not matter.

Ashiana did not matter.

Not even the sapphires mattered as much anymore.

He had scoured the island from stem to stern, digging at every logical hiding place he could think of, at every spot she had ever shown any interest in. All he found were mud and rocks and roots—not a sign of the sapphires. It was just possible she had been telling the truth about that. They might very well *be* gone.

He had had all nine in his hands, for one second on his ship. He had felt that strange bolt of energy. He could only hope it meant something, that the brief reunion of all nine might have done some good.

He had separated the sapphires again, but at least the curse would be on his own head now. That he could live with.

The path opened onto the beach. Determined to enjoy a few hours in the sun, he walked across the warm sand and into the water. He had only gone a short way out when he saw that his pleasant afternoon was not to be.

Glancing to his left, he saw her, in the water around a curve in the shore.

She was about fifty yards away, but close enough so he

could make out what she was doing. She stood poised over the waves, her back to him, her petticoat knotted up around her hips and a net in her hands.

A net. How the devil had she made a net?

And of all the buggering beaches on the island, why did she have to choose the same one as him? It was bad enough that they had thought alike in choosing to go fishing; this was too much.

A host of emotions simmered through him. He ruthlessly throttled them. All but one.

His blood boiled with a heat that had nothing to do with anger or the sun. She had tied her tattered skirt up to keep it out of the water—and revealed every perfect inch of her creamy legs and thighs. Even at this distance, the sight made his lower body tighten in response. The little wanton had no modesty at all.

She suddenly bent closer to the water and cast her net, and the short skirt bared her smooth, pale backside . . . so round, so soft, so vulnerable.

Desire shafted through him. Pure, male lust unlike any he had ever felt. In seconds he was hard, groaning with a hunger heated by memories, sharpened by days of abstinence, made raw by the knowledge that she would soon belong to another.

That thought struck him like a fist in the gut. He shoved it aside and feasted on the look of her as she straightened: her thin garments, now soaked and transparent, the ends of her black hair, wet, that clung to her hips, and the lush white curves of her buttocks, framed by the bunched-up petticoat.

He shuddered in the grip of overpowering need. Another memory lanced through him—of her in the water, in the pleasure pavilion, when she had teased him, half-naked in his arms. She had been acting then. Had thwarted him with her games and her tainted kiss.

But there were no poisoned candies here. No Ajmir. No Emperor. No one to rescue her.

Nothing but the two of them and the sun-warmed water.

He turned, raised his arm, threw his fishing pole back toward the beach; like a javelin, it stabbed the sand.

Dropping beneath the surface, he swam toward her, his body a blaze that could not be cooled even by the sea.

Ashiana's first cast had caught nothing.

Gathering in her net with a frustrated sigh, she spread it between her hands. The waves lapped about her bared thighs. She stood still for several minutes until the fish returned, flashing around her ankles.

Concentrating intently, she waited for the moment when her supper would be unsuspecting.

She heard a splash behind her and stiffened. Moving only her head, she looked about the inlet and didn't see anything. Still, a little frisson of fear went through her. There were sharks in these waters. Saltwater crocodiles. Barracudas.

She glanced down and searched the clear sea all around her, her heart thudding. It would be unusual for them to hunt this close to shore in daylight. She saw nothing but the bright-blue fish. Exhaling slowly, she tried to relax. Her arms were growing tired, but she was not going to give up.

Gripping the net, she returned to her crouched pose.

She was about to cast again when suddenly the fish all darted away. She felt movement in the water behind her.

Turning, screaming, she tried to leap to one side. Something warm behind her ankle tripped her.

Strong hands caught her before she could fall. Ashiana realized only then that the shape bursting up out of the surf was Saxon! And it had been his leg tripping her.

Her startled cry choked out as he lifted her from the water with one steely arm and crushed her to his wet body. His other hand speared into her hair. She tried to draw a breath and drew his breath instead as he sealed his mouth over hers. He molded their lips together in a deep, hot, ravaging kiss that sent a shattering wave of sensation through her entire body.

Her surprise and alarm fled under the power of his

passion for her. His tongue slicked over her lips, thrust inside, slid over her tongue until she tasted nothing but him—salty, tangy, masculine. He explored, caressed, claimed every curve of her mouth with that wet, darting part of him.

Whimpering under the forcefulness of his onslaught, she tried to pull away, needing to ask a hundred questions, but his hand in her hair held her still as his mouth worked over hers, hungry, bruising. His thick beard rasped the tender skin of her jaw and cheek. A tremor cascaded through her that left her trembling with desire. She heard—felt—him groan in response.

Locked against him, lost in him, she could no longer find the will to resist. Ashiana pressed her hands against his shoulders, but her fingers, palms, wrists all felt shivery and weak.

Had he missed her as she had missed him? Had he been as lonely as she these past days? Had he ached for this too?

Was he at last willing to understand, to forgive?

She knew that Saxon had never been able to express his feelings with words; his bold caresses were his way of calling peace, of bringing them back together.

Sighing into his mouth, Ashiana buried her hands in his thick blond hair, holding on for all she was worth. She returned his kiss in full measure, opening her mouth fully to allow him in, her tongue dueling with his.

He made a growling, primitive sound deep in his throat. Still holding her captive against him, he slowly lowered her body, rubbing her against his dripping, naked chest, until her feet returned to the sandy sea floor. The water sluicing off him soaked her. Bending his head, he captured the peak of one breast in an openmouthed kiss, suckling hard through wet cotton and lace. Ashiana cried out as tendrils of fire, lit by his tongue, unfurled within her.

He suddenly yanked her *kor-set* down from her breasts. The delicate fabric, damaged by salt water and days of sun, gave way beneath his hands with a tearing sound.

REFUND

IN OR CANCEL

ARD

ARRIVAL DATE: _____

ARRIVAL TIME: _____ ROOM #: _____

LENGTH OF STAY: _____

NAME: _____

ADDRESS: _____ ZIP: _____

NO. IN PARTY: _____ NO. OF ROOMS: _____ TYPE OF ROOMS: _____

HOW TAKEN: ☐ PHONE / ☐ VERBAL / ☐ MAIL   DATE TAKEN: _____

RES. TAKEN BY: _____   PHONE #: (_____) _____

PAID BY: CASH   CK   VI   MC   AX   DIS   DIN   AMT. PAID: _____

CARD #: _____   EXP. DATE: _____

REC. BY: _____   DATE PAID: _____ CC AUTH. #: _____

Ashiana flinched, filled with a sudden, uneasy feeling that she had not guessed his motives correctly.

This felt frighteningly like the first time he had taken her.

"Saxon?" Ashiana wanted to slow down, wanted the caring, the tenderness she had felt with him. She tried to pull free but his arms were too strong and his hands too fast. His palms whisked over the wet, taut peaks of her breasts, a second before his tongue found one bared nipple, drawing a gasp from her lips. His teeth grazed her, ungently.

"Saxon?" she asked, suddenly afraid. "Saxon, wait—"

Her plea ended in a ragged breath as his blunt fingers sought the triangle between her thighs and thrust into her dampness without warning.

A wordless cry tore from her throat. He urged her hips forward, his arm about her back, holding her still while he delved into her. Shocked, she looked into his eyes and saw . . .

Nothing.

His gaze was flat, distant, utterly emotionless.

Bitterness replaced the joy she had felt only moments ago. His contempt for her had not changed! This was not a warm, healing reunion for him; it was a cold, physical act. He was using her, like the whore he had proclaimed her to be.

She pressed her fists against his broad shoulders. "Saxon, please—"

His mouth silenced her as his arm shifted to subdue her struggles. Ashiana choked out a protest deep in her throat, but he held her so tightly that he fastened her arms to her sides. Even through his breeches, she could feel his heat, his urgency, the hardness of his arousal—and knew she was no match for his physical power.

Having known his tenderness before made his unfeeling methods now all the more anguishing. Her hope shattered into painful shards. She was a naive fool! She had revealed her feelings to him, but he could not settle for throwing them back in her face. He had to dishonor her, dishonor all they had shared, in the worst way.

She was nothing to him. Nothing but a female body on which to ease his lust. He did not care for her at all.

He tore his mouth from hers and buried his face in the tangled hair against her neck. He didn't even look at her as he positioned himself between her thighs and tore at the fastenings of his breeches. She was crying now, silent tears that came not from fear or pain, but from sorrow. Holding her waist in both broad hands, he lifted her up and brought her down against him in one swift movement.

His sudden entry cut off her sobs. She inhaled sharply, her head tipping back, her hair dragging in the water.

His fingers wrapped through the tangled strands at her hips. His mouth trailed over her bared throat, making her shudder even as she strained away from him. He thrust himself into her, taking her hard and fast.

She cried out as every movement of his hips took him more deeply within her, his rampant maleness filling and stretching her. To her deep and abiding shame, Ashiana felt a gathering storm of pleasure building, spinning, winding upward from deep inside her.

But the lightning flash of release never came.

A shout tore from his throat as he exploded within her, pulsing and flowing. His thrusts gradually slowed, then stopped, but he still held her clasped against him. She could feel him breathing heavily against her neck. All she wanted in that moment was to run, run as fast as she could and never look upon him again.

But when she tried to push free, he would not let her go.

On the contrary, he held her closer. She could feel him shaking. His arms tightened around her until she could scarce breathe.

The next instant, he suddenly lifted her from him, coldly disengaging his body from hers, and set her on her feet. He did not say a word, did not touch her again, did not look at her.

Head bent, he refastened his breeches, then turned and strode through the water, toward the beach. His rigid back and broad shoulders glistened in the sun as he strode away. Having taken his pleasure of her, he left her standing there, her entire body shivering, her *kor-set* and *pet-ti-koot* in disarray.

Her throat constricted. Tears came in a rush, bursting forth with all the hurt and shame she felt. He had told her in no uncertain terms what he felt for her. Contempt. She was nothing to him. *Less* than nothing!

How could he be so cold? How could he close himself off from her so completely, after what they had shared aboard his ship?

Unless lust was all he had ever felt for her.

Ashiana fell to her knees in the water and covered her face with her hands, sobbing, unable to look at him. He was *incapable* of feeling anything more. Incapable of caring, of loving, of feeling *any* gentle emotion.

Of forgiving.

And she would never forgive him! Not after this!

A sudden burst of anger and humiliation made her raise her head and shout a single word after him.

"Why?"

Chapter 20

Peering into the light morning rain, Saxon stood at the water's edge for half an hour and still could not believe his eyes.

It took that long to grasp that he was not seeing a low bank of clouds, a whale, or an illusion brought on by sleepless nights. After almost thirty days on this accursed chunk of sand, he was indeed seeing the one thing he most wished to see.

A ship.

He blinked, wiped the rain from his eyes, stared.

A ship. There was no mistaking it.

Doubt and disbelief instantly gave way to hope, which just as quickly turned back into doubt. From the crow's nest, the ship's watchmen might see the tiny island—but they wouldn't stop here. Saxon turned, thinking fast, tension singing through every muscle. He ran toward the trees.

His signal fires had been doused daily by the monsoon; they would be useless. Blast the weather anyway. His— their—only hope lay in the reflecting device Ashiana had made. *If* the sun that occasionally broke through the clouds would cooperate.

He raced through the forest, tearing aside every bit of greenery in his way, ignoring the path and taking the most direct route to her encampment.

Even as he crashed through the undergrowth, he felt a cold knot in the pit of his stomach at the thought of seeing her again. He had avoided her since their encounter in the water. He told himself it was because he still felt furious with her. Nothing could quell that.

But beneath it lay anger at himself. Anger that he had no control over his actions whenever he came within yards of her. Anger that she still held some mysterious power over him, even after everything that had happened. Power to make him think of her. Of nothing *but* her.

And the far more startling, disturbing power to make him feel.

Days of lightning, pounding rain, and thunder could not block out her tears and her shouted *why*. They had haunted him, slashed him more deeply than the *Valor's* shattered glass.

Long, brooding hours of denial had finally forced him to admit—to himself—that some of her barbs had been on the mark: if he blamed her for breaking her betrothal vow, he had to blame himself as well. He had taken her roughly, ruthlessly, had never given her a choice in the matter, both that first time on his ship and here in the sea.

None of that, however, changed the fact that she was an Ajmir spy, a deceitful wench, a liar born, who would say or do anything to carry out her duty.

Determined to hide his vexing thoughts, Saxon buried them under an indifferent expression as he broke through the trees and into the clearing where her shelter lay.

He jerked to a halt, dripping rain and sweat. His brusque greeting died on his lips.

The little structure was not there anymore.

Only the poles remained, bent and twisted by the storm, an eerie bamboo skeleton, the mats torn away. One glance took in the rest: her food supplies were missing. Her shells and baskets had been broken, ripped apart, scattered. Animal tracks littered the sand.

Fear sleeted through him with one horrible thought: she had been set upon by predators—and he hadn't been here to protect her.

He moved toward the ravaged shelter, his steps wooden.

As soon as he had a closer look, however, his anxiety faded.

There were no traces of blood, no signs of a struggle. The tracks had been mostly washed away by rain, but the ones he could make out were only her small footprints and the tiger's broad paw-prints.

The other marks made him suspect langur monkeys as the culprits who had played havoc with the baskets and shells. On the far side of the camp, he discovered a long scrape in the sand that led into the trees. It looked as if the mats had been bundled together and dragged away.

She had done this. She had taken everything and left in a hurry. Probably so that he could not find her again.

Shaking off the last of the chill that had seized him, he relaxed and cursed himself. What the hell was wrong with him that he could still feel fear or anything else for the treacherous little *chokri,* after everything she had done?

Thoroughly annoyed with himself, he searched for the signaling device. He found it leaning against a tree, either left behind or forgotten. Picking it up, he decided he had more pressing matters to deal with at the moment than a runaway spy. He would track her down later.

With one last scowl about the abandoned camp, he started back toward the shore.

He could only hope that the shiny bits of metal from the *Valor* would be enough to catch the meager sunlight.

Two hours of searching for her turned up nothing.

"Ashiana!" Saxon tried not to let his frustration show through in his voice for fear of scaring her off again. "Ashiana! I've sighted a ship. They saw my signal and they're coming for us."

He had crisscrossed the island's forest in a grid pattern, but could find no clue as to where she had gone. He had caught a glimpse of her tiger, prowling among the trees, but there was no sign of Ashiana. The scrape of the dragged mats had ended in a tangle of vegetation—as if she had vanished into the air.

He was beginning to worry, and that irritated him.

"Ashiana!" He stopped and leaned one hand against a huge gray *sal* tree. At least it had stopped raining, for the moment. "Where the bloody blazes have you gone off to?" he growled under his breath.

"What kind of ship is it?"

Saxon straightened and spun about. Her disembodied voice seemed to come from the humid air itself. He turned fully around and saw nothing.

"Look up," the voice suggested.

Tilting his head back, Saxon sighted his quarry at last.

From high in another giant *sal* several yards away, she peeked at him over the edge of . . . he wasn't sure what it was, but it appeared to be some sort of platform of sticks and bamboo lashed together with vines.

How the devil she had constructed it up there—much less why she hadn't settled for simply moving to a new location—was utterly beyond him. She had moved her entire shelter, more or less, into the tree. It must have taken days of strenuous work.

He felt a surge of admiration at her ingenuity, and at the unexpected strength that lay beneath her delicate exterior. He ruthlessly subdued the unwelcome feeling.

"It's the kind of ship that's going to get us off this blasted sand pile," he said sarcastically. "Who the devil cares what kind of ship it is?"

"How do I know there is a ship at all?" she asked warily. "You might be lying, just to lure me down there for your own . . . purposes."

"I don't have time to argue. The ship will be here any moment."

"You haven't answered my question."

"If you want me to come up there and get you, I will."

"I doubt that you could," she shot back.

His short fuse already sizzling, Saxon stalked over to the tree, but was forced to a halt when confronted with the thick, smooth trunk. There didn't seem to be any footholds, and it was much too big around to shimmy up. How in the *hell* had she gotten up there?

He stepped back and glared up at her. "What the devil

made you want to live up there with the monkeys in the first place?"

"I much prefer their company to yours."

"It's a deserted island, for God's sake. You didn't need to move into the trees to avoid me."

"I did not wish to be ambushed again!"

Her declaration knifed through him. He finally understood what she was saying: she had gone to all this work, all this time and trouble, probably strained herself to exhaustion—solely to save herself from his physical attentions.

The thought struck him like a blow, right to the center of his chest. Had he hurt her that badly?

He clenched his jaw, willing the guilt and other, softer feelings away.

"Ashiana, come down from there," he said gently. "There *is* a ship. They might be here already." He paused, adding, "I give you my word I won't touch you."

"Your *word*," she choked out. "I doubt your word will protect me!"

"How about if I tie my hands behind my back?"

"That I would like to see."

"I could also leave you here." Saxon knew he didn't mean it, but apparently she believed him.

He heard her gasp. "You would, wouldn't you?"

At the sadness in her voice, he almost took it back. He gritted his teeth and let the threat stand.

Her face disappeared from the edge of the platform.

A moment later he heard her moving about. Then an airy whoosh and a rustle of wet leaves overhead splattered him with raindrops.

To his utter amazement, she appeared on the ground at the base of a tree a short distance away, clinging to a vine she had wrapped about her waist.

He blinked, again feeling grudging admiration at her daring. "Where did you learn to do that?"

"I was raised on an island much like this one. You may not believe anything I say, but it was the truth." Letting go of the vine, she stood poised to run, as if he were a predator more terrible and unpredictable than her tiger.

Saxon crossed his arms over his chest. There was that word again. *Truth.* "Are all Ajmir princesses taught to swing through the trees?"

"I was adopted."

She seemed to think that should explain it. Abandoning the subject, he stepped toward her. She backed away, eyes narrowed.

"I am not going to attack you," he said, feeling irritated beyond all reason that she should be so cautious of him.

"Pardon me if I find it difficult to believe what you say."

She remained tense but did not flinch as he came near; he knew it must take courage to face the one thing she found more threatening than the worst monsoon or a tiger's claws.

Him.

It was only when he came closer that he could see her clearly in the shifting light that penetrated the jungle. She looked drawn and tired. Dark circles showed beneath her lower lashes. Her skin had lost any hint of freckles or sun, as if she had not ventured beyond her sanctuary. And he didn't have to touch her to know that she had lost weight; his eyes knew her body that well.

"Are you all right?" The concerned words slipped out before he could snatch them back.

"Oh, stop," she said with a humorless laugh. "You have already done enough. Didn't it make you feel better?"

He instantly regretted his soft inquiry. "Didn't *what* make me feel better?"

"The way you tricked me, just as you *think* I tricked you," she accused. Her blue eyes, so large against her pale skin, suddenly glistened. "When you took me in your arms and kissed me, you made me believe that . . . that you cared for me. But then you showed me quite clearly that you do not!" Her voice wavered, then strengthened. "Did it not make you feel better to take your vengeance on me?"

Saxon felt as if she had just slashed him with a blade of ice. Vengeance? She thought he had sought her that day to take *vengeance?* That had had nothing to do with it. It was desire. It was hunger that could not be sated. It was the fact that he had no control over his response to her merest presence.

. . . That even knowing her for a lying spy, knowing she belonged to another, he still could not keep his mind, his eyes, or his hands from her. He wanted her even now.

But he wasn't about to tell her that. He was not going to apologize. He was not going to trust her. Not her. Wanting could be ignored. *And that was all it was, damn it. Wanting.*

"It would be impossible," he said rigidly, "to have any measure of vengeance for what you have done, little thief."

"I think you managed quite well." A tear slid down her cheek and she whirled away from him, clearly not wanting him to see. But it was too late.

That single tear had burned him. He couldn't even speak.

With her back turned, she railed at him. *"You* are the thief here, not me. Let us at least be clear on that. Call me what you will, but your reasons and your actions have been no better than mine!"

Saxon refused to listen to her accusations. "I did not spend two hours tracking you down to argue. Are you coming or do I have to carry you?"

He reached for her. She shied away and spun about, her eyes glacial. "I can walk quite well, my lord." She addressed him frostily. "I do *not* need to be carried."

With a low curse, Saxon turned and started back the way he had come. But he found himself walking slowly so that she would not have to tire herself keeping up.

"Your entire problem," she commented as she followed him, "is that you seem to think that you are better than me. But then arrogance is a common trait among you English."

She said "you English" with brittle contempt, classing

him with the worst of his people, purposely trying to irritate him.

To his unending annoyance, it worked.

"You will soon have ample opportunities for comparison," he tossed back.

"Why is that?"

He glanced at her over his shoulder. "The ship that is coming to our rescue. You asked what kind it was. The answer is that it is English."

Saxon set Ashiana down on her feet a few yards from the beach, within the forest shadows.

He dodged her open hand as it came at him, grabbing her wrist. "I'll have no more of that, damn it." His left cheek already stung from where she had slapped him when he picked her up. He had caught her the second she tried to flee to her treetop sanctuary.

They stood frozen, glaring at one another. Carrying her in his arms had been sheer torture; her tattered garments covered little, and the heat of her body had seared right through to his. Her wriggling efforts to get away only enflamed him further. He was breathing raggedly—and it had nothing to do with carrying her feather-light form all the way across the island.

"You are hateful," she hissed, trying unsuccessfully to wrench her arm from his grasp.

Saxon didn't have time to argue her opinion; one glance at the harbor revealed two white boats lancing through the waves, headed for the beach. He could see uniformed Royal Navy officers and seamen in each—heavily armed.

They were only being cautious, not knowing who had signaled or what awaited them. The ship that had anchored in the inlet, Saxon noted to his relief, was what he had guessed from a distance: a modest-sized fourth-rate. He had almost feared that the gods had tossed Greyslake into his path once more, but it seemed they had something else in mind for him.

He turned back to Ashiana, still holding her wrist. "I want you to stay put," he commanded. Capturing her chin with his free hand, he tipped her face up and emphasized his order with a steely gaze. "Don't let them know that you're here until I call for you."

He could tell by her mutinous glare that she meant to run the minute he let her go.

"I will now have the help of several dozen Englishmen to track you down," he warned. "And it's not that big an island."

The defiance melted right out of her at his threat, though her eyes still expressed in no uncertain terms that she wished him condemned to Shiva's darkest lair. "As you command, my lord."

It bothered him that she refused to call him by his given name.

It shouldn't, but it did.

He let her go abruptly. "These are not the same men that attacked the *Valor,* so everything should be fine. But if anything happens to me, run for that bloody tree-house of yours and don't come down until they're gone."

Her eyes widened and she started to say something, but she stopped herself. Her expression returned to cool disinterest. "Very well."

"And do *not* make trouble." He turned to walk out of the trees.

"I will do whatever I must to get you out of my life, *angrez,*" she assured him in an icy whisper.

He stopped in his tracks, his back to her, and retorted in the same tone, "Believe me, *chokri,* the feeling is mutual."

Exasperated by the way she provoked him, Saxon clamped down on his temper and went down to the shore to greet their rescuers. He glanced back over his shoulder, casually, just once. Ashiana stood where he had left her.

Leading the dozen men up the beach was a tall young officer wearing a perfectly spiffed blue-and-white uniform, every gold button polished to a high gloss. With his white wig, keen green eyes, and gleaming saber, he looked like he had just stepped out of a Royal Navy muster poster. Saxon held out his hand. "Greetings, Captain. You're a welcome sight."

"Good God!" The man's wary expression became a smile. "An Englishman! Of what ship, sir?"

"The Indiaman *Valor*. She went down about a month ago."

The captain shook Saxon's hand vigorously. "Storm?"

"Fire." Saxon saw no sense in making accusations—against another Navy captain—that he could never prove.

"Blasted bad luck. We hadn't heard a word of it, Mr. . . . ?"

"Captain," Saxon corrected. "Saxon D'Avenant."

The man's eyebrows shot up to the brim of his tricorne. "Of the D'Avenant shipping family? The late Duke of Silverton's son?"

"The same."

The man sheathed his sword and shook Saxon's hand again. "Captain Andrew Bennett, of His Majesty's sloop *Crusader*. An honor to meet you, sir."

"The honor appears to be mine—isn't it a bit unusual for a Navy captain to leave his ship for a shore party?"

"I insist on taking whatever risks my men take." Bennett smiled rakishly. "I trust you won't inform the Admiralty of my nefarious lack of respect for regulations."

Saxon laughed, feeling an immediate kinship with the man. "You can trust me on that score." He found himself shaking hands and accepting introductions from the other officers before he could get any more information out of them. "If you hadn't heard of the wreck, that means none of my men returned to the mainland?"

"Not that I know of." Bennett shook his head with regret. "But we came out of Fort St. David on the east coast over a month ago."

"Lucky for me that you came this way. What's your destination?"

"Home, Captain. And it's not luck at all. In another week or so, ships in these lanes will be thick as pickpockets at St. Bartholomew's Fair. Half the Navy has been ordered back to England. Trouble with the French." His expression turned grim. "Afraid we haven't time to turn back and take you to the mainland. Home will have to do instead."

Home. God, how long had it been since he had seen Silverton Park? Saxon nodded, slowly. There was no reason for him to go to the Andamans now; the sapphires weren't there. And if fourth-rates like the *Crusader* had been ordered home, he could guess that the more powerful third-rates would be on their way back as well.

Including the *Phoenix.* England was where he would find Greyslake, he thought with a violent shot of anticipation.

"Home will do quite well," Saxon said at last.

"Excellent."

"Are you the only survivor, sir?" one of the officers asked.

"No, there is one other." Saxon turned toward the forest, tensing. "Ashiana?"

She stepped out of her hiding place hesitantly and stopped a few paces beyond the trees, eyes wide at the gathering of uniformed men arrayed before her.

Saxon heard the quick intake of masculine breath all around him. Possessiveness seared through him. He cursed himself for having damaged her corset; she was trying to cover herself, and her tumbled hair helped, but the Navy men were getting more of an eyeful than they would in a brothel.

He silently cursed her as well, for the innocent way she blushed and dropped her gaze to the sand. Now that she had an audience again, she had apparently decided to renew her act.

"It's all right," he said to her in clipped Hindi. "Come on."

Trembling, she walked slowly forward.

Bennett exhaled and spoke in a dry, wondering whisper. "This would be your ... wife?"

"Hardly."

The sarcastic denial was no sooner past his lips than Bennett doffed his coat. "A passenger on your ship, then?"

"Something like that."

Bennett crossed the sand and met Ashiana halfway. Saxon felt a gnawing in his gut as he watched the Navy captain gently wrap his large coat around Ashiana's slim shoulders; he buttoned it at her throat, smiling down at her. She looked up at him with an expression of surprise and gratitude.

Saxon had to clench his fists against the sudden impulse to choke the life from his rescuer.

None of the men around him noticed his reaction; they were too busy being entranced.

Bennett bowed, took Ashiana's hand lightly in his, and kissed it. "A pleasure to make your acquaintance, my lady. Captain Andrew Bennett at your service. The *Crusader* and every man aboard are yours to command."

Saxon ground his teeth at the display of gallantry. "She doesn't speak much English."

Bennett gave him a perplexed look. "Why, she looks as British as a queen! What are the lady's origins?"

Saxon wrestled with the urge to say that she was not a lady by any stretch of the imagination. She was about to spend months at close quarters with these men; it was wisest to afford her whatever protection possible.

"She was born of English parents but raised in India." His gaze settled on Ashiana's bright eyes, her glossy hair, her full lips—and knew he was the only man present looking at her face. The rest kept subtly glancing at her legs: bare, tempting curves that peeked out from the bottom of Bennett's blue coat.

Saxon decided to embellish the tale.

"Her father was an earl, I believe. From Kent or something like that. Quite wealthy. Crème de la crème. She was separated from her family at birth. They'll be thrilled to have her back. Probably see that you receive a knighthood, at the very least." His eyes met Ashiana's. "Beyond her parentage, to be honest, I really don't know her all that well."

He doubted she understood either his words or the undertone of irony.

"Have you any belongings you need to gather?" Bennett addressed Saxon, but kept his gaze on Ashiana. "We really should be off. No time to tarry when the King calls, you know."

"We'll be along straightaway," Saxon assured him. "Let me speak to her in private and see if she has *anything* at all that she would like to take along."

He knew the irony of that statement would also be lost on Ashiana.

With one last bow, Bennett finally deprived himself of her presence and ordered his men to ready the boats.

Saxon crossed the sand in three strides and took Ashiana by the elbow, keeping a smile pasted on his face while his fingers dug into the thick navy-blue wool of her sleeve. Bennett's uniform swamped her, covering her from neck to calves, the epaulets drooping halfway down her shoulders. It brought out the jeweled azure of her eyes and made her look very small and very vulnerable.

Saxon vowed to ignore it. "Do *not* think to play your games with these men," he warned in low, tight Hindi.

She jerked her arm from his grip. "*You* are the only one playing games anymore. *I* have been nothing but honest since the night I told you the truth. Now please tell me what that man said. Will they return us to the mainland?"

Saxon turned her to face him. "They can't. If we want to get off this sand heap, we have to accompany them to their destination. England."

She gaped at him as if he had just announced they were to sail to the moon. "*England? I* cannot go to England!"

"I'm afraid you haven't any choice. They've been ordered back by the King and they haven't time to ferry us about."

"I will stay here, then!"

"You are not staying here." He said each word flatly, distinctly.

"I can do quite well on my own. You know that I can. I do not need to be rescued. I will wait for another ship!"

Saxon vividly imagined what a shipload of sailors with

less honor than Bennett and his men might do if they came upon her stranded alone. "I am not going to leave you behind."

She blinked, her eyes suddenly swimming with tears. "There is no need to keep pretending. You've had your vengeance. I know that you don't care about me."

"I am only thinking of myself," he snapped, not sure whether he was trying to convince her or himself. "If I leave you here and you *somehow* make it back to the mainland, you'll go straight to the Ajmir. When you tell them you've failed, they'll send another assassin after me. One who can do the job."

Her eyes flashed defiance, but her lower lip quivered. "I am either going to the mainland, or I am staying here."

"You are coming with me."

"You cannot keep me prisoner! You cannot force me to go anywhere!"

He smiled humorlessly. "Allow me to remind you that you are my slave girl. Given to me by the Emperor. Lock, stock, body, and soul. I can keep you as long as I like and force you to do whatever I please."

"I was *never* the Emperor's to give and you know it," she replied hotly. "That was all a ruse."

"Really? Dozens of Europeans witnessed it. They would verify my story to anyone who inquired."

She began to shake with repressed fury. "I am not going to England!"

"If I have to carry you, I will. And if I don't do it, I'm sure that Navy nabob will." He jerked his head in Bennett's direction. "He's the proper officer and a gentleman type. He would never leave a helpless female stranded on an island."

"I am *not* a helpless female!" Fresh tears slipped from Ashiana's eyes. Her fingertips dug into the gold-embroidered cuffs of Bennett's coat. "And if you make me go to England I will . . . I will despise you even more than I do now!"

"Have you anything you wish to take along?" he said

tightly, not liking the way her tears made him feel. "Such as—"

"I shall find Nicobar." She turned and stepped away from him.

Saxon caught her by the collar. *"That* was not what I meant and you know it. We can't take a bloody tiger on a Navy ship."

Gasping, she glared at him. "I cannot leave him behind! And he was quite fine on your ship!"

"This is a small warship with ten times the men and not an inch to spare. They don't have cargo holds. Nicobar is not going."

Anger blazed in her eyes. "You are hateful!"

"Just like all the English," he retorted mockingly.

"No!" she spat. "Only you! *Some* Englishmen seem quite nice."

He ignored her insult, the reference to Bennett, and the dangerous flare of jealousy that cut through him. "I am giving you one last chance, Ashiana. We are leaving. Where are the sapphires? You had damn well better tell me the truth and tell me now."

Her eyes turned to blue ice. "The sapphires are *gone.*"

Saxon glared down at her. He had no proof that the jewels were still here—but he could not believe her, not after all her other lies. "You are a liar born, *chokri.* Someday I am going to come back and find them, if it's the last thing I do."

"You cannot find them, because they are lost at—oof!"

Without warning, he scooped her into his arms. "It is time to go."

"Put me down!" she cried. "I do not need to be—"

He cut off her protest by tucking her head against him and squeezing her so tightly she could not free her hands to strike him, much less twist away. He stalked across the beach toward the waiting boats, and knew it was not concern that she would break and run that had made him pick her up.

It was the desire to send a territorial message to every man watching.

"Is the lady unwell?" Bennett asked with concern as Saxon approached.

"The lady is overcome with joy that we are leaving."

He hoped none of the men could overhear the Hindi curses Ashiana was muttering against his throat.

Chapter 21

London

From the deck of the *Crusader*, the city looked impossibly huge, a shadowy sprawl of buildings that extended as far as Ashiana could see. Down in the streets, among the inhabitants, every step she took on English soil felt strange and overwhelming, even with Andrew Bennett's large and reassuring presence beside her.

Saxon had left the ship just as soon as they anchored, saying he would return with a coach shortly. He'd been gone for two hours now. She didn't know whether she should feel relieved or upset about that; she was too tense at the moment to feel anything but nervous and numb by turns.

After waiting over an hour for Saxon's return, Andrew had taken her for a short walk, escorting her to an eating establishment where he bought her a hot drink called "choc-o-lat." They walked back to the dock slowly, while she tried to take in her new surroundings.

She shivered, and it wasn't just from the cold and the odd white flecks, like pristine motes of dust, that floated down out of the sky in the last flame-red rays of sunset. She tried to catch one of the white crystals on her finger, but it melted the instant it landed on her skin.

Andrew laughed. "I told you about snow, didn't I?"

"Yes, you did. Made of water, light as air, cold as ice. I thought you might have been making it up to tease me."

Ashiana's English had much improved during her months on the ship.

"I can get you another blanket when we get back to the ship."

"No, thank you. I am fine, really." She gave the captain a tremulous smile. She was already wrapped in his big blue coat and two wool blankets. He had offered his hat as well, but it had slid down to her nose, and she had handed it back with regret. "Is it always this cold in England?"

He gave her a sympathetic look. "This is barely an autumn nip in the air, my lady. It's only November. The real winter weather won't set in until next month."

Ashiana absorbed that information with dismay and returned her attention to the streets around them, her heart thudding. For eight months at sea, she had had precious little to do but prepare for this day. She had applied herself to the two pursuits she thought might do her some good: mastering English and learning about England. But nothing that Andrew or the other officers had told her could have prepared her for her first sight of London.

Nothing.

The city seemed so big that just imagining how many people must live here made her dizzy. Every detail that greeted her eyes seemed so odd, from the flat little stones that covered the narrow streets ("Cobbles," Andrew explained), to the way the buildings were made: of rocks and bricks and wood, cramped one upon another, each layer overhanging the one below.

Many of them had huge, gaudy signs, painted with pictures and letters in bright colors, suspended from elaborate metal brackets. From the deck of the ship, she had also seen tall spikes here and there, soaring above even the highest roofs, all the way to the horizon ("Church steeples," Andrew said).

More surprising still was the jostling crowd of people that thronged the streets, even as the day's light faded: brawny laborers, Navy sailors with their now-familiar uniforms, lavishly dressed men wearing white false hair and large hats.

And the noise! By Hanuman's tail, how could the English stand such noise? As if the clatter of booted feet and hooves and carriage wheels on those hard cobbles wasn't enough, people shouted at one another, and at the carriages, which raced past without regard for the safety of those on foot.

Raucous laughter and conversation spilled out of certain of the buildings ("Taverns," Andrew explained). Then there were the men pushing carts, piled high with fish or shoes or strange-looking red fruit ("Apples," Andrew laughed), each ringing a bell and yelling about his wares. Small, very loud boys darted through the crowd, crying out the news of the day and waving large pieces of paper with writing on them ("Penny-post newspapers," Andrew pointed out).

But what struck Ashiana as strangest of all were the women.

She could hardly believe her eyes upon seeing that women and girls of all ages mixed quite freely and boldly with the men, neither modestly lowering their gazes nor covering their faces. All these people couldn't possibly be from the same family, yet only a few ladies had male escorts. Many went about with other women in pairs or small groups. Some were even *alone*. More amazing still, she saw men and women greeting one another, talking together, touching. In public!

Some of the women wore expensive-looking garments, while others appeared to be beggars, with children clinging to their skirts. Still others wore quite different clothes: garish colors and low-cut gowns that revealed much of their breasts, and a great deal of face paint. Ashiana asked why these women looked so different, but Andrew flushed and muttered that he wasn't sure.

After a second she guessed: courtesans! She could hardly believe they would be so brazen as to walk the streets, rather than keeping to their pleasure pavilions.

All in all, the scene looked like a riot. In her land, calm and dignified deportment was the rule, even among the lower classes, and most especially in public. Andrew had explained to her that etiquette was quite important in England—but it seemed no one else had been informed.

Ashiana huddled into the scratchy wool blanket, wrapping it tighter around her, feeling as alone and out of place as a tiny *machali* fish swimming through a strange, cold sea.

When they reached the *Crusader,* Andrew took her elbow to help her up the steep gangway. "I know London must appear overwhelming at first, my lady, but I think you will get along quite well. Your English is excellent."

"You are v-very kind."

"Not at all. It's true. You've just the hint of an accent left, and it's charming."

They reached the main deck and he escorted her toward the rail, where they watched for Saxon in the crush of people below. Ashiana tried to let Andrew's confidence in her make her feel better. It had been a long while since she had spoken her native tongue; at times over the past few weeks, she had even found herself dreaming in English.

She told herself it was a necessary evil; she had no way of knowing how long she would have to be here. How long before she could finish her duty and return home, to her clan, to her family.

"Andrew." She turned toward him. "I wish to thank you again for giving up your cabin for me. And for taking so much time to teach me English. It was all very nice of you."

"'Twas nothing. A pleasure to be of service. I hope the voyage was not too uncomfortable for you."

"No, not at all."

Ashiana kept her voice light and turned back toward the docks. She didn't want to hurt Andrew's feelings by revealing just how miserable she'd been these past months. Or the real reason she was grateful for his cabin: it had made it easier to avoid Saxon.

The two of them had seen little of each other, except at supper each day, and then only in the company of the ship's officers, where they barely managed two civil words to one another.

She couldn't help feeling angry and awkward and embarrassed in Saxon's presence, after the way she had revealed her feelings to him on their—*the,* she amended—island, only to have him show he felt nothing for her in return but lust and contempt. In eight months, he hadn't changed his opinion one bit. He would never forgive her for being a spy, for taking his sapphire, no matter how valid her reasons had been.

She had once imagined there was some caring and tenderness beneath Saxon's harsh exterior—but she had only been naive, seeing what she wanted to see. He was incapable of giving in to emotion. At least *gentle* emotion. Anger he managed quite well.

Never again would she let herself be so vulnerable, so foolish, as to reveal her feelings. To wish that he was something he was not. To wish for something between them that could never be.

Avoiding him was the easiest way to accomplish that.

The only way.

Andrew paced beside her. "If D'Avenant doesn't return for you, my lady, you are welcome to stay at my family home."

"I am sure that will not be necessary." Ashiana felt regret at having to decline his offer; Andrew was a kind, pleasant companion. She did not relish the idea of staying with Saxon . . . of being alone with him again. Not for a minute or a day or any length of time.

But she knew she had no choice; her duty was not yet finished. Eight of the sapphires were safely hidden, back on their—*the,* she corrected herself firmly—island, but Saxon still had the ninth one. She must get it back from him.

She was determined, though, that this time she would not take it by lies and deceptions, but by reason and persuasion. She must make Saxon see that it was the right thing to do. That would be the best way, the right way, to get the sapphire back.

It would also satisfy a much deeper need she felt: to make that stubborn, impossible, infuriating man understand that *honesty* was her true nature, not lying and deceit. She would convince him of that, he would give her the sacred stone—and then she would take it and return to her island home, where she belonged.

Andrew tapped his boot impatiently. "I can't believe D'Avenant would have this much difficulty locating a coach. Perhaps we should wait inside."

Ashiana was about to agree when one of the large, boxy horse-drawn vehicles pulled up at the foot of the gangway below. The door in its side opened and Saxon stepped out, still wearing his borrowed Navy uniform.

Ashiana's heart beat faster. She told herself it was only relief, nothing more. Relief that she would be able to finish her mission, *not* relief that he had come back for her.

Trembling, she turned and spoke quickly to Andrew. "I suppose this is farewell, Captain." Her throat felt so dry, she could barely talk. "I thank you again for your generosity."

He took her hand, bowed, and looked as if he were going to kiss it. He hesitated and darted a glance toward Saxon, who was still on the dock, conversing with the coach driver.

Andrew lightly brushed his lips over her fingers. "It has been a sincere pleasure, Lady Ashiana. And I do hope this is not farewell. I'll be in town a short while before the *Crusader* gets her orders. May I . . ." He glanced again toward Saxon, who was now at the bottom of the gangway. "May I see you while you're in London?"

"Yes, I would like that." Ashiana smiled, pleased at the thought of having at least one friend in this strange place. "But I do not know where it is I am going."

"Everyone knows the D'Avenants. I don't think I'll have trouble locating you. I do wish—" Andrew fell silent suddenly.

"You do wish what?" Saxon's low, casual voice came from behind Ashiana, rolling over her nerves in a way that made her tingle. She couldn't force herself to turn around.

"Er . . . I do wish the lady good luck in locating her parents," Andrew finished.

"I'm sure."

Ashiana heard sarcasm in Saxon's tone. She finally turned around, bestowing an irritated look on him. He had not been at all pleasant to Andrew the entire voyage. From the very beginning, she had sensed a growing dislike between the two men that she couldn't understand. Perhaps Saxon simply disliked all Navy officers; whatever his reason, he didn't have to be rude to the man who had rescued them. "Andrew was just saying that he would like to visit while I am in London. And I—"

"I'm not sure that will be possible."

To Ashiana's annoyance, Saxon didn't even deign to glance down at her; he kept his level gaze on Andrew, over the top of her head. She caught the scent of liquor on his breath and her temper flared hotter. *That* was why he had left her waiting in the cold? Because he had gone *drinking?* For him to be so inconsiderate showed just how little she meant to him. The hurt made her unreasonably angry. "I must at least return his coat. I would give it back now, but I'll freeze without it."

"We'll have it sent."

She could not understand why he was being so disagreeable about something so minor. "I wouldn't have needed to borrow it in the first place if you hadn't taken so long hiring a coach."

"This is not Bombay or Madras or Daman, my *lady,*" he said coldly. "I cannot simply snap my fingers and have a dozen slaves come running."

No, she thought bitterly, *you haven't a dozen slaves. Just one. One who doesn't mean a thing to you. Merely a warm female body that is yours for the taking whenever you please—or so you would wish.*

Arguing was getting her nowhere. Ashiana turned and smiled at Andrew. "I'm afraid this is farewell for now, Captain. I must say, you are one of the kindest Englishmen I have ever met."

She heard Saxon mutter something rude under his breath behind her.

Andrew took her hand again, though this time he did

not kiss it. "I'm certain your parents will be very happy to have you back, Lady Ashiana. And proud. It's been a pleasure to see you blossom these past months. You've truly become an English lady."

Ashiana's smile melted away like the snow that dusted her cheeks. "No, I could never be that. Never."

In the puzzled silence that followed her declaration, Saxon thrust out his hand toward the captain. "Bennett."

"D'Avenant."

"Thank you."

"Certainly."

From Ashiana's perspective, their handshake looked as bruising as it was brief.

Without another word, Saxon motioned that she should precede him down the gangway. She had time for only one last, fleeting smile back at Andrew before Saxon's broad shoulders blocked the captain from view. Turning, she started down the inclined plank.

She felt Saxon's hand at the small of her back, and trembled. It was the first time they'd touched in months.

It seemed an innocent gesture, but her reaction was anything but. The unexpected, swift response startled her; she drew in a quick breath through parted lips. Tingling raced along her limbs, to the very tips of her fingers and toes. The heat of his hand seemed to burn through the layers of wool and cotton she wore, straight to her skin.

She tried to ignore the sensation—and the wild tangle of emotions that his merest touch drew from deep within her. She tried to focus her attention instead on the cold breeze, on the coach that loomed in the waning light.

Terrifying questions suddenly rained down on her, about what might await her in the land of the Ajmir's enemies, this place that had been home to the mother she had never known.

Sitting in the darkness on his side of the jouncing coach, Saxon stared out the window, tried to ignore the throbbing ache in his groin, and cursed himself for being ten kinds of an idiot.

He never should have given in to the urge to touch her.

That one brief moment when he impulsively placed his hand against her back had set him ablaze. Even through the layers of clothing, his fingers had felt the delicate curve of her spine, the gentle flair of her hip, the roundness.

The feel and scent of her filled him, blocking out even the longed-for English smells of fallen leaves and chimney smoke and the fresh November bite in the air. All the familiar, mundane, achingly sweet sights and sounds of home were lost on him.

He could think of nothing but the fact that he was at last alone again with Ashiana—that he wanted to take her right here, right now. Rip that bloody Navy coat off her, wrap her creamy legs around his hips, and bury himself to the hilt inside her. Close the distance she had built up between them. Join the two of them together until she thought of no other but him.

He braced one arm on the open window, gripping the wood to try and hold himself in check.

She loathed his touch as much as she loathed him. That much was clear from the way she had avoided him on the ship. And he could hardly blame her, after that last time on the island. He had sworn to himself then that he would not lay a hand on her again. He would not force her. He would do nothing more to hurt her.

Turning his head, he let himself look at her. Ashiana sat huddled in the folds of her blankets, watching the lights of London pass by, her eyes wide. She was trying hard not to let her teeth chatter, but every so often she failed and he could hear the light clicking mingling with the noise of the horse's hooves and the wheels clacking over the cobbles.

He couldn't help but admire her courage; once England had become inevitable, she had set about preparing herself to face it, learning the language she had resisted so long, and pestering the *Crusader*'s crew for every detail about their homeland.

After only a few days at sea, she had also tired of wearing the scratchy uniform donated to her by a thin young midshipman; gathering up all the borrowed cotton garments she could, she had sewn herself a modest *choli* bodice and *salwar* in the Hindu style, accented with bits of gold braid from old uniforms, topping it off with an oversized waistcoat. She had taken it all and pieced it into something unique.

That seemed to be the way she handled whatever life threw in her path.

Annoyed at that warm, gentle thought, Saxon folded his arms over his chest. "The white flakes are called 'snow.' "

"I know," she replied without looking at him. "Andrew told me."

Biting back on oath, Saxon stared out the window once more, dropping his attempt at conversation. *Andrew.* She had spent so much bloody time with that popinjay Bennett, she'd even picked up his refined speech patterns. She not only sounded English, she sounded upper-class English. The trace of an accent only added to her exotic allure.

Bloody Bennett. It had been easy, at first, to condemn her for being so cordial to him. Easy to think she had simply chosen a new target for her lash-fluttering games. But Ashiana had been nothing less than completely decorous with the captain and everyone else. She had been friendly but never flirtatious.

In sum, she made it damned impossible for him to keep labeling her a whore as he had on the island.

The entire voyage, she'd spent most of her time in her cabin. Saxon had at least made sure she would be there alone. He'd had a little talk with Bennett a few days out, when it looked like the dandiprat might have more in mind than English lessons.

The captain or any man aboard, Saxon had put it succinctly, would find himself the guest of honor in a funeral at sea if they so much as touched the hem of her handsewn skirt.

Bennett was no coward—and he had a fully armed warship crew at his command—but he wasn't a fool. Apparently realizing that Saxon was not making an idle threat, he had backed off.

"Where is it exactly we are going, my lord?"

Saxon swiveled his head toward her. *My lord.* He was getting bloody tired of that. And of the way she looked at him as if he were a stranger. A *stranger,* for Christ's sake. After he'd been inside her so hard and so deep she had shuddered with pleasure and shouted his name.

He speared her with a glare. "Why is it exactly you insist on calling me 'my lord'?"

She looked at him as she had for months: with eyes of sheer sea-blue ice. "Is that not proper? Andrew tried his best to instruct me in etiquette, but he—"

"*Andrew* is a lord as well. He's the son of a bloody peer. It is also proper for you to call him 'my lord.'"

In the shifting night shadows, he could see her tilt her head to one side. "He asked me to call him by his given name."

Saxon fumed silently and glanced away; he couldn't argue with that—and he wasn't going to ask her for his name or for anything. Let her call him Beelzebub, for all he cared. What did it matter? She could not wait to get away from him and return to her people; he did not want her in his life. Their feelings were completely mutual.

If the time ever came when he *did* want a woman in his life, Saxon thought decisively, it would be a woman like his wife Mandara: sweet, innocent, loyal, trustworthy.

Truthful.

But he kept hearing Bennett's farewell in his mind. *It's been a pleasure to see you blossom these past months, my lady.* All that blasted bowing and fawning and complimenting—and the way Ashiana had smiled in return—was enough to make him retch. Was that what she wanted? Was that really what she admired in a man?

Was that what she got from her betrothed, her prince?

"Where are we going?" she repeated.

"My family's town house in Grosvenor Square."

She flinched at his tone but made no other comment, returning to her perusal of the passing streets.

He ground his teeth, wondering again whether it was wise to take her home. He *should* find her a room in an inn somewhere, put her beyond temptation's reach. Only one thing kept him from doing so: whenever Greyslake got around to slithering into town, Saxon wanted Ashiana where he could keep her safe.

That was the reason he had taken so long getting the coach. He had been trying to track down an old friend, a man who had served the D'Avenant family for years, though not as a servant.

Only after an hour's search, another half hour of catching up on old times, and several celebratory glasses of rum had Saxon been able to get down to business.

The man and his associates would keep an eye out for the *Phoenix*, which had not yet arrived, and keep Saxon informed of Greyslake's every move in town. They would also keep watch over the D'Avenant family. And Ashiana.

Vengeance might be sweet. It might be a dish best served cold. But when one sought vengeance against a cunning, high-ranking officer of His Majesty's Navy, in London, it also had to be cautious, carefully planned, and kept absolutely secret.

Saxon was jolted from thoughts of the complicated net he was weaving when the hackney coach lurched to a stop. The driver appeared at the door and helped Ashiana down.

Saxon stepped out behind her, gave the man a silver coin—borrowed earlier from the ever-helpful Captain Bennett—and sent the coach on its way.

Then he turned toward the door. He stood on the wet pavement, looking at the lacquered wood and the gold engraved knocker, snow falling all around him. The physical ache he felt from Ashiana's nearness suddenly competed with a different ache.

It had been more than ten years since he had stood on this spot. Ten years. He could not even remember what season it had been when last he had seen his family. The time that had passed and all that had happened, all that had changed, suddenly weighed down on him like iron.

Forcing aside the sense of loss and frustration and regret, Saxon raised the knocker and let it fall. He looked down at Ashiana in the light of the oil lamps that flanked the entrance.

"Welcome to London," he said softly.

She started to reply, but one of the efficient servants was already opening the door. The red-and-blue-liveried footman stuck his head out into the cold and squinted into the lamplight. "Yes? Oh, is this Naval business? The Duchess is at supper and I—"

"Come, come, Townshend," Saxon reprimanded lightly. "I haven't changed all that much, have I?"

The footman took a closer look and his hand flew to his forehead. "As I live and breathe! Lord Saxon? By the graces! By all the graces!"

Saxon smiled as Townshend stood staring in open-mouthed shock. "I hate to interrupt everyone's supper, but do you suppose we might come in?"

"Yes! Yes, of course! Forgive me, my lord." He opened the door and ushered them both inside. "By the graces! We received no word that you were coming!"

"It's a long story," Saxon said dryly, feeling weary even as he told that much. "How is everyone? I've had no news since I saw Julian last year."

"Quite well, sir, quite well." Townshend was busy trying to help Ashiana remove the tangle of blankets, his expression pure puzzlement at the coat she was wearing beneath. "I shall fetch your mother posthaste."

Before Townshend could move, Saxon heard his name called from the rear of the house, a breathless query that was almost at the edge of a sob. A second later, Penelope "Paige" D'Avenant, Duchess of Silverton, all five feet two inches of her, appeared at the far end of the hall, one hand still holding a damask napkin while her other rose, trembling, to her lips. "Saxon?"

He shook his head in wonder, filled with warmth and love. "Three score years of age and she can still pick out one of her children's voices from half a house away."

The napkin slipped from her fingers as she dashed across the marble floor in a flurry of blue silk, tears and laughter sparkling equally in her gray eyes. "I'm not a day over fifty-five, you teasing scoundrel!"

He opened his arms and caught her, hugging her and spinning her around while she laughed and cried all at once. He felt his own throat close.

"Sorry to be away so long," he said gruffly. "I've missed the family so much. I love you, Mother."

Other servants came running, filling the entry hall with cries of surprise and jubilation.

"Clements," Townshend instructed one of the under-footmen, "run and fetch Lord Maximilian."

"No," Saxon protested, not wanting to disturb his gravely ill younger brother. "Don't wake him. Let him rest."

It was too late, for a tall blond figure dressed in breeches and boots, waistcoat and cotton shirt came down the hall, his nose in the open book he held in his hands. "What the devil is all the fuss about? Is there a fire?" When he raised his head and removed his spectacles, he came to a dead stop, blinking at Saxon.

"Max?" Saxon cried hoarsely, unable to believe that the hale and hearty young man before him was the sickly boy he had last seen ten years ago.

"Good God," Max breathed, tucking his spectacles in the pocket of his waistcoat with an absent gesture. He strode forward, his mouth curved into a broad smile. "This couldn't be the legendary, long-lost Saxon D'Avenant?"

"Max!" Saxon grabbed him in a bear hug, lifting him right off his feet. He felt like his heart would burst. "Max! Thank God you are well!"

"He recovered months ago," their mother explained happily. "Like a miracle. He's not been abed a day since." She wagged a finger at her youngest son. "Though he does need to stop going about with a book in hand all evening and learn to be on time for supper."

Saxon felt like shouting with relief and joy and dropping to his knees in thankfulness at the same time. That brief moment aboard his ship, when he'd held all nine sapphires in his hands, must have done it. The curse was lifted.

"I've a feeling I have you to thank?" Max asked quietly when Saxon finally released him.

"Yes. Sweet Jesus, yes, it's over." Saxon could hardly believe the sight of his little brother standing on his own two feet. "It's finally over."

As if to prove his strength, Max punched him on the shoulder. "Now what the bloody blazes is this? Have you gone off and joined the Navy?"

Laughing, Saxon started to explain while he shared greetings and handshakes with every servant in the house, with the zest of a man celebrating the happiest day of his life.

It wasn't until his mother cleared her throat and called for silence—twice—that the uproar quieted.

"Saxon," she said patiently, "would you like to introduce us to this lovely young lady and perhaps explain why she is wearing a Naval uniform?"

All present turned as one toward Ashiana, who stood trembling in the doorway, still wearing Bennett's coat.

A bit of Saxon's good mood evaporated. "I'll need to speak with you in private, Mother—"

"Well, you can at least reveal the poor child's name!" Paige was already wrapping a motherly arm about Ashiana's shoulders and drawing her closer to the group. "We're so sorry to have ignored you, my dear. I hope you'll forgive us. This is all quite a surprise!"

Ashiana kept staring at Saxon as if she'd never seen him before. It appeared her command of English had failed her.

"Her name is Lady Ashiana," he said. "I'm not sure of the last name. She's the ... uh ... the long-lost daughter of an earl." Saxon decided it would be easiest to stick to the story he had told Bennett, at least publicly.

"I see." Paige gave him a curious glance, but immediately returned her attention to Ashiana, who was shivering so badly, it looked as if her knees might give way. "Oh, you poor dear. You look exhausted. Eugenie?"

The summoned maidservant wound her way through the crowd. "Your grace?"

"Please escort Lady Ashiana to a guest room so that she can rest. And find her something suitable to wear. And fetch her some tea from the kitchens. Would you like that?"

"Y-yes," Ashiana said in a small voice, still looking at Saxon, her expression strange, almost like amazement.

"Mother . . ." Saxon growled.

"You can explain everything later, Saxon," Paige said.

He bit back an oath, watching his mother and Eugenie help Ashiana up the stairs, realizing just how difficult it was going to be to keep temptation at arm's length.

Chapter 22

G uest or prisoner?

That question kept tormenting Ashiana even as she finished the last bite of her breakfast and set the beautiful silver tray on the table beside her bed. She hadn't cared much for the salty little fish, but the hot buttered bread had melted irresistibly in her mouth, and the sticky, clear paste made with sugar and bits of tangy fruit tasted delicious. She couldn't remember what Eugenie had said it was called. Mar-mal-something-or-other.

It was also a pleasant surprise to discover that the English favored tea, though she did not understand why one should wish to pour milk into it. She tried to let the soothing aroma of the dark brew calm her nerves as she got up from the bed and walked to the hearth, warming her hands on the tiny, fragile cup.

Eugenie had explained that the servants kept a fire burning in every room of the house at all times. Ashiana thought that rather dangerous, though with the freezing English weather, she could easily understand why it was necessary.

She settled herself in a chair as close to the crackling flames as she dared get, drawing her knees up and wrapping her borrowed nightclothes more closely about herself. Last night, the Duchess and Eugenie had presented her with an array of garments to choose from, and Ashiana had selected the warmest ones: a soft, white cotton gown and a deep-purple velvet robe. The fur at the cuffs tickled her nose as she raised the cup to her lips.

Despite the thick robe, the fire, and the tea, she could not stop shivering, wondering.

Guest or prisoner?

The Duchess had offered all this kindness before she had a chance to speak privately with Saxon. Today she would know the truth—that Ashiana was a spy. Today everything would change. Ashiana knew that Saxon thought of her as nothing but his possession. When he had forced her to come to England with him, she doubted that he had intended for her to be welcomed as an honored guest.

She had no idea how long he meant to keep her; she knew only that, regardless of how she was treated, she must change his opinion of her, convince him to give her the sapphire, and return home as soon as possible.

Trembling, she rose from the chair, unable to stand the futile tears that welled up at the thought of leaving Saxon.

She had thought him incapable of feeling gentler emotions, incapable of knowing love. She had thought that was simply the way he was—until she watched him reunite with his family last night.

The emotional scene in the foyer had shocked her with the truth: he wasn't a harsh, uncaring man. That wasn't it at all! He clearly cared deeply for his mother, his brother—even the servants.

He just did not care for her.

The realization left her stunned, and hurt her more deeply than she could bear. The agony of standing there, alone, in the hall, seeing the true depth of feeling he could share—and knowing he would never share even a speck of that tenderness, that caring, with her . . .

Pacing back to the bed, Ashiana set her half-finished tea on the tray. She must stop torturing herself with thoughts of him! Vishnu help her, she must not let herself feel this way about him! Caring for Saxon D'Avenant could only bring her pain.

She wiped her eyes and tried to stop pacing. Attempting

to distract her thoughts and find calm, she examined the chamber's strange contents for the first time in daylight.

Decorated paper covered the walls, its deep amber designs fuzzy beneath her fingers. The bed perched on tall legs that extended upward into skinny pillars at each of its four corners, topped with a voluminous length of fabric. She had seen canopies at home, but wondered what it was doing on the bed. When she had asked last night, the Duchess had smiled and said it was intended to catch drips when the roof leaked.

Ashiana thought she was joking, but couldn't be sure. These English seemed a most practical people.

Beneath the tall windows that lined one wall of the room sprawled a long, well-stuffed piece of furniture. She ran her hand over the sloping back and bent down to look at the feet—carved like the paws of animals, complete with *claws.* How odd! She noticed that the half-dozen spindly-legged tables and matching chairs scattered about also had such feet.

Rising, she stepped closer to the tall, slender cabinet in an adjacent corner, peering through its glass front to the white circle marked with black figures beneath; the device's pendulum made a constant tick-tick-ticking sound that had kept her awake half the night. *Clock,* her memory supplied. She had seen a similar device aboard Andrew's ship.

The smell of woodsmoke rose from the hearth, mingling with the more delicate scent of flowers; a great bouquet in a blue lacquered vase made a brilliant display, reflected in the mirror that topped a fabric-draped table against one wall. Eugenie had brought them with breakfast. Ashiana could not name even one of the flowers, and thought the English must be magicians to grow such delicate blooms in such a cold land. Beneath the spray of blossoms, small porcelain figurines of English ladies danced along the tabletop, amid brushes and combs and silver boxes of every shape and size.

Of all the furnishings that filled the room, only the bristly carpet beneath her bare toes was familiar. It looked just like those at home in the Maharaja's palace, with its swirling pattern of blues and golds.

With a sigh of longing, she sat on the rug, folded her legs, and rolled backwards until most of her weight was balanced on her shoulders. Comfortable in the yoga position, she closed her eyes, trying to find refuge in meditation from the question that troubled her.

Guest or prisoner?

Only minutes had passed when a knock sounded at the door. "Finished with breakfast, miss?" Eugenie popped in.

"Yes, thank you. It was very good." Ashiana opened her eyes but remained on the floor in her yoga position.

Eugenie stopped in the doorway, her expression curious, her eyebrows arched so high they touched the lacy edge of her white cap. She recovered her customary smile just as quickly and walked to the bedside table without a word.

Blushing, Ashiana unfolded herself and got to her feet. Perhaps English ladies did not practice yoga.

Eugenie picked up the silver tray. "The Duchess would like to come see you, if it is not too early."

Her tone was pleasant, but Ashiana's heart pounded. Now it would come. Now the Duchess knew the truth, and she would despise Ashiana every bit as much as her son did.

"Of—of course," she whispered, her thoughts so scattered, she forgot to ask the name of the mar-mal-something-or-other.

"Very good, miss."

No sooner had Eugenie left with the tray than the Duchess came to the door. "Ashiana? May I come in?"

The question sounded so polite, it made Ashiana all the more nervous. "Yes, your grace," she said, dropping into a curtsy as the lady entered. She hoped she was doing it right; Andrew had tried to show her aboard the *Crusader,* but the result had elicited more laughter than learning.

The Duchess closed the door behind her. "Saxon has told me everything," she said quietly.

Ashiana could not say a word or even raise her eyes.

She felt a blaze of color wash her cheeks as she wondered what "everything" included.

"Now, now, my dear," the Duchess said, taking Ashiana's hands and helping her up out of the awkward curtsy. "None of that. You need not be embarrassed."

Ashiana was amazed to hear sympathy in the woman's voice rather than anger. "Y-your grace, I—"

"The first thing you must learn is that my name is Paige." The Duchess squeezed Ashiana's hands, smiling, a sparkle in her silver eyes. "Actually, it's Penelope, but I've always hated that. Too stuffy and dull. My friends have always called me Paige. I do hope it will be all right if I call you Ashiana?"

"Yes. Of . . . of course. But . . ."

"Please, Ashiana, feel free to speak your mind. I always do. Shall we sit while we talk?" She led her to the long, overstuffed piece of furniture beneath the windows.

Ashiana did not know how the Duchess could still smile and be kind to her—unless Saxon hadn't told her the truth, which Ashiana could not believe.

"How is it that you don't hate me?" she blurted.

"Hate you?" The Duchess laughed, her white teeth as bright as the morning sunlight. "Oh, my dear, no."

"But didn't . . . didn't Saxon tell you what . . . what happened?"

"Yes, he told me all of it." The Duchess's smile curved into a wry expression. "Well, not precisely *all* of it. I am his mother, after all. But I think I have a fair idea of what he left unsaid."

Ashiana blushed furiously and dropped her gaze to her lap.

"Here now." The Duchess laid a gentle hand on Ashiana's arm. "You have nothing to be ashamed of. If there is one thing I understand in this life, it is the D'Avenant men. Goodness knows, I was married to one for twenty-six years, God rest his soul. I don't hold Saxon blameless in all this, and I don't think you've done anything so terribly wrong."

"How can you say that?" Ashiana asked wonderingly. "Don't you know about ... about the sapphires?"

"My dear, I've known about those sapphires for longer than I care to remember."

"But didn't Saxon explain that I am a ... spy?"

"And that you lied to him, and stole the jewel from him, and almost killed him."

Ashiana raised her head, amazed at her calm tone. "That was accidental—the almost killing him."

"Yes. And he also told me about your father being murdered by Englishmen. And about how the Ajmir adopted you, when you were so young and all alone. Everything you have done has been for the love of your family." She paused for a moment, pursing her lips. "Though I don't think Saxon quite understands that. Men can be rather thickheaded at times."

Ashiana swallowed hard, speechless that the Duchess understood. Not only understood, but sympathized.

"To set out alone on such a dangerous mission took great courage," the older woman continued, admiration in both her tone and her eyes. "I'm not sure I would have been so brave. Certainly not when I was as young as you."

Ashiana looked at the Duchess with wonder and respect. "There has been such hatred between our families for so long. How can you forgive so easily?"

"Partly, I think, because hatred and fighting and war are much the work of men. We women are the ones who must forge the understanding, who must heal the wounds, if the world and life are to go on."

Ashiana had never thought of it that way, but realized it was as true among her people as the Duchess said it was among the English. Perhaps it was true among all people. She liked the Duchess more and more; the lady had keen insight as well as a gentle heart.

"Partly, too," Paige continued, a bit of sadness creeping into her tone, "is that I know that we—our family—are greatly to blame for all the trouble over the jewels."

"You do?" Ashiana felt more astounded by the minute.

"I loved my husband very much, but he was not a

perfect man by any means. If not for what he did all those years ago, you would not be sitting here right now."

"Why?" Ashiana asked suddenly, feeling herself close to the answer she had wondered about so long. "Why did he steal the sapphire in the first place?"

The Duchess glanced heavenward, sighing. "How can I explain? I suppose I should start at the beginning. You see, my dear, the D'Avenant family, we are . . ." She paused, searching for the right words. "We are known to be somewhat eccentric, a bit outside the norms of English society. Generations of D'Avenants have been raising eyebrows all over England for scores of years. It has always been tolerated because we hold title to a dukedom, and English society has never met a duke they didn't adore. We are also quite wealthy and well-connected, both in shipping and in politics. The tongues that wag do so cautiously."

Ashiana listened politely, noting that the Duchess related all of this merely as fact, without boasting, without apology.

"My husband, Brandon D'Avenant—" A smile touched the older woman's lips. "—was perhaps the most notorious black sheep in a family known for black sheep, and he—"

"Black sheep?" Ashiana interrupted.

"I'm sorry, my dear. Your English is so excellent that I forget you don't know all of our sayings. A 'black sheep' is a . . . hmmm. I suppose the closest word would be 'rascal.' Have you heard that one before?"

"Yes," Ashiana said, mirroring Paige's grin.

"I don't think Brandon would object to being called a rascal." The Duchess's gaze flicked heavenward again. "In any case, he was a second son and he thoroughly enjoyed the life of a black sheep. He believed he was entitled to it. He indulged himself quite scandalously." Her humor faded. "Mostly in gaming and drink. He had a terrible problem with liquor when he was a young man, before we married. It made him attempt the most insane things. One night, someone wagered an enormous sum and proclaimed that he had finally thought of the one feat that Brandon could not accomplish: steal one of the Nine Sapphires of Kashmir."

Ashiana inhaled, beginning to understand. "And he accepted the wager."

"Yes." Paige frowned, smoothing her striped skirt. "At the time, he gave no thought to the consequences. It became an obsession with him. Brandon always had a tremendous need to prove himself. Yet in his heart, he was an honest man. I believe that if he hadn't been so caught in the grip of drinking, he never would have become a thief. He never would have stolen your people's jewel."

Now it was Ashiana's turn to touch the other woman's hand soothingly. "I understand."

The Duchess smiled warmly. "I hoped you would. The only way to stop all the hating is through understanding. There is more to the story than that, of course, but I think . . ." She paused, then nodded. "I think Saxon should be the one to tell you. Actually, that is what I've come to see you about."

Ashiana stiffened, her heart thudding. "He wishes to see me?"

"No, he's gone off with Max for the day. He asked us all to keep an eye on you until he returns this evening."

Ashiana swallowed hard. She had her answer. "He means for me to be kept as a prisoner, then."

The Duchess's laughter returned. "Oh, no, not at all. That was what I most wanted to tell you, Ashiana. I think you must learn to take what Saxon says to you with a grain of salt. He is—"

"Salt?"

"Oh, yes. Sorry. To 'take with a grain of salt' means that you shouldn't take everything he says completely seriously."

Ashiana furrowed her brow, confused. "And why, as you say, do I need to take Saxon with salt?"

"A grain of salt, my dear. Because despite all of his blustering on about your being a spy and the most scheming and deceitful woman in the world since Cleopatra—" She raised an eyebrow, adding thoughtfully, "In fact, maybe it was *because* of all that blustering on. In any case, I could tell that, beneath it all, he cares for you, very much."

"No." Ashiana denied it instantly, fiercely, protecting her heart from what she could not bear to hear. "No, you must be mistaken." Saxon might *want* her, but he did not care for her. She could not believe it. Any gentleness he might have felt had been snuffed out when he discovered she was an enemy spy. She knew all too well what he felt for her—from the cold way he looked at her, from the brusque way he spoke to her, and most of all from the callous, contemptuous way he had taken her on the island.

But she could hardly explain to Paige that she knew Saxon's feelings from the difference in his lovemaking.

"No," she repeated miserably. It was the only word she could manage.

"Trust me, my dear," Paige insisted. "As I said, I know the D'Avenant men."

Ashiana bowed her head, fighting sudden tears, hope fluttering wildly in her chest. "Your son has been away many years, your grace—"

"Paige," the Duchess corrected.

"Paige." Ashiana raised her head. "He has been away ten years. Years can change a man."

Paige glanced out the window into the morning sunshine, smiling softly, her voice almost a whisper. "There is something far more powerful than years that can change a man. Unfortunately, each of them has to learn that for himself, in his own way, in his own time."

Puzzled, Ashiana was about to ask her to explain, when Paige rose suddenly, again taking Ashiana's hands in her own.

"My dear, I also want you to know that you are welcome in my house. You are my guest for as long as you like."

"I cannot stay. You are most kind, but I must return to my people as soon as possible. My duty . . ." Her throat constricted and she could say no more, the word *duty* warring in her mind and heart with what Paige had just told her.

"I see." Paige looked a bit sad. "Well then, for as long as you are here, I hope you will consider yourself an honored guest and look upon me as a friend."

Touched, Ashiana felt a soothing warmth settle over her heart as she stood. "I will." The last thing she had expected to find in England was such a generous, intelligent, kindhearted friend.

"I'm glad." Paige hooked her arm through Ashiana's and started toward the door. "Now then, we've much to do! Even if you are only here a short time, we must get you properly outfitted. We can hardly have you going about in my old robe, can we? I think we should keep to the story about you being the long-lost daughter of an English earl. It will make everything easier. And vastly more interesting! Would that be all right?"

"Yes," Ashiana agreed.

"Excellent. The first thing we must do of course is pay a visit to a draper. You will look simply smashing in all the wonderful colors I have never been able to carry off. With your midnight hair and blue eyes, and that lovely accent, the shopkeepers will adore you! Now then, there used to be an excellent draper down on the Strand called Osgood's, but that closed years ago. I suppose Amelia Farrell could accommodate us. She's in the West End. And there's a splendid milliner there as well. Then we'll pay a visit to a shoemaker, and a *parfumerie*—"

"Parfumerie?" Ashiana's head was already spinning.

"It's called 'shopping,' my dear." Paige laughed. "I can guarantee you'll adore it!"

Chapter 23

A shiana's dark-red skirt rustled as she descended the stairs to the foyer. The scent of candle wax warmed the air, and she could see servants lighting the sconces and chandeliers for evening. Tension gripped her as she headed for Saxon's study, step by reluctant step. Her heart beat unsteadily while she considered how best to pose the question she must ask him.

Fatigue slowed her pace as well. Today had been an exhausting whirl of linens and laces, boxes and parcels, shopkeepers and measuring tapes. The more she saw of London, the more its strangeness frayed her nerves. The crowds and the noise had given her a headache. The damp cold had settled into her bones until she wondered whether she would ever feel truly warm again. Even the air had seemed difficult to breathe, thick with overpowering smells and dust and competing perfumes and the crush of too many people living too close together.

Reaching the bottom step, she paused and tried to take a deep, calming breath, barely managing the merest gasp because of the tightly laced corset and petticoats she wore. She had almost forgotten how much she despised the English undergarments; it had been such a joy to go without them aboard Andrew's ship.

What bothered her even more were the long white gloves that covered her arms from fingertips to elbows. The seamstress had insisted upon them after all but fainting in shock at the tattoo on Ashiana's left arm. Ashiana didn't see why she should have to cover up the beautiful work of an Ajmir artisan.

At least Paige had relented on the matter of footwear. Ashiana had not been able to walk in the tight-fitting, pointy little instruments of torture she had been shown. She was deeply grateful to the shoemaker for offering a compromise: satin slippers, not unlike those she was used to at home.

Her steps barely whispered on the marble floor as she turned down the hall and edged uncertainly toward the third door on the right.

She felt a bit dizzy, and knew it was because she had eaten precious little since her tea and toast this morning; it seemed she was the first vegetarian the English had encountered. Her distaste for their food had the Duchess completely baffled.

Through it all, Ashiana hadn't uttered a word of complaint or offered one critical opinion. She could not repay Paige's kindness by appearing ungrateful. Besides, her aversion to life in England did not matter.

She would be leaving as soon as Saxon gave her the sapphire.

Stopping before the study door, she touched a hand to her elaborately curled and pinned hair, wondering what miracle Eugenie had used to make it all stay in place the entire day.

She wondered, too, whether Saxon would like her new appearance.

Willing away that thought, she told herself it didn't matter and knocked on the door.

"Come in."

He sounded almost cheerful. She opened the door, just a bit, keeping her gaze on the polished wood floor and holding tight to the knob to stop herself from shaking. "Mr. Townshend told me that you had returned from riding. I thought I should . . . that is, your mother . . . M-may I speak with you?"

"Yes, but you'll have to stop hovering in the doorway and come over here."

Ashiana raised her head, surprised by his light, almost teasing tone. She clung to the doorknob another instant before she let it go and stepped inside.

He stood on the far side of the room, leaning against one of the tall windows, his muscular form outlined by the gray light of the autumn evening. Looking relaxed, he stayed where he was as she came in, his boots crossed at the ankle, a glass of amber liquid in one hand. His attire was casual, buff-colored breeches and waistcoat and a cotton shirt with the sleeves rolled up, a cravat half-untied about his neck. The wind had tousled his hair and deepened the color in his bronzed cheeks.

As she stepped into the chandelier's light, his expression changed, making her breath catch in her throat. His eyes widened, sweeping from her coiffed tresses to her slippers and back again. He swirled the liquor in his glass with a flick of his wrist. "I see that my mother spent the day introducing you to every shopkeeper in the West End."

Ashiana stiffened, waiting for the sarcasm or disapproval. It never came.

After a second, she realized he didn't seem to object to his mother's kind treatment. "Yes. I mean . . . that is—she has been most generous. Too generous." She looked down at her skirt, smoothing her gloved hands over it. Paige had called the color *cran-ber-ee.* "This is just a gown that the seamstress had on hand. The others will be arriving in a few days."

She wasn't sure he heard her; his silvered gaze kept tracing over her with a look that held both the surprise of discovery and the intimacy of a caress. Her blood pounded in her veins.

Taking a sip of his drink, he turned to look out the window. "The color suits you. Makes you look . . . pretty."

Ashiana felt amazement and warmth chase through her, one after the other. Had he just given her a compliment? She couldn't remember ever having heard one from him before—but then again, she had never seen him in such a pleasant humor before. There was a calmness, a lightness about him. Almost like happiness.

Ashiana took a few silent steps closer, but stopped on the near side of a heavy, carved desk. She thought it wise to keep something large and solid between them, unsure whether his mood would last after she asked what she had come here to ask.

What you just saw in his eyes was merely desire, she admonished herself. *What Paige said could not possibly be true. You must think of your duty. Your duty and home. And Rao.*

She looked past Saxon's shoulders out the window, watching night's first shadows steal over the gardens at the rear of the house. Her throat felt dry. "You are happy to be home."

"Yes." He didn't turn around, but she could hear the pleasure and pride and satisfaction and firmness in that one word.

"Your mother said you spent the day with your brother Max?" She cursed herself as a coward, dancing around the one question she truly needed to ask.

"I was getting to know him." Saxon turned partially toward her, leaning one shoulder against the window, smiling down into his glass. "Last time I saw him, he was barely more than a boy, so sick he couldn't get out of bed. Now he's a man. Hell of a man at that. Speaks five languages and knows more about science and politics and literature than any professor at Oxford. Hell of a shot with a pistol, too. Says he rigged up a chair with carriage wheels and used to have the servants take him outside to practice target shooting when Mother wasn't around." Saxon's smile widened until his eyes crinkled at the corners. "Can't ride worth a damn, though. I was giving him a lesson."

Ashiana felt Saxon's happiness seep into her. He loved his brother, his family, very much. *Loved* them. Every bit as much as she loved the Maharaja and her family.

She felt a tearing emptiness inside, seeing him so at peace, standing so close that she could *feel* the depth of love in him—and knowing he could never give that love to her.

Not to her.

He slanted her a look. "What else did my mother tell you?"

His question caught her off guard. She gazed down at her white-gloved fingers, splayed on the smooth, dark top of the desk. "Her ... her favorite subject seems to be her children. She mentioned that Maximilian inherited her love of learning, Julian her sense of humor, and the oldest one—"

"Dalton," Saxon supplied.

"Yes, that Dalton inherited her flair for getting into trouble."

When she didn't say anything else, Saxon moved away from the window, coming closer. He set his glass on the desk between them, resting his knuckles on the polished top. "And?" he asked expectantly.

"And?" she echoed.

"What about me?"

"Oh." She tried to remember Paige's exact words. "She said that you favor your father. Something about sheep and grains of salt."

His expression reflected complete puzzlement. "I see. And what else did my mother expound upon while the two of you were emptying the shops of London?"

Ashiana's stomach knotted as she remembered the question she had asked his mother, the question Paige had insisted she pose to Saxon himself. She still could not make herself say the words.

"She ... well ... she did talk quite a bit about how much she loves history. She said she has studied it all her life, and even named each of her sons after a famous historical personage. Except for you, of course, because you were born during what she calls her 'medieval era.' "

He gave her a pained look. "You said that you wanted to speak with me. What is it you wanted to talk about?"

Ashiana looked down at her hands again, realizing that his good humor had faded and her respite had ended. "S-something I asked your mother. She said I should ask you."

"Ask."

The indifference that he had bestowed upon her for months had slid back into his voice. And it hurt. Oh, Vishnu, it hurt. Worse than it ever had before.

"It's about the . . . the sapphires," she began. "Why you wanted them so badly. It has something to do with your brother Max, doesn't it?"

He flinched and straightened. "That's none of your business."

"Paige said she would answer my question, if you did not. But she felt you should be the one to tell me."

Saxon grimaced and snatched up his glass. "My mother's problem is that she allows her feelings to cloud her judgment. I am both fortunate and eternally grateful I didn't inherit that quality from her." He turned his back and stalked to the window.

Ashiana remained quiet, giving him time, as Paige had advised.

After a long, silent moment, her patience was rewarded. Saxon's shoulders relaxed. He shook his head and exhaled slowly. "I can't for the life of me understand why my mother thinks you deserve to know this. But I don't suppose it matters anymore, now that he's well. It's over. And you've caught me in a generous mood." Tilting his head, he half-emptied his glass. "Yes, it had something to do with my brother."

"Then if . . ." Ashiana took a gasp of air. "If they don't matter to you anymore—" Another gasp. "—will you give me the sapphire you have and let me return home?"

He jerked toward her, so fast that liquor sloshed over the edge of his glass. "No."

She flinched at his vehemence. It was the answer she had expected, but it made her no less exasperated. "Why *not?* You just said it doesn't matter anymore—"

"I said no."

Stubborn, unreasonable, unyielding man! "I wish you would tell me," she requested, clenching her gloved fists, "why the sapphires mean so much to you. I told you why

I needed to have them, but you have told me nothing. When I asked Paige—"

"The curse," he snapped.

"Curse? What do you mean?"

"Oh, please. The curse that struck my father, because he stole that blasted stone all those years ago. The curse that slowly drained the life out of him. The one that almost killed Max." His voice faltered, then strengthened. "The goddamned curse that demanded that all nine sapphires had to be reunited in the hands of the thief or one of his blood heirs."

Ashiana felt as if she had just been struck by one of the carriages that sped through the London streets. "That was why you wanted the stones?" she asked breathlessly. "To save your *family?* To save Max from this curse?"

"You expect me to believe that you never knew?"

She adopted his tactic of answering a question with a question. "And what would you have done with the sapphires, once you had reunited them?"

"I'm not a fool. I wouldn't want Ajmir assassins and Ajmir spies—" He punctuated the last word with a glare. "—chasing after me for the rest of my life. Once I was sure that Max was all right, I meant to give them back."

Ashiana gaped at him, stunned as the truth in his words washed over her. She felt behind her with one trembling hand and sank into a nearby chair. He hadn't come after the jewels out of greed or selfishness or arrogance, but out of . . .

Love.

Love for his family, for his brother. Love that had been strong enough to drive him through ten years of searching and suffering and even torture. It tore her apart to know that he could feel love *that* deeply. She had misjudged him so terribly, for so long.

"Why didn't you ever tell me?" she asked bleakly.

He made a strangled sound. "I was supposed to reveal everything to *you?*"

Ashiana winced and closed her eyes. He didn't have to add that she had been his enemy from the beginning. That he *still* considered her an enemy. A possession, a soft body to warm his bed, but an enemy. It all rang through loud and clear.

She raised her chin, every bit as stubborn as he was, clinging to the hope that she could make him believe in her as she now believed in him—make him understand that he must do the right thing and give her the stone.

"Our reasons were the same, don't you see that? I was fighting to save my family, just as you were fighting to save yours. I did whatever I had to do, and so did you. How can you condemn me if you do not condemn yourself?"

His only response was a cool, piercing stare.

"I know you will never believe this, but I didn't know about the curse. The Maharaja never told me. He *never told me*. Just as he never told me that Ajmir warriors had tortured you. I thought—"

"You thought your people were paragons of virtue and all Englishmen were marauding pirates."

Ashiana couldn't answer. For the first time, she felt anger—true anger—at her own people. They had played on her feelings, told her only what they wanted her to know, to enflame her hatred against him. So that she would take the stone and kill him without a thought.

She almost had.

They had used her.

Tears burned behind her eyes and spilled over. "They kept it all from me." She hung her head, feeling more alone than she could ever remember being in her life. "I know you don't believe that, but it's the truth."

She heard him set his empty glass on the desk with a clatter. Expecting him to storm out, she felt astonished when he instead came to stand beside her chair.

And when he reached down with one hand and tipped her chin up, his gentleness stole her breath away.

His eyes still burned, his lips were still pressed together in an unyielding line, but it seemed the fury had melted out of him.

"If I had been in their place," he said slowly, "I

wouldn't have told you either. If you had any sympathy for the enemy, you wouldn't have made much of a spy."

Ashiana gripped the padded arms of the chair, shaking with emotion. He believed her. Perhaps for the first time ever, he believed her. That small scrap of trust filled her with pleasure, with more warmth than his touch, with feelings she couldn't begin to name.

But as she looked up at him, a chilling realization struck all else aside.

"This curse—it is on *you* now, isn't it?" she gasped. "You reunited the stones, but you separated them again!"

He shrugged and withdrew his hand. "It doesn't matter. Max is well, and I feel fine."

She relaxed a bit. "Did it affect your father right away, then, after he stole the first sapphire?"

Saxon looked thoughtful, his brow furrowed. "No." Then he only shrugged again. "It doesn't matter," he repeated.

Ashiana almost groaned. It did matter!

He mattered.

And because she had lied to him on the island, insisted that the sapphires were gone, it would be her fault if anything happened to him. She could not live with that.

She realized then that she was going to have to be completely honest, not later but now. She had hoped to persuade him that she was not deceitful by nature; this final piece of the truth would either convince him of that, or prove to be the last lock that would seal his heart against her forever.

She hadn't planned on making such a huge leap of faith so quickly. But she had no choice. Not when the curse put his life in danger. Taking as deep a breath as she could manage, she braced herself and said it all in one sentence.

"It matters but we can do something about it because the other eight sapphires are still on the island."

He swore and clenched his fists. "I *knew* you were lying about that! Blast you, woman, you looked right into my eyes and *swore* they were lost!" His gaze cut her. "Do you *ever* expect me to trust *anything* you say?"

"I didn't know about the curse!" she cried. "If you had been honest with me, I would have been honest with you!"

"It's too late to argue about who lied to whom first, damn it."

"I couldn't tell you before, but I am telling you now. I *am* being—"

"Where on the island?"

Ashiana tucked in her chin. He wasn't interested in the fact that she was being honest, or how much it was costing her. He neither noticed nor cared that she was taking an incredible risk, trusting him.

But why should he care? she cried inwardly, the thought piercing her like a sharp needle. *He still considers me the enemy.* She cared for him—more deeply than she had ever dared acknowledge before this moment—but he did not return her feelings in the least.

"They are not *on* the island exactly," she whispered. "I hid them at sea."

"At *sea?* How in the name of God did you hide them at sea?"

"I'm a very strong swimmer." She looked up at him from beneath her lashes.

He looked dumbfounded, then angry. Whether with her or with himself, she couldn't tell. "Of course. I should have guessed. Anyone who knew the islands well enough to be able to make watertight mats and build a blasted tree-house would probably be able to swim, too."

"What is important is that I know where they are. We have to take the one you have and reunite them before it's too late."

"I can't leave London now. There's a little matter of business I have to attend to. I'll leave in a few weeks."

"We will leave," she corrected.

He looked at her askance. *"You* don't trust *me?* I told you I'm going to give them back."

"You can't give them back. I have to do it. If you go anywhere near the Ajmir, they'll kill you. They know who you are! How do you think I knew which man to dance for in Daman? You would never have the chance to say a word of explanation before they cut your throat."

"I'll wrap the blasted sapphires in swaddling and leave them on the doorstep," he said sarcastically. "I am not taking you with me. Now where exactly are they?"

Ashiana remained stubborn. "If you don't know where they are, you'll have to take me along."

"I don't need you," he retorted. "Now that I know they're in the sea, I'll find them soon enough."

"It is a very large sea. And I'm a strong swimmer. You don't know how far out they are. You don't even know if you'll be well enough to look for them once you get there." Her voice broke as she pointed that out.

"That's not what this is about at all, is it?" He glowered at her. "You just can't wait to get back to your people. Back to your *prince.*"

Ashiana bit her lower lip. "Did you intend to keep me here forever?"

He didn't respond, but his eyes said it all: he wanted her. But fierce as his physical desire was, it was just that. Physical.

She had been an enjoyable bedmate, but she was no more important to him than the cravat he wore or the amber liquid in his glass.

She could not bear the silence of Saxon refusing to speak. "I am an Ajmir princess," she said with pride. "I must go back. Even if you locked me in a room and kept me prisoner, I would find some way to get home."

His gaze narrowed. "Knowing what you know now, your *duty,* your *clan* still mean more to you than anything?"

She blinked back tears. "When you disagree with your family, do they mean any less to you? Do you love them any less? Even if all the years and miles in the world parted you from them, would you *ever* stop trying to get home?" She choked back a sob and motioned to the window. "Think of how happy you felt today. Is it so difficult to understand why that is what *I* want?"

He stood towering over her, his fists clenched so tightly,

she could see him shaking. Suddenly he spun on his heel and stalked to the door. "You'll only have to suffer England a few more weeks. As soon as I've finished my business here, I'll take you back to your family."

John Summers, Sixth Earl of Greyslake, spent his first morning back in London half-naked in bed at his fashionable town house; this sanctuary was one of the only places in which he didn't mind exposing the scars burned into his arms and hands. Gulping down coffee liberally laced with rum, he perused the newspapers.

The Daily Post, The Grub Street Journal, The London Evening Post, The Courant, The Gazette—he featured prominently on the front page of every one of them. Chortling, he lit a cigar and clamped it between his teeth.

"Look at this one." He smacked the bare rump of the expensive young lady dozing beside him. " 'All London has cause for celebration as perhaps the greatest hero of the year reached our shores yestereve. Captain Greyslake of His Majesty's sloop *Phoenix,* at personal risk to life and limb, did gallantly rescue every sailor from the unfortunate Indiaman *Valor* and grant one and all safe passage home to these fair climes. It is believed he will receive not only a full pardon from the Admiralty for being late in returning to London when recalled, but will accept a much-deserved promotion—' "

The girl moaned and pulled a pillow over her head. Greyslake whacked her with the paper.

"Pay attention when I'm reading to you, damn it. It's not every day you have the honor of servicing a national hero. Show some gratitude."

Picking up a pair of shears from the bedside table, he clipped the article and placed it in the pile with all the others, to be enjoyed in detail later. Grabbing his coffee, he drank between puffs on the cigar then picked up the next paper on the silver tray.

He hadn't expected things to turn out quite this well. He had thought he might have to do a bit of dodging with the

Admiralty to explain why the *Phoenix* had trailed in long after the rest of the fleet.

It seemed poetic justice that the "rescue" of the *Valor*'s sorry crew made such an excellent alibi. What a perfect finale to D'Avenant's death.

In truth, he was late because he had resumed his course for the Andamans—where he left his ship with a few selected men and conducted a clandestine search of the islands.

Which proved fruitless.

Greyslake frowned. Even the glowing praise he was reading in *The Daily Advertizer* could not erase that disappointment. He had wanted those bloody sapphires—almost as much as he had wanted D'Avenant dead—but they were nowhere to be found. His search for the jewels had begun eight years ago as pure vengeance: he wanted to leave the D'Avenant family forever cursed. But he certainly wouldn't mind becoming one of the world's richest men.

Unfortunately, the only information his spies had been able to glean on the islands were rumors: about secret plans and an adopted English girl, a princess, who had recently been banished from the clan.

Probably just rumors. But from the description, it had sounded exactly like the wench in D'Avenant's cabin.

Greyslake chewed his cigar. It was too late now to regret not taking the chit with him. Whatever information she might have known had died with her. The *Valor*'s boats had barely gotten clear of the sinking ship before it exploded and went down. None of the survivors had seen her. Only bodies floated among the debris in the darkness.

She was dead, with D'Avenant, at the bottom of the sea with the *Valor* for their coffin. Greyslake would have to settle for that satisfaction.

He turned the page, deciding he had had his full of stories about himself, for now, and could turn his attention to London's other news. As he scanned the columns with little interest, a familiar name leaped out at him.

D'Avenant.

His gaze swooped back. The lit cigar tumbled from his

mouth along with a searing mouthful of curses as he read the headline.

D'Avenant rescuer to receive medal.

"Son of a bitch!" Greyslake exploded out of bed, the paper clutched in his shaking, scarred fists as he read the rest.

Captain Andrew Bennett of the sloop Crusader, *whose miraculous rescue of a member of the famed D'Avenant family this publication reported here Monday last, will receive a medal for meritorious service from the Admiralty at a ceremony Wednesday next. Captain Bennett will be honored for saving the life of Captain Saxon D'Avenant of the East India Co., and a lady passenger from aboard his ship, the rescue of the crew of which is reported elsewhere in these pages. Captain D'Avenant and the lady were located only after suffering terribly during weeks upon a deserted island in the Indian Ocean, which story this reporter is presently endeavouring to secure. The lady is believed to have been separated at birth from her British parents . . .*

"Goddamned buggering son of a *bitch!*" Greyslake crushed the paper between his hands, fury and disbelief slashing through him. D'Avenant was still alive! For nine years Greyslake had wanted only two things—the sapphires and D'Avenant's death—and now he had neither!

He flung the wadded paper at the cowering woman in his bed. "Get up. Get out!"

She needed no more urging, didn't even pause to cover herself with a sheet before she ran for the door. Greyslake kicked it closed behind her, then picked up the silver tray piled with half-empty dishes and sent it flying against the far wall, finding no satisfaction in the shattering porcelain.

Breathing hard, he tried to get a grip on himself and think of what action to take. D'Avenant probably knew everything already—not only that Greyslake was back in London, but exactly where he was. The bastard didn't even need his network of informants, for Christ's sake— Greyslake's whereabouts were splattered all over the bloody papers!

And here he was sipping coffee in his own bed in his own town house! He might as well paint a target on his back! They were probably outside even now—

Greyslake ran to a secret compartment in the wall and withdrew a pair of pistols and a favorite knife. Grabbing a fistful of clothes from his armoire, he yanked them on without summoning his valet. He had to get out of here. Secretly, quietly, fast.

From what the paper reported, D'Avenant had been in town for over a week. He'd had time to plan. To choose a strategy. To protect his family, to protect—

The girl.

Greyslake stopped, his shirt half-buttoned. Calm settled over him as confidence returned in a rush.

The girl.

Walking around the bed, he snatched up the crumpled newspaper he had thrown, opening it on the mattress and smoothing it out until he could read the smeared ink. He scanned the article, seeking her name.

Lady Ashiana.

He committed that to memory and tossed the paper aside. From what his spies had managed to glean in the Andamans, she had something to do with the gems. Now he would have the opportunity to wring the information out of her. Personally. Eagerness washed over him. She was the key.

He would have the sapphires *and* D'Avenant's death, all wrapped up in one neat package. All he needed to do was get his hands on the girl.

And he knew exactly how he would do it.

Chapter 24

Well over a thousand people had crammed into the Drury Lane Theatre for the evening's six o'clock performance. The galleries and pit overflowed with peers and ladies, maids and footmen, dissipated lords eager to visit the latest comely young actresses backstage, and noisy crowds of young bucks dropping by just for a scene or two on their way to the coffeehouses. Those who weren't busy talking to one another stamped their feet and banged sticks on the wooden seats, impatient for the curtain to rise.

Saxon took it all in with a gut-churning combination of wariness and unease. Greyslake had disappeared two weeks ago, vanished just hours after he arrived, even as Saxon's men lay poised to spring their trap. They could find no trace of him, but the slippery snake would have to surface sooner or later; the *Phoenix* was scheduled to leave London in three days.

Three days. Before then this deadly duel that had skirmished from London to India and back again, over years and seas and continents, would finally end. Three days. Saxon burned for vengeance now that it hovered within his reach. Burned with the nightmare images that now tormented him even during daylight: his wife, his Mandara, dying an agonized death in his arms on the Kashmir plains. For her, he would have justice.

Three days.

If he was going to find and finish Greyslake, he had to

lure him out, taunt him into making a desperate move in
the open. But Saxon was not about to play games with the
lives of his family.

Two things made him feel better this night: the tiny candles that lit the lavish D'Avenant family box, just to the
right of the stage, left them almost in darkness, illuminated
only by a wisp of a glow. And some of those dissipated-
looking lords and noisy young bucks down there were
Saxon's own hand-picked men.

Still, as he scanned the audience, he could not shake the
feeling that they made a quintet of most appealing targets:
Ashiana, Paige, Max, himself, and Julian, who had finally
returned home from the East last week.

Paige leaned forward from her seat beside Max and
spoke to Ashiana. "I know you'll enjoy this, my dear. One
cannot truly know England until one has seen Shakespeare. Are you certain you're quite well, though? Your
sniffles seem to be getting worse."

"Oh, no. I am quite all right." Ashiana sneezed.

Saxon, sitting at Ashiana's right, offered his handkerchief. "Her cold couldn't have anything to do with the fact
that you've been giving her the grand tour in the middle
of December, could it, Mother?" he said disapprovingly.

The Duchess opened her fan with a snap. "I would
hardly call a few afternoons in the local shops, an im-
promptu ride in St. James's Park, and tea with Lady
Kilvert and her daughters 'the grand tour.' "

"You have barely allowed us to go out anywhere,"
Ashiana added, waving aside the proferred handkerchief
and using her own.

"I've already explained ten or twelve times why that's
necessary. I also think it's foolish for you to be out in this
weather when you're not used to the climate. And it appears I've been proven right." Saxon jammed the linen
square back into his waistcoat.

Since learning of Greyslake's return, he had restricted
the ladies' activities, and accompanied the pair as much as
possible, but his mother was not one to listen to reason or
let the threat of a little violence ruin her enjoyment of life.

Tonight she had been adamant in her insistence on a grand evening out to celebrate the holidays, and steadfast in her confidence that Saxon could protect them from any harm.

Max scanned the audience through a pair of opera glasses. "I would hardly say you've been gathering dust at home, Mother. It hasn't been all that bad."

"That's right." Julian leaned forward from his seat on Paige's left. "You two ladies have been like a pair of snowbirds, twittering about everywhere from Charing Cross to the Strand and pecking at us poor men to carry your packages. Peck, peck, peck—"

"Oh, stop it, you." Paige tapped Julian with her fan, but her smile was brighter than the chandelier that lit the stage below. "I'm just so happy to have three of my sons all home at the same time. I can't help it if I'm in the mood to go out and celebrate. And there are Christmas gifts to be bought."

"Yes, convenient of you to grace us with your presence just in time for Yuletide, Jules," Max said.

"I pride myself on timing." Julian looked down the row and winked at Ashiana. "Who could resist wassail and plum pudding *and* the company of two such lovely ladies?"

"Timing, hell," Saxon commented. "You're just lucky you left Bombay with a guardian angel on your shoulder. The winter gale that blew you into port could just as easily have sent the *Rising Star* to the bottom of the Channel. All that money you spent repairing your ship would have been wasted."

Julian flashed a smile. "We all have guardian angels, Sax. Some are invisible, some aren't. What angels require most is someone to believe in them."

Saxon shot his brother a glare, catching his double meaning. He'd already heard this particular lecture. What he couldn't believe was how easily Julian had forgiven Ashiana after all she had done. Julian had been angry at first, upon hearing that the sapphire she had taken from Saxon—the one Julian spent months searching for—had been on the *Valor* all along. But when Ashiana had explained her reasons, Julian had been quick to forgive her. He had also commented that it was a trait his older brother obviously didn't—but should—share.

Ashiana sneezed again.

"Bless you," Saxon growled.

"Thank you," she replied with cool formality. "You are most kind, my lord."

Saxon returned his attention to the audience, trying to ignore Ashiana, just as she had been ignoring him all evening. He was discovering, however, that it was impossible to ignore and protect at the same time.

He had moved his chair so close to hers that their arms touched. The gown she wore—black velvet, embroidered in silver at the bodice and sleeves—left her shoulders bare. The occasional brush of her skin against the cloth of his coat sent heat and tension radiating through him.

The fact that she did not flinch away from the contact only intensified his desire, as did the scent she wore. It was an intoxicating blend of Eastern spice and English roses that a perfumer had mixed especially for her.

She wreaked havoc on his senses and his concentration—and that was dangerous.

"Oh, look, Ashiana," Paige said brightly. "There's that charming Captain Bennett. Didn't you decline an invitation from him to be with us tonight?"

Ashiana waved her fan and smiled at Bennett, who sat with a group of Naval officers on the opposite side of the theatre. Saxon had already noticed them, but saw no familiar faces other than that six-foot popinjay, and no reason to point him out.

"Actually, I was *instructed* to decline," Ashiana said, casting a meaningful look Saxon's way. "But Andrew has asked me to join his family and some friends after the play for a late supper, and I accepted."

"You didn't tell me that." Saxon pinned her with a narrow gaze.

"I did not see the need. Andrew is certainly not a threat to my safety. You know him quite well."

"We all do, after the past two weeks." Max grinned.

"Late supper with Bennett. Tea with Bennett. Whist with Bennett. Luncheon with Bennett."

The Duchess nodded. "I think it's been very sweet of the kind captain to visit, since Ashiana hasn't been able to get out much."

"Has not been *allowed* out," Ashiana corrected. "And Andrew will not be in London much longer. His ship is being sent to help blok-ed a French port."

"Blockade, dear," Paige amended.

"About bloody time," Saxon muttered under his breath. "The 'kind captain' is getting to be such a fixture at the house I'm thinking of having him stuffed and hung over the hearth."

"Sax, your taste is all in your elbow. He'd clash with the decor," Julian quipped. "What with that big gold medal dangling about his neck and all."

Ashiana fixed a glare on Saxon. "I think it was terribly rude of us not to attend Andrew's medal ceremony. It was not his fault that his name was connected with ours in the newspapers."

"I believe it's time for us all to stop twittering, please," Max admonished, consulting his pocket watch. "The curtain is about to go up and this is a very serious play."

"I thought you said it was a comedy," Julian protested.

"The Merchant of Venice is considered a comedy by most, but it contains some quite powerful and intriguing themes. For instance—"

"Themes?" Julian groaned. "God, anything but that. I thought this was going to be fun."

"Shakespeare *is* fun," Max countered.

Julian shook his head in despair. "We have to get you out more often, lad. Your life has been too dull."

"Yes. It has," Max retorted, "and don't call me 'lad.' You're only four years older than I am. Perhaps I have devoted myself to my studies, but—"

"You can tell *me* the themes of the play, Max," Ashiana interrupted, gently but deftly deflecting his rising anger. "I would like to know."

Turning away from Julian, Max smiled at finding a

more receptive audience. "I really think it's one of the Bard's best. All about justice and forgiveness. In the fourth act, Portia, the heiress, has a marvelous speech that begins, 'The quality of mercy is not strained'—'strained' in this sense, of course, meaning constrained or compelled . . ."

Saxon returned his gaze to the audience while Ashiana listened with rapt attention to Max's impassioned dissertation. She asked questions and offered comments at appropriate points, though she couldn't possibly be half so interested as she appeared. She was merely being kind to make up for Julian's teasing.

Kind. Another of her admirable qualities, he thought with surprise. Like her courage and ingenuity, Ashiana's kindness was so subtle, so deeply a part of her, that he hadn't really noticed it before.

Or had he? Thinking about it, he realized it had been there all along: on his ship, when she hid Wyatt from the press-gang. On their island, when she tended his wounds and offered him a soothing drink in a pineapple shell. At the town house, when she kept silent about how much she disliked the food and the weather and everything else about England. He was the only one who knew her well enough to recognize her unhappiness.

He simply hadn't allowed himself to appreciate her kindness before now. Just as he hadn't allowed himself to appreciate anything beyond her physical beauty. He kept rigidly reminding himself that he didn't want a woman like her in his life. A woman he couldn't trust . . . couldn't forgive.

Couldn't care for deeply.

Not the way he had cared for Mandara. It was impossible.

Wasn't it?

The curtain rose and Max finally stopped talking, leaning forward to blow out the candles at the front of the box as a hush fell over the audience.

Saxon sat taut as a bowstring in the darkness, thinking not of dangers that might lurk on all sides, or of the words of the players on the stage, but of the questions that

Ashiana had asked in his study. They taunted him, re-proached him, tore at him.

I was fighting to save my family. Our reasons were the same, don't you see that? How can you condemn me if you do not condemn yourself?

Did you intend to keep me here forever?

"Are you all right?" Ashiana whispered suddenly, her face so close to his, he could feel her breath on his cheek.

"Would you please stop asking that?" he hissed back.

She turned her face to the stage. "Pardon me." She kept her voice so low, he had to strain to hear it. "You looked as if you were in pain. I thought—"

"If I feel a curse coming on, I'll tell you."

He could not see her in the darkness, but he swore he could almost feel the heat of her blush, their cheeks were so close.

She slanted him a disapproving look. "I do not think you are taking this at all seriously."

"At present there are far more serious matters that require my attention. You are the one who should be concerned about your health." He lifted her hand from where it lay on the arm of her chair, feeling the warmth of her skin even through her white silk glove. "You haven't been eating enough. You're almost frail."

She shivered. He couldn't tell if it was because of his touch, or because she wasn't well. He wished to God he knew.

"I—I can find very little that is palatable to eat in this country of yours. I will be fine as soon as I return home."

She tried to withdraw her hand, but Saxon held on, lacing his fingers through hers. "You're trembling," he whispered. "If you have chills, you really should be back at the town house. In bed."

She began trembling worse than before. "I have had chills since the day I set foot in this frigid country of yours. Tonight is n-nothing out of the ordinary."

Saxon disagreed. Tonight felt very much out of the ordinary. Ashiana rigidly returned her attention to the play. But she did not try again to take her hand out of his. And he did not let her go. Holding her firmly yet carefully in the darkness, he stroked his thumb over the silk of her glove.

She felt light, fragile, as if she would float away without the heavy gown to hold her in place. Raising his eyes, he could just make out the contours of her cheekbones, far more pronounced than they had been before.

It was almost ironic. She had been constantly keeping watch over *his* health, asking if he was well, watching for any sign of illness that might indicate the curse had begun to affect him. And all along, she was the one who was—

A sudden, chilling thought iced through him.

What if it was affecting her instead?

His heart clenched, then began to pound. It couldn't be. It made no sense. But then the fact that Max had been stricken had made no sense either. He tried to thrust the wild fear aside, grasping for some handful of logic.

She was thin because she wasn't eating. Her sniffles were the result of the cold weather. *England* was having this effect on her, not the curse.

"Ouch," she whispered, glancing at him with a frown.

"Sorry." Saxon relaxed his grip on her hand and forced himself to take a deep, slow breath, trying to recover his balance. He felt shaken. Stunned. He had been utterly unprepared for the forcefulness of the feelings that had rushed through him at the thought of anything happening to Ashiana.

Tearing his gaze from her face, he swept a keen glance over the audience, filled with a renewed sense of purpose. Three days. He would be finished with Greyslake within three days, and then he would leave and reunite those damned sapphires once and for all. He was not going to let Ashiana go back to her family until he was sure she was well.

However long that took.

That thought both bothered and pleased him. He tried to concentrate on the play and the hundreds of people in the theatre rather than the dozens of uncomfortable questions chasing through his head. Max might find this fun, but to Saxon the first act seemed interminable.

Then, halfway through the second, Ashiana suddenly slumped forward in her chair.

"Oh!" Paige gasped.

"Bloody hell!" Saxon hissed, catching her and lifting her into his lap, his heart slamming against his ribs. He hadn't heard a shot, the hiss of a blade, an arrow, anything. "What happened? Did something hit you? Are you all right?"

She shook her head groggily, pushing at his hands as he tried to check for wounds. "I am not hurt. I just felt dizzy."

"Oh, dear," Paige whispered. "I'm so sorry. This is my fault. It was thoughtless of me to cajole you into coming with us when you aren't feeling well."

Saxon kept running his hands over her neck, her arms, checking for any sort of injury, even a pinprick. "You're sure nothing struck you?"

"No," she insisted, trying to get out of his lap. "Now please let me return to my seat. I will be fine."

"The devil you will." Saxon stood up, lifting her in his arms. "Sorry to cut the evening short, Mother, but I'm taking her home."

"Perhaps that would be best," the Duchess agreed. "Have Cook make her some nice hot soup."

"Max and I will stay with Mother and see that she keeps out of trouble," Julian offered.

"Good. I'll trust both of you to keep a sharp eye on everything." Saxon turned and started for the steps at the rear of the box. "See you all back at the town house."

"There is no need to take me home," Ashiana protested. "I just felt a little light-headed. I will be fine."

"Yes, you will." Saxon carried her down the steps, along the adjoining corridor, and into the theatre foyer, ignoring both Ashiana's objections and the curious looks of the footmen who opened doors for him along the way. He paused only long enough to collect their cloaks, wrapping Ashiana in both her cape and his own.

"This is entirely unnecessary." She tried to wriggle out of his arms as he picked her up again, but was foiled by the thick layers of fabric. "You are the most *stubborn, infuriating*—you are a . . . a . . ."

Saxon grinned wryly as her English failed her and she had to resort to Hindi epithets. He stepped outside and called for one of the two family coaches. The streets surrounding the Drury Lane bustled with footmen and drivers and Londoners out for their evening stroll. The cold night air stole Ashiana's voice just for a moment, but she found it again quickly enough.

"I know why you are doing this," she said accusingly. "You just want to keep me from meeting Andrew later."

"Bloody Bennett has nothing to do with it. You're not well and I'm taking you home."

"Do not pretend that you care about me. I don't think you ever cared, from the very beginning! I have never been anything to you but a possession. Another . . . another notch on your bedpost!"

He looked down at her in amazement, seeing her hurt and fury clearly illuminated by the oil lamps that lit the street. "Where the devil did you hear *that* expression?"

She was struggling so fiercely, he finally gave in and set her on her feet, keeping one arm firmly about her waist.

"I have heard that and more!" she cried. "In the shops, at tea. Everywhere. English ladies do nothing but gossip when they are among themselves. They talk of everything. Just as in the harem. And it did not take many days in London to learn of your reputation!"

"And what, precisely, is that?" he asked lightly.

"Do not make a joke of it. You know what I mean. All your women. You have helped yourself quite glut . . . glut-ton-oz-lee—"

"Gluttonously?"

"Yes, gluttonously! I learned that word yesterday and I think it applies perfectly to you! You have helped yourself quite *gluttonously* to the bedroom pleasures of untold numbers of women. And yet you were the one who called *me* a whore."

Saxon's humor vanished. He took her face carefully between his hands. "I haven't called you that in a very long time, Ashiana."

"But you still *think* it." Tears pooled in her eyes. "That is why you will not let me go anywhere with Andrew. Because you think I mean to give myself to him—"

"*No.* That's not—"

"How could you think that of me? How could you?" She shoved his hands away and stepped back, wiping at the tears that wet her cheeks. "You are the only man I have ever been with. *You.* You are the only man I have ever *wanted* to be with—"

She gasped and clapped a hand over her mouth to stop the words, too late, her expression wide-eyed with complete mortification.

Before Saxon could respond, Ashiana swayed weakly, her knees buckling. She would have fallen in the cobbled street, except that he caught her and lifted her gently in his arms.

Chapter 25

As the coach sped through the London streets toward home, Saxon held Ashiana cradled in his arms, trying to warm her with a fur throw and his own body heat. She was groggy and weak, but her pulse beat strongly in the slender column of her throat.

He stroked her pale, damp cheeks, brushing away her tears and the tangled strands of her black hair. Self-loathing burned in his throat at the memory of having called her a whore; it was perhaps the most untrue thing he had ever said to her. He hadn't said it since their argument on the island, but his words had obviously cut deep wounds.

It seemed that was all the two of them had between them: untruths and half-truths, hurt and desire and anger.

And tenderness.

Saxon closed his eyes in frustration at the emotions knotting inside him. Tenderness. That was definitely among the feelings he had for the woman in his arms. It had been there for some time; that fact had slammed home to him in the gut-wrenching moment when she collapsed in the theatre.

How bloody long had he been deluding himself?

Ashiana stirred and instantly drew his attention. Her lashes fluttered and she took a startled gasp of air and tried to sit up.

"Easy," Saxon said soothingly, holding her still. "You're all right. You got dizzy again."

At the sound of his voice, she squeezed her eyes shut and groaned. "I do not suppose I . . . I fainted in the theater and . . . and dreamed the rest?"

"No." He tried to keep the pleasure and satisfaction out of his voice. "The rest was real. You almost fainted, but it was just before the coach pulled up."

He could feel her wince. "I should not have said what I . . . I mean . . . I did not—"

"You didn't mean it?"

"No—I mean yes. I . . . oh, this is so unfair!"

"Unfair? That you want me?"

"No. Yes!" She tried to turn her head away, but in doing so only nuzzled his arm. "Why do you always have to *do* this to me?"

"What is it that I always do to you?"

His finger traced along her cheek, gently turning her face back to his. In the wavering light of the coach lamps, he could see the dark uncertainty swirling in her eyes.

"Confuse me," she whispered. "Drive me mad. Make me answer questions that have no answers." With a sob, she buried her face against his coat, escaping his gaze as she added, "Make me speak the truth when I have no wish to speak the truth."

"The truth?" he asked in a low, gentle voice. "That I am the only man you have ever wanted?"

Her heart was beating so frantically hard, he could feel it even through the fur and the cloaks.

"Yes."

Her admission made fire and softness steal through him. He lifted her closer, lowered his mouth to hers.

"Saxon?" she whispered, her lashes dusting her cheeks.

His pleasure deepened at hearing his name on her lips for the first time in months. His kiss was his reply.

He took her mouth so gently, so tenderly, she opened like a flower touched by the sun. Warmth and wanting flowed swiftly from him to her and back again tenfold. Her lips parted at his gentle urging, and he felt a sweep of desire take him, unlike any passion he had known in his life, at once fierce and hesitant, commanding and yielding.

His tongue delved lightly, teasingly, tasting and remembering and rediscovering the unique sweetness that was Ashiana. She was fire and spice, petal-softness and exquisite mystery, as rare and precious as the scent she wore and a hundred times more entrancing. His arms closed about her, holding her closer. Tighter, stronger.

He lost himself in that kiss, felt his control slipping, felt emotion taking over as he had never allowed it to do before. He did not want to let her go.

Not now, not in three days, not ever.

That stunning thought shuddered through him, as powerful as the hunger that set his body ablaze. He broke the kiss, only to rove along the smooth curve of her jaw, his lips finding the sensitive spot behind her ear.

"Saxon," she breathed on a sigh, moving in his embrace. "Saxon, I cannot free my arms."

"Really? How convenient." He smiled, nuzzling his cheek against hers. He had wrapped her snugly in the fur, thinking only to keep her warm. But now that other possibilities had presented themselves ...

"Convenient for whom?" she whispered in protest, but even as she said it, she was turning her head, her mouth seeking his once more.

He kissed her lightly this time, his lips brushing hers with a feathery touch, then another after another, until she was shivering in his arms.

"Chills?" he asked teasingly.

"Yes," she sighed. "Oh, yes."

"I thought I was warming you up."

"I'm very ... warm. But, Saxon, I don't think we should be doing—"

"This."

His mouth came down on hers more powerfully and he kissed her deeply, long and slow, lingering over her like sun over water, blazing, encompassing, yet all the hotter for being reflected back by the shimmering currents. When he finally raised his head, her eyes sparkled with sea-deep color and unmistakable passion. The fire in her gaze as she looked up at him echoed what she had said earlier, as clearly as if she were again speaking the words aloud.

You are the only man I have ever wanted.

The truth, the trust, the power she was placing in his hands with that look made him ache so deeply he had to close his eyes against the feeling.

Words suddenly spilled out of him on a ragged breath. "I'm sorry, Ashiana, for ever calling you a whore. I never should have said it. It's not true and it's not what I think."

When he dared look down at her again, he could see fresh tears in her eyes. "What *is* it that you think, then?" she asked hesitantly. "If not because of ... because of that, why are you always so angry when I wish to see Andrew?"

Saxon gritted his teeth, which he had been doing so often of late, his jaw ached. "It's dangerous for you to go out anywhere."

"Why?"

"I explained why."

"Not to me. You explained only that this man named Greyslake is in London, and that he might mean harm to your family."

"That's the truth."

"But why would Greyslake have anything to do with me?"

"Because he thinks you are connected to me."

A heartbeat passed ... two ... three.

"And am I?" she whispered.

"Are you what?"

"Connected?"

"You're a guest in my family home."

She swallowed, dropping her gaze. "I see."

Saxon grimaced. *God, woman, don't do this to me. I don't know what you are to me. Don't ask it now. Not now. Not in the darkness when we're alone for the first time in so bloody long and you're so soft and so sweet and so right in my arms.*

"It's the truth, Ashiana."

"It's only part of the truth. You have never explained

why this Greyslake intends to harm you. You simply expect me to accept your commands without question. You always have. Tell me," she said coolly, "is it that I do not merit an explanation? Or do you think a woman would simply be too dull-witted to understand the complexities of male thinking?"

Saxon sighed in exasperation. How the devil had they gotten onto this subject when he had had something vastly more interesting in mind? "You are anything but stupid, Ashiana. You are the most deucedly quick-witted woman I have ever met."

"So it must be that I do not merit an explanation." Her voice became very small.

"Damn it." His temper ignited at being forced to answer questions he didn't even want to think about. He didn't know what to say.

Everything had been so simple with her in the beginning. Their mutual distrust and dislike had fit him like an iron glove, made it easy to classify her into neat, manageable little categories. Slave girl. Spy. Liar. Whore. He knew how to deal with those.

Now ... he had no new category in which he could place her. And he needed one. Needed some sense of control. Without it, he felt like he was floating in a void of darkness—like the day his ship went down and he swam through the smoke-blackened waters, not knowing whether to reach for her or swim toward the air that he needed to survive.

He abruptly returned to their original subject. "Why is it so bloody important to you to see Bennett anyway?"

"Because he is one of the only friends I have here in London."

Saxon froze. "Has it been so terrible?"

"Yes."

The pain that edged that one word was like a fist in Saxon's gut. He was damned, and he knew it right then. He didn't want to let her go—but she could not wait to leave. If he forced her to stay here against her will, she would hate him. If he took her back to her family and her prince, he would hate himself.

Damned.

"All right, Ashiana," he said tightly, shifting her so that she wasn't so temptingly arrayed over his lap. "You deserve an explanation about Greyslake. But first you need some food and some rest. I am not going to have you fainting on me again."

At his brusque decree, she only nodded her reply.

He held on to her and glared out at the passing town houses, unable to look at her, unable to feel anything but simmering frustration. Blast it, when he had first agreed to take her with him to the islands, he had thought . . .

Once she had fulfilled her duty, once she had seen the sapphires safely returned, he had thought she would . . .

Hell, he wasn't sure what he'd thought. But it wasn't that she would be so eager to leave him.

As he watched the passing streets through narrowed eyes, another thought hit him in the gut. Ashiana's feminine softness and intelligence and warmth were slowly, subtly entwining into his life—and it hadn't even been a year since he had lost his Mandara.

Lost the wife he had sworn never to forget.

He closed his eyes and felt it all claw through him. Betrayal and desire and damnation.

Sitting on the rug before the hearth in her room, dressed in her black velvet gown, two woolen blankets, and the fur throw from the coach, Ashiana at last began to feel warm. She had thawed almost completely by the time Saxon returned and set a silver tray piled with food on the floor beside her. He picked up a pewter mug of steaming liquid and placed it in her hands.

"Eat."

She sniffed the fragrant, spicy liquid. "What is it?"

"Leek soup. Guaranteed by Cook herself to be suitable for vegetarians."

Ashiana took a swallow and made a small sound of relief at the heat it spread through her.

"You could have asked the kitchen staff to prepare something special for you before this, you know," he admonished.

"Paige was doing her best. And I did not . . . I did not wish to be any more bother than I already have been."

And it really does not matter because I am going home soon. I will be healthy as soon as I am back on the Andamans. Healthy and . . .

She couldn't bring herself to add "happy" to that. Or to say any of it out loud. But as Saxon settled himself beside her, leaning back against the hearth, she could tell by his hard expression that he knew what she was thinking.

In unnerved her, the way he seemed to be so attuned to her that he could guess her thoughts. It made her feel vulnerable—and she did not like being so easily read by him when he was still so much a mystery to her.

She dropped her gaze from his penetrating silver eyes, staring into her soup. "You said you were going to explain. About Lord Greyslake?"

"I'll talk. But only if you eat."

Ashiana looked up at him from beneath her lashes, but his request was easy enough to comply with. At least it wasn't an order. Finishing her soup in one long drink, she looked over the platter. He had brought cheese, bread, apples, a bowl of something thick and white made with rice, and a whole pile of plump little sugar-dusted rounds of bread. "What are these?"

"Pastries. Try one."

Ashiana took off her gloves, picked up one of the odd little spheres, and bit into it. It was sweet and sticky, filled with a thick, creamy paste in the center. She polished it off in three bites.

Saxon smiled, and an odd gleam came into his eye. "You see, you can't judge all of England by kippers and roast beef. Just as you can't judge all of our weather by November and December."

She picked up another pastry. "I am eating," she pointed out, trying to persuade him to begin his explanation.

He sighed heavily, drew up one knee, and rested his arm

across it. "John Summers—the man who is now the Earl of Greyslake—was once my best friend," he began without prelude. "Since we were lads. Until the day those bloody sapphires came into my life. My father gave me the jewel he had stolen, on the night he died."

"And asked you to reunite all nine?"

"Yes. He would have preferred to trust it to my older brother Dalton, but Dalton wasn't here, so he had to settle for me."

Ashiana heard the resentment in Saxon's voice and almost asked about it, but didn't wish to distract him from the story at hand. She remained silent, remembering what Paige had told her about dealing with D'Avenant men.

Patience.

"Naturally, I told Greyslake everything," Saxon continued. "He wanted to help. He wasn't an earl then. He was just a second son, like me, with no lands and little money to his name. We set off together for India on my ship, the *Silver Viking.* Thought it would be a grand adventure."

Saxon ran a hand through his hair. "Greyslake's older brother the Earl and his sister went with us on that voyage. We were all friends. The two of them were escorting her to Bombay, hoping to find her a suitable marriage among the newly wealthy set at the English settlement there."

"But could she not find a husband here? There are so *many* people in London."

"Eligible men in London generally seek either beauty or wealth in a wife, and unfortunately Faith was ... to call her plain would be kind. And the Greyslakes never had much of a family fortune. A great many young ladies in her situation go to India each year, hoping to use their titles to catch husbands. They're collectively known as 'the fishing fleet.' "

Ashiana let her expression show what she thought of that unkind term. Rather than interrupting him, she ate and let him continue.

But he didn't.

He remained silent for a long time, his eyes on the polished leather of his boots, the crackle of flames the only sound in the room. Just when she was about to speak, he started again, his voice low and taut.

"There was an accident, when we were less than a week out of port. A fire. Fires are common enough aboard ships, but I should have been paying more attention to my command and less attention to thoughts of sapphires and adventure. The *Silver Viking* didn't go down, but both Greyslake's brother and sister were killed. Trapped by the flames."

"Oh, Saxon, by all the gods," she whispered, horrified.

"Greyslake almost killed himself trying to save them. They were the only two remaining members of his family."

"And he blamed you for their deaths?"

Saxon let his head fall back against the hearth, looking up at the ceiling. She could tell that he blamed himself, even now, after all these years.

"Saxon," she pleaded, "fires *do* happen all the time aboard ships. Andrew told me that is the most dangerous thing about sailing, that we were lucky to survive the fire that sank the *Valor.*"

Saxon seemed trapped in his memories; he didn't even react to Andrew's name. "A Company board of inquiry found me innocent of any wrongdoing, but Greyslake . . . the loss was too much for him. It twisted him inside. He got it into his head that I had purposely murdered them. He knew my—" He flicked Ashiana a pained glance. "—my reputation with women, and convinced himself that I had found Faith irresistible and seduced her, then murdered her to keep her quiet."

"No," Ashiana cried, unable to imagine that Saxon's best friend could have believed that of him.

"That fire killed the man I knew as John Summers, just as surely as it killed his brother and sister. He vowed to take the sapphires, so that *my* family would be left cursed forever. And then he vowed he would take my life."

Ashiana gasped, stunned by the depth of Greyslake's hatred, anguished that friends could turn so horribly into enemies. She understood now why Saxon considered

Greyslake so dangerous ... but sensed there was even more to all of this.

"Is there no chance for forgiveness between you?" she asked softly.

"No," he snapped. "Not after he ..." Saxon closed his eyes, as if each breath caused him pain. "Not after he took ..." He stiffened, his whole body rigid, then shook his head. "I'm sorry, Ashiana. I can't ... tell you any more. Not ... now. Not yet."

Ashiana felt fresh tears in her eyes, not for herself, but for him. She wasn't even touching him, but she could feel the agony that raged through him as if it wracked her instead. Greyslake had done something, taken something from him, hurt him so badly that it was beyond all forgiving.

Forgetting her hunger and the cold and anything but Saxon, she leaned forward, letting the blankets and the fur slide from her shoulders. "Sometimes it is very hard to speak of the past. You do not have to tell me. I will not ask anything more."

She lay her hand over his. His gaze swept up to meet hers, pain and memories and longing and something more swirling in his silver eyes. Suddenly he pulled her into his arms, holding her, breathing raggedly into her hair.

"God, Julian was right about you."

"Right?" she asked softly, wrapping her arms about his back and returning his embrace.

"You are an angel."

Ashiana meant to ask what an angel was, but never had the chance. Saxon showed her that he had other uses in mind for her mouth. Her lips. Her tongue. Slowly, tenderly, he kissed her, until the tension and pain seeped out of him and into her and she accepted it all and soothed it away. She felt the need in him as he tangled his fingers through her hair, lowered her to the rug in front of the fire, one hand seeking and finding the softness concealed by her bodice.

"Wait," Ashiana pleaded in sudden panic. "No, please wait ... I must not do this."

His expression clouded over. "Why, Ashiana?" he asked raggedly. "Is it that you still want to go back to *them?* Back to your clan? Your prince?"

Ashiana squeezed her eyes shut, unable to think, barely able to hear over the pounding of her heart. When she did not reply, he thrust himself away from her.

She could have lied. Should have lied. But she could not make herself lie to him. Not anymore.

"What I want," she said painfully, "what I need, is to feel the sun on my face and the sand beneath my feet, to feel the breeze that comes from the Bay of Bengal. To never again feel crushed by noise and people and customs that make no sense to me. To be with my family, and know their love and respect and pride because I have done what I promised I would do. For all the rest of my days . . ."

She slowly, reluctantly opened her eyes. The hurt that showed on Saxon's face almost tore a sob from her throat. He turned his head and stared into the flames.

". . . And what I want most of all," she finished softly, "is to have you beside me for every minute of every one of those days. And nights."

His gaze shot to hers.

Tears blurred her vision. *"But I cannot have that!* You cannot come with me! The Ajmir would kill you!"

Before she could see clearly again, he had taken her into his arms. "Damn it to hell, Ashiana—"

"And I will not stay here and be your miztriz!"

"My *what?*"

"Miztriz! It is a word I overheard a woman whisper about me in one of the shops. I have been introduced to ladies who are someone's wife or mother or sister or aunt or grandmother or cousin—but I don't fit any of those. I am a miztriz."

"Mistress," Saxon said tightly. "It means—"

"Please do not tell me the meaning! I do not care to know what it means. I can guess."

Whore, her mind whispered. Hard on its heels came

other painful words, memories from her childhood: *feringi.* Outsider. Foreigner. Different.

She had worked all her life to stop those whispers, and they followed her still, reminding her that she didn't fit in, wasn't accepted, didn't belong. No matter how kind Saxon's family was, she was an outsider among them—just as she had been that first night in the foyer. She had no place here.

There was only one way to silence the hateful whispers forever: finish her duty, return home, and become Rao's wife. A heroine to the clan.

An Ajmir princess, forever.

She pulled out of Saxon's embrace. "I can guess what *miztriz* means and I cannot deny that it is accurate!"

"It doesn't even begin to be accurate!"

"It is. I do not belong here. I have never been anything more than a possession to you and I will not *be* that anymore!" she sobbed. "I cannot." Her heart cried out all the rest that she did not dare say aloud: *I cannot bear to touch you this way, to care for you this way, and know that I must leave you. It hurts too much to let you into my heart and then tear you out again. So much I wish to die!*

"God damn it, Ashiana, you are—"

A loud knock interrupted him. Saxon got to his feet with a curse.

Ashiana rapidly straightened her bodice and her hair, cheeks burning as she realized how inappropriate it was for Saxon to be here, alone, in her room like this. A proper English lady would have known that.

A proper Hindu girl would have known it, too.

She wasn't a proper anything. Except perhaps a proper *miztriz.*

Saxon opened the door an inch. "What?" he snapped.

"Sorry, sir. Urgent, sir. One of your . . . er . . . associates just came to the back entrance. Says he went to the theatre and missed you there. He has news he must tell you immediately, my lord. I've shown him into your study."

Saxon muttered another oath. "Tell him I'll be down in a minute."

He shut the door and stalked back to Ashiana's side. Bending down, he lifted her chin on the edge of his fist. "Wait here," he commanded quietly. "Don't move. Not one inch. I'll be back shortly and we will finish this discussion once and for all."

He kissed her, a quick, hard, possessive kiss. Ashiana didn't protest. It was useless to tell him there was nothing more to discuss.

When he left the room, she felt her earlier chill return in an icy rush.

He was her warmth. *Saxon.* Hotter than any fire, brighter than the sun, more comforting than the thickest furs, stronger and more potent than wine.

And she was going to have to get used to living without him. When she returned to the heat-drenched islands that were her home, she knew she would be colder than she had ever been in England.

She sat staring down at the patterned rug, neither thinking nor moving. Saxon had only been gone a short time when a knock came at the door.

"Come in," she said, surprised that he had bothered to knock. She cleared her throat and repeated it more loudly, realizing she had barely whispered. "Come in."

To her surprise, it was Eugenie. The maid smiled. "Lovely to see you've got a bit of color back in your cheeks, miss. Are you feeling better? Captain Bennett is below, in the parlor. Something about a late supper?"

"Oh! I forgot all about Andrew. Thank you, Eugenie." Ashiana went to the door, then went back and picked up her gloves as an afterthought. She didn't intend to go to the late supper with Andrew and his family as she had promised, but she could at least look presentable when she went down to apologize for leaving the theatre so abruptly.

She paused to glance in the mirror, hoping no one could tell she had been rolling about on the floor in a torrid embrace.

Miztriz.

Forcing the hateful word to the back of her mind, she followed Eugenie down to the parlor.

"Andrew," she greeted him as she stepped inside. "I am so terribly sorry I left the play without a word to you. I was not feeling well, and Saxon thought it best to bring me home."

He looked concerned. "Are you quite all right?"

"Yes, thank you. I have what the Duchess calls 'the sniffles.' I am feeling better now."

He smiled. "Excellent. My coach is outside, and my family are so looking forward to meeting you."

He had a sparkle of almost boyish excitement in his eyes, and Ashiana felt terrible for having to decline. She shook her head. She would certainly welcome an escape from the rest of the discussion Saxon had promised, but she wasn't going to run off like a coward. And she certainly wasn't going to leave with Andrew; that would make everything disastrously worse. "I am afraid I will not be able to join you tonight."

"Another time, then?"

"I hope so," Ashiana agreed, already escorting him back to the foyer.

"Do you think you might come out just for a moment, Lady Ashiana? I have a lady friend who has been simply dying to make your acquaintance, and she was so disappointed to miss you at the theatre. She had her driver follow my carriage over."

Ashiana hesitated. She really should check with Saxon before going anywhere. But he was busy, and Andrew seemed so eager; if this one simple request could make up for so rudely missing his medal ceremony and tonight's supper, it was the least she could do.

Besides, she was with Andrew. She was completely safe.

"Townshend," she said to the footman at the door, "I am going to step outside a moment. If Lord Saxon comes looking for me will you let him know I will be right back?"

"Certainly, miss." Townshend hurried to fetch her cape, then draped it about her shoulders.

Andrew offered his arm. "You do me a great favor, my

lady. My friend said she would hold me in eternal esteem if I managed an introduction to the mysterious young lady from the East."

Ashiana smiled at seeing the happiness in his eyes. They stepped outside and Townshend shut the door behind them. As Andrew led her down the steps and into the darkness, Ashiana shivered, feeling the night-sharp cold seep through her in seconds.

Two coaches waited at the end of the walk, the drivers hunched in voluminous cloaks and wool scarves. Andrew approached the second one and tapped on the door.

To Ashiana's surprise, the figure who waited inside was clearly not a lady. "Andrew," she said in puzzlement, "what is—"

"What the devil, man," Andrew exclaimed with surprise. "Where are her paren—"

Someone leaped out of the darkness and struck Andrew from behind at the precise moment a leather-gloved hand cut off Ashiana's scream.

The man leaned out the door and smiled in the light of the coach lamps. "Don't you appreciate my little surprise, *Lady* Ashiana? Ah, I see you remember me."

Chapter 26

Ashiana was half-lifted and half-thrown into the coach. The instant the gloved hand came away from her mouth she screamed, an ear-splitting cry for help. But the driver had already whipped the horses and the team lunged into a gallop. The coach raced away into the night even before the curtained door slammed behind her.

"Shut up, damn you." Greyslake shoved her into the corner of the seat beside him.

She struck at him with her fists and started to scream again. Greyslake clamped a hand over her lips.

"Save your breath. You're too late to save your gallant friend Bennett. I'm sure his death will make all the papers—hero tragically killed on the street while visiting the man he rescued. Too many footpads, vagabonds, and highwaymen on the roads these days. Dangerous to even step outside one's door."

Ashiana made a sound of anguish in her throat. Andrew! She struggled, but Greyslake's hand choked off her air and his weight crushed her against the seat. His voice had a high-pitched, cruel tone that terrified her.

"My dear, you have no idea how long I have been waiting to renew our acquaintance. I had hoped to catch you at that fool Bennett's medal ceremony, but D'Avenant was too smart to let you attend. I anticipated that. So I did the next best thing and made friends with Bennett. He was quick to accept a fellow Navy captain into his circle."

Ashiana tried to slow her frantic breathing, her racing

323

heartbeat, tried to think. Where was he taking her? What did he intend? If he hadn't killed her outright he must have something far worse in mind.

The answer pierced her heart.

He meant to use her as bait! To lure Saxon to his death!

She tried again to call out but no sound passed his hand. She fought him, kicking and wrestling against his hold.

"Enough, wench!" Greyslake released her mouth just long enough to strike her with the back of his fist. Ashiana's head snapped to the side. Her cheek ached and burned and her mind reeled dizzily. She tasted blood on her tongue.

"Don't make me damage you just yet," he said silkily, covering her mouth once more and jerking her head around so that she was forced to meet his dark, unfeeling gaze. "I've waited too long for this. Do you think it was easy convincing Bennett to keep my presence a secret? I told him I had read about you in the papers, that I had been sent by your long-lost father the Earl. I said your parents wanted to surprise you. Tonight's supper was to be your reunion celebration."

Ashiana felt her heart sink. Andrew had always been so hopeful that she would find her English "parents." Greyslake seemed to know exactly how to play on his victims' weaknesses.

"I was right there at the Drury Lane tonight," Greyslake continued with relish. "Waiting in my coach at the rear of the theatre. I told him I would have your mother and father with me and that we would give you a ride to the party. I even told him to use that line about meeting a lady friend so you wouldn't guess and ruin your surprise." His pleased expression vanished beneath fury. "But then you left early."

Ashiana's heart redoubled its pace. Paige. Julian. Max. Had he hurt any of them?

Greyslake leaned to the side and parted the window curtains. "You can scream all you want now. No one will help you. Not in this part of town."

Ashiana tried to stop shaking as he slowly removed his

hand. Her cheek throbbed where he had struck her. Her tongue felt thick in her mouth. "There is no need to do this," she said quickly, desperately. "You have already had your vengeance. You have hurt Saxon before—"

"Not half so much as I'm going to hurt him now." He shoved her back against the seat again, pinning her there, grabbing her wrist in a painful grip. Her other arm was wedged behind her back. "Shall I begin?"

Ashiana felt herself go pale, but she wouldn't give him the satisfaction of hearing her beg for mercy. "You cannot hurt him by hurting me. And he will not come after me. I mean nothing to him."

Greyslake laughed. "You forget I was his friend once. Why do you think I selected you? I could have abducted one of his brothers. Or his mother. *You* will make him careless. I've been following you for days. Watching you with him. You mean even more to him than his wife did."

Ashiana gasped.

His *wife*.

Suddenly she knew what it was that Saxon had been unable to tell her earlier. Understanding flooded in.

"You killed her," she breathed.

"That was only the first part of the payment I will exact," Greyslake snarled. "Now the rest begins. But we have time. You will not die so quickly as she did. I want to make him *watch* while I take you."

He leaned closer, so close she could see the flat, lifeless brown of his eyes. "First, my pretty bit of bait, you will tell me everything you know about the sapphires."

"Sapphires?" Ashiana pressed her head back against the seat cushion, straining away from him.

And struck upon a plan.

"Don't try my patience, wench. The Nine Sapphires of Kashmir. The jewels that will make me one of the richest men in the world."

"What . . . what is it you wish to know?"

She moved her hand, the one trapped behind her back, up toward the curls pinned at the nape of her neck. Years of yoga exercise had made her more flexible than

Greyslake could ever guess. If she could just keep him talking—

"Where are they?" His fingers tightened about her other wrist.

Ashiana gasped in pain. "I do not know." She inched her hand up ... up ... her fingers straining to reach one of the long hairpins that held her coiffure in place.

From inside his coat, Greyslake withdrew a long, wicked-looking knife with a serrated edge. "You will tell me. Now. Or I will slice off an ear to send as a token to D'Avenant."

Ashiana's fingers closed around the jeweled head of the pin. "The sapphires are hidden at ... at ..."

"Where?" He placed the edge of the blade beneath her earlobe.

She yanked the pin free, twisted her wrist, and stabbed the point into his hand.

Greyslake yelled with surprise and snatched his hand back, dropping the knife. Before he could recover his hold on Ashiana, she lunged to one side, scrambling desperately for the handle that opened the door. She threw all her weight against it.

It opened far more easily than she had guessed. With a startled cry, she fell outward with the door as the coach raced around a turn and onto a bridge. Greyslake shouted curses and grabbed for her cloak, too late. She hung suspended for one terrifying second before she fell.

She tried to roll but her knee, her elbow, her side all struck the ground painfully hard. The cobbled street knocked the breath from her. She barely missed being crushed by the coach wheels.

She lay on her side, dazed, until the sound of Greyslake shouting at his driver brought her to her feet. They were on a bridge that spanned a huge river, but she could barely make out the shadows of buildings along the banks; there were no street lamps here. The only light came from the moon.

"Help!" she screamed. "Someone help me!"

The few people evident in the shabby-looking area took one look at the unfolding scene and fled.

The driver had yanked his team to a stop and Greyslake was already leaping out of the coach. Ashiana turned to flee—only to see a dark-haired man on horseback bearing down on her.

He brandished a pistol in each hand.

Ashiana froze, screaming, certain she was about to be killed.

"Get out of the way!" the stranger yelled, aiming over her head and firing.

The explosive report of the pistol shot rang in her ears, followed by another. It took Ashiana a second to realize that he was not shooting at her, but at Greyslake and the driver.

"I'm supposed to be protecting you!" the man shouted. Reining in his lathered horse, he holstered the empty pistols and leaned down, holding out his arm. "Come on!"

Ashiana didn't need a second urging. But she wasn't quick enough. Her moment's hesitation had been one moment too long.

Greyslake's knife hissed through the air and struck the man in the shoulder. Her rescuer fell backward with a grunt of pain, tumbling from his horse.

Before Ashiana had time to react, Greyslake was beside her. He grabbed her about the throat with one arm and yanked her back against him as a shield.

"I'll kill her!" he shouted as the man got to his feet. "Back off or she dies!"

Ashiana gasped air in terrified gulps. Greyslake locked his arm about her throat with such force that one quick snap might break her neck. He was wounded; she could feel blood soaking into the back of her cloak. The driver was nowhere to be seen. Her rescuer jerked the knife from his shoulder with a low curse and crouched as if he meant to lunge toward them.

Greyslake backed toward the bridge railing. "Stay away, damn you. Send your horse over here."

The man didn't move.

"Do it!" Greyslake snarled.

Still no reply.

Greyslake suddenly lifted her in his arms, up over the slender metal railing. Ashiana screamed. She could hear the icy river currents rushing by, so far below she could barely see them in the darkness.

Greyslake held her balanced on the edge, pushing her out so far her fingers couldn't reach the railing. If he released his arm from around her throat, she would fall.

"*Now,* you bastard!" Greyslake yelled. "Send your buggering mount over here or—"

The clatter of hoofbeats sounded from the end of the bridge.

"*Ashiana!*"

"Saxon!" She managed only that strangled cry of mingled relief and love and terror before Greyslake's arm tightened. She could move her eyes just enough to see Saxon riding up on an unsaddled horse.

"Stay back, D'Avenant!" Greyslake shouted, his voice getting higher. "I'll kill her!"

Saxon threw himself from his horse, his eyes never leaving hers. He wasn't wearing a cape or coat. Ashiana's heart hammered when he tossed the single pistol he held to the stranger in the dark clothes.

The man caught the pistol and aimed it at Greyslake's head.

Saxon took a step toward the railing, his hands held away from his sides. "It's over, Greyslake. Let her go."

"How did you find us, you son of a bitch?"

Ashiana could hear Greyslake's breathing becoming labored. If his arm weakened, he would drop her. She gasped for air, for courage as new tendrils of fear wrapped around her. She focused on Saxon's deep voice.

"One of my operatives came to tell me you had been spotted at the theatre. As soon as he said it, I knew Ashiana was in trouble." His eyes burned into hers. "I felt it."

Greyslake ground out a curse.

"And the footpads you hired weren't up to your usual

standards," Saxon continued. "Bennett managed to fight them off. He told me what your coach looked like. But I already knew where you would go."

"I *wanted* you to find us," Greyslake shot back. "I knew the Scuppers and Blood tavern would be the first place you'd look. But by the time you got to our old haunt, you would have only found a piece of her. I was about to take an ear to leave with the note telling you where to go next."

Ashiana's stomach lurched. In her heart, she reached out to Saxon for strength against the terror and cold that made her tremble.

"It's over," Saxon hissed. "Let her go. You don't want to do this."

"This is *justice,* you murdering bastard! Two lives for two lives!"

"It's *my* life you want." Saxon raised his empty hands. "If you kill her, Logan will shoot you. I'll still be alive. Think about it, Greyslake. *I'll still be alive.* Let her go and it will be you and me. Whatever weapons you want. One to one."

Ashiana sobbed at what Saxon was offering.

She could hear the river lapping hungrily ... such a long, long way down.

Greyslake seemed to hesitate, breathing hard.

"John," Saxon said quietly, "you don't want to do this. You know I never touched Faith. You know I didn't murder them. It was an accident."

"No! It was you! *You* took the last of my family!"

"The fire took them. There was nothing anyone could have done. Not you, not me. We can't always explain a tragedy, John. There isn't always a reason."

Sensing Greyslake's distraction, Ashiana tried to move. He struck her again with his fist, even harder than he had before.

Saxon swore savagely. "If she dies, you die!"

Ashiana could barely hear Greyslake's reply over the buzzing in her head.

"Then we die."

He pushed her over the edge.

* * *

Saxon lunged forward an instant too late. Ashiana fell without a sound. Not a cry, not a scream. Greyslake's blow must have knocked her unconscious.

Logan fired but Greyslake was already moving, diving toward Saxon, knocking him to the ground before he could reach the railing.

"You're too late!" Greyslake laughed.

Saxon's fist smashed into Greyslake's jaw. He tried to shove him aside, his only thought of Ashiana, but Greyslake's hands closed around his throat. Logan rushed at them but they were already locked in furious combat. He couldn't get a clear opening to strike at Greyslake with the knife.

"Go!" Saxon choked out.

Logan obeyed without argument, dropping the knife and kicking off his boots. He dove into the river.

Saxon's hand shot out and closed around the blade's hilt. There was no time to think of life or death or forgiveness or vengeance.

He had to save Ashiana before she died in the icy Thames.

Greyslake fastened both hands about Saxon's wrist, wrestling for the blade—but the blood running down his arm made his hand slick. The death struggle ended almost before it began.

Saxon turned the knife, forced it upward.

And buried it to the hilt in Greyslake's chest.

Greyslake screamed, a keening wail of vengeance thwarted. But even as his body jerked with a death spasm, a smile curved his mouth.

"Two lives," he breathed with his last gasp, blood bubbling on his lips.

Saxon shoved free of Greyslake, feeling no pleasure in vengeance, no relief in victory, no justice for Mandara's murder, no mourning for the man who had once been John Summers.

He felt nothing but gut-wrenching terror as he leaped up

onto the railing. He saw only rushing water and huge chunks of ice below.

"Ashiana!"

The hoarse, anguished shout tore out of him as he dove into the freezing river.

Chapter 27

Saxon sat alone in his darkened study. No fire, no candles, only blackness and cold. Slumped in his chair, he faced the windows. He had drawn the curtains to shut out the light of the December afternoon. In one fist he gripped a crystal decanter, emptied to the last inch of gin.

In the other, he held a long, limp glove.

The white silk was dry now. He looked down at it for the first time in hours. He could see the bloodstains. Even in the darkness, he could see them. And the mud ground into the fingertips. Mud from the river bottom.

All he could think, through the numbing haze of alcohol, was that her hand had been so much smaller than his, her fingers so delicate and slender.

His fist tightened about the glove. His hand started to shake, then his arm, then his entire body, lashed by emotions that threatened to tear loose and rip him apart.

He heard voices murmuring outside the door, the click of the latch whispering open.

"Sax?" Julian said quietly.

Tell me you found her. Sweet Jesus Christ, tell me you found her.

He knew that was not what he was going to hear. Not after three days of searching.

"Sax, they've . . . they've stopped going in. It's too cold. They don't think . . . There's no . . ."

Julian's voice broke and he gave up trying to speak. Saxon didn't respond. He knew what Julian meant to say.

Even if they find her now, there's no chance she's still alive.

His breath left his body in one shuddering exhalation. He tried to lift the decanter again but couldn't find the will. He stared into the darkness, listened to the silence pressing down on him. When he finally spoke, his voice was a dry whisper, hoarse and laced with gin. "You know, I can still smell her perfume in here. She was only in this room once and I can still—"

"Don't, Sax," Julian asked softly. "Don't do this to yourself."

"She died alone. Alone in the cold."

His hand opened and closed reflexively around her glove; he had found it a mile downriver from the bridge, caught in a tree branch. It looked as if she had struggled, fought, grabbed for life—only to be snatched away by the currents.

It was her left glove.

The one that had covered her Ajmir tattoo.

Saxon felt moisture on his face. It took him a moment to realize what it was. Tears. Emotions rose up, hot and unstoppable. "I killed her," he said roughly. "England killed her. She told me once she was a strong swimmer, but she was weak from not eating. I never should have forced her to come here."

"A madman killed her," Julian corrected forcefully. "You did your best to *save* her. You searched until we dragged you out of that river and brought you back here by brute strength. There was nothing anyone could do, Sax—the whole crew of the *Rising Star,* Logan and all our operatives, Bennett and his men. Don't blame yourself."

Saxon blinked and turned toward his brother, but didn't see Julian or anything else. Gone. It was gone. He had accomplished all that he had worked for, all he had thought he wanted. Max was well. Greyslake was finished. But he felt as if he'd lost . . .

. . . Something so vital, he couldn't begin to define it— except to know that he could never replace it. His life. The light.

Julian crossed the room and picked up a taper from the mantel. Lighting it, he carried it to the desk.

"Put it out, Julian. Put it out and leave me alone."

"After we talk." Julian set the sconce on the desk. The sapphire that Saxon had placed on the polished wood top two days ago sparkled in the flame's light. He had taken the jewel out that first morning, when his brothers had brought him home and locked him in here and posted servants at the windows to keep him from going back to the river.

He had sat glaring at it, as if it possessed some answer, some power, some way of calling her back.

Next to it, still in the box, lay the Christmas gift Ashiana had bought him. His mother had brought it in this afternoon, hoping it might help him, somehow, to know that Ashiana had loved him.

It was the *Valor*, a small-scale model, perfect in every detail. She had had it made for him.

Julian sat on the edge of the desk. Saxon glowered at him. "Get out," he said without emotion.

"How long are you going to sit here in the dark drinking and blaming yourself and shutting everyone out?"

Saxon set his jaw, looking up in stony silence.

"Doesn't it remind you," Julian asked carefully, "of another time you and I sat in the dark like this?"

No reply.

"When I found you in the Maratha village." Julian persisted. "You were grieving then, weren't you?"

Saxon slammed the decanter down on the desk and thrust himself to his feet, turning away, clamping down on the emotions that threatened to explode within him.

Julian kept talking. "I was just too blind to see it then, much less help you through it. But you were grieving. Over a woman. Who was she?"

"Get out."

"Do you think this is what she would have asked of you?" Julian continued mildly.

"What?" Saxon roared.

"That you stop living. Is that what she would have

wanted? Is that what *either* of them would have wanted?" Julian's voice dropped to a low, accusing tone. "Do you really think they were both such selfish, demanding bitches?"

Saxon spun with a wordless snarl and grabbed Julian by the coat front, jerking him to his feet and slamming him up against the nearest wall. He drew back his fist, barely stopped short of knocking his brother to the floor.

"That wasn't it at all, was it?" Julian said quickly, not even flinching. "It's not them. It's you. You've done this to yourself. You blame yourself for their deaths and the guilt is tearing you apart."

Saxon stood there breathing harshly, shaking, his arm still poised.

"You want to take a shot at me?" Julian asked softly. "Will that make you feel better? Go ahead. But when you're done beating the hell out of me and beating the hell out of yourself, they'll still be gone."

"It should have been me," Saxon ground out. *"It . . . should . . . have . . . been . . . me!"*

"But it wasn't."

Saxon shoved away from him, fury and grief and anguish blistering through his chest. With a savage sweep of his arm, he snatched up the decanter and threw it the full length of the room. It shattered against a painting on the far wall, slashing the canvas, splashing gin everywhere, scattering shards across the floor.

He slumped forward, bracing his arms on his desk, feeling the pain of the past days, months, years, raining down on him all at once like hail made of hot steel.

Julian stepped closer. "There was nothing you could have done to prevent their deaths, Sax. Sometimes there is no blame. No explanation. You did the best you could."

Saxon swore, one short, expressive oath. Hadn't he recently used Julian's exact words himself? "It's not only that. There's more to it. It's . . ." His voice trailed off.

"Tell me."

"It doesn't matter anymore."

"Tell me."

At his brother's insistent prodding, words tumbled out before Saxon could hold them back. Sharp, agonized words. "I once said to Bennett that I didn't know Ashiana all that well. But I did. I knew her better than I've ever known any woman in my life. I wanted her more. I—" His voice choked out on a dry rasp.

"Say it," Julian urged. "Say it out loud, Sax."

Saxon straightened with a jerk, his head snapping around and the truth spilling out in one breath. "I loved her more! *I loved her more than I loved Mandara!*"

Julian stood silent a long moment. "The Maratha lady you were mourning?" he whispered.

"My *wife*. I married her, Julian. I thought I would never love *any* woman enough to marry, but I did. Then that murdering bastard killed her and I just cast her aside. Forgot her. Like she never existed."

"She obviously meant a great deal to you," Julian argued. "Anyone could see that. You sought justice for her death and you got it."

"But I fell in love with another woman. *Less than a year after she died.*"

"And how long would have been long enough?" Julian challenged, striding around to face Saxon across the desk in the faint light. "How long? A year? Two? Ten?"

"I made a vow."

"And you honored it."

Saxon swore again. "You couldn't begin to understand."

"I understand you better than anyone. You're like a bloody bull terrier once you get your teeth into a promise. Just look at the way you went through hell and back again to keep that vow you made to our father."

"When I give my word, I keep it."

"And you did. And it's done. Now let it go. *Let your Maratha lady go.* What is it you're waiting for, Sax? Forgiveness? She can't come back and give it to you!"

Saxon froze, his heart flickering as fast as the candle flame. Was that what he wanted? Some sort of absolution for the guilt he felt over the death of his innocent wife? Someone to tell him it was all right to stop mourning her?

He shook his head. It couldn't be that simple. "I vowed I would never forget her and I've done nothing but dishonor her memory for months."

"Dishonor?" Julian said incredulously. "You are the most honorable man I know. Just the fact that this is tearing you up so much proves that." He straightened, folding his arms over his chest. "Sax, do you have any idea how much I've admired you, all my life? How much everyone in this family admires and respects and loves you?"

Saxon lifted his gaze to Julian's.

"No, of course you don't," Julian said irritably. "You've been too bloody busy keeping vows to the dead. Trying to prove yourself to our father. Trying to make up for what happened to your Maratha lady. Well, I've got news. Our father is never going to come back and tell you how proud he is of you, and your wife is never going to come back and forgive you." Julian braced his hands on the desk and leaned closer. "*Stop living for them,* Sax. Those of us in your present would greatly appreciate it if you would come out of the past. If it's forgiveness you want, you'd better start by forgiving yourself!"

"Nice speech." Saxon raked a hand through his hair. "I thought Max was the philosophical one. Are you finished?"

"Not yet." Julian picked up the sapphire from the top of the desk. He grabbed his brother's hand and slapped the jewel into his palm. Then he turned and walked away.

"What the hell is this for?" Saxon growled.

"You'll figure it out."

With that, Julian left and closed the door behind him.

Saxon sank back into his chair, staring at the stone, furious that his brother had provoked him into such an emotional outburst.

But then, slowly, his anger faded and he began to understand.

Julian had done this on purpose. Stirred up all the feelings and thoughts crowding his heart and his head, so that he couldn't shut them out anymore.

As Saxon watched the sparkling facets of the sapphire

dance along the walls in the light of that single candle, he began to feel. Longing and love washed over him with a single name. *Ashiana.*

And for the first time, those emotions came without guilt and regret and all the rest of the trappings he had clung to so long.

Ashiana could have filled up his life, just as the sapphire's light filled up this room—with fire and beauty and shimmer and spirit that were beyond any price. She could have made him whole, truly whole.

If only he hadn't been so obsessed with honoring the past, so locked up in memories that he hadn't realized he was living only half a life.

Mandara had been innocent and sweet, and would have made a fine, gentle wife. But she never would have been strong enough to truly balance him. To complete him the way Ashiana could, to join with him as two sharing one life, in all things.

Start by forgiving yourself.

Saxon realized then that he had had everything backwards. Julian was right.

His problem wasn't that he had not held on long enough, but that he had held on *too long.* And in doing so, he had missed the sweet promise of the present. The future.

Forgive.

He closed his eyes as he closed his fingers around the sapphire.

"Mandara," he whispered to the darkness. "Mandara, it is time for me to let you go."

Chapter 28

"**B**y all the graces!"

"Hello, Mr. Townshend." Ashiana smiled weakly, her weariness lifting at the footman's astounded expression. Snow swirled around her in the bright morning sunlight. The hackney driver who had brought her home held her elbow; partly to keep her upright, she thought generously, but mainly to ensure that he would be paid. "I am so sorry to be such a surprise."

"My *word!*" Townshend blinked from her to the coachman and back again, apparently unable to move.

"This . . . this gentleman was kind enough to bring me home, but he did not quite believe that I would pay him." Ashiana coughed, a deep, wracking cough that left her breathless for a moment. "Would you be kind enough to do so?"

"Of course, my lady." Townshend instantly dug into his waistcoat and handed the man several silver coins, then took Ashiana's other elbow to help her inside.

Letting go of her at last, the driver bobbed a quick bow. "Sorry, miss. Hope ye'll fergive me, miss. Can't blame a man fer not believin' ye lived in Grosvenor Square, what with ye lookin' like that."

Ashiana knew that her matted hair and ruined velvet gown made her look like she belonged on the impoverished street where she had hailed him. "I understand. It is quite all right. Thank you."

Townshend dismissed the man with an impatient gesture

and closed the door. "Lady Ashiana, wherever have you been? Everyone has been so—"

"Please, I know that I have a great deal to explain, but first you must tell me—"

"Ashiana?" Paige's astonished voice rang out from the far end of the house. Ashiana's fatigue suddenly competed with a surge of warmth and happiness at seeing the Duchess. Paige came running into the foyer in a flurry of pale-yellow silk. "That *was* your voice I heard! Oh, my dear girl!"

Before Ashiana could utter a word of greeting or apology or explanation, the petite duchess had thrown both arms about her in an astonishingly strong hug, heedless of the dirt caked on Ashiana's gown. "Wherever have you *been?*" Paige cried. "We thought you were dead."

Ashiana returned the hug, feeling more than just relief at finally being safe; her heart was filled by the Duchess's affection and concern. It almost brought tears to her eyes, but she was too tired to even cry. "I am fine, really. But please you must tell me—is Saxon all right? I was so afraid for him on the bridge! Was he hurt?"

"No, no. He escaped unscathed. Greyslake is dead. Captain Bennett is well, and Mr. Logan and everyone else—but what happened to *you?*"

Ashiana could not speak for a moment. Saxon was all right! The fear and tension that had knotted her stomach finally unwound—but that was all that had kept her on her feet. She felt such relief that her legs went weak. Paige instantly led her to the nearest settee.

"Oh, Paige, I do not know where to begin." Ashiana coughed, shivering at the dark, terrifying memories that closed in, now that her concern for Saxon had been relieved. "I tried to swim but the river was so fast, and so cold." She closed her eyes and shuddered. "I tried to make my way toward the shore. I grabbed a branch, but I could not hold on. And then I . . . then . . ."

"What?"

"I am not sure. I do not really remember. The next thing

I knew, I awakened in the darkness, in a very dirty, very small hut. I am not sure you would call it a house."

"But where?" Paige exclaimed. "We checked at all the homes along the river. We checked with physicians, with the magistrates—"

"I am not sure who these people were." Ashiana shook her head. "Only that they were quite un . . . un-plez—"

"Unpleasant?"

"Yes! Their eldest son found me on the riverbank, un . . . un-con . . . asleep."

"Unconscious," Paige supplied.

"Yes, and he brought me home. They were very angry with him. My body was so cold that they could not find my heartbeat. Then they became frightened. They could tell from my clothes that I was someone of importance. They were afraid they would be blamed for my death, so they did not take me to the—the word that you said just now?"

"Magistrate?"

Ashiana nodded. "They did not wish to become involved." She paused, exhausted but able to smile ruefully now that she was safe. "I gave them quite a scare when I awakened. I am not sure how long I had been asleep, but it must have been some time. A day, I think, perhaps two. I was terribly weak and ill. They still thought I might die, and argued over what to do with me."

"But why did they not bring you back here?"

"I asked them to, but they demanded money in order to do so. I told them I had none and pleaded with them to send word here, that you would see they were rewarded. They decided it would be better to wait until I was well and escort me here themselves, so that they might collect payment for their troubles."

"And are they here?" Paige looked toward the door, her expression furious.

"No." Ashiana coughed again and could not speak for a moment. "I could not bear that they would keep me, when I knew you must all think me dead. I slipped away as soon as I felt strong enough. This morning."

"I will have them arrested at once for kidnapping you!" Paige declared, leaping up from the settee.

"No, please." Ashiana caught her hand. "They were not unkind, and they did take care of me. They were just afraid of what might happen to them. And they are so poor, they could not resist the chance to make some money. They had a great many children."

Paige still looked upset. "You are too kind by half, my dear."

"I know what it is like to feel afraid," Ashiana said simply. "Do you think we might send them some small amount for rescuing me?"

"I will send one of the servants with a few guineas." Paige frowned. "And a stern warning never to try such foolishness again."

Relieved, Ashiana smiled. "Thank you, Paige. Now, please, where is Saxon? I have so much to say to him."

The Duchess squeezed Ashiana's hand. "I'm afraid you will have to wait until he returns, my dear."

"Returns?" Ashiana echoed with disappointment.

"Yes. He and Julian left for the Andaman Islands last week, aboard the *Rising Star.* Saxon means to return the sapphire to your clan for you."

Every emotion in Ashiana's heart vanished beneath a storm of shock. Then all her feelings burst together in an explosion of love and pride and stark fear that left her heart thudding in her chest. She couldn't speak, couldn't even think of words that would express what she felt.

Paige sat beside her again. "He was devastated to lose you, Ashiana. It is only a miracle that he did not die in the river trying to save you. I have never seen him so emotional. I feared the grief might be too much for him—and then he got this idea into his head. He said he had to carry out your duty for you."

Stunned into utter silence, Ashiana closed her eyes, feeling tears wet her lashes as the full breadth of her love for Saxon swept through her. What other man would do this—face his mortal enemies to complete a mission that was not his own.

It was not the act of a man who considered her merely a possession, a *miztriz*.

He loved her!

She remembered that night on the bridge, his eyes burning into hers, the way he had tried to sacrifice himself to make Greyslake set her free. Perhaps he had not been able to say the words, but his every action had expressed it vividly. *He loved her.*

She remembered, too, her last thought in the river when she felt life slipping—that she did not want to leave him. And her first and only thought upon awakening in that filthy hut—that she was glad to still be in the same world as Saxon.

She loved him. Oh, by all the gods, she loved him. Being so close to death had shown her just how priceless and beautiful and fragile life could be—and every precious bit of it resounded with his name.

"Saxon," she whispered, opening her eyes.

Then the fear overwhelmed everything else she felt—frantic terror for his life. "Paige, he must not do this!" She grabbed the older woman's arm. "The Ajmir will never believe him. They will kill him!"

Paige looked doubtful. "But he seemed so confident."

"Saxon is *always* confident," Ashiana exclaimed. "But I am afraid that this time he may have taken on a task that is truly beyond him!"

Paige went pale. "But the *Rising Star* left under full sail. They are far out to sea by now."

"We must send another ship to catch him, to bring him back!"

"But they could search for weeks and not find him."

Ashiana groaned, her head spinning. "Then we must rely on another way to save him. We must find a way to get *me* to the Andamans before he arrives. If I can speak with the Maharaja . . . I might be able to make him understand."

"But, my dear, you are not well—"

"Paige, you mentioned once that I was courageous for my age. Please believe me when I tell you that everything

I have done came not from courage, but from love. And I have never loved *anyone* as I love Saxon. This means his *life*, and I must do it!"

Paige didn't argue further. She summoned servants and began issuing orders. She called for a carriage, instructed Eugenie to pack Ashiana's things, asked that Cook make a cough remedy with lemon and honey, then helped Ashiana to her room so she could wash and dress.

"You know, my dear," the Duchess said a short time later, hurriedly seating Ashiana at the dressing table and helping dry her hair while the maids packed. "I suspected from the very first moment I saw the two of you together, in the foyer, that you and Saxon loved one another."

"You did?" Ashiana whispered, genuinely surprised, her heart beating unsteadily.

"Yes. And I must admit, I had ulterior motives for being so kind to you."

"Mo-tives?"

"Yes, dear. 'Motives' are reasons." Paige turned to pick up a hairbrush. When she turned back, Ashiana thought she saw sadness reflected in the gentle woman's face in the mirror. "You see, I have four sons, and I love each of them with all my heart and soul. But I ... I also had a daughter."

Ashiana remained silent as Paige brushed her hair. Patience, it seemed, worked as well with D'Avenant women as it did with D'Avenant men. Before she could guess where this daughter was, Paige explained.

"It was a few years after Max was born. She would have been my youngest. But she lived only a few days."

Ashiana met Paige's silver gaze in the mirror, seeing the tears that Paige was trying to blink back.

"She would have been a woman grown now," Paige whispered. "With a husband of her own. Perhaps children."

The Duchess set down the brush and perched on the velvet-padded bench, laying a gentle hand on Ashiana's cheek. "I never knew my daughter, but these past weeks, it has almost been like ... like having ..."

She could not continue. Ashiana leaned over and hugged her. "Paige," she whispered, her throat tight, "my mother died the day I was born. She was English and I have spent years hating her for that. Resenting her. But . . ." Suddenly she was speaking through tears. "If she had been anything like you, I think I would have loved her very much."

Paige hugged her hard and then sat back. Both of them drew their hankies at precisely the same time. Glancing at one another, the two of them suddenly laughed in the midst of their tears.

"Oh, Paige, you are such a treasure. You *all* are." Ashiana felt a wave of emotion as their laughter faded—something familiar, yet surprising. Almost like . . . homesickness.

She realized then that it was not going to be easy to leave England. There was so much she would miss.

But the love she felt for Saxon was far stronger. She could not lose him now. To have come so far only for him to be killed at the hands of her—

No. She would not think of it. She would save him. She was the only one who could do it.

But the enormity of the journey that lay ahead was almost overwhelming. "Paige, how can I possibly get to the Andamans before Saxon?" she whispered. "If only I had wings!"

"I cannot supply wings, my child, but I can supply the next best thing." Paige smiled confidently. "As I explained once before, we D'Avenants are *very* well connected."

Chapter 29

Andaman Islands

He was still alive.

Saxon took that as a good sign, but he had doubts about how long his present condition might continue. He walked through the thick forest of *sal* trees, escorted by Ajmir guards, his hands tied painfully behind his back. The blazing heat quickly baked him dry, but the clothes that had clung to him with seawater soon clung to him with sweat.

He could only hope that Ashiana's adopted father, the Maharaja, would prove to be an understanding sort.

Ashiana. Even after eight months, just the thought of her name was enough to make him ache. Carrying out her duty was the only thing that had gotten him through the long voyage from London. Someone had to give the sapphire back and tell the Ajmir where the other eight were located; it was his way of honoring everything she had meant to him.

At least he had come alone. He had insisted on it. Only after a heated argument with Julian had he left the *Rising Star* this morning. No one was to follow him. The bloody sapphires had already cost him too much. He was willing to risk his own life to do this, but no one else's.

He had planned to lie low near the beach and make his way to the palace at nightfall, but the Ajmir guards had captured him before he had even reached the shore. They had appeared out of nowhere in their swift *cata maran* water craft, netted him like a blasted fish, and relieved him of the sapphire. If he were the paranoid type, he would have thought they had known he was coming.

Being logical, he had to chalk it up to his own bad luck and their extreme good sense in posting sentries at all times—even in broad daylight. What he couldn't understand was why they hadn't cut his throat on the spot.

The guards closed in more tightly around him as they entered the palace grounds. They didn't bother to blindfold him—which did not bode well for his future, he thought grimly. If they were not concerned about an enemy seeing the way into their palace, they didn't intend for him to live long.

They hurried him inside through a hidden entrance, down a corridor so dark he couldn't see. They walked for what seemed a half hour along sinuous, unlit hallways, and he felt the air grow cool and damp. They were going deep underground.

With a sharp turn to the right, they passed through a door and into what felt like a large chamber; he couldn't see because the sudden glare temporarily blinded him.

One of the sentries shoved him forward and pushed him down to his knees. He felt cold marble beneath him and heard the door close, then a deep male voice speaking in clipped Hindi.

"*Namaste, angrez.* Greetings, Englishman."

His eyes finally adjusted, but what caught his attention was not the richness of the room, or the man sitting on a throne at the far end of the chamber.

It was the woman kneeling on a red tasseled pillow beside that throne.

"*Ashiana!*" He surged to his feet, only to be forced back to his knees by one of the guards.

The man on the throne said something, but Saxon didn't hear. His heart was pounding so loudly it blocked out all other sound. Time wrenched to a halt in a mind-numbing moment of shock. *She was alive!* She wore Hindu silks in vibrant shades of blue, with sheer veils over her hair and face, and she kept her gaze on the floor, but it was unmistakably her. She sat with her fingers interlaced on her lap, and he could see the rose tattoo on her left wrist. That beautiful, precious, indelible Ajmir tattoo.

Ashiana didn't say a word, didn't look up, didn't acknowledge him in any way.

After that first frozen second, the relief and joy and thanks to any and every god that might be above were swiftly buried beneath questions.

How the devil had she gotten here? How long had she been here? Had she purposely let him believe she was lost?

Had she faked her own death on the Thames?

Had she been that desperate to get away from him?

He couldn't believe it. "Ashiana—"

"*Chuppi!* Silence!" the man on the throne demanded.

Saxon tore his eyes from her and looked at the Maharaja for the first time. The Ajmir leader's appearance only complicated Saxon's doubts: the dark, brawny, severe-looking man wearing regal blue *jama* and *shilwar,* a jewel-studded turban, and a hate-filled expression was much too young to be Ashiana's adopted father.

He fixed Saxon with a glare. "*Angrez,* you will not speak to her. You will address me." With a single flick of his hand, he dismissed the guards, his jeweled rings flashing in the light.

"*Maf kijiye.* I ask pardon," Saxon said, in the least hostile Hindi he could manage. "May I have the honor of knowing whom it is I am addressing?"

The man didn't bother with the traditional formal flourishes. He stated his name flatly. "Maharaja Rao Chand Ajmir."

Rao. The name lanced into Saxon. *Prince* Rao! Now the Maharaja. Saxon speared Ashiana with an accusing stare as pain and betrayal shot through him. Even as he watched, Rao reached down and touched her, resting a hand lightly but possessively on her shoulder—and she did not flinch away from the contact.

He had thought she was dead. He had grieved for her.

He had spent months at sea mourning her, remembering every detail of her face and form and spirit and laughter, and *she had returned to her prince!*

Even as his mind denied what he was seeing, the enormity of his self-delusion raked his heart. He had thought she cared for him, at least as much as she cared for her family and her home. But it seemed she was exactly what she had insisted all along: an Ajmir princess, whose loyalties and love obviously lay with the Ajmir.

She just sat there at Rao's side, passive, head bent. She wouldn't even spare him a glance.

"Ashiana," he demanded hoarsely, "look at me—"

"Princess Ashiana does not converse with strangers," Rao pronounced.

Saxon pierced him with a look that could have seared the gold off his throne. "Ashiana and I are hardly strangers. And we have done a great deal more than converse."

The innuendo made Rao's eyes widen. Ashiana obviously hadn't chosen to share that information with her betrothed.

Or was Rao already her husband?

Blinded with jealous fury, Saxon couldn't stop himself. "She is mine, Ajmir. I have made her mine and she will always *be* mine. Forever."

"What happened in the past is of no interest to me. And her future is of no concern to you, *angrez."* Rao spoke in a cool, regal tone and confidently removed his hand from Ashiana's shoulder—but Saxon could feel the heat of his anger even across the distance that separated them, and saw the fierce grip he took on the arms of his throne.

"What happens to Ashiana is always of concern to me," Saxon retorted. "How did she come to be here? And what happened to her adopted father?"

"He is dead," Rao said sharply. "His heart gave out when he was told that Princess Ashiana had failed in her mission and been taken away on an Englishman's ship!"

For the first time, Ashiana reacted to what was being said. She winced visibly and seemed to fold in upon herself, as if the weight of the entire palace was pressing down upon her.

Saxon suddenly realized that he had completely misjudged her mood. She was not being passive and uninterested; she was dispirited, devastated. Her beloved adopted father had died thinking she had failed him—while she had been aboard the *Valor,* making love to her people's greatest enemy.

Only the knowledge that any move toward the throne would likely cost his life kept him from going to her and pulling her into his arms.

He had to settle for another exchange of furious stares with Rao. "She did not fail in her mission," Saxon said tightly. "You have the ninth sapphire. Those apes of yours relieved me of the jewel as soon as they captured me."

"The sacred stones were only part of her duty. The other part was to kill the enemy of her people and see that he could cause no further trouble. The fact that you are here and breathing, Englishman, is proof that she failed."

Saxon tore his gaze from Rao and fastened it on Ashiana again, willing her to raise her head. "It wasn't your fault," he said in English. When Rao tried to silence him, he only spoke louder and faster. "The Maharaja's death was not your fault. Your duty is done. You did your best and if that isn't good enough for this high-handed son of a bitch, that's not your problem."

Ashiana finally raised her head, and he could see that her sheer veil was damp with tears. He could see, too, the indecision and pain in her eyes. And the love.

It stole away all his doubts and left only love in their place. "Ashiana, I—"

Rao's angry voice sliced between them. "The Princess wished for me to see you and speak with you before I decided your fate. I have seen you and spoken with you and I see no reason to change my mind—"

"Rao!" Ashiana spoke for the first time, turning toward him. "You said—"

"Chuppi!" Rao snapped. Then, looking down at her, his expression softened in a way that made Saxon's gut clench.

Rao leaned over, whispering something Saxon could not hear.

Ashiana's only response was a glare. A glare that made joy and pride jolt through Saxon. The spirit and fire that he loved so much were still there.

He had not lost her. Not yet.

Rao straightened and turned back to Saxon. "I shall remove that smile from your face quickly, Englishman. You will be executed in the morning. The clan Ajmir demands your life for your crime."

"Rao, no!" Ashiana cried, grabbing his arm.

The Maharaja ignored her. "Because she has told you where the other sapphires are, we cannot risk allowing you to live. You would steal them. Greed is too much a trait of your race. You die at first light, Englishman."

"You have changed, *premika.*"

The sadness, the disappointment in Rao's voice penetrated the black haze of grief that had wrapped itself around Ashiana. The two of them were alone in Rao's lavish apartments; he had granted her a private audience.

These rooms had once belonged to her adopted father. Many times, she had come here to play chess or sing to him or harass him into putting aside matters of state to join her for a walk about the grounds.

Shaking, she turned from where she stood at the edge of the terrace that led to the sculpted gardens beyond. "*I* have changed? Rao, *you* have changed! You were once a man of your word."

"I promised only to meet the Englishman and speak with him, Ashiana. I did both."

Ashiana took a deep breath, listening to the warm, familiar sounds of evening descending on the palace, trying to control her temper. "You must realize by now that he came here in peace! His only intent was to return the sapphire. Exactly as I told you."

"Ah, *premika*. You are a woman. You cannot understand the cunning ways of men."

Ashiana clenched her fists. She had been afraid of this.

The late Maharaja had possessed wisdom and gentleness; she could have explained everything to him and persuaded him to spare Saxon's life.

Rao would be far more difficult to convince.

"I will tell you what cunning is," she said accusingly. "Cunning is persuading me to tell you the truth, and then using my words against me. Yes, Saxon knows where the other eight sapphires are. I told you that. But I only told you to prove my point! If he intended to *steal* the jewels, why would he have risked his life coming here, to the Andamans? He had one of the sapphires, and he could have gotten the other eight with little trouble."

Rao paused beside a heaping platter of fruit in the corner and picked up a mango, turning it over and over in his hand. "You did not tell me *all* the truth, Ashiana."

She flinched at his low, angry tone. She had not told him of the intimacy between her and Saxon because she had come here to save Saxon, and intended to leave with him. She hadn't seen any need to torment Rao with images of them together.

She had also feared it would so enrage Rao that he would lop off Saxon's head at the first opportunity.

But then Saxon had ruined her carefully laid plan for a truce, unable to resist asserting his male claim over her; they were practically the first words out of his mouth! Men were utterly impossible to deal with. Especially these two. They were both equally stubborn and quick-tempered and possessive. And they had gotten so caught up in that side issue that Rao had completely missed the point of the meeting.

"Why, Ashiana?" Rao set the mango down without taking a bite. "Why did you not tell me?"

"Because I knew you would react this way!"

"And how should I react? To think of that thieving Englishman forcing himself on you—"

"No." She turned and looked out at the gardens again, at the fountains splashing so gently in the twilight. "That was not what happened between us, Rao."

He crossed the chamber in two quick steps, grabbed her

shoulder, and spun her around to face him. "Are you telling me you *gave* yourself to him?"

"Would you have me lie to you?" She felt desperation rising. "Please, Rao. Please, you must spare him!"

"*Spare* him?" Rao shouted. "I should have instructed my guards to drown him in the sea like a diseased rat. I never should have let you convince me to waste my time listening to him!"

"But you *didn't* listen to him!" She placed her hand over his. She and Rao had known one another since childhood. She tried to appeal to the gentle heart she knew he possessed. "You do not understand, Rao. He came here to do *my* duty. He came not to take, but to give."

Rao made a frustrated sound and turned away from her. "Englishmen live by violence and greed."

"Saxon is a man of great honor."

"I cannot believe you are arguing for the enemy's life!"

"He is not my enemy!"

"His blood is *English!*"

"So is *mine!*"

Rao spun toward her, clearly astonished to hear her claim the heritage she had denied so long.

Ashiana couldn't take another breath, feeling just as surprised as he, barely able to believe the words that had just passed her lips.

But after a moment, the words didn't seem incredible at all, and the air seemed easier to breathe than it ever had before, and her tense muscles relaxed, and she repeated what she knew was the truth.

"So is mine," she whispered, with the same quiet pride with which she had once declared herself an Ajmir princess. "You and I both know that I am half-English, Rao."

A myriad of expressions chased over his features. Denial. Outrage. Hurt. "You do not know what you are saying."

Seeing the pain she caused him, Ashiana dropped her gaze to the gleaming marble floor. "I know what I am."

"You cannot believe that you are one of *them.*"

She shook her head. "I am not one of 'them,' but I am

not one of 'us' either." She raised her head and looked around at the familiar, magnificent room, at the jeweled ceiling and lapis walls and plump silk *musnad* pillows, and felt sadness and peace. "I am ... different."

She had known that since childhood, hated it, fought it. But now, for the first time, she accepted it. All her life, she had wanted to belong. But now ...

Now she knew she belonged to herself. And to Saxon.

"Ashiana, you came back to me," Rao said huskily. "I thought you were dead but you came back to me. And now you are telling me that you don't wish to stay?"

"I am sorry." It seemed so insufficient to heal his hurt, but she could no longer deny the truth, not to him and not to herself. What she felt for Rao was affection, perhaps even a kind of love—but what she felt for Saxon was the passionate love of a woman for a man.

"Where will you go?" Rao demanded. *"England? Did you love it so much?"*

"No." She sighed heavily. "I did not love England. England is ... How can I explain it? If you took all the strangest buildings you could imagine, and all the strangest people, and the strangest behavior and weather and noises, and put them together in one place, that would be England."

"And you wish to return to *that?"*

"My place is with *him,"* she whispered. "If he were to go to a land where there was no sun and no moon and no stars, I would go with him. If he lived always at sea aboard a ship, I would live with him. If he had no home and walked the earth and never settled in one place, I would take every step with him."

Rao stared at her, speechless.

"If there were any way to say this without hurting you, I would," Ashiana cried. "I love him, Rao. Please spare his life. If not because you believe him, then for me. If you kill him, you kill me. Take his life and you cut out my heart."

Rao dropped his gaze and remained silent a long time. Sensing a softening in his attitude, Ashiana tried to appeal to his reason. "The clan is safe, Rao. You have the sapphires. All nine. I told you where the other eight are. You will know them by the cloth fastened to the reef."

When Rao finally looked up at her again, his dark eyes seemed haunted. "Your part in this is done. I will personally hide the last sacred stone with the others beneath the sea. You have done your duty."

Ashiana felt pride and peace and happiness at his words. "Then let Saxon live. He only did what he did because of the curse." A hint of accusation crept into her tone. "The curse that neither you nor the Maharaja told me about when I left."

"It is best never to have sympathy for one's enemy."

"Yes, of course," Ashiana agreed, mocking him softly. "Because then war and killing and the rest don't make any sense at all, do they?"

"You are a woman," Rao said dismissively, as if that should explain her inability to grasp the grand, higher meaning of war. "And the curse is no longer important."

"But Saxon separated the stones—"

"If, as you said, he had them all in his hands when the explosion on his ship occurred, then they were separated by an accident, not by a thief. The curse is upon thieves."

His assurance made Ashiana feel satisfaction as well as relief. "Then the fact that Saxon is not cursed is more evidence that you should let him live! He is obviously not a thief!"

Rao furrowed his brow, pondering that point. His next words astounded her.

"I will spare his life—"

"Oh, Rao!" Ashiana exclaimed, running across the room to throw herself at him in a joyous hug.

He wrapped her close.

And finished his sentence.

"If you will stay here and marry me."

Ashiana froze, then pulled back. "Rao!" she gasped. "After what I have told you—"

"It does not matter," he said savagely. "I love you."

Ashiana blinked at him. She had not realized, until this

very moment, how strongly Rao felt about her. She had assumed that his feelings for her were like hers for him—affection, but not passion.

She had clearly assumed wrong.

"Rao," she whispered, "you would still want me as one of your wives, knowing that . . . I have been with someone else?"

"Yes, *premika*," he said raggedly, clasping her to him. "Yes. I have known you most of your life. I know that you could never be happy in that foreign land with him. You will be happy here. I will give you all the joy you could ask of life, and more. We will travel, if that is what you wish. And you will be my *only* wife."

Ashiana closed her eyes. It was an incredible sacrifice for him to make. For a Maharaja to marry a *feringi* girl, a foreigner, was unusual. For him to make her his *rani vadi*, his first wife, his queen, was unprecedented. To make her his only wife was unheard of.

And it made no difference.

"I love Saxon," she said, as gently as she could, trying to pull out of his embrace. "I belong with him. I will always love him."

Rao raised his head to look down on her, framing her face tenderly between his broad, dark hands. "In time, it will fade, *premika*. You will come to love me as I love you. I *know* you."

Before she could say a word, he went on. "Ashiana, it would kill me to lose you a second time. I cannot do it. I will set the Englishman free, because it is what you wish. He is the Ajmir's most hated enemy and I risk the entire clan by letting him live, but for you, *I will do it.* But if you truly do not wish to stay, I am afraid . . ."

He dangled the sentence and the image of the executioner's blade in her mind. Ashiana felt like screaming. He was offering her an impossible choice: to save Saxon's life, she must face a life without Saxon. "I . . . I must have time!"

"We have no time, *premika*. He is to die at dawn. If you wish to save him, you must tell me now."

Ashiana felt as if the entire world had been snatched out from beneath her. Rao had forced her into a corner. And the worst part of it was that she could tell how much he hated forcing her. He truly loved her and thought he was doing what was best for the future.

But he held Saxon's life in his hands—and left her no choice but one. Ashiana stopped resisting his hold, and made the most painful promise she had ever given.

"I will do as you ask," she said through tears. "After Saxon is safely away from the island ... I will marry you."

Chapter 30

In such a magnificent palace, Saxon might have hoped for a bit more comfort in the way of a cell. Perhaps a nice dank dungeon. But it seemed the clan's fierce reputation was more than rumor; the Ajmir did not take prisoners in battle. He was apparently the first unwilling guest they had had in some time.

They had locked him in one of the cages in the Maharaja's menagerie, outside, surrounded by six armed guards. They left his hands tied, and bound his feet as well, but at least they had removed the cage's previous occupant—a huge tiger that looked like it might have been one of Nicobar's larger relatives. The guards had debated about making the two of them share quarters before they took the animal out and placed Saxon inside. He wasn't sure they had been joking.

Long after darkness fell, Rao paid a personal visit, striding out of the darkness, a torch in his hand.

The guards all fell to their knees, but their ruler waved them to their feet, spoke to them in low tones, and sent them to wait a few yards away.

Leaning against the bars of his cage, Saxon sat up with as much dignity as he could manage. "Come to gloat, Ajmir?"

Rao smiled slowly, the flame and the moonlight reflecting the hatred in his expression. "I have just come from speaking with your executioner, *angrez*. I wanted to make sure he did not sharpen his blade. We would not want you to die too quickly. It will take him two or three strokes."

Saxon listened to the details of his death sentence without emotion. It was the chance he had taken in coming here. He had only one concern, and he voiced it quietly.

"What will happen to Ashiana?"

Rao looked dumbfounded, as if he had expected rage or groveling instead of a question about her. He recovered quickly. "My betrothed is not your concern."

Saxon forced back a grin. *Betrothed.* She was not yet Rao's wife.

Rao braced his legs in an arrogant stance. "You think you mean something to her, *angrez*, but you are wrong. She will forget you quickly after you are dead. In her heart, she knows she belongs here, with me."

"You obviously don't know her at all if you think that is what is in her heart."

The barb struck home. "I spoke to her not an hour ago," Rao shot back. "And she told me she is joyously anticipating our marriage. And the wedding night."

Saxon fought the jealousy and possessive fury that sizzled through him. It could not be true. "She would never forget so easily what she and I shared."

"Your death will make it easier for her."

"Will it?" Saxon taunted.

"She never felt anything for you." Rao's dark eyes gleamed in the light of the torch and his smile widened. "She was merely doing exactly what we sent her to do. She fooled you into believing her and delivered both you and the sapphire directly into my hands."

Sharp, poisonous fangs of doubt sank into Saxon's confidence. Part of him refused to believe it, but part of him flashed back to all the times Ashiana had adamantly proclaimed that she belonged with her clan. Together with the image of Rao bedding her, the memories savaged what was left of his control. "Touch her and I'll kill you," he vowed with soft malice, his temper slipping its leash.

"By the time I take her, you will already be dead. But enough of this," Rao said abruptly. "I will see that you are brought a final meal, *angrez*. Use this time to make peace with whatever gods you claim to believe in. You die in a few hours." As he stalked away, he tossed a parting gibe over his shoulder. "Sleep well."

Ashiana was dreaming.

It was a familiar dream: Saxon's mouth warm and insistent on hers, his body heavy and hard, his hands masterfully arousing her. She sleepily remembered throwing herself down on the pile of pillows near her terrace, muffling her sobs in the mounds of silk. She must have cried herself to sleep.

The dream was such a pleasurable escape from reality, she let herself doze and gave herself over to the fantasy. Saxon's touch was glorious.

But after only a moment, he stopped. She moaned softly in protest as he lifted his mouth from hers.

"Sorry, love. We have to go."

Ashiana's eyes flew open. Never had her dream spoken to her before! Darkness cloaked her sleeping chamber; he had extinguished all the oil lamps. Moonlight shimmering in through the open terrace illuminated the golden head bent over her, the muscular body pressing her down into the pillows. Panic for his life tore a strangled cry from her throat. *"Saxon!* How—"

"Shhh, love." He silenced her with another kiss.

Ashiana wanted to shout at him in terrified fury. *How had he escaped? What was he doing in her private apartments? He should be running for his life! She had just managed to convince Rao to spare him, but if he were caught here in the harem—*

He started to rise, his mouth still sealed over hers as he lifted her from the pillows. She could tell from the tension in his body that he knew the danger they were in. She felt desperate to make him leave. *Now.* Even as her heart thundered and her senses reeled under his potent power, she tried to wriggle free of his arms.

His arms tightened around her. He was breathing unsteadily. "We have to hurry," he said roughly.

But then his kiss suddenly deepened.

He angled his head and opened her lips wider, his tongue sweeping and sampling. His embrace held equal parts fierceness, gentleness, and care. Longing and memory ignited inside her, drew a ragged moan from her throat that sounded nothing like protest. They had been apart *so* long. Too long. An eternity.

Before she could stop herself, her arms stole round his neck.

"Damn," he groaned. She nibbled at his lower lip. *"Damn."* He held her closer and their kiss became a cascade of kisses, those brief, light, feathery brushes of their mouths that turned reason to fog and left her as shivering and breathless as a newborn kitten in his arms.

Some distant shred of sanity cried out: they could not do this! He had to run! She must convince him to escape. Without her. She had made a promise. She had to stay . . . here . . .

They might be discovered at any moment! Both their lives were in danger. But risk only sharpened their desire. Need. Urgency to steal one moment that might be their last.

Hungering, caressing, loving, they fell together onto the pillows.

There was a swift, impatient sweeping away of breeches and silks, and she felt skin against skin. The weight of him, so heavy, so right, pressing her down into the soft bedding suddenly seemed the only reality in her world.

The rough satin of his tongue thrust into her mouth and out again in a quick, aggressive claiming that left her languid. His fingers sought her heat, brushing against her intimately, finding her already damp and throbbing.

She cried out softly and he captured the sound and echoed it back in deeper tones. Tenderness tempered his sensual power even as the velvety steel of his arousal parted her. She grasped fistfuls of his hair, urging him closer. *"Saxon, I need you."*

He turned his head to kiss the rose tattoo on her wrist and took her in one powerful thrust.

His hard length slid into her to the hilt, dragging a low,

aching cry from her lips. Her head tilted back, her hips arching upward at the sweet pressure and throbbing of him inside her. His possession sent fiery sensations splintering through her, fanning outward from her belly to her fingertips. Dream and reality and memory and pleasure blended as he moved back and forth and back again, hot, sliding, pulsing.

It had been so *very* long, but her body adjusted and remembered and held him within. Their breath rasped together in hot, moist kisses and sighs as they rose, higher, faster. Wrapping his hands through her hair, he gazed down as he drove himself into her with a passion she had never felt from him before. His eyes glittered like diamonds afire.

He plunged deeper, harder, every motion of his hips defining the depths of her femininity. Together they formed a whole, a circle of two that could never be broken. She felt like a goddess, worshipped by his body, caressed by his silver gaze.

And then Ashiana knew no thought but bliss, no feeling but the rich, hot joining of their bodies as Saxon sent her to the peak and beyond. The pleasure twining within her suddenly exploded in a flare of ecstasy. She had no voice but a ragged whisper of his name which he captured hungrily.

The tenderness of his mouth on hers as all the heavens expanded and shattered within and around her was more exquisite than any feeling she had ever known, like life ending and beginning anew.

She heard a groan tear through him and he joined her in release, embedded deeply inside, spilling his breath and his life and his seed into her. They held one another, silently accepting and belonging to one another. She could feel him breathing hard, his chest pressing against her breasts. Saxon allowed them to savor the sweet moment only an instant before he withdrew from her body and stood, drawing her up with him.

"Saxon, you should—"

Her breath whooshed out as he pulled her against him in

a sudden, fierce embrace. "I'm not leaving without you, so let's just skip the discussion completely."

He kissed her to reinforce his declaration, and Ashiana abandoned logic and objections. Leaving with Saxon would mean betraying her promise to Rao—but staying would mean living a lie. This was the right thing to do, and she knew it with all her heart.

Before her drugged senses had time to drift back to reality, Saxon had picked up her clothes and started to dress her hurriedly. She still felt languorous from their lovemaking. "H-how did you ever *find* me?"

"Your perfume. You're still wearing the perfume you had made in London." He nuzzled the soft hollow of her throat, where her pulse heated the scent of spice and roses, just for a second before he grabbed his own clothes.

Her mind was clearing rapidly. "But how did you *escape?*"

"The new Maharaja has an arrogance problem," he growled. "He dismissed four of the guards, and the two who were left decided to sleep in shifts. One didn't lock the door all the way after he untied my hands and brought my final meal. No one will find them until morning."

"Saxon! You didn't—"

"No. They're tied up and enjoying sweet dreams in the forest. No one goes tramping about in the forest at this time of night, do they?"

"I was the only one who ever did."

"And I've got you right here." Moonlight shone on his white teeth as he smiled. With a quick move that caught her by surprise, he lifted her in his arms and shifted her over his shoulder.

"You don't have to cart me off like a sack!" she protested.

He stepped to the edge of the terrace, glancing around, listening intently. "I'd like a hand free in case we encounter trouble. You don't have any weapons in here, by chance?"

"No." It was the truth, and she was relieved. She couldn't bear the thought of Saxon hurting one of her clan any more than she could bear the thought of them hurting him. "Put me down and you'll have two free hands."

"No second thoughts?" he asked warily.

"What do you think, my love?" she replied softly.

"London it is, then. One-way passage for two." He lowered her to the ground and pulled her beside him into the darkest shadows at the edge of the palace, peering into the night. "By the way, how *did* you get here from England?" he whispered curiously.

"Your mother's friend Alexander Fox. She hired him to bring me here in his racing sloop."

Saxon made a strangled sound. "You risked your life sailing with that reckless gray-haired rakehell of a smuggler?" He slanted her a glance. She smiled lovingly in reply.

Shaking his head in disbelief, he grabbed her hand. "My daring little tiger-tamer and seafarer." He muttered something about supervising his mother's social associations more closely, but he was already leading Ashiana forward at a crouch.

Her heart pounded as they moved quickly and silently through the gardens. Saxon stopped only when they reached the inner wall of the palace grounds. Beyond lay the terraced hillside that led down to the beach.

They heard a voice from a few yards away on the other side of the wall. Both froze.

"Sentries?" Saxon whispered, looking at her.

She shook her head. "They patrol the ramparts on the shore at night."

"Wait here until I see if there's a safe way down."

"Saxon—"

"No arguments." He started to rise, then stopped. He captured her in a sudden, tender embrace. "I love you, Ashiana."

The startling words came to him so naturally, so easily, she felt as if she had just been sent soaring into the clouds. He kissed her hard and repeated it again. "I love you. You are mine, Ashiana. Forever. *Hamesha ke liye*. Forever mine." He released her just as suddenly and leaped up onto the smooth stone wall.

His sweet declaration opened up the last gates that guarded her heart, and all her love for him came flowing out on one breath. "I love you Saxon. Forever—"

But he was already gone, disappearing into the darkness. She wasn't even sure he had heard her.

Shaking, Ashiana knelt in the shadows beside the wall, the sound of Saxon's deep voice, so husky with emotion, still echoing through her mind, her heart, her soul. *I love you.* She had thought he would never be able to say those words aloud, but he had declared it without hesitation.

She crouched in the darkness, waiting for him to come back, filled with wonder and love and fear. As soon as she saw him, she was going to tell him, show him, quite firmly and in detail just exactly how much she loved him. She waited, her hair tangling in the breeze, her pulse rushing in her ears.

But Saxon did not return, and she heard nothing more from the other side of the wall.

Then a pistol shot rang out.

She jumped to her feet, scrambling over the wall with an agility she had not known she possessed. Saxon was nowhere to be seen on the hillside below. She nearly screamed his name—but heard voices coming toward her. Before she could think whether to hide or race down the hill after Saxon, Rao's voice shouted from the darkness.

"Ashiana!" He came at a run with a dozen heavily armed men, some bearing torches.

"Rao! What—"

He shouted orders to his warriors, sending them down the hill. Striding toward her, he caught her arm. "I cannot believe you would go with him!"

"How did you—" A barrage of gunfire sounded from their left and she lost the rest of her question in a horrified gasp. Turning, she finally saw Saxon, halfway down the hill, diving behind a low hedge for cover. The Ajmir marksmen had split up; the other half of the group appeared a few yards above Saxon on the right, raising their flintlocks.

The hedge would never be enough to protect him. "Rao,

no! He has no weapons! Let him go! You gave me your word—"

"I *did* let him go."

"You? But he said—"

"I had to make it look as if he escaped! I could not simply let him walk away in the morning, Ashiana. The clan would never understand. I had to do it secretly. I instructed the guard to leave his cell unlocked." He glowered down the hill in Saxon's direction. "I told him exactly how he would die and said that you did not care for him. I cannot believe he did not run for his life!"

"Not all Englishmen are cowards, Rao. You do not understand him! He loves me!"

The marksmen on the right started firing. Saxon flattened himself against the ground, but he was pinned down with nowhere to run.

"Rao, make them stop!" she cried. "They will kill him!"

"Do you think my men would miss at this range?"

The flat tone of his voice made Ashiana tear her gaze from Saxon and look up at Rao, aghast. "I don't understand."

"They will not kill him unless I give them the signal." He released her and moved back, holding out his hand in entreaty. "It is your choice, Ashiana."

The marksmen on the left fired again.

"Rao, I am begging you!"

"I love you, Ashiana," he said fiercely. "I will cherish you. You will forget that *angrez*—"

"I love him! I will never forget him!"

At a signal from Rao, the warriors began firing at will.

Ashiana closed tear-filled eyes against the hellish sounds, against the hellish choice she had to make. "Make them stop!" she pleaded.

"Only you can make them stop, *premika.*"

With a sob, Ashiana placed her hand in his and let Rao pull her into his arms.

"Ashiana, no!" Saxon yelled, unable to believe what he was seeing in the torchlight on the hillside far above him.

He couldn't tell what Ashiana and Rao were saying up there, but she had looked down at him, back at Rao, then taken Rao's hand *and gone straight into his arms.*

She was not struggling or trying to get away in the least. Rao wrapped one arm lovingly around her and tucked her face against his shoulder. He called out to his warriors. The marksmen started advancing on Saxon from both sides.

He was going to be sliced to ribbons by the crossfire if he didn't get out of here right now.

He surged to his feet. "Ashiana!" he shouted in agony.

Rao raised his head and glared down at him with a look that Saxon felt as much as saw was utterly triumphant. A bitter, cold lump filled his throat. She had lain with him only moments ago, cried out with need, with what he thought was love. But Ashiana needed something he could never give her, a happiness she could find only here. She truly could not bear to leave her family, her island home.

Memories flashed through him, words Ashiana had said over and over.

I am an Ajmir princess.

I belong with my clan.

They are my family and I love them.

She had made her choice, and he had to let her go.

For love, he had to let her go.

As he stood there, stunned, a hail of bullets suddenly struck dirt at his feet and flew over his head. One grazed his shoulder and knocked him to the ground. The message was clear and he didn't need any further reminders. The Ajmir were perfectly willing to kill him now and rob the executioner of his fun with the dull blade in the morning.

He felt a hot, anguished tearing in his chest as he turned and raced down the hill, the warriors close on his heels. He reached the shore, ran across the white sand, threw himself into the sea.

And left the spice and fire and heartbeat and breath of his life behind as the dark waters closed over his head.

Chapter 31

J ulian rubbed his bleary eyes and blinked down at his pocket watch with a sigh. It was a quarter past ten. Sitting in the small office that he and Saxon had borrowed, he could hear the sounds of the Company's Bombay settlement coming to life for the evening: merchants and junior officials and seamen making their way toward punchhouses and *nautch* parties and card games.

Glaring down at the accounts he had been studying, he slid his watch back into his pocket and tried to ignore the temptations—though God knew he needed a night off. Hell, he deserved one, after putting up with his brother for the past three months.

Saxon had been driving him completely around the bend. After returning to the *Rising Star* in a black mood with a bullet wound in one shoulder, he had said only three things: he had given the sapphire back, Ashiana was alive, and he never wanted to hear her name mentioned again. Ever. Or else.

Even Julian didn't dare test that "or else." What baffled him was why the devil Saxon insisted on staying in India. If it was really because he wanted to build a replacement for the *Valor,* as he said, they could have returned home and had the ship made the traditional way, at the Company shipyards at Deptford. Relying on the settlement's few shipbuilders and Indian materials made the whole process take twice as long. The new vessel was still up in the stocks, half-finished.

Julian stretched and yawned and looked back down at the pages of figures before him—estimates for sails and rigging. He had volunteered to look them over, sending Saxon off to bed; the man was going to drown himself in work if someone didn't put a stop to it. The long hours were murder on Julian's good humor, but helping with the new ship was the best way to keep a close eye on Saxon. And his brother definitely needed someone to keep an eye on him.

Trying to put palm wine and pretty courtesans out of his mind, Julian turned the page with a sigh. A knock sounded at the door.

"Bloody hell." He groaned and got to his feet. "Phipps, if that's you, I'm going to wring your scrawny neck. I told you I don't have time to join your card party, so stop bother—"

As he opened the door, the rest of the rebuke died on his lips. Two women stood in the shadows just to one side of the entrance, both draped in dark silks that hid their faces. One stepped forward into the circle of light that spilled out the door, and lowered her veil.

"Julian," she said quietly but firmly, "I need your help."

"This had better be good, Julian," Saxon warned as he followed his brother up a ladder and onto the deck of his half-finished ship. The pungent smells of freshly cut wood and sawdust and tar clung to the sultry night air. "What the hell is so important that I have to see it at three in the morning? What have you been drinking?"

"Nothing. Not a drop," Julian swore, flashing a smile. There was a definite spring in his step as he led the way to the aft hatch and down the companionway that led to the ship's cabins. "I've made an improvement in the captain's cabin, and I couldn't wait to show it to you."

They came to a stop at the far end of the passageway, and Julian raised the lamp he carried. The light shone on a door of carved teak. "Look at this—"

"A door?" Saxon asked laconically. "You got me out of bed at three in the morning to show me a door?"

Julian paused with his hand on the latch. "It's not the door but what's behind the door, Sax. You'll love it, I promise." He tripped the latch, pushed the portal open an inch, then stepped aside and motioned for Saxon to precede him. "After you, Captain."

Gritting his teeth at his brother's annoyingly mysterious mood, Saxon shoved the door open, shot Julian an irritated look, and stepped inside.

When his head swung around to view the promised surprise, his boots and his heart both slammed to a halt.

Ashiana stood on the far side of the cabin, starlight spilling in through the mullioned windows behind her, glistening on her royal blue Hindu silks and flowing *peshwaz*. Her gaze was unflinching, her expression calm, her fingers interlaced in front of her.

Saxon felt as if all the air had suddenly been sucked out of his lungs. He barely noticed when the door swung shut behind him. He spun on his heel too late.

Julian spoke from the other side of the thick teak, laughter in his voice. "I told you I had made an improvement in your cabin. Isn't that an improvement?"

"Julian!" Saxon grabbed the latch and tried to yank it open.

The door wouldn't budge.

"Sorry, Sax," Julian said brightly, jiggling the latch from his side. "There seems to be some sort of locking mechanism on this door. What do you know about that?" He jiggled it again. "I can't get it open."

"God *damn* it, Julian, what the hell have you—"

"I'll never be able to get a locksmith out here at this hour," Julian mused. "I'll have to bring one first thing in the morning."

"Not if I kick the blasted thing down first!" Saxon growled.

"I wouldn't advise it, Sax. I'll just end up having to fetch a physician as well as a locksmith in the morning. This door is solid teak. You said you only wanted the best."

"Julian!" Saxon roared.

"Don't worry, I'll be back first thing. Or at least by ten. Well, maybe eleven. I'll bring breakfast. Meanwhile, I'm going to go find myself some brandy and cigars and take some much-needed time off. Ashiana?"

"Yes, Julian?" Her voice sounded soft and meek amid all the masculine bluster.

"Are you sure you'll be all right?"

"Yes."

"See you in the morning, then. Good night."

Saxon listened with disbelief to Julian's retreating steps as his brother walked off whistling.

"Please don't blame him for this," Ashiana said hesitantly. "I asked him to help me. I didn't think you would see me willingly."

Saxon rounded on Ashiana and fixed her with an agonized glare. "Do you mean to torture me *forever,* woman?"

She started to apologize—but Saxon didn't hear the words.

He could only think of how beautiful she looked. So wrenchingly beautiful. Living with the family she loved had obviously been good for her: she had regained the weight she had lost in England, and her eyes sparkled, and her skin looked warm in the light of the candles on the table beside her.

It was only then that he noticed anything beyond Ashiana. The room had been completely furnished: tables, chairs, sea chest, water basin.

Bed.

"Saxon, I . . ." Her tongue darted out to wet her bottom lip and desire shot through him. "I had to speak with you . . ."

Her voice was as soft and warm as her expression; the dulcet tones raked him like a hundred sharp knives.

He closed his eyes to shut her out. "Does your *husband* know you are here?"

"I do not have a husband."

"Widowed already?" Had she only come to him because something had befallen Rao?

"Rao is well. I never married him."

Saxon's eyes flew open. His heart beat once ... twice ... then began to pound against his ribs. Hope tore through him, but he throttled it. He had had ample time to hope and give up and hope again these past months. Three months. *Three.* "Then what the hell have you been doing on that island all this time?"

Her breasts rose and fell rapidly, and he realized that her calm exterior was only a facade, and crumbling rapidly. She answered his question with a question. "Why did you remain in India, after I had so obviously forsaken you by choosing Rao?"

Saxon almost retorted something sarcastic.

Then the vague explanation he had given to Julian leaped to mind.

Instead, to his vexation, he found himself speaking the truth, grating it out, word by painful word. "Because, stubborn idiot that I am, I kept hoping you might come to your senses."

She turned and moved away before he could get close enough to touch her. Her hand trembled as she reached up and rested her palm against the window. "Julian explained that you stayed to build a new ship."

Her tone was tremulous, vulnerable, as if she were afraid to believe he could still love her, after what she had done.

He felt tenderness steal through him, and he could not force it back. "That was part of the reason I stayed. I wanted a ship built with Indian materials and English techniques. A blend of the best of both." His voice dropped to a heavy whisper as he slowly crossed the distance between them. "I'm calling her the *Lady Valiant.* Why didn't you marry Rao, Ashiana? What have you been doing for three months?"

She rested her forehead against the glass. "I *had* to promise to marry him. I had to stay or he was going to kill you. He didn't want to set you free, but he agreed to do it if I would stay and become his wife. He scheduled our wedding for the festival of Diwali next month."

Saxon's breath came in sharply as surprise and regret

tore through him. Why the hell hadn't he thought of that? She hadn't *chosen* to stay with her people; she had been *coerced* into doing it. She hadn't done it for herself.

She had done it for him.

Her self-sacrifice touched him deeply. He felt such love for the delicate, courageous, maddening, intoxicating woman before him, it made his heart beat erratically. He reached up and gently laid one hand on her shoulder. She trembled beneath his touch, but again moved away from him.

"Ashiana, what's wrong? You didn't just come here to tell me when your wedding will be." As his confidence grew, lightness crept into his tone. "I don't think I'm on the guest list."

She smiled and suddenly her eyes gleamed with unshed tears. "I am not going to marry Rao—"

"Then marry me."

"Saxon, wait—"

"I have waited long enough. I want you to marry me, Ashiana. I love you and I've never stopped and I never *will* stop."

She closed her eyes, her expression one of pleasure and relief and wonder. "You can forgive me so easily?"

"Forgive you for what? For sacrificing yourself so that I could go free? I don't have to forgive you for that. I love you for that." He caught her at last, taking her face between his hands, gently, filled with soft emotions that made him ache. "Though it is something you are never to even contemplate doing again." He dusted kisses over her lips, her cheeks, her eyelids. "How did you escape from your promise to Rao?"

"I . . ." He finally stopped distracting her with kisses long enough to let her answer. "I did not escape, not really. First he had to make sure the sapphires were safe. He went and put the last sacred stone with the rest, and he moved them, to another location beneath the sea. I don't even know where they are now—"

"Thank God."

"I kept hoping I could make him understand, make him

see that I would not forget you. But he would not listen. He insisted we would marry during the festival of Diwali. But then ... then something finally happened to convince him, and he had to agree that I would never forget you."

"What happened?" Saxon prodded.

"I discovered that ..." Shaking, she pulled out of his embrace, as if needing distance before she told him the rest. He could not understand why she seemed fearful of his reaction. She walked back to the windows. The words finally flowed out, all on one wavering breath.

"I discovered that I am carrying your child."

Saxon closed his eyes, then opened them again, but she was still there, and this wasn't a dream, and he felt as if he would burn to a cinder with the feelings that flared through him.

His child. His love was carrying his child.

"Ashiana," he said thickly, the only word he could manage as he realized the real reason for the changes he had noticed in her—the added weight that softened her body, the glow that warmed her skin. "And I thought it was the *islands* that had been good for you ..."

Emotion choked out his voice. But when she turned toward him, she must have seen the love and fire and pride and passion shining in his eyes, for tears suddenly coursed down her cheeks. "It was not the islands." She smiled, opening her *peshwaz* and resting one hand over the gentle swell of her abdomen. "It was you, here."

He reached for her, swept her into his arms, kissed her until they swayed with the power of it, and when he lifted his head long enough to allow them both a breath, he held her with a fierce possessiveness, and kissed her again. It was a long time before he gave her the chance to finish her explanation.

She said the rest into his shirt. "Even Rao had to agree that while the clan might accept me, they would never accept your son or daughter. He released me from my promise, and even let Padmini come with me. We left the island and came here to Bombay to seek passage back to England, but then I was told that you were still here, and I thought—I hoped—that you might have stayed because you still love me. But I was so afraid to see you, to tell you. I was so afraid you would not . . . would not believe the babe is yours."

He stroked a hand over her hair. "Then what made you risk coming here and telling me?"

"I love you, more than I was afraid for myself." She raised her head, caressing her hand along his stubbled cheek. "*I love you. Forever.* I told you in the gardens, before you leaped over the wall, but I wasn't sure you—"

His mouth came down on hers in a kiss that bound her to him, bespoke his love and passion, and found it reflected back tenfold. She was his and he was hers in a way that had never been true before. Brushing his lips over her cheeks, he said everything that needed to be said.

"It doesn't matter what happened before, love. And I have no doubt the child is ours. As soon as I left you behind on that island, I felt as if I had lost half of my *soul.* But I thought you would be happier on the Andamans. I couldn't force you to come with me. I couldn't destroy your free spirit, when that is one of the things I love so much about you." He kissed her again, his voice turning husky. "One of so many things."

She returned his kiss and threaded her fingers through his hair.

"Will you not miss your home?" he asked gently.

She shook her head. "It is not blood or birthplace that make a home. It is love. My home is with you, my love, now and forever." Smiling, she cuddled against his chest. "But would it be possible for Padmini to come with us?"

"Padmini?" He started walking her slowly backward toward the bed.

"My maidservant. She is a good friend, and I think she would be helpful in the kitchens. She knows many excellent vegetarian dishes and—mmmm."

There was definitely a "yes" muttered somewhere among the sweet nothings Saxon whispered in her ear as he lifted her in his arms and laid her on the bed.

She sighed at the whisper of silk parting beneath his

fingers. "And ... and Nicobar? We could stop and pick him up from our island on the way home. Tigers do quite well in the cold Himalayas, so I don't think he'll mind the English climate—" She gasped as Saxon distracted her with an extremely well-placed kiss.

"Nicobar too," he agreed thickly. "And you may dispense with wearing the gloves you dislike so much. Perhaps even corsets. I'm willing to negotiate on undergarments."

"But won't I be rather scandalous?"

"No, my love." Saxon stretched out beside her, sharing her smile, loving the sparkle of her sapphire eyes in the candles and starlight as he gently welcomed her home. "You'll be completely a D'Avenant."